COURT

~OF~

SHADOWS

COURT
OF
SHADOWS

A HOUSE OF FURIES NOVEL

MADELEINE ROUX

HARPER TEEN
An Imprint of HarperCollinsPublishers

HarperTeen is an imprint of HarperCollins Publishers.

Court of Shadows
Text copyright © 2018 by Madeleine Roux
All rights reserved. Printed in the United States of America.
No part of this book may be used or reproduced in any manner whatsoever without
written permission except in the case of brief quotations embodied in critical articles
and reviews. For information address HarperCollins Children's Books, a division of
HarperCollins Publishers, 195 Broadway, New York, NY 10007.
www.epicreads.com

Library of Congress Control Number: 2017959289
ISBN 978-0-06-249871-7

Typography by Erin Fitzsimmons
22 23 24 25 26 LBC 6 5 4 3 2
❖
First paperback edition, 2019

For Mom and Pops

And of course, for The Smidge

Macbeth shall never vanquished be, until

Great Birnam wood to high Dunsinane Hill

Shall come against him.

—WILLIAM SHAKESPEARE, *MACBETH*

Nature, with equal mind,

Sees all her sons at play;

Sees man control the wind,

The wind sweep man away.

—MATTHEW ARNOLD

We should forgive our enemies, but not before they are hanged.

—HEINRICH HEINE

Prologue

Year Two

𓊪𓏏𓏭𓉐 𓈖𓏤𓏏𓏭 𓂝𓏤 𓏭𓉐

Journal of Bennu, Who Runs

They emerged from the tree like worms from the earth. More shadow than mass, they slithered out from between the groaning cracks in the trunk before making their way to the clearing. The roots of the tree were as thick around as horses, broad and gnarled, never touched by man and rarely even glimpsed by him. The creatures came out of those roots gradually at first, but as twilight dipped into evening, they arrived at a steadier pace, a slow drip that became a constant stream.

Where did they come from? Was the tree hollow inside to hold so many children? How deep down into the earth did the roots go? Was that where the creatures lived when shunning the cool green air of the forest? Were they made of mud or rock or wood, or were they flesh like me?

I had come so far, untold miles, to witness this rebirthing with my own eyes, though I had witnessed many oddities in Per Ramessu and Bubastis, and though I had struggled through the unknown territories swarming with painted strangers and curious animals. I had seen a woman swallow a cobra whole to no ill effect, watched a woman's face melt like wax under the breath of an angel, and taken meals with men who claimed to be older than the sands of my home.

But this . . . It blackened my heart to see this, to see nothingness given shape, to see a tree, tall as any palace, act as fleshly woman and create life. Life that walked and breathed, each creature with a different face. They were not ugly, these creatures, but nor were they like any man I had seen before. Dark lines like tattoos covered their skin, though even in the dim light I could see that they were carved into the flesh, and carved deep. The creatures glistened and moved with unnatural grace, as if floating along the dewy grass.

Owls, horned and menacing, sat in the smaller trees around me, hooting in a low rhythm. All manner of snake and spider had come to watch, an army of glittering black eyes and scales. I noticed that it was a kind of music, frogs and crickets singing in concert, aided by the low moan of what sounded like a deer. The music echoed in my chest, ancient and primal, and I shivered, huddling beneath the fur I had scavenged along the trail from a fallen animal. The forest stank of new growth and suppurating rot, a rich earthen smell that seemed to pulse with its own life.

I wondered where my protector had gone, the beast man who had come with me from Egypt and guarded me through so much. But he was gone, and in the distance I heard an angry howl. Had they taken him? Was he in pain?

Life. Everything here was life, almost to suffocation, all things growing and expanding, spreading through the loam and the water with no civilization to curtail it. How lonely and cold it was, to be the only man for what felt like an eternity in every direction.

But I remained.

None emerging from the tree noticed me, though I made no attempt to make my presence secret. After all, I had been summoned here, sent by women with visions, guided in daylight by a winding Sky Snake that threaded its great, terrible body across the clouds. I'd listened and I'd followed, and crossed seas and mountains and valleys to this place. To the tree. To Father.

At last the tree slowed its creation, and all those it had made circled around it. The music of the forest grew louder, painfully loud, drumming in my chest like a fist striking harder and harder. I could do nothing but cower under my fur, feet wet with mud, and wait, watching as the tree opened once more, the great rift in its trunk sighing out one last figure.

Had I known true cold before? Had I known the face of real and evil magicks? No, this changed all. I was in the presence of something out of time, out of calculation, a being without a beginning and without end.

He was their king, and this, this was his court. My king. My Father. At once, all eyes turned to me, black as beetles and shining. All of them smiled, though I did not wish to know why. I felt suddenly hunted and knew this could be my death—those were not smiles of welcome but marks of insatiable hunger.

Father came toward me and the song grew softer, more like a chant, now with reedy, ghostly whispers chasing through the rhythm.

The words blossomed with sense as this forest king saw me and approached. He was taller than the others, with a sharp, jagged face, a trembling hand's sketch of a human's features. Nose of hawk, chin of lion, cheeks of sphinx, hair of ravens. His eyes, deepest black, danced with faint red pinpricks of light, and he wore moss, vine, and feathers, fashioned into a robe that floated out from his shoulders.

He reached toward me with fingers curved and sharp, and I knew that what I held in my arms, what I clutched protectively to my chest, would soon be his. The whispers! The whispers gnawed at my brain, making me weak and forgetful.

Why had I come? The nymphs had offered me sanctuary. This was not meant to be my end . . .

All Father of the Trees, All Father of the Trees, All Father of the Trees . . .

I could hear nothing but the whispers now, not even my own thoughts. If I survived this forest, I knew not if I would ever think another thought again.

"You have come so far to bring me this . . ." *His voice was the very crack and creaking of branches in a storm, it was the rush of wind through leaves, the babble of water over stone.* "To bring me her."

Is it for you? Have I made a mistake? Perhaps it was made for no one. It must never be found!

Then his fingers touched the book clasped to my chest, and there was no power left in my body. The hundreds of black eyes hunting me had stolen my strength, and their chant had put me almost to sleep. He took it from me. He took it, and I failed.

"Sleep now, Bennu, one who has known hunger and exhaustion and fear. Sleep now, safe among the boughs. Your secrets are safe with me."

Chapter
One

North of England
Spring, 1810

It was not the first time I had stared down the barrel of a gun, but I sincerely hoped it would be the last.

Then again, this was at least a change in my normal routine. I had come to know the numbing effects that boredom could have on even the most bizarre chores. At first, the novelty of cleaning up after guests annihilated by Poppy and Mrs. Haylam's magicks had kept it interesting. But hefting buckets of gore, scrubbing bloodstains from wood tiles, and scraping bird droppings from Mr. Morningside's carpets had quickly grown tiresome. Life, even in a house of dark wonders, could become drudgery. I'd begun to lose count of the villainous boarders whom I'd had a hand in killing. It still made me ill if I thought too much about just what I was employed at Coldthistle House to do.

"Och, you're not concentrating one jot, Louisa."

Behind the curved hammer of the pistol, Chijioke grimaced. There was an exhausted twitch to his eye, and his hand shook a little as he pointed the weapon at my face. Hazy sunlight fought through the grime on the library windows, pale dust motes dancing around us like afternoon fireflies.

"Just promise me it isn't loaded," I said, grumpy.

He rolled his eyes at me and snorted. "For the fifth time, it's empty. Now focus, Louisa, or was that just a lucky fluke that saved your life?"

I tried to concentrate, but now his questions were only making me more distracted. In truth, it was a combination of things that had saved my life on the day Lee's uncle decided to try to take it. There had been Mary shielding me with her peculiar magic, and Poppy using hers to lance George Bremerton's head like a boil. I shuddered at the memory of it—nightmares of that day visited me often, and I knew in my heart they were unlikely ever to leave.

There were the hideous dreams, and there was the even crueler reality of Mary's absence. I missed her. Months had passed since I had gone to Ireland, hoping to conjure her again with a wish thrown into a special spring. According to Mr. Morningside, Mary, as an Unworlder spirit, neither dead nor alive, should have gone to the Dusk Lands, a place like limbo; I should have been able to conjure her back with the same magic that had brought her into existence in the first place. But my wish had fallen into the spring, only to plop into the water and drop like a stone.

In that horrible moment, I'd at least fancied myself free of Coldthistle House. I'd left the spring and drunk my way through Dublin to London and then, reluctantly, back to Malton. Those few things I had stolen from the house went far when sold, but not far enough. I'd thought to strike out on my own, to find some measure of independence working as a barmaid. Alas, my quarrelsome nature was not tolerated in town the way it was at Coldthistle House. In no time, I was broke and unemployed once more. Perhaps it was fate that was forcing me back to Coldthistle House; perhaps, on some level, I just missed the dastardly place.

Chijioke must have read the dismay on my face. He sighed and nodded toward the pistol pointed at my nose, as if to remind me that he was doing this for my own good.

Outside, even through the tightly shut windows, I could hear the sounds of merry voices. All that week, workmen from the neighboring property had labored to raise a massive tent on the lawn of Coldthistle House. Well, part of it was on the house property—half, to be specific—and the other half landed on the pastures to the east, those tended by the kindly shepherd who had taken me in for an afternoon. The purpose of the festival tent remained a mystery, and my thoughts shifted from poor Mary to whatever Mr. Morningside might have planned. The workmen took their tea down on the lawn, their deep, boisterous laughter an unusual sound on the somber Coldthistle grounds.

"Go on, lass, you're trying my patience now!"

Chijioke was nearly shouting in my face, that tired tic in his eye gone as he snarled in earnest.

"Very well!" I cried back, finding at once the focus that had eluded me. It came, as it had before, out of anger. There was no smoke or loud pop of magic, no descent of sparkling dust, nothing quaint or worthy of a children's story in what I could do—I simply focused all of my mind for an instant and the Changeling power within me stirred, transforming the pistol in his hand into a rabbit.

Chijioke gasped, looking as shocked and befuddled as the baby rabbit squirming in his grasp.

Then he laughed and loosened his grip, letting the darling little animal curl into a curious, snuffing ball in his palm. It was a charming enough sight—the callous-handed gardener of Coldthistle cradling an ivory bunny no bigger than a snowball.

"Very funny," he said, eyeing the rabbit with a cocked eyebrow. "So your power wasn't a fluke after all. What will you name it?"

I turned away from them both and trotted to the dirty window, going on tiptoes to gaze down onto the lawn. The white tent was nearly as large as the barn. A red, green, and gold flag topped each of its attractively curved and then pointed peaks. The pennants were simple, unadorned, and I couldn't help but wonder what they meant. Perhaps, with the weather changing, this was meant to be a May Day celebration. Yet that seemed altogether too whimsical for Mr. Morningside. He could do nothing pleasant without there being some sinister motivation.

"Louisa?"

I glanced back at Chijioke and his new little fuzzy companion. It was not to last. In another blink the rabbit was gone, and Chijioke again held a weapon in his hand. "Alas, nothing at all. No matter how hard I try, I cannot seem to make the spell last."

He gave me a sympathetic shrug, tucking the pistol into the back of his trousers and joining me at the window. We both gazed down at the fool courtyard and watched the workmen finish their tea and return to the pavilion, each doing their best to avoid the holes dotted around the yard.

"This time it might be for the best, lass," Chijioke said. "That wee thing would've been lunch for Bartholomew before sundown."

"He certainly has been eating more," I agreed. "And growing. Soon you'll be tending to him in the barn. Poppy will be riding him up and down the lawn."

Out of the corner of my eye I saw Chijioke wince.

"You truly don't know what all this is about?" I asked, using a little pile of books to lever myself up for a better view. There was a shallow ledge to the window, enough that I could rest a knee on it and crane my neck down to see the lawn.

"I suspect only Mrs. Haylam knows, though it would not surprise me at all if she were just as in the dark. I've no reason to lie to ye, Louisa. But if you find out first, ye best share all of it with me."

I squinted, but of course could see nothing, even when the slit of an opening at the front of the tent ruffled in the wind. Muttering, I let my forehead touch the glass of the window. Using my powers—*Changeling* powers, or so Mr. Morningside claimed—had left me feeling slightly fragile. "If this were any other boardinghouse, I might think we were hosting a wedding."

He laughed and leaned onto the ledge next to me, flicking the necklace that had slipped free of my gown and now swung visibly from my neck. "Have those on the mind, do we?"

God, the necklace. I had hoped to keep it a secret, and now my unladylike climbing and crawling had dislodged it from the partlet tucked primly into my bodice. I snatched the spoon up with my hand and tucked it back into my frock. Jumping down from the window ledge, I turned away, trying to find shelter among the bookcases. "It isn't what it looks like."

"Oh aye? Because it looks like a lot of sentimental rubbish to me."

"This *sentimental rubbish*," I said hotly, turning and finding the door, "saved my life."

After nearly dying at the hands of George Bremerton, I'd thought often of leaving permanently. I still did. But if I fled now, abandoning Lee and what memories of Mary lingered, what would that make me? A thief and a runaway I might be, but I would not also prove disloyal. Perhaps if Mary somehow returned and Lee found happiness or at least peace, maybe then I could leave. Maybe then . . .

Chijioke called after me, but I was drained from our practice and now saddened. I felt the weight of the spoon on a chain around my neck and closed my eyes, taking quick steps to the corridor. There was no thinking of the spoon without thinking of Lee, who had died in my scuffle with his uncle. Well, died, but only briefly, his life renewed by Mrs. Haylam's magic and

Mary's sacrifice. Dead. Renewed. That hardly covered it, the scope of what I had done, what I had *chosen*, as a fate for my friend.

No, not a friend; a shadow of a friend now. Though he lived at Coldthistle and could not leave it, I had not seen a glimpse of Rawleigh Brimble in weeks. He skulked and hid like a shadow, and not a single part of me could blame him.

"Louisa! Neglecting your chores again, I see . . ."

My swift exit was cut short by Mrs. Haylam, tidy and clean as ever, her gray hair knotted at her nape, her apron starched and blindingly white. She tucked her dark hands in front of her waist and looked down her nose at me, sniffing.

"Just on my way to retrieve the linens for the Pritcher Room," I murmured, avoiding her sharp gaze.

"Of course you are. And you'll see to the Fenton Room as well after, and bring in the wash. There will be no more lazing about with the Court convening."

I could sense Chijioke's eyes went as wide as mine did at that. "The Court?"

Mrs. Haylam was a fearsome woman at the mildest of times, and now her eyes flared as she turned to make room for me to pass and pointed down the hall. "Does it sound like I'm in the mood to be interrogated, girl?"

"Right. Pritcher, Fenton, the wash," I whispered, trotting by her.

She caught me by the ear and I twisted, crying out in sudden pain. Lord but the old woman was far, far stronger than she looked.

"Not so fast, Louisa. Mr. Morningside wishes to see you. Something urgent, he said, and I wouldn't tarry if I were you." She gave a mean little laugh as she let go of my ear.

Eager as I was to be away from her pinching fingers, I did not relish the thought of going downstairs and through the green door to see my employer. Our interactions had been mercifully few since my return from Ireland. In the hall I cowered like a wounded dog, glancing fitfully between Mrs. Haylam and the way to the stairs.

She had already forgotten me, rounding on Chijioke, berating him for wasting time with silly serving maids in the library.

I decided to flee before she caught me staring, and I whirled, retreating down the hall while holding my wounded ear. As I went, I saw what looked like a shadowy foot disappear around the corner, vanishing as whoever had been watching escaped up to a higher floor. The footsteps were already growing softer, but I knew them. Lee. Mary's sacrifice and my decision had resurrected him, but in exchange, he lived with nothing but darkness fueling his spirit. I hardly understood it, and he was not amenable to discussing the changes he had undergone.

Pausing, I listened to the footsteps as they diminished, pressing the spoon under my dress to my chest. I had doomed him, and I had doomed our growing friendship, too, souring it as I seemed to sour everything in my path.

"Louisa! Downstairs! Now."

There was no room for argument in Mrs. Haylam's voice. My many duties awaited, but first, I had the unenviable task of meeting Mr. Morningside once more.

Chapter Two

"**L**ovely Louisa, there you are."

He was in a disturbingly good mood. Every short glimpse of Mr. Morningside lately showed him to be irritable and vexed. Shouting matches raged at all hours between him and Mrs. Haylam. Complaints about noisy, lead-footed servants disturbing his work. And wasn't the foyer awfully drafty? But now, sitting behind his massive desk, his menagerie of birds clustered around him, Mr. Morningside smiled at me. Brightly. Too brightly.

I curtsied and waited for him to invite me to sit, which he did, giving a small, elegant wave of his hand. Reams of parchment that had seen much better days littered his office. Huge, leather-bound books were stacked high on the floor. Quills with broken nibs, their feathers splattered with ink, had been abandoned in every corner. He was hard at work at something, though nothing on the pages looked intelligible to me. Scribbles, I thought, unintelligible little pictures.

He sat back in his chair while I took just the very edge of mine, my hands squeezing each other fretfully in my lap. I had yet to enjoy a wholly pleasant or even mundane interaction with this man . . . creature . . . *thing*. Given his too-friendly smile, this afternoon's visit would be no different. Mr. Morningside cleared a space in the mess on his desk, haphazardly gathering up the old parchments and stacking them on the right side of the polished wood.

"Tea? Something stronger? How are you enjoying the spectacle out on the lawn? It's soon to be far more exciting. The Court convening here . . . It's been, let me think—" And here he began tabulating silently on his long fingers. "Oh sod it, who knows? Who cares? It's been a very long time, and now we are to host the Court. *Such a delight.*"

"Forgive me for saying so," I began carefully, "but you don't look particularly delighted."

"Do I not?" He showed yet more white, even teeth with his next smile, but it only had the effect of being even more unsettling, forced. Aggressive. "Well, my questionable delight over hosting the Upworld's finest fops and fools is a topic for another time, Louisa. We have far more pressing matters to discuss."

He served tea in his ornate cups, each decorated with tiny, fine birds. Without my asking him to, he also removed a round bottle of what looked to be brandy and poured some in with my tea, scooting it quickly across the table. Given the smell wafting off the cup, he had given me rather more brandy than tea.

"It isn't yet three o'clock," I pointed out mildly, eyeing the concoction.

Mr. Morningside tipped his head to the side, ceding the point, then took a gulp straight from the brandy bottle and tented his fingers in front of his nose, studying me. My mind raced. He was generally so unflappable. What could be upsetting enough to call for that much brandy this early in the day? Did it have something to do with Mary? Had she returned from the Dusk Lands after all? Or perhaps he had concerns about Lee, who had become like the house ghost, often heard but rarely seen. Then there was, of course, George Bremerton's people, the cult of zealots that had sent Bremerton to Coldthistle in the first place with the mad idea of killing the Devil.

I sighed and picked up the tea, waiting. What had my life become that these were the anxieties swirling around in my mind?

"I've received a rather curious letter, Louisa. Quite honestly, I do not know what to make of it." Mr. Morningside ruffled his luxuriant black hair and then reached for one of his desk drawers, withdrawing a folded piece of parchment with a broken green seal. Even at a distance, I could smell the distinct scent of juniper emanating from the paper. "It's left me speechless."

"Now that *is* odd," I mused.

"Yes, yes, please enjoy a chuckle or two while you still can. I doubt you will feel so blisteringly superior when you hear the contents of the letter," he said, his eyes, yellow and dancing, flamed with annoyance.

Setting down the tea without drinking it, I frowned and reached for the letter, but he tugged it away, keeping it just out of my reach. A few of the birds perched around him tittered as if amused.

"Not yet," he said, shaking his head. "You may read it soon, but first I must know something, Louisa." Mr. Morningside leaned toward me, setting his jaw and grinding it back and forth a few times before saying softly, "How *are* you?"

I stared. "How . . . am I? What sort of question is that?"

"A friendly one," he replied. "A genuine one. I realize I have been . . . preoccupied of late, but I do honestly worry. That ugly business with Bremerton would leave any normal person catatonic with shock. I know you must feel a certain amount of confusion still, what with Mary's ritual not working. You appear to be taking it all in stride, but as you know, looks can be deceiving."

"I'm . . ." I cast about for a suitable response. It hurt to realize just how baffling that question could be. How was I? Unsteady, terrified, disheartened, utterly lost in a sea of strange forces and even stranger revelations about the world, about myself, about the nature of good and evil, God and the Devil. I was . . . "Getting along. Yes, I'm getting along, sir."

Mr. Morningside lifted one dark eyebrow at that. "A genuine question deserves a genuine answer, Louisa."

"Very well, then I'm surviving. I survive, usually by trying not to think too hard about what you are and what this place is. I clean the chamber pots and wash away blood. I sweep and muck out stalls and put my hands over my ears at night if a guest is screaming. If I thought too hard about any of it, about who I am and what I've seen and done after less than a year of employment here, then I might not *appear* to take it in stride.

So while your question may indeed have been genuine, sir, it was also foolish."

My voice had risen to almost a shout, and I did not apologize for it, nor did Mr. Morningside seem taken aback or offended.

He placed the letter on the desk between us, tented his fingers again, and nodded slowly, chewing briefly on his lower lip as he continued regarding me. His gaze flickered once to the letter, but then fixed on me. I refused to squirm under the scrutiny.

"Would it please you to see your father?"

I laughed. Scoffed, really, and gave a distinctly piglike snort. Pointing to the fine parchment of the letter, I said, "Malachy Ditton could never afford paper that fine. If he has, it's a deception, some way to part you from your coin, and you'd be a dolt to believe a word of it."

Mr. Morningside's eyes grew huge, almost innocently so, and his lips parted. "Oh." Still looking dazed, he reached for the letter and began opening the creased pages, laying bare a long, long note written in a scrolling, beautiful hand. I had never seen letters with so many flourishes and loops. The entirety of it appeared to be written in Gaelic.

"My father can hardly scratch out his own name," I murmured, transfixed by the sheer loveliness of the penmanship and that delicate perfume of juniper and forest drifting from the paper. My eye swept to the bottom and the signature, a name I did not recognize. It looked like *Croydon Frost*. "There must be some mistake . . ."

"There is no mistake, Louisa," Mr. Morningside said gently. "This letter is from your father. Your *true* father. Not a man of flesh and blood and mortal spirit but a Dark Fae, the source of your Changeling magic."

Chapter Three

At once, I was a child hiding in the cupboard again. My stomach felt as if someone had thrown a sack of bricks into it. I had few memories of my father before he left, though the ones that remained were potent in all the worst ways. One could never forget the sound of a hard slap, or the mother's grief that came afterward. I spent more time hiding from his moods and his drunkenness than I spent in his arms hearing stories.

He did tell me one tale that stuck. "Remember, my girl," he would say, bouncing me on his knee in one of his few moments of sobriety and kindness, "every man has his limits. From the smallest to the tallest, they all have a weakness. You have to know it, girl, but you have to know yours, too. See, I can drink one bottle of whiskey and keep my feet, but two more cups after that and *bam*! I'm on the floor. You drink the bottle and keep your feet. You don't be tempted by those last two cups, you hear? See the wall before you crash into it."

"What a father," I breathed. I had all but forgotten that I was not alone. Mr. Morningside stared at me, but I felt no pressure behind the look. At last I reached for my tea and drank it, all in one gulp, fighting back a cough from the heat of the liquid and the strength of the brandy.

"Can I refuse to see him? Can you refuse him for me?" I

asked, pushing the cup and saucer away from me.

"Of course I can. Is that what you wish?"

"I had one father already, and I can't recommend the experience. How do I even know this one is telling the truth about our relation? It seems so . . . far-fetched." But it would explain my odd abilities, which, one year ago, I would have found very far-fetched indeed.

Mr. Morningside nodded, tapping the letter on his desk with one fingertip. "You aren't curious to read what he has to say?"

"Curious?" I searched the wall behind him, looking from bird to bird, watching them preen and sleep. "Morbidly so, perhaps, but I think I feel more . . . disappointed. The father I already have let me down, but I accept that now. I've worn that around and grown accustomed to the feeling. I don't think I'd like to be let down that way again."

I pushed away from his desk and stood, aware suddenly that I felt dizzy. It wasn't the brandy, or that wasn't the only culprit. For so many years my father had railed against my mother, accusing her of all manner of ridiculous things. Foremost among them? Infidelity. And now here was proof that at least one of his suspicions was true. I shook my head, silently deciding that it wasn't worth giving this stranger and his story too much credence.

Why would anyone go to the trouble of finding you if it wasn't the truth? Why would anyone care about a futureless, penniless daughter?

"There is another possibility," Mr. Morningside said quietly.

I had already begun to leave, but I stopped and took a few tentative steps back toward him. He folded the letter neatly and held it out to me. "You might be pleasantly surprised. You might even find kinship with him, considering that you're both of the Unworld."

"Or it's just a bunch of nonsense and he's some kind of criminal," I replied. "Isn't that more likely? Coldthistle House lures the wicked, you told me that yourself."

He inclined his head, still offering me the letter. "I'm familiar with the criminal set. Nothing in this note leads me to believe he has ulterior motives. He sounds quite educated, in fact," he explained, pausing for effect. "And wealthy."

It was bait, and I was stupid enough to take it. No, not stupid, *desperate*. I still had little money to my name, only a scrimped pittance I'd saved from my wages. A wealthy father was what every poor girl hoped for, wasn't it? Something out of a fairy tale. . . . I reached out for the letter but stopped, holding myself back.

What about my life had ever been a fairy tale?

"No," I said, making a fist. "I don't think I want it, not even if he's the richest man in the kingdom."

"It's not mine to keep," Mr. Morningside pointed out. "Burn it, if that suits you better, but I think you should be the one to decide its fate. And your own."

My stomach throbbed again, and I blinked hard against the dizziness rising like a tide again in my head. I half expected the paper to burn my fingers when I touched it, but it was ordinary. Not that I took any comfort in that. Tucking the note into my apron, I curtsied and went to the door, eager to be alone, eager to dispose of the letter and never think of it again.

"It's silly anyway," I said as I left. "I have no idea how to read Gaelic."

Behind me, Mr. Morningside laughed. I turned to find him cooing over one of his parrots, grinning, his old wry self returning. He seemed strangely satisfied. "You're a clever girl, Louisa. I'm confident you'll figure something out."

had watched the commotion on the lawn from many different angles—my chambers, the library, the kitchens, the first-floor salon—but never from the roof. The thought of doing so then came only out of desperation. As I climbed upward through Coldthistle House, dodging distant voices so as to remain alone, I felt the panic subside a little, as if by leaving Mr. Morningside far below in his cave-like offices I could escape the tide of confusion altogether.

The relief was only temporary, lasting through my search for a way out onto the upper battlements. I had not returned to the topmost floor of the mansion since my first ugly encounter with it; I knew that the Residents, the shadow creatures that haunted Coldthistle, lingered there in their greatest concentration. But they had been strangely absent from my life in recent months. A new fear struck me—that maybe their scarcity was somehow related to Lee's death and subsequent return to life. After all, I had seen his shadow bleed back into his body, bringing with it breath and, seemingly, a second chance.

And it had been Mrs. Haylam's strange magic that had done so. I winced as I avoided the large ballroom-like expanse on the top floor and the evil book that resided within it—there was so much more to think about than just my "father's" letter. Had I done the right thing by bringing back Lee—a decision that had resulted in the loss of Mary? Mary, whom I was still desperately hoping to bring back, too? I had gone to the magical spring in Ireland to make my wish that she return, but perhaps I had done something wrong. Or the magic hadn't taken. Or I had misinterpreted entirely how I might bring her back again. . . .

Ah, and then the sickness in my gut returned. I hurried down the hall, finding the air musty and warm up on this floor. A thin, rickety banister ran along the corridor, giving an open and dizzying view down to the levels below and the main foyer. Dust fell like soft snow from the rafters. The walls, decorated with Mr. Morningside's paintings of reedy, gawping birds, were hung with a medieval tapestry that was rapidly disintegrating into faded tatters. The wood and stone behind were black with grime. Though I saw no shadow creatures as I scurried onward, I nonetheless felt their cold, unsettling presence. I was certain they watched; it was impossible to be alone in Coldthistle House.

I at last reached a door, stooped and dark, with a decorated knob that looked like it had not been touched since its installation. The air around me felt too close, and I breathed hard as I took the little handle and tugged, expecting to find the door locked, and of course it was. Taking a step back, I closed my eyes, letting the ill feeling in my stomach do what it would. I needed that discomfort, that pain, and I focused hard on it, feeling it deeply, until it felt like the warm, dusty air was choking me.

With one last deep breath, I wrapped my hand around the spoon hanging from my neck and pictured it becoming a key. A tiny key, decorative and old, one small and delicate enough to fit into the lock on this miniature door in front of me. My hand flashed hot, and when I opened my eyes there was just such a key nestled in my sweaty palm. I fit the key in the lock, wondering if it was even possible that I could conjure the correct thing. But I had.

The room beyond opened to me after a few hard pulls on the door. It was a dirty, forgotten attic, crowded with moth-eaten linens and damaged furniture. One of the mansion's many chimneys ran through it awkwardly, the brick body of it poking through the middle of the room. I scuttled through the attic without giving the mess a second look, spying another door on the far side, one with a grimy window peeking out into the open air.

The small key I had conjured fit that lock, too, but the door wouldn't budge. I gave the stubborn thing a shove, and then another, growing warmer and clammier as I put my shoulder to the wood and really pushed. The door swung open too quickly, and I tumbled out into the late-afternoon winds, finding the edge of the roof much too soon. I gave a short shriek of surprise, feeling nothing but the void as my forward movement sent me reeling over the slates.

There was no banister to catch me. God, how could I be so stupid? My hands flailed in every direction, trying to find purchase, but it was too late. I was going to fall.

And then I wasn't. It happened in an instant, a strong arm hooking around my middle and yanking me back to safety. I screamed again, grabbing the arm at my waist and leaning back, sending us both sprawling onto the dark slant of the roof.

I breathed heavily, closing my eyes, shifting to the side, and rolling off my savior. Leaning on my elbows, I looked up to find Lee, dressed in his shirtsleeves, staring down at me. That was almost as shocking as going end over end off the roof.

"What are you doing up here?" he demanded.

He looked different. He *sounded* different.

Of course he does, you fool, he died and came back to life. It would change anyone.

"Forgive me," I blurted out, struggling to gain my feet. His hair was still curled and golden, but longer now, unkempt. There was a dark, haunted look to his turquoise eyes, and a gaunter hunger to the hollows of his cheeks. His clothes were rumpled, and he was not wearing a waistcoat or jacket. Lee turned away, hiding his face. He went to the edge of the roof and stared down, perching there like a gargoyle.

My heart was pounding at the sight of him. He had tried to save me twice now. And what had I given him in return?

"Why are you here?" he asked again. His voice was hushed. A snarl.

I wiped my sweaty palms on my apron and crossed my arms over my stomach, finding the wind at that height bracingly cold. "I needed to be alone. I didn't mean to intrude . . ."

"Well, you seem to be intruding," he said. And then, as if he couldn't stand to be rude, even if he had every right to be, he added, "I'll just go."

"Please don't." It was unfair of me, but I hadn't seen him in so long. I felt suddenly desperate to keep him there. He sighed softly. "We never . . . I owe you an apology. Several. Hundreds, maybe. It was just . . . I thought in the moment it was the right thing to do, and I couldn't let you go, not like that. I'm sure that sounds very selfish."

He still refused to look at me. Lee tucked his hands behind his back, and I saw that they were pale and scratched. "So give your apology, then. If you must."

"Forgive me," I said quietly. They were words I had wanted to say to him for months, but they hurt, and they came out in a whisper. He probably could not even hear me over the whip of the wind. "Forgive me, please," I said, louder. I tried to rub some warmth back into my arms. "Everything with your uncle happened so fast. One moment he was trying to kill me, and the next you were shot. You didn't deserve to die, Lee; you were only trying to help. I made a devil's bargain, I know that, and I should pay the price for it. Not you."

"Should Mary have paid?" he growled.

My eyes snapped shut. That hit the mark. "No. I'm trying to mend that, too. Apparently I can only break things, not put them back together."

At that, he snorted. "How very sad for you."

The wind tugged at his hair and he settled it, irritated. Far down below us, the workmen on the lawn called to one another, then laughed about some jest we could not hear.

"I will not stop looking for Mary," I told him resolutely. "There's a special spring . . . I know it's the key, and I'll find a way to get her back. And . . . And I will never stop trying to make amends for what I did to you. You have no idea how sorry I am, Lee."

After that, we were both silent for a long, shivering moment. His shoulders drooped and then he looked to the side, one eye finding me, studying me. "So why are you dawdling here with me if you're so eager to be alone?"

I thought I heard a sliver of his old, jolly demeanor seeping through. His tone was not as harsh, but he also did not appear ready to accept my apology. He might never.

"Believe it or not, I received the most astounding letter. From my father."

His brow furrowed. "I thought your father—"

"A different one. My real father, supposedly. I honestly have no idea what to think."

"What does it say in the letter, then?" He turned away again, grumbling. "Not that it matters one jot to me."

I felt a wry smile tugging at my mouth, but I held it at bay. Perhaps one day he would speak to me like a friend again. The only thing I could do was keep trying. "Well, that's the other tricky bit." Taking one tiny step toward him on the ledge, I pulled the folded letter from my apron pocket. "It's all in Gaelic, and I can't read a word of it."

"Your dear friend Mr. Morningside wouldn't help you?" he sneered.

The urge to say something smart was difficult to fight. He deserved my kindness and patience, and so I took a deep breath, unfolding the letter and looking at the unfamiliar words. "He isn't my friend, and no, he wouldn't help me. He just said something unbelievably condescending and sent me on my way." I pursed my lips and sighed. "As usual."

Lee vented a husky laugh, glancing over his shoulder at me. He looked ready to say something, but his eyes caught on my necklace. I looked down; the key had reverted to its former appearance. The spoon he had given me as a gift. The letter shook in my hand, and I could see Lee's eyes turn blacker and blacker, as if pure ink spread across the whites and turquoise, revealing the living shadow within.

His eyes were black for only a moment, then he seemed to struggle with what to say, fidgeting, whipping his head around and away from me. At his sides, his fists clenched.

"You still have the spoon," he said, hoarse.

"Of course I do." I put the letter away, realizing that I would find no solitude there on the roof, and no help.

Lee nodded and looked out over the hills rolling up to the boundaries of Coldthistle House. The wind pulled at his hair again, but this time he let it. "Louisa . . . you should go now. Please, go now."

And I would have, I really would have, but as I turned to go I saw a shape in the distance, hurtling out of the sky. As soon as it appeared, a cold, deep dread iced through my bones. I felt frozen in place, petrified, a part of me I could not name but *hear* whispering words of warning. It was like Mr. Morningside's green door, an ancient calling, though this one did not say come closer, but hide.

It was like a star falling in an arc from the heavens, brilliantly gold. The object came closer and closer, and both of us watched in stunned silence as it shimmered overhead, a wail going with it, before the flash of gold careened out of the heavens and landed with a thud in the fields to the east.

I did not heed the warning in my bones. Without another word, we both fled back into the attic, running toward the little door and whatever poor fool had just fallen from the sky.

Chapter
Five

reathless, we tumbled out into the sunshine to find the laborers in an uproar. They had heard the thunder as whatever or whoever had fallen into the east fields landed. It had not been a smooth arrival, as a great cloud of dust and grass and feathers hung in the air, visible even from the kitchen door.

"Move!" It was Chijioke. He exploded out of the house, pushing past us, rushing toward the tent on the lawn and the confused workmen. Lee and I hurried toward the fields as Chijioke intercepted the men, herding them back toward the tent, calling, "Back to work! All of you! Nobody is paying you to make a fuss!"

I heard them complaining in return, but ran on anyway. It was difficult to keep pace with Lee, whose long legs sent him bounding ahead. I muttered and cursed my long skirts, holding them up and pelting for the rickety fence guarding the borders of Coldthistle property.

"Lee! Wait!" But I called to him too late. He reached the fence and stopped short, falling hard to the ground as if he had run headlong into a wall. Whatever shadow magic Mrs. Haylam had used to resurrect him tied him to the house, and he could no more pass beyond the limits of the house than a horse could fit into a mouse hole.

Gasping for air, I paused next to him, leaning down and putting a gentle hand on his shoulder. His shoes and trousers were scuffed by the dirt, and he pushed blindly at my fingers.

"Are you all right?" I asked.

"No," he muttered. "Leave me be."

I looked between him and the cloud of dust in the field just beyond. Lee shooed me off again and I stood, gathering my skirts and climbing the low fence. "I'll go and have a look," I told him. "Stay here and I will let you know what I find."

He ignored me, climbing to his feet and dusting off his muddied trousers.

As I turned toward the crater in the fields, that icy sensation lanced through me again. I shivered and wrapped my arms tightly around myself, rubbing at my elbows. It was such an odd feeling . . . to be perfectly aware of the lovely spring sun overhead while my body felt plunged into the depths of winter. I blinked, gasping, watching as a puff of my own breath bloomed into the warm air. How was it possible? But then, I should've known better than to question the curiosities of this new and darker world I found myself living in.

The whisper in my bones rose again, stronger, and with it came a physical tugging, as if the warning inside could slow me down, turn me from the hole in the ground, and march me back to the house. I still wore the small silver pin Mr. Morningside had given me, a token that allowed me to pass beyond the boundaries of Coldthistle. Even so, I felt ill and numb with strange frost.

The noise around me dimmed until there was only the inner voice, panicked and desperate.

Foolish child, turn back from here. Turn away from this place.

Though the words were strange to me, I somehow knew their meaning. Turn back . . . Some hidden voice inside wanted me to turn back. It was a woman's voice, thin as a knife's edge. I fought the urge to flee, watching as the cloud of dust kicked up by the fallen object began to dissipate. A figure took form, hunched, and while my steps grew slower from the cold, the image became clearer and clearer.

How could anyone survive such a fall? Yet the person righted himself and moved closer, ducking through the particles of dust as if parting a misty curtain. The moment he appeared in full, a surge of light blinded me, painful, a spike of heat cutting through the cold. I grabbed for my head and flinched, falling back, stunned by the agony. The voice did not throb now but screamed, wraithlike and wailing as the pain crested—

Cursed sky sentinel! Priest thief!

I must have doubled over from the intensity of it, hands clasped on my knees as I fought to regain my balance and strength. An instant later I felt pressure on my back. A hand. The sensation gradually ebbed, and when I could breathe again I found a young man standing next to me, his full, dark brows knitting with concern.

A kind of yellow glow surrounded him, then faded, and at last I could make out the details of his face. He did not look bruised or battered from the fall, and even his very fine gray suit was untouched by the impact.

As I beheld him, the voice whispered to me one last time, repeating itself. It was ghostly and stern, like a mother turned ghost.

Cursed sky sentinel. Priest thief.

"Priest thief?" I murmured. It didn't make any sense at all. In fact, looking at the young man, strong and well-groomed, with dark brown skin and a mane of wild black hair, I couldn't imagine he could be any manner of thief. He looked every ounce the impeccable London gentleman, though I had never met anyone of his particular origin.

"Sorry, could you say that again?" He still looked racked with concern. "Are you well, miss? You look ill."

"M-me?" I stammered, laughing. "Am I well? You . . . How did you do that? I saw you fall so far; how could you possibly survive a fall from such a height?"

The young man opened his mouth to answer, but a second figure emerged from the haze of dust and grass. She, too, was dressed in clean, gray colors, in a cut of suit not so different from the boy's. For a woman in men's trousers, she did not seem the least bit ashamed of her odd attire, striding toward us with her head held high, a cocky sway to her full hips. She was beautiful, suffused with that same yellow glow around her shoulders, and with her large sapphire eyes and yellow hair, she might have been the boy's opposite.

"Frightening the local wildlife, are we?" she drawled. She was far taller than I, and in my shocked state I could hardly find the outrage to respond as she approached us and put a finger under my chin, tilting my head upward. Nobody but Mr. Morningside had ever studied me so closely or with such cool intensity.

"You will of course excuse my sister," the young man said, batting her hand down and away from my face. "She has all the subtlety of a bull."

"Wings, dumpling," the girl added, ignoring her brother. "He has wings, that's how he managed. Not his most graceful entrance, I'll warrant . . ."

They both had crisp London accents to match their tailored clothing, though I also heard a hint of something foreign that I did not recognize. There were stories, of course, of the wealth coming to England from the East Indies, and I had to wonder if these two hailed from that region, though she might have been from any town in the commonwealth. How they could be related, I did not know.

They have wings, you fool; they're not from any region on known Earth.

Sheepishly, I glanced around the young man's shoulder. I saw no wings of any kind, big or small. The girl noticed me looking.

"Ha. Not the kind you can see with your eyes, my dear. Not usually, anyway."

"I'm Finch," the boy said, giving a polite bow and then

gesturing to his sister. "And this charming creature is Sparrow, my twin. I had no intention of making such a cumbersome entrance, but it seems protective measures at Coldthistle House have been improved since our last visit."

Finch and Sparrow? Was everyone around here obsessed with birds?

"Your twin?" I repeated, glancing between them.

"Ah, you see, our kind attain physical b-bodies in an unconventional way," he said with a charming stammer. "We start as just little motes of light, and when we perform our first act of service, whomever we helped, well, that's who we come to look like. Sparrow and I were 'born' at the same time, which is why she's my twin."

"That's rather lovely," I said, thinking it over.

I watched as they both turned toward the mansion, leaving behind the immense crater in the field. Far in the distance, beyond the hole, I noticed a cluster of sheep on the hill. A furry herding dog there watched us, too, wagging its tail before it gave a few short barks and disappeared at a run.

Cold lingered in my bones, but I slowly followed the two strangers, wondering how exactly they could fly about on unseen wings. It had to be believed, since they had fallen so far and apparently sustained no injury greater than a ruffled hair.

"You've been here before?" I asked, still confused but eager to make conversation. Ahead, I saw that Lee had vanished, though Chijioke was waiting for us by the fence, leaning on it, a faded work cap dangling from one hand.

"Loads of times," the girl, Sparrow, replied. Her long blond hair was pulled back in a severe and intricate braid, the crown of which arced over her head and then ended in a dizzying knot at her nape. They wore matching gold rings on their right pinkie fingers. "Still utterly hideous, I see. Henry should really stop hiring so many maids and invest in a painter or two."

"We're here for the Court," Finch said, glancing over his shoulder at me. He had a noble face, with a broad nose and easily smiling lips. And were I less baffled by their sudden appearance, I might even have counted him handsome. "It, well . . . It seems there has been some trouble here lately, enough of it to convene the Court. Which means . . ."

"Somebody's in trou-ble," Sparrow finished, singing her way through it with a sneer. "Henry's gotten himself into a mess, surprising literally no one."

"Oh," I said, fiddling nervously with the spoon around my neck. "Yes. There was something of a scuffle here a few months ago. I never realized it had caused so much attention. It must be severe if you came here from, um, from wherever you're from to look into it."

The young woman stopped short, spinning swiftly on her heeled boot. She squinted down at me, a sharper counterpoint to her brother. Another chill shot through me, the whisper in my bones giving a menacing hiss. Whatever or whoever this strange voice was, it clearly had no love for these two strangers.

"Who *are* you?" Sparrow asked, leaning toward me. "Or rather, *what* are you?"

"Irish?" I glanced between them, squeezing the spoon in my fist. "An Irish chambermaid?"

Finch smirked, quirking his lips to the side as he chuckled. "You think you're clever, do you?"

"Not particularly."

"Don't lie to me, clever thing," Sparrow said, narrowing her eyes. "I can have the truth from you whether you want to give it or not."

"That won't be necessary," Finch put in with a grumble, placing an arm between his sister and me. She leaned away from me, but only a little. "She means to ask what your name is, I think, and also what you *are* are."

I did not like the way this girl had chosen to menace me when I had done nothing but show concern over their well-being. Curiosity was not a crime, and her instant cruelty rankled. Though I would never have her height, I could still do my best to appear dignified and unimpressed.

"You first," I replied tartly. "I may have your names, but I still have no idea what *you* are."

"Are all of Henry's servants this ignorant?" she sighed, rolling her eyes. She propped both wrists on her hips and gave yet another heaving sigh. "We're Upworlders, Adjudicators, which is why the very sight of you makes me feel ill. And since you make me feel fit to vomit on my shoes, that means you're one of

Henry's lot. Or something fell. So out with it, mm? You're not a bairn, too tall. A soul whisperer? A witch? Definitely not a succubus, too plain."

"How kind of you," I muttered bleakly. Before she could insult me further, I added, "My name is Louisa, and according to Mr. Morningside, I'm a Changeling."

"A skin changer?" It was a brief moment of triumph, as Sparrow's eyes widened and she reeled back as if scalded. She looked, satisfyingly enough, frightened. "I thought you were all but gone. You're *supposed* to be all but gone."

"Apparently not," I told her with a shrug. "But if it makes you feel any better, I'm the only one I've ever met."

Sparrow's lip curled as if smelling something unpleasant. Her eye caught on the silver pin shining on the shoulder of my apron and she flicked it, hard. "No bloody wonder the Court is being convened," she spat, throwing up her arms and turning as she stalked toward the fence and Chijioke. "He's lost it for good this time—the jailers are in the cells and the inmates are running amok."

Chapter
Six

hijioke did not welcome the strangers with a smile.

He brooded over the fence railing, humming a melancholy tune to himself as we drew near. I could only surmise that he had met Finch and Sparrow before, and judging by my brief interactions with her, she had also left a not-so-kindly impression on Chijioke. He didn't so much as glance at Finch, but he did glower noticeably at Sparrow.

"You can stay right where you are on the other side of that fence," he said by way of greeting. Then he gave me a quick smile and a gesture. "Not you, of course, Louisa; you're always welcome with us."

"The ages certainly have eroded courtesy here at Coldthistle," Sparrow said with a theatrical laugh. I didn't much relish the thought of climbing clumsily over the fence and making a fool of myself, so instead I simply went and stood as close to Chijioke as I could.

Finch stopped a polite distance from us and rolled his big dark eyes at his sister. "What my twin obviously means to say is that we came ahead for the convening of the Court. We have no expectation of hospitality, but it only seemed proper that your employer knew of our arrival."

Chijioke nodded and slapped his floppy blue cap back onto his head. "Mighty polite of ye."

"Now, now, be generous," Sparrow said, syrupy. She batted her eyelashes, but Chijioke simply stared at her. "We came a long way and we're weary. Could we not at least enjoy a bit of tea? A nip of brandy?"

"Ha," he said, turning away from the fence. "No."

"We don't need to ask permission, you know. We have the right of passage."

"Och, lady, you could have every right in your world and mine, and it could be carved on your forehead and I couldn't be bothered. I'd sooner invite a scorpion into my boot." He gestured to me again, and absent a stile, I was forced to scamper back over the rickety fence. At least Chijioke offered me a hand of assistance, though he never took his eyes off the well-dressed twins behind us.

"Don't trust them," he whispered as he helped me down. "Not the nasty one nor the one with all the friendly smiles. They're not our kind, and they're not here to help, whatever they may say. Keep to yourself and keep close to the house; Mrs. Haylam says everything will be topsy-turvy with this Court going on. There's danger afoot, lass, and we best stick together."

I nodded, keeping my head down. Enough problems swirled in my head; I did not need to add more to that morass.

Before we could start back toward the house, I noticed a shadow moving toward us at great speed. It flickered in and out of sight, leaping forward invisibly and then appearing again closer to us, and then closer. It made a soft popping sound, as if it broke through an unseen barrier each time it emerged. Chijioke did not seem bothered by it, but I heard the girl Sparrow groan.

When the shape was close enough to touch, it took solid form at last, and Mr. Morningside came through, stepping out of a black and shifting portal. He adjusted his fine cravat, walking toward the fence and the twins, never breaking his stride as he went. When he passed us, he gave a subtle wink.

"The Beast himself," Sparrow said, shaking her head. "We were just talking about you; were your ears itching?"

"Not exactly," Mr. Morningside replied. Their appearance did not seem to upset him, and he leaned jauntily against the fence, regarding the twins with a twinkle in his golden eyes. He was taller than the two newcomers, but only just. He buffed his nails on his striped coat and basked as languidly as a cat. It was strange, I thought, to see him out of doors and in the sun. It was like seeing a fish happy to be on land.

"I thought I felt a nasty indigestion coming on," he continued. "Then I realized it was only our esteemed guests arriving. Jostles the innards, the presence of Upworlders, doesn't it?" Perking up a little, he turned to me and cocked his head to the side. "Did you feel it as well, Louisa? Something must have alerted you to their presence."

"I did feel cold and strange," I admitted with a shrug. "Not sick so much as frozen. But I saw them, too, a great glowing shape that fell out of the sky and into the east fields."

"Frozen," he repeated, lifting one brow.

I pointed, and Mr. Morningside followed my fingers, leaning to the left to see around the twins. Then he chuckled and smoothed his hair back with one palm. "What a landing! I'm sure I remembered to warn the shepherd about the new protections around the place."

Finch crossed his arms over his chest, glowering. "I'm sure you didn't."

"Intentionally," Sparrow added. "Not the best way to begin the proceedings, Beast, given you're the one on trial. Punishing the wicked to sate your ridiculous bloodlust should be enough, but here you are, causing even more trouble."

Mr. Morningside clucked his tongue, spreading his hands wide. "That's awfully hostile, Sparrow. The Court can be more than a trial—why, I thought we could make it civil. You know, more of a meeting of the minds. We are all just trying to coexist peacefully, are we not? I'm going to throw a grand ball for you all. It will be a diverting change from your usual life of toil and sobriety."

"Distractions only make you look more desperate," Sparrow replied coolly. "And more pathetic."

"Doubling down on the hostility, are we? That's all right, that's all right." He waved off her glare and then just as breezily beckoned them across the fence. I took a step back, remembering Chijioke's words of warning. "You're free to come and go, though I will ask you not to interfere with my staff or their duties. We're expecting guests of a more . . . mundane nature, and they must not be neglected. As you said, my *bloodlust* must be sated."

I saw Finch shiver at that. Did they know what went on at Coldthistle House? Was it simply accepted, even among these so-called Upworlders? I wondered if they would try to stop Poppy or Chijioke, though I couldn't imagine them being more dangerous than the employees of the mansion. They might have wings that I could not see, but otherwise they appeared quite normal. Normal. Was any of this normal? Surely they had as many secrets as we did.

"There is tea waiting in the downstairs salon," Mr. Morningside continued, turning back toward the house with a flourish. "You will show them in, won't you, Louisa?"

For a moment I said nothing, staring at him and then Chijioke. The groundskeeper gave me a single nod and I swallowed my trepidation, waiting behind to see the "guests" inside. After a similar hesitation they breached the fence, though they did so much more gracefully than I, buffeted up and over as if on a strong, perfect wind that carried them safely to the ground. As they did, the gentle glow around their shoulders brightened and I felt another twist of cold in my guts.

I heard their shoes whisper softly over the grass as we left the fields behind. There were fewer fresh holes in the lawn now that Bartholomew was a few months older; he seemed more interested in eating and napping than trying to dig his way back to Hell. Poppy called it "murder sleep," some kind of ritual he had to undertake after helping her with Colonel Mayweather's demise. Coldthistle House reared up before us like a skeletal stallion, dark and unwelcoming even awash in sunshine. The spring light never seemed to really touch the place, as if always a shroud of winter hung around it. And the house, unsettling as it was, was not to have a moment's peace—the drive was cluttered with three teams of horses, each pulling an ornate carriage. Chijioke rushed on ahead of us, and Mrs. Haylam swept out of the front doors, walking swiftly to the descending folk, the next batch of evil souls to be reaped for Mr. Morningside.

"Maybe the side door," I said, changing course.

For I did not want to see their faces. It was hard enough knowing they were all irrevocably doomed.

Chapter
Seven

woke the next morning in a deep fog. Somehow I made it down to the kitchens for a meal at dawn, but I had no memory of dressing myself or fixing my hair, and I could not remember tying the laces on my boots or pinning a cap to my head.

But there I was, sitting in the chilly gloom before sunrise, warmed only by the meager heat left by the baking ovens. The room smelled oddly . . . empty. Normally my first meal of the day saw me enveloped in the tantalizing scents of fresh scones and meat roasting for supper. Sometimes Chijioke packed the little smokehouse off the kitchen and brought in a tray of pig's belly musky and woodsy with the perfume of oak. None of those smells met me today, not even the usual hot blast of bergamot from Mrs. Haylam's morning tea blend, steaming away in a cup just for me.

Today the room was odorless. Colorless, too. The fog in my head and my heart thickened, and the walls, table, and floor all looked dead and gray. I waited alone, wondering if Chijioke and Poppy had gotten an early start—there were human guests to tend to now, and that would require more work from all of us.

I waited for a long time for Mrs. Haylam to bring me my food. Most days she appeared at once, but this was strange. . . . Where was everyone? What was taking so long?

At last I heard her quick, clipped stride as she approached from the larder. Face cold, hair as severe and neat as ever in its bun, she did not even glance at me with her one good eye but instead slammed down a giant tray in front of me. It was laden with meat, an entire haunch of it, the shape of it still intact. I knew little of butchery, but even to my eyes it did not appear to be from swine or goat. Not mutton, then, but what . . .

"Porridge will do," I told her, but she was already gone, bustling out toward the foyer with a tea set.

The meat in front of me was the only thing I could smell, pungent and unappetizing. The odor reminded me of worms, gray and watery. A knife large enough to be a cleaver was stuck into the haunch, down all the way to the bone. I picked up a small fork from the table, one that did not look at all equal to the task of tackling this monstrous leg.

My stomach growled. Something compelled me to eat, though the thought of chewing even a single bite made my guts roil. I carved a piece from the leg, the meat flabby and limp. The carving sent a twinge through me, and while I put the meat in my mouth I felt a tear slip down my cheek. What was the matter with me? I chewed and it tasted horrid, just on the near side of rancid. I sliced at the leg again and a burst of pain exploded from my own leg.

The chewed meat stuck in my throat. There was no tea to help me gulp down the awful stuff. I couldn't stop the tears anymore, and my face grew wet as I tried to force another bite down. No, I could not go on. . . . It hurt too much and tasted too sickly. I cried and looked around the kitchens for help, freezing as I noticed the walls had disappeared. Where was I? What was this? The walls had become trees, gnarled and black, though they shifted, unreliable, as if dozens of figures moved among the branches. Eyes glowed from every direction, watching me.

The pain in my leg was too much then. I pushed away from the table and tried to stand up, deciding it was better to flee. At once, I tumbled to the floor, crying out as I looked down and saw that my right leg was missing from the knee down. Gone . . . It was . . .

The meat I had forced down came back up and I retched, weeping, floundering on the floor. The leg was not normal. It was too familiar, too sleek. . . . My own. I had eaten my own flesh. And now I was choking, dying, helpless and scrambling across the floor.

Suddenly, from the mass of twisted trees all around me, a single figure came forward, eyes blazing like coals. It wore a crown of antlers and it spoke with a voice like thunder.

"Wake up," it said, reaching to help me up. "Slumber no more."

The world, the real world, slammed back into place with a scream. My own. I almost flew out from under the blankets, frantically pushing them down around my legs until I could verify that my leg was still there. A dream. No, a *nightmare*. I wiped at my face, finding it slick with perspiration and tears.

An instant later the door burst open and I shrieked again, then sighed and flopped down to the tick.

It was Poppy, eyes wide with shock, and she vaulted onto the bed beside me, placing a small, cool hand on my forehead.

"Are you well? Is that a fever? Oh, Louisa, you do not look good, not even a little bit!"

"That's very kind, Poppy," I muttered, closing my eyes.

"I would send Bartholomew to nurse you but he is very sleepy right now. He refuses to wake unless there is meat to be had!"

"Please," I whispered. "Please . . . no talk of meat just now."

"Should I fetch Mrs. Haylam?" she asked, frowning and sticking her little elfin face right up to my nose. "You really are amazingly sweaty, Louisa."

"Just an unpleasant dream," I told her with a thin smile. "I'm sure I will recover my wits shortly."

"Oooh," Poppy gasped, leaning back on her knees and then twirling one pigtail around her finger thoughtfully. "Do you know, I have had many strange dreams, too! They are not all bad. Sometimes I am a fat little bird screaming into the wind on a boat. I like those ones. But some of my dreams have been distressing. Mrs. Haylam says there are dark things lurking at Coldthistle these days and that we must, must, must protect each other."

Pushing myself up onto my elbows, I rested back against the pillows and nodded. "Chijioke said something similar. The Upworlders don't seem that bad."

Her eyes went wide again and she shoved a finger into my face, wagging it back and forth. "Shush! Shooosh, Louisa! Nobody must hear you say that. I will not repeat it but you must promise not to say that again. Mr. Morningside would be ever so cross if he heard you speak that way."

"Why?" I shooed her hand out of my face gently and fixed the blankets over my lap. Outside, I heard the familiar and comforting sound of the birds calling to one another as dawn broke. "What's this Court business about? It was such a big secret and now it's all anybody can talk about."

Poppy shrugged and let go of her pigtail; then she hopped off the bed and began rummaging in my chest of drawers, pulling out my usual housemaid attire and stacking it on the bed. "It is all new to me, too, Louisa, but Mrs. Haylam says the nasty Upworlders will be coming with the shepherd and his dumb daughter. They will all sit in the tent outside and decide if Mr. Morningside is too stupid to go on."

"Too stupid to . . ." I had to laugh, pressing a knuckle to my lips. "Well, that will certainly be a lively debate. But come now, it must be more serious than that. Is he really in trouble?"

She nodded emphatically, braids swinging, and fetched my boots from across the room. "That mean George Bremerton got too close to hurting Mr. Morningside. There could be more like him coming, and I think that's what everyone wants to argue about, what to do with those folk what want to hurt Mr. Morningside."

That made just a smidge more sense. "I see. That does sound troublesome. . . . What will happen if they decide he's, um, too stupid to go on?"

"I don't rightly know, Louisa, nobody does," she said sensibly, finishing her work and standing next to the bed with her hands crossed in front of her waist. "I only know that I don't like when the shepherd and his angels come. They eat everything in sight and make my tummy hurt. You must promise not to like them with me."

"Very well," I said, crawling out of bed. She had done such a neat job of gathering my clothes, I did not want to disappoint her with hesitation. "I promise not to like them, but only if they give me a reason. I did not like all of you at first, remember?"

Poppy chewed her lip, swaying back and forth as she considered my question. "I think that is fair." She dug in her own apron pocket, her small fist emerging with a folded piece of paper. "Louisa, what is this?"

The letter. She must have found it in my apron as she gathered up my garments.

"Just . . . nothing important. It's a letter I meant to read yesterday." The day had gone by in a blur, first with meeting Mr. Morningside, then being ambushed by Lee and the arrival of the Upworlders. My chest felt funny and hot as I looked at the folded parchment. Could it really be from my father? My *real* father? And how the devil was I supposed to read it?

"Oh, well, you must not forget again," she said, tucking it

back into my apron, where she had most likely found it. "But you cannot read it now, Louisa, there is no time at all to waste. I will help with your laces and give you a nice braid, but then we mustn't tarry. Mrs. Haylam wants to see all of us, and she is in a cross mood. I think the angels make her tummy hurt, too."

Though I had been at Coldthistle House for only about seven months, it was the first time Mrs. Haylam had called us all together.

Well, most of us. Mr. Morningside was not to be found in the early morning chill of the kitchens. I moved subtly closer to the ovens, rubbing my hands for warmth. The sun had only just appeared, and the springtime rays had yet to suffuse the house with their heat. Outside, through the open kitchen door, sheep bleated to one another in the fields beyond the fence, and just above that came the uneven, growly hum of Bartholomew as he snored. I could see nothing but his tail curled on the stones, the end of it dipped black as if he had stuck it in an inkwell.

Chijioke stood to my left, arms crossed, his clean workman's shirt smelling of Mrs. Haylam's lavender soap. I was surprised to see that Lee was in attendance, standing in the corner just in front of the larder. His clothes were rumpled, though he wore a coat now, one far simpler than the gentleman's attire he had brought to Coldthistle in the autumn. He avoided my furtive glances, eyes fixed on Mrs. Haylam, who stood before us in front of the large kitchen basin. Poppy munched on her breakfast, sitting at the table and swinging her legs.

It all felt terribly normal, and I wondered what it would be like to have this breakfast somewhere else. In a normal place. Chijioke, Lee, and Poppy could be normal friends, if only we had mundane jobs and no violence on the horizon. Was it foolish to hope for such a thing—foolish to even consider it?

Clearing her throat, Mrs. Haylam made eye contact with each of us in turn. Perhaps I was imagining it, but she looked at me the longest. I shrank under her inspection, aware that I had dressed in a hurry and did not look my tidiest.

"Well. At last we can begin," she said, and nothing more needed to be said about my tardiness. "As you all have undoubtedly noticed, there are a few changes here this spring. The visiting Upworlders are to be tolerated, nothing more and nothing less. If I hear of any of you beginning trouble with them out of turn, I will be unhappy in the extreme. Do not disappoint me."

"And if they start trouble with us? What then?" Chijioke asked, shifting.

"They will not."

"But if they do?" he pressed.

Mrs. Haylam snapped her head toward him, narrowing her eyes. "Why do I have the impression you are eager to vex them?"

"Because they're insufferable gits, that's why."

The old woman nearly smiled, but caught herself at the last moment, her lips pulling up into a half smirk before she regained control. "Be that as it may, you will restrain yourself. The Court is an unusual occurrence, naturally, and one that we should not draw out. The sooner those outlanders leave our house, the better. We want to resolve a disagreement, not start a war."

"Excuse me," I said, taking a tiny step forward. "But what exactly is this Court? Nobody has explained it to me. Not in full, anyway."

Mrs. Haylam sighed and glanced at the ceiling. "You will not be required to participate, Louisa, just see to your regular chores and tend to the guests. If Chijioke or Poppy has need of your assistance, you will be told."

"But—"

"*You will be told.*" She raised her voice just enough to silence me. "Now, I want all of you to stay alert and tell me at once if you think the Upworlders are interfering with your work at the house. Do not wander to town and do not take any unnecessary trips off the property. This is just a temporary disruption, and I expect us all to complete our work as if these were ordinary days."

Nobody spoke up after that, and a brief pause taken, Mrs. Haylam added, "Rawleigh is a permanent member of the house now, and as such I have asked that he take a position as valet. He will see to the gentlemen staying with us for the next month. Which brings me to our *guests* . . ."

I looked in Lee's direction, but he remained determined to avoid me. He stared at Mrs. Haylam and then at the floor. It was hard to imagine him acting as a valet with his messy hair and clothes, but perhaps she would force him to clean up before taking up his job in earnest. Of any of us, he would be the most familiar with the duties and mannerisms of a valet, having been the only one wealthy enough to employ one of his own in the past.

It was cruel to stare at him, and I wondered if he felt furious at the thought of having to work in a station so beneath him. And with me. He had already been shot by his uncle, died, and been revived with shadowy necromancy; this further punishment made me feel ill. Worse still, I had no interest in hearing about the newcomers to the house. Now that I knew Lee had been an innocent wrongly drawn to Coldthistle, I would always be concerned that another mistake was being made.

"The pavilion outside has been constructed for the Court, yes, but it will also be used by our guests. We are to host the nuptials of Miss Amelia Canny of Dungarvan and Mr. Mason Breen of London. Never have a more villainous pair of families darkened our doorstep. You are to serve them with all due deference and see to their needs, until you are called to escort them violently from this mortal coil."

Chapter
Eight

stayed behind in the kitchens to have my breakfast once the house meeting ended. For a moment, sipping my tea and gazing at the fire in the hearth, I felt again the terror of my dream return. Shivering, I held the teacup with both hands, breathing in the fragrant steam and letting it banish the chill of the nightmare. It seemed I had stepped from one nightmare to another, left to huddle alone in the kitchens while I dreaded the work ahead of me and the guarantee that I would meet these Canny and Breen families, come to know them, and then watch as they were extinguished.

Slowly, I meandered to the open kitchen door and leaned against the frame, watching as the laborers finished the work on the pavilion and cleaned up their tools. I wondered if I would miss them, having grown accustomed to their workaday chatter. It had been such a curious dash of normalcy to the otherwise constant strangeness of Coldthistle. But now they were leaving, trading boisterous jokes as they trundled off. They knew better than to even look in my direction; one brawny, sun-reddened man had shouted vulgarities at me on my first day. Mrs. Haylam marched him from the property, and I could only speculate on his fate after that.

Bartholomew dozed at my feet. He had doubled in size over the winter, no longer so much resembling a sweet, small pup but a frizzy bruiser of a beast. A wiry mane had grown between his ears and down his back, giving him the appearance of a far wilder, fiercer creature. Still, he had not outgrown his puppy ears, which flopped charmingly onto the stones as he rolled onto his back and tucked his paws up to his belly.

Crouching down, I scratched his neck and listened to his sleepy growls of contentment. I closed my eyes and took another sip of tea, and fancied I was far away, just a normal country girl outside a cottage in Ireland, patting her dog and having her breakfast before a day of tutoring or darning. That made me remember the letter still hidden in my apron and I stood, closing my hand over the place where it waited. What if that life of tutoring and darning was possible, and I needed only reach out to this so-called father for help? Or better yet, what if he shared his unimaginable wealth with me, and right that moment I could be sleeping in, a woman of means in a stately home, nothing to do but call on friends and make small talk with well-perfumed ladies. . . .

A duo of distant voices drew my attention. At first I assumed it was the twins, Finch and Sparrow, but instead I noticed Lee skulking in the shadows of the barn across the yard. He was talking to somebody, though I could not at first make out whom. A moment later, he took a step deeper into the eaves of the barn, leaning on a horse stall and fixing his hair. Beside him stood a vague shape, what might have been a person but was merely a shadow. A shadow of a girl.

"I told you not to get mixed up with him."

I cursed in surprise and dropped my teacup, watching it shatter on the stones. Bartholomew yelped and leapt up, circling once and sniffing his tea-stained tail before trotting off to find a quieter place to nap.

"You gave me a shock," I said, irritated. "I'll fetch a broom. . . ."

"In a moment." Mrs. Haylam emerged from the kitchens, and in the transfer of light from dark to bright, her rheumy eye seemed to glow. "He's a creature of shadow now; there's naught but that left inside him. That pretty skin he wears is just a mask, and when it rots and falls as a man's flesh does, you will see the truth in what I say."

An image of his eyes, consumed with blackness, revisited me in a flash.

"If he's that changed, then it's my fault," I said. "I made the choice to revive him."

"You will never receive gratitude if you feel entitled to it all the time," she replied with a sniff. "He may eventually come to thank you for what you did, but he's just as likely to despise you. I told you not to meddle."

"Aye," I sighed. "You mentioned that once or twice."

"Do not begrudge him his choices after you made such a grave one for him," Mrs. Haylam added, and unexpectedly, she placed a hand on my shoulder. At first I thought it was a gesture of motherly sympathy, but that was foolish—I felt a strange heat wash over me, warmth spreading from where her hand touched my frock. As I watched Lee and the shadow, the black shape took greater form, resolving itself into a lovely young woman, who spoke back to him and tugged at her skirt flirtatiously.

"Is that a ghost?" I breathed.

"Of a kind. Another creature of shadow tethered to this house. He can see them as they once were, for he dwells with the shadows now. Don't look so sad, Louisa; you should be pleased that he has found a friend." Mrs. Haylam took her hand away and the girl vanished, leaving only her dark silhouette on the floor in front of Lee. "Finish your breakfast and off you go. The Canny girl is already moaning about the accommodations, and I don't have the patience for it today."

And I do?

She must have heard my grumbling sigh.

"Louisa."

"Aye, Mrs. Haylam," I said, watching Lee slip away into the barn with his new friend. The letter in my apron felt suddenly heavy. Present. A rich father. Maybe I deserved a change; maybe I really could leave and find a new life somewhere far away. For forever.

"And clean up that broken cup. I don't need anyone slicing open a foot, least of all that good-for-nothing hound. . . ."

I stared at the shattered porcelain and felt her shoulder as she hurried back into the kitchens. The lawn was empty. The workmen had gone. In a sunny, dusty corner somewhere Bartholomew slept, his rumbling snores the only sound in the yard.

Spilled tea spidered into the cracks between the cobbles, speeding toward my boots. I took one step away from it, watching tea mingle with mud, and put my hand over the letter in my apron.

Spilled tea and broken cups. There had to be something better on my horizon.

Amelia Canny was a pinched, ugly girl with shockingly black hair and beady brown eyes. On another face, with more finesse and ease, her features might have been pretty, but if a painter had envisioned her, it looked as if they had rushed, slapping on a too-big nose and a retreating glance.

She flitted from bureau to bureau like one of Mr. Morningside's birds, moving excessively while accomplishing absolutely nothing.

"Lottie twisted her ankle and couldn't make the journey," Amelia was informing me, inspecting a massive bonnet studded with red silk flowers. Red, in fact, was her color of choice. Everything from her expensive bags to her light summer frock was done in crimson. "Silly girl said she needed to be off her feet for a month. A month! Can you imagine the luxury of it? And her, just a lady's maid! I shouldn't be surprised at all—she's always been lazy like that."

Amelia whirled and pinned me with her dark eyes. "*You* won't be lazy, I suppose?"

It was a question, but only just. I heard the implicit order. "I'm a hard worker, miss."

"What did you say your name was again?" She arranged and rearranged the bonnet until the sunlight coming in through the greasy window shone off the beads on the brim.

"Louisa."

"Louisa what?"

"Ditton, miss," I said, appending that *miss* with a tight smile. I rather envied Lottie, who didn't sound lazy at all but like a genius for finding a way to escape this simpering ninny.

"You're Irish," she pointed out.

Yes, obviously.

"County Waterford, miss."

Her eyes lit up, which almost made her appealing for a moment. "My family is from Dungarvan, but I shan't be going back to that shabby little place. Do you know what Mason's father said to me yesterday? He said, 'What good could come of a place with dung in the name?' And you know something, Louisa? He was right. I'll be a London woman soon. But you must know *Dung*arvan. Can you believe it? That we should meet all this long ways away, and both of us from such different worlds."

I thought of the letter in my pocket and winced. If this was what having money did to a person, then perhaps I ought to burn the parchment after all.

"How fortuitous," I choked out. "Was there something else you needed, miss?"

She needed her pillows fluffed and her bedding switched, to

a pattern with something red, naturally. I had already unpacked her traveling trunks and aired out the gown she wanted to wear that evening to supper. My hands had never touched so much buttery-soft silk.

"Only . . ." Amelia went to the window, peering out into the yard for a moment. Her room faced the north, and from her room, one could see the hidden path that led to the spring. She gestured me over and I obeyed, standing next to her and following her gaze to the wooded trail. The trees there looked menacing, and never quite recovered all the leaves they had lost in the autumn. What little foliage remained looked cruel and black. I hadn't remembered the wood around the spring being so dense, but perhaps I had never viewed it from this vantage.

"You seem like a sensible girl," she said, curling a thoughtful knuckle under her chin. "Lottie never wants to give me advice. She thinks it's improper for a lady's maid to weigh in on the comings and goings of her better. But I think she's a bit of a dullard."

I was admiring Lottie more and more. It was tempting to claim that I was also dim-witted, but part of me wondered what exactly Amelia had done to land at Coldthistle House. Just being rich and terrible was not crime enough, surely.

"I believe I am quite sensible, aye," I said carefully.

Amelia sighed and leaned against the window, resting her forehead on the glass. She traced a heart shape over the pane and gazed wistfully at the forest. "Do you think God forgives sin if it's done in the name of true love?"

I blinked at her for a moment.

Obviously not, considering where you are.

"I . . . think it would depend on the nature of the sin," I told her.

Nodding, Amelia shut her eyes and then turned them toward her feet. Then she softly murmured, "Lying?"

"That could be forgiven, I'm sure."

"Stealing?" she asked.

"Stealing is not all that bad," I said. That one I meant, as I had done my share of thievery at that very house. Then I remembered that I was to act as her lady's maid, and she would not want a known thief rummaging through her possessions. "At least, it's wrong, of course, but I . . . I can see that being a forgivable sin if love hung in the balance."

She nodded again, and in a voice so quiet I almost missed it, she whispered, "And murder?"

Now we were getting somewhere.

I was about to answer her, but she put up a perfumed hand, shushing me. Her eyes blazed, and it was as if a different person were staring out at me, not a dainty girl obsessed with bonnets and red blankets, but a crueler creature who had seen and done as much or more as I.

"Aye, you heard me, Louisa, but I will not say it again. And I believe you know of what I speak, for I was not always wealthy and as you see me now, but I knew the sting of hunger and destitution. But I wanted my dear Mason and now I have him, and I would have done anything in the world to lift myself out of that old and ugly life and live in comfort with my true love."

To that I gave a single nod, deciding it would be better to be her confidante. Clearly I had underestimated Amelia, though now I saw the truth in her eyes.

"Of course you understand," she added, the fire in her gaze lingering. "When I was small I would see the ladies in their fine carriages go by and I told myself: one day that will be me. Whatever it requires, whatever sacrifice I must make, it will be me. And now you are meeting me, Louisa, and perhaps you will leave this chamber and say to yourself: one day I will have what she has."

Again, I tried to speak, but Amelia would not allow it.

"No, no, there is no shame in thinking so. Girls like simple Lottie are not like us. She is content to be told she has nothing and she will do nothing about it." With a flounce, Amelia turned away from the window and trailed toward her bed, sinking down onto it heavily. "Listen to me! Chattering on and on. . . . And why? I cannot say. But I feel I can trust you, Louisa. Is that so? Can I trust you?"

"Oh, you can spill your secrets to me, miss," I said with a curtsy. But my mind was only half there. Amelia's rant had given me an idea, and the sooner I could leave her presence, the sooner I could act upon it. "I am a solitary creature and speak to no one. It's a lonely place, Coldthistle House, and often silence and secrets are my only company."

Chapter
Nine

The warm, close mustiness of the library was a comfort after Amelia's endless twaddle. Over many months I had managed to put the place in some kind of order, sweeping the dunes of dust away and shelving the books that had collected on the floor in toppling towers. Nobody had seen me tiptoe down the hall and into the room. Lee was no doubt playing valet to Mason Breen; what Poppy and Chijioke were plotting I could only guess.

I cleared a spot in the back of the library near the windows and behind a row of shelves. If anyone wandered by, they would not see me shirking my chores. Leaving the mysterious letter on the windowsill, I began searching among the rows and rows of books for something useful. Mr. Morningside—or so I assumed, for I could not even imagine what Mrs. Haylam might read in her spare time—had amassed a collection of dramas and romances. I smirked and kept searching, fingers brushing across dozens of love stories. When I had still been at Pitney, it was a common fantasy to think a wealthy, available bachelor was waiting out there somewhere. Those vague notions were for the prettier girls, who had at least a minuscule chance of landing a solid match, one that would at least provide them shelter and his modest income. A vicar, perhaps, or a soldier.

I had never entertained any such dreams, though I had to

admire Amelia's certainty that whatever grave sin she had committed to win Breen and climb fortune's ladder was worth it. And here I had a chance to do so by simply reading a letter.

Simply. There was a barrier, of course, to understanding the contents of the note. My parents had taught me snippets of Gaelic as a child, but only as far as it was needed for songs and fairy tales. But I had been taught languages at Pitney, and if I could just find a suitable translation guide, or even side-by-side comparisons of English to Gaelic, I might stand a chance of deciphering the letter.

After all, it was mine. Why shouldn't I read it? Anyone would be curious, and now the bait of a new and better life hung there, just ahead and above me, shining like a brass ring.

Something in that library would help me reach up and take it. Or so I thought. And hope remained for the first hour of searching, but waned as I slumped into the second. I would soon be missed. Nuncheon was approaching, and if I did not appear in the kitchens to help serve, then Mrs. Haylam would come looking. Nothing about her mood that morning made me want to cross her, and so I glanced through book after book. Each promising book contained nothing but translations without a single passage of Gaelic for comparison. Some, those with titles all in Gaelic that made the fires of hope burn a little brighter each time I glimpsed them, were unintelligible from cover to cover. I was accomplishing nothing other than creating a mess for myself that I would soon need to tidy.

At last, I spied a book with a green cover on the bookshelves nearest to the door. The spine was decorated with gold leaves, and read *Dagda, The Warrior* and just next to that, *Dagda, An Laoch*. This could contain the side-by-side comparison I might use as a base of knowledge. Breathlessly, I scurried back to my hiding place, crawling into the windowsill and tucking up my knees. Cracking the cover, I flipped through the first few pages, feeling a hot, prickling sensation climb from my chest to my neck and higher. Useless. The book was useless. Another full English translation with little to help me.

That book, perhaps the thirtieth I had found and discarded, made something come loose inside me. Furious, I let out a cry of frustration and hurled the book across the room. It landed with a dull thud in the corner. Nobody came running. I was alone and foolish, red and sweating with anger. I picked up the letter and tore open the seal, cursing at it as I took it in both hands and began to tear, enraged, ripping it cleanly down the middle.

And then I stopped.

Fury. Rage. It must have pulled at the power inside of me, for in front of my eyes the words began to change, as legible and clear as if I spoke the language fluently.

I had changed it. I could change a spoon into a knife and into a key, but with enough need and desperation, shift language to language. It was astounding. Gasping, I watched the words shimmer as they waited to be read, my so-called father's looping hand preserved in all its intricate beauty.

My Dear Louisa, it began. *At long, long last I have found you.*

My entire body shook as I read the letter, carefully holding the two halves together. I read it once, twice, and then a third time, leaning back against the windowsill for support. He had lived not far from where I was born, and described my mother, our town, even our house, with perfect detail. There was no mention of love for my mother, only passion, and then embarrassment when he realized their liaison would produce a child. Me.

> *I fled north, and in my confusion I failed you both. I always knew I would return to look for you, child, but I did not know whether I would have the courage to offer the apology you so dearly deserve.*

He spoke of riches made from hunting rare flowers and ambergris for perfumes. *Enfleurage.* If what he said was true, my father—my real father—was the kind of person who knew what *enfleurage* was. Wealthy. Posh.

That was one sharp barb to bear; the second came in the next paragraph.

> *Strange powers have always run in my family, and through my blood you are gifted or cursed, however you choose to interpret it. Perhaps, as I did, you always knew that you*

*were different. Or maybe you have yet to know the full
depths of what you are. This strangeness in your blood can
be harnessed to take you far, or you can crumble under the
burden of society's expectations. Whatever you choose, I should
be there to shoulder the burden with you, as I am the architect
of your fantastic reality.*

Another surge of anger burned through me. While this
coward was off picking flowers and making a fortune, we were
scrabbling in the dirt to eke out a living, crowded into no more
than a shack while my father—my false father—drank himself to death. None of this needed to have happened. I did not
need to end up with my cruel grandparents or the crueler Pitney
School. I need not have endured beatings and neglect. I need
not have run away and drifted to Coldthistle House.

Bitter, furious tears spilled down my cheeks. I set the letter aside and wept, wishing for even the smallest comfort of
friendship or understanding. I missed Lee. I missed Mary. One
or both of them, once upon a time, might have known what to
say to me in that dark despair. The sadness soon twisted into
spitefulness. Perhaps I *should* invite this monster to the house
of monsters and rob him of everything he had. Maybe it was
better to have a worthless drunk for a father than whatever this
person fancied himself.

By his absence he had made me small and poor and blighted
with dark magic.

I wiped at the tears on my face and folded up the torn letter, placing it back in my apron. It was no use wallowing there in the windowsill, not when tantalizing thoughts of revenge danced in my brain. As much as I was loath to admit it, he was right—this shirker, this thief, this *Croydon Frost*—I could wither or rise, and I would not let his letter or his existence make me crumble.

The mess of books I had made would have to wait for later. I stormed out of the library and into the hall, startling one of the shadowy Residents, one that had apparently been attempting to eavesdrop on me. It reared back and vanished in a puff of black smoke. I cared not, for there was nobody it could tattle to who wouldn't soon have the truth of it from my mouth. Farther down the corridor I found Poppy sweeping the landing, her head bent over her work as she hummed an idle tune.

"Oh! There you are, Louisa, Mrs. Haylam was—"

"Not now," I said, brusque, quickly turning at the landing and bolting down the stairs. "She can find me later!"

"But she will be cross with you! Louisa!"

"I don't care."

I felt alive with anger, speeding along on a current of fire. When I reached the foyer, I could hear Mrs. Haylam in the kitchens preparing the afternoon meal, but I quickly dodged out of her sight and toward the green door leading to Mr. Morningside's office. As usual, the air beyond the door was close and unsettling, but I banished any thoughts of hesitation and flew down and down, then through the antechamber littered with portraits.

Money. One could do so much with money. I could recover the life that had been stolen from me, yes, but I could do more. Chijioke and Poppy were employed through contracts at the house, and they certainly relied on the room and board provided. But what if *I* could provide? They had become my friends, and with a true fortune I could change all of our lives. I could buy a house—no, a mansion—and let Chijioke, Poppy, Lee, and that massive dog live however they chose to, without the burden of killing and concealing.

That thought was even more inspiring, pushing me faster. My only misgivings came when I at last reached the door to his office and felt an unmistakable tension waiting on the other side. He cursed, loudly, and slammed a fist on his desk so hard the entire house around me seemed to rattle with his rage.

Taking in a deep breath, I tapped on the door. It was a soft and sheepish sound, which was why I jumped when Mr. Morningside's voice thundered through, unnaturally strong.

"What?"

And again I made a tiny sound, this time with my voice. "It's . . . It's Louisa. I wanted to speak with you about my father."

There came a sigh and then a pause. He muttered something and groaned, "Go away, Louisa."

"No. No, I won't go away. I want to speak with you right now—"

The door blasted open, revealing Mr. Morningside at his desk, both fists digging into the wood as he snarled at me.

"This is a very bad time," he warned.

Carefully, I took a few shuffling steps inside and cleared my throat, trying not to cower in the face of his displeasure. His office had become even more of a mess, and his normally coiffed, perfect hair had come undone, tousled to the side. Opened books, quills, and parchment were scattered before him, though one strange journal sat directly in front of him, between his fists. It looked handwritten, but it was just filled with drawings and scribbles.

"I want to meet this man," I said, drawing the two halves of the letter from my apron. "I've . . . Well, I've read what he has to say and I'm not satisfied. I believe he owes me a debt, a large one, and I intend to collect. I want his money, you see. I have plans for it."

A wicked, slow smile spread across the Devil's face, but he did not change his posture. "Translated it, did you? Who helped?"

I balked. "Nobody helped me, I did it on my own."

"Indeed. And with what materials? There are no Gaelic dictionaries in the library, to my knowledge. . . ."

"It doesn't matter how I did it," I shot back, irritated. "I want to meet him. Can you arrange it?"

At last he relaxed a bit, sitting back in his chair and fixing his hair with a snort. His cravat was askew and he addressed that, too. "I'm afraid, little bird, that it does matter. You tell me how you managed to translate the letter and I will arrange this revenge for you."

"It isn't revenge," I spluttered, looking at my feet.

"It obviously is, Louisa, and there is nothing at all wrong with that. Just as you stated, he owes you a debt, just as you owe me an explanation." Mr. Morningside lifted both dark brows and nodded toward the letter. "How."

He probably could have just as easily guessed how I managed it, but I obliged, slapping the torn letter onto the desk amid his terrible mess. "With my powers. I'm a Changeling, so . . . so I changed it."

His golden eyes narrowed dangerously. "Just like that?"

"Just like that."

Leaning back farther, he rubbed his chin and studied first the letter and then me. Finally, his eyes slid to the journal opened just in front of him. "That's remarkably advanced for someone so newly awakened. You're absolutely certain nobody helped?"

I nodded, growing impatient.

He slapped the journal on his desk and chuckled, looking boyish, even excited. "How badly do you want to meet this man? How badly do you want to enact these *plans*?"

"Badly," I replied, feeling again that surge of anger and the determination that came with it. Croydon Frost owed me a different life and I would not soon forget it. "Very, very badly."

Mr. Morningside tented his fingers and peered at me over the top of them, giving me a cat's languid smile. "Very, very badly, is it? Badly enough to make a deal with the Devil himself?"

Chapter
Ten

emember, my girl, my drunk of a father used to tell me. *Every man has his limits. From the smallest to the tallest, they all have a weakness. You have to know it, girl, but you have to know yours, too. See the wall before you crash into it.*

Surely this was my wall, standing before the Devil while he offered to strike a bargain with me. I looked at the birds behind him, and they all stared back at me, the little liquid beads of eyes trained on me. They were silent to a one. It felt like a bad omen, as if even these animals couldn't believe that I was seriously considering saying yes.

But I was. I did not know if I was in control or out of it, but at least it was a feeling besides regret and loneliness. I had a purpose now, one I saw clearly: I would meet this Croydon Frost and punish him for what he did to me and my mother, punish him for the punishment of the father I had actually suffered, and most of all, punish him for cursing me with this Changeling's body.

And if I could rob him of some of his riches and use them to escape all the strangeness I had come to know, then so much the better. Better still, I could help my friends out of employment that forced them to murder.

Mr. Morningside's eyes glowed, as bright and enticing as embers on a cold night. Still, I was not reckless enough to lose all sense of caution or propriety. I tucked my hands behind my back and rocked on my heels, choosing my next words very carefully.

"May I know the terms before I agree to them?" I asked.

"You may," he said at once. "I'm only making a modest request."

I nodded and took a deep breath. "All right, then; what is it that you want?"

He sat back down and reached for a brandy decanter hidden under a mountain of creased papers. Pouring himself a drink, he sipped it slowly and tipped his head back, regarding me down the length of his thin nose.

"I've been struggling to make sense of a rather important journal," he said. At once, my attention fell on the scribbly pages in front of him. "Yes, that. I won it for a dear price at auction. Cadwallader's of London. Funny old place; they only deal in rare goods from our side of things."

"The Unworld," I murmured.

"And the Upworld, and anything but the mundane," he explained, taking another drink. "Had a lovely trio of shrunken heads that day, but my real interest was in this journal. Cadwallader knew it, too; said an odd fellow gave it to him for a song, thought it was an old bit of junk."

Mr. Morningside put down his cup of brandy and flipped the leather cover on his desk, closing up the journal. He then nudged it toward me. I came up flush to the desk and leaned down slightly to get a better look. It was yellowed with age and some of the pages had suffered badly from water. A strip of leather dangled from the edge, a means to wrap up the journal and tie it shut. There was nothing at all written on the cover.

"Honestly, it does look like an old bit of junk. It looks perfectly ordinary to me," I said.

"There's nothing ordinary about it," Mr. Morningside replied with a chuckle. He opened the cover and turned it, showing me the scribbles more directly. They were rows and rows of minuscule pictures. I picked out a bird and what looked like a wibbly line, possibly a wave. There were larger drawings, too. A long blue snake filled the bottom half of the page. "It belonged to a young man I'm very interested in. There are languages similar to what he used, but this journal is written completely in a shorthand of his own devising. I've been unable to translate anything but a few stray words here and there."

I stood back and smiled, finding that Croydon Frost's letter and the journal were now right next to one another. A translation. It hardly seemed like the sinister sort of demand one would expect from the Devil.

"And you think that I can read this journal because I translated my father's letter?"

"Precisely," Mr. Morningside replied, cheerful. "If I prayed, you would be the answer."

"What's so important about this journal?" I asked. If I was

going to learn the terms of this bargain, I wanted to know everything.

"That's not your concern," he assured me. "It's a big job and it may take up most of your time. I'll make sure Mrs. Haylam knows that you will be less available for your usual duties. I'll arrange a quiet space for you to work, and for now I'd like to keep this our little secret."

My ears perked at that. A secret? If Mr. Morningside didn't want anyone to know about the journal, then perhaps my being in possession of it would put me at an advantage. It might give me leverage over him. Or it might put me in danger. Both possibilities seemed equally likely. I glanced at the journal again, fighting my natural tendency toward curiosity.

"Is this going to get me in trouble?" I asked.

"It's my journal, not yours, Louisa. If anyone should ask questions about it, you can come to me and I'll handle everything." He stood and fixed his cravat again, putting his fingertips lightly on the desk. "Give me proof that you've translated in full, say, the first entry, and I will arrange for your father to come. Whatever you choose to do with him is fine with me. You say when he comes and when he goes, and that will be that."

It all seemed so simple. Unnervingly simple.

"Sometimes . . ." I sighed and pinched my lips together. "Sometimes I cannot make my powers do anything unless I'm upset."

He was already reaching for one of the scattered pieces of

parchment on his desk and a quill. Dunking the nib in ink, he wrote in huge, looping letters: CONTRACT.

"Is that so?" he asked, uninterested. For just an instant, he glanced up from his work, and if I didn't know better, I would think he looked truly happy. Relieved. "Well then, I suggest you find a solution to that problem. You want to be a rich girl, don't you, Louisa? You want to have your revenge. . . ."

"That's not the only thing I want."

He paused, eyes glistening with renewed interest. "Oh?"

"My plans, remember? I want you to let Chijioke and Poppy out of their contracts. And Mary, too, if she ever returns. I know they have some kind of arrangement with you and Mrs. Haylam. I'd like Lee to come with us, too. There must be some way to free him from the house."

Mr. Morningside tilted his head to the side, then squeezed his eyes shut. "Let me think . . . Ah yes, Chijioke and Poppy signed three-hundred-year resolutions with us. They are bound to serve the black book so long as it remains here at the house. Three hundred years have not passed, Louisa. You are asking me to let go of nearly my entire staff."

"So? Replace them. You can find some other Dark Fae to do your bidding, can't you?"

He scoffed at that. "Actually, your kind are *not* so easily replaceable. But I see your conundrum. A mere letter to your father is not much of a prize, I suppose. And I do admire your tenacity. Haggling with the Devil. You don't see that one every day."

Grinning, he put quill to paper. "Mrs. Haylam is fanatical about order, so this will deeply unsettle her. Do you know how this house works, Louisa? How we work? This is a little atmosphere in balance. My workers and I reap the souls of the evil; the shepherd sees to the souls of the good, or occasionally the unconventionally evil. These contracts keep the whole apparatus running smoothly. . . . You are asking me to tip a carefully balanced scale."

I swallowed, sensing he was going to refuse me.

"But on the whole, it does feel like a fair bargain to me. After all, without this translation, I will be facing greater scrutiny from my peers, and that is not something I desire at all." He glanced around at the office, his eyes coming to rest quite noticeably on the nearest perched bird. "No, scrutiny of the house will not do at all."

I said nothing as he drew up the contract. It was not all that long or complicated, and I read it over several times while he waited patiently, turning his back to me and fussing with his birds. One hopped onto his elbow and he chucked it under its feathery beak.

I, Louisa Rose Ditton, hereby enter into a forever binding contract with Henry I. Morningside. In a period deemed reasonable by both parties, I will fulfill my portion of the contract, which includes:

A full, written translation of the agreed-upon journal

A statement attesting to its accuracy

Secrecy regarding its contents unless otherwise stipulated by H. I. Morningside.

The second party, H. I. Morningside, will make every possible effort to bring, by force or otherwise, Mr. Croydon Frost to Coldthistle House for a length of time I deem appropriate. His lodging, food, and furnishings will be provided gratis by Coldthistle House. Disposal of any corpse or corpse-like material will be undertaken by H. I. Morningside or his associates. Successful translation of the provided text will also nullify the sworn contracts of Chijioke Olatunji, Poppy Berridge, Mary Caywood, and Rawleigh Brimble, subject to their consent.

Failure to produce the translated journal will result in immediate termination.

So it is sworn by both parties under laws earthly and otherwise, on this May the 29th, 1810.

I spun the quill in my fingers and read the contract once more, searching and searching for some clever point of deception that he might use to trick me. The line about termination did seem a bit troubling, and I put the contract back down on the desk and pointed to it, waiting for him to turn around and notice. He didn't.

"Termination," I said. "You mean you'll let me go from the house if I don't finish the translation?"

At last he turned around, still cooing over the bird on his arm. It was a common raven, but its eyes sparkled with unnatural intelligence. Mr. Morningside gave me only half attention, one eye dancing in my direction. "That's your interpretation. It simply says 'termination,' does it not?"

"Oh, so you'll kill me over a silly journal?" I pushed the contract back toward him. "No, thank you."

Mr. Morningside rolled his eyes at me, placing the raven back on its perch. It cawed softly and began cleaning its feathers. "Always so dramatic."

"What other meaning would it have?" I demanded. "I want that line clarified or I won't sign."

"Fine."

As I watched, the ink on the parchment describing the penalty for my failure blurred and rearranged, the letters re-forming to say, *Failure to produce the translated journal will result in a wage cut and the forfeiture of H. I. Morningside's pin.*

The pin. I touched where it was stuck to my apron. That little thing was my only guarantee of freedom from the house. It would be terrible to lose it, but it at least seemed like a far fairer, and clearer, punishment.

"Very well," I said, drawing in a huge breath. I felt shaky and light-headed as I touched the quill nib to paper. My nerves were obvious in the quality of signature I gave. But it was signed. I had done it. I blew out that breath and straightened, locking eyes with Mr. Morningside. He gave a slight nod and reached for the contract, adding his elegant signature right next to mine.

With a snap, he sanded the signatures to keep them from running, then folded up the contract and unearthed a stub of wax from the mess on his desk. He held the black wax over a candle, turning it evenly back and forth. I watched it grow slick and runny, and felt a pit growing in my stomach. Had I really just signed a contract with the Devil? Had I gone completely mad?

"Now, that bit of business done, I think we can get you to work, yes? Let's see . . . Why don't we say you'll be finished in one week? That seems like more than enough time."

And there it was, the rub I should've seen coming. *Stupid girl.*

"One week! That isn't reasonable at all! You must understand that I'm very new to this. . . ."

"And you're also entirely capable. Have a little confidence, my dear! A little pride! The Court convenes any day, and this is a pressing assignment, Louisa. An assignment I would not entrust to just anyone. One week is more than enough if you put your mind to it."

"The Court?" I echoed. "This has something to do with your trial?"

He gritted his teeth and smeared the melting wax over the folds of the contract, pressing his signet ring into the spreading glob. "It might. Does that change your decision? Not that it matters, of course; you *did* sign."

"*I know I did.*" I closed my eyes tightly and covered my face with both hands. God, but I wanted to strangle him. A week. If I could somehow find a way to consistently use my Changeling powers, then it might just be enough time. If not . . . "I will do what I can."

"And that's all I ask, Louisa." Mr. Morningside picked up the journal and trotted around the end of his desk, flashing me a brilliant smile before inclining his head toward the door. "Now, let's see if we can't find a cozy hideaway for you and this wee book of secrets."

Chapter
Eleven

My idea of cozy and Mr. Morningside's idea of it obviously did not align.

He led me into the circular rotunda outside his office and then to the right. I had never even looked there, as I assumed it was just the narrow area allowed by the spiral staircase. To any nonchalant passerby, it would appear unimportant, but now I saw that a curtain hung there. It was dark red and the bottom of it had been embroidered with silver thread in the pattern of locks and keyholes.

Mr. Morningside strode up to the curtain, the leather journal tucked under his arm. He swept aside the crimson fabric, revealing a hallway beyond. An impossible hallway. It looked to go on forever, dotted here and there with heavy iron-bound doors.

It looked, quite frankly, like a row of prison cells.

"But how . . . ," I murmured, hesitating in front of the curtain. It was hard to see much, as the only light bleeding down the corridor came from the rotunda in which we stood.

"Only a fraction of my artifacts and sundries fit in the house itself," Mr. Morningside explained, gesturing me forward. "A man of my taste and interests requires a good deal of storage."

Cautiously, I took a few steps down the dark hallway, and just as they had when I first visited Mr. Morningside's office, candleholders on either side of me flamed to life. Pale blue fire burned at our sides as we journeyed forward, and each new flicker made me jump. We passed several doors, and I began to count them out of curiosity.

"Here will do," he said.

We had stopped six doors in, though clearly there were many, many more ahead of us, vanishing into the gloom that the blue glow of the candles could not reach. Mr. Morningside simply touched his open palm to the door, and a locking mechanism released. The hinges squealed as he pulled on the handle, and we were both met with a blast of stale, cold air.

"As a rule only I would be able to enter," Mr. Morningside told me, holding the door while I stepped inside. "But that pin allows you to do more than just leave the grounds."

"Then I could have come in here whenever I wanted?" I asked.

"Indeed. If you had known it existed," he replied. "I wouldn't let that knowledge go to your head, Louisa. As you discovered, there are dangers in this house, and I cannot promise that poking your nose into every corner and cranny will be good for your health."

I thought at once of the large room upstairs, and the dark book that waited there, guarded by the shadowy Residents. My fingertips tingled at the memory, still burned from where I had touched the book, a touch that should have killed me but instead left only a permanent mark. That had been luck, really, and though I might never lose my inquisitiveness, it would be better to temper that curiosity with care. Accordingly, I took only a shallow step into the chamber, allowing Mr. Morningside to close the door behind us and stride into the unlit room.

He disappeared into the heavy swaths of shadow, and then I heard a crackle and a fireplace to my left filled with bright sapphire flames. The chill in the air lifted, and as Mr. Morningside made his way back to me, the candelabras on the wall blossomed with fire, too. The growing light revealed a large study, tidier than the upstairs library, with wall-to-wall shelves covered in all manner of antiques. I moved slowly along the wall toward the hearth, finding urns, daggers, dried flowers, a jar of teeth, and a tiny skull. Musical instruments I did not recognize, one like a flute but curved, and candles of every color, unlit but marked with runes and incantations. An unfinished portrait of four figures leaned against an ornate cupboard. The walls behind the shelves looked like those of a cave, as if this underground wonder had been scooped out of the earth ages ago. A charming collection of mismatched rugs was scattered across the bare earth floor, and the whole place smelled like cool, clean mud.

Mr. Morningside waited for me at a desk near the fireplace. A big, overstuffed chair was there, too, and he pulled it out, angling the fluffy seat toward me. He left the journal on the desk and crossed his arms, his foot tapping impatiently.

"I suppose you're going to tell me not to touch anything in

here," I said, taking the proffered chair.

"Oh no, Louisa, by all means, please go digging through my personal belongings," he said with a snort. "Rummage at your own risk, but do try to remember that time is of the essence. Wouldn't you like to free your friends sooner rather than later?"

He tapped the leather journal and pushed off from the desk, crossing briskly to the door. "I'll tell Mrs. Haylam to leave some dinner outside the door if you disappear for too long. There should be fresh parchment and quills in the desk, but don't be shy if you need replacements. . . ."

"Wait," I said, twisting in the chair. Mr. Morningside stopped in front of the door, his pointed chin turned toward me, one lock of black hair falling in front of his catlike eyes. "This place . . . The journal. Why do you trust me with these things? Poppy and Chijioke could help you. Or Mrs. Haylam. Why me?"

Laughing softly, he shook his head and brushed the hair out of his eyes. "Poppy and Chijioke are not Changelings. Mrs. Haylam has the eyesight of a vole. A vole with one eye, even. You are uniquely suited to this task, and I do so love efficiency."

That wasn't good enough, and perhaps he sensed it, because he did not immediately leave.

"You really can't do this yourself?" I asked, waving my hand over the journal. "That doesn't seem right; after all, you're the—"

"*I* am many things, but I am not the right tool for the job," he interrupted, and now his impatience had returned. Mr. Morningside's mouth curled, but not pleasantly, and he set his gaze on me like an accusatory finger. I felt suddenly cold inside again, blood turning to ice as it had at the sight of Finch and Sparrow.

"Besides, I need to make this house appear as if it all runs smoothly. There are extra eyes on us now. You're special, whether you appreciate that fact or not," he said, a desperate edge to his voice. "Dark Fae are special. I did not ask the others because they are not Changelings. Perhaps it's for the best that you're going to meet your father one day. Maybe when you meet him you will understand how few of you there are left, how spectacular your gift truly is."

Chapter Twelve

It was almost impossible to work with my mind split in ten different directions. A part of me wanted to chase after Mr. Morningside and demand more answers from him, but I had made myself a promise, and fulfilling that promise would bring me answers, too. It would also, fortune allowing, provide a way to protect and free the people I had come to consider friends.

Indeed, if my blood father was also one of the Dark Fae, then he would have even more knowledge of our kind than Mr. Morningside. The thought spurred me, and invigorated what I already knew would be draining work. Using any kind of magic left one exhausted, and now I would have to fight off that tiredness to translate this odd journal. As indicated, there was plenty of parchment and ink for me to use, but first I would have to learn how to consistently harness my powers. *One segment*, I told myself, *just translate one segment and Mr. Morningside will have to fulfill his end of the deal.*

I reached for the journal and flipped it open to the first page. What was I expecting? No introduction. Nothing in English. The blocks of tiny snakes and waves and birds captured my imagination for a moment. What must it be like to think this way? To write not with words but images? Or maybe to the author, these *were* words. Yet it seemed somehow more fluid, more emotional, than what I was accustomed to reading. Paragraphs of little images were followed with bigger sketches, and those I could decipher, no Changeling powers required. Mr. Morningside must have seen the sketches, too; perhaps that was what convinced him the journal was an artifact of interest.

As long as I stared at the snakes and rivers, they remained snakes and rivers. My focus was drifting. This was a dangerous room, filled with distractions. Concentration. Determination. I had a job to do. But how?

Apparently the key to unlocking my powers whenever I needed to was close at hand. My mind wandered, and as soon as it did, the anger quickly followed. While my eyes roved over curiosities and treasures amassed over who knew how long, my pulse quickened at the thought of owning such a place. And I might have. I might have done a great many things if I had been given the childhood and upbringing owed me by Croydon Frost.

Heat. A surge in the blood. There it was, that outrage, that fury, and the sound of thunder gathering in the back of my head. Just as steady was the flicker in front of my eyes as the tiny pictures became text. English words. My right hand sprang into action, hurrying to copy down the paragraphs as they came to new life in front of my eyes.

Well, that was one thing I could thank my blood father

for—he was an endless source of anger, and I would use that well until it dried, until he was standing before me ready to reveal what he knew.

But until then: the journal.

Year One

𓊪𓏏 𓈖𓆓𓏏 𓋴𓏤 𓀠

Journal of Bennu, Who Runs

Before, none of the books existed and none were required. I think I was a happy boy before the books, but afterward nothing was the same.

Meryt and Chryseis summoned me to the usual meeting spot, and I knew this was an unusual time. Our prayer hour was midnight, but the little spiny mouse had sneaked under the crack in my door, a note tied to a collar of beads about his neck, at just past dawn.

They needed me. It was time.

We met at the birthplace of the book. It had emerged from the water, slick but otherwise undamaged, and sat there like a stone baking in the sun. It had appeared the day the moon overtook the sun, in the last days of Akhet, while the river was swollen and overflowing. We had no word for what it was at first, its pages not papyrus but something smoother, the language inside a mystery to us all. Meryt said, let us call it "Spells" or "Book," and we three agreed. If one of the gods had sent it, then surely it was filled with spells for us to one day learn.

My feet knew the path to the place by the water, and I slipped on silent, bare feet across the night-cooled sand to the grassier banks. A striped snake slithered along beside me, and then another, but I paid them no attention. Though a chill hung in the air before Apep could banish it, I felt hot with fear, and sweat dripped down my arms to my fingers.

Date palms sheltered the meeting place, fronds draped in front of a low stone hut no taller than a man. The snakes followed as I stepped into muddier terrain, the wet earth sucking at my feet as I dodged into the hut. The two women waited for me on their knees, their heads bowed over the book. It always looked shiny and slick, despite having been pulled from the river weeks ago. When we touched it, it felt like warm calfskin.

The women were in meditation, and had been almost

constantly since the book arrived.

I waited, impatient, eyes always on the strange thing between them, its cover glittering, embossed with what looked like eight ovals. Perhaps they were eyes.

Suddenly, both of the women before me began to shake. The tremors were terrible, contorting their bodies in every direction, as if their bones had vanished, as if they were not humans of flesh and blood at all but empty sleeves of skin. A thick violet foam exploded from between their lips, running down their chins and staining their clean white garments. Meryt swayed back and forth, arms flailing, her face bending so low that her forehead brushed the book. It was cursed, I thought. An accursed thing brought forth from the river to trick us.

I rushed to Meryt, taking her dark brown shoulders in my hands and squeezing.

"Come back to me!" I shouted, shaking her, but the spell that gripped her made her too strong, and I flew back against the wall, dazed.

As quickly as the tremors had begun, they ceased. Chryseis opened her eyes first, blinking as if she had just had a long, deep nap. She wiped at the foam on her chin and then studied it, turning her hand this way and that, though it did not seem to trouble her.

"You frightened me," I said, climbing back to my feet.

It was amazing. She looked herself again, a healthy glow on her cheeks. Her golden-brown hair was twisted into braids around her face, and in that moment she appeared almost like a goddess.

"Did you see her?" Chryseis spoke to Meryt, who was now also awake and no longer shaking.

"Yes," she whispered back, eyes big with wonder. "She was beautiful."

"So beautiful," Chryseis agreed. "Impossible to describe . . ."

"But what did you see?" I begged. "Are you both well?"

"There is no time," Meryt told me, rising from her knees. She took me by the hand to the corner, where her personal satchel had been laid flat near a brazier. With purple foam still on her chin, she took the bag and emptied it, then returned to the middle of the room, taking up the strange book and shoving it into the satchel.

"What are you doing?" I asked her. "We should not move it!"

"It is not safe here," Meryt said, and she sounded sure. Chryseis joined us, helping her close the satchel and lift it over my head. The book was amazingly heavy, and I sank under its unnatural weight.

"It must be taken far away," Chryseis added. "The voice says you must go, Bennu, you must take the book north and you must not be seen. There can be no delay; she must be reunited with her husband."

"Who? Who told you these things?" I felt tears coming to my eyes. This was so fast, and so unfair! Why must I leave my family? Why had I been chosen for this, and by whom?

"She appeared to us, a beautiful lady all in purple," Chryseis explained, turning me toward the door. "As soon as she came, I felt whole. Perfect. As if everything around me was made of pure love."

"The snake, the bird, the spider, the cat, the dog," Meryt said, "she is mother to them all."

"I wish I could have seen her," I replied in awe, hesitating to leave the hut. My shoulder already ached from the cruel weight of the book. "I, too, have always protected the creatures here and worshipped those who made them. Why did she only come to you?"

Meryt guided me toward the dark outside the hut, pressing firmly on my back. "Yours is the most important task of all, Bennu. There are other forces that would see our order destroyed, demons in black and winged things. You must take her north, now, before she can be found."

"But how will I know the way?" I asked, feet touching the cold sand. "I have only once been farther than Tanis and seen the sails billowing on the sea, but never once boarded one."

"You will have help," Chryseis said. Her eyes glittered with urgency. "When the moon is full again you will have help. Our lady is sending you a guide, under the full and milky light; she promised it would be so."

"Go!" Meryt cried hoarsely, pushing me again. In the darkness, the purple stain on her chin looked like blood.

"Go!" Chryseis chimed in.

They chanted it at me as I left the hut, limping with the heavy book dragging from my shoulder. I yelped and nearly tumbled into the river, shock and fear making a tangle of my feet. Outside the shack, snakes and spiders had gathered in such quantity that I could hardly find a safe place to step. My stomach churned. It was a crescent of wriggling black tails and legs. None of them moved or made to bite, enthralled or ensorcelled into submission. And as I dodged to the patch of reeds far from the hut, they each of them slithered and skittered and turned, watching me go.

Chapter
Thirteen

A rich purple sunset darkened the horizon when I finally pulled myself from the house cellar. Mr. Morningside was not in his offices, and I stood ready to present him with the first fruits of my labor. I would not say I thought of handing over that first entry with eagerness—unease had settled in my stomach, a general agitation that I could not understand.

It was tempting to categorize what I had read in the journal as nonsense, but I had read Mr. Morningside's book and called it silliness only to realize that what he had seen and described was true. If Mr. Morningside's fantastical book held scraps of truth, then so, too, could this journal. Yet the only connection I found between my employer and the journal was the mention of an odd book—the tome in the attic of Coldthistle had been filled with illegible scribbles and burned to the touch. Mr. Morningside even claimed that anyone not of the Unworld would have died from contact with it. Perhaps there were more like it, although ours was decorated with only one eye.

Tired, I forced myself to stand in the kitchen doorway and face the last comforting tendrils of the sun's heat. I shielded my eyes from the light, finding it made my brain throb after so much time in the cavernous storage room below. I found the yard unusually bustling—Mr. Mason Breen and his betrothed played a lazy game of lawn bowls against Sparrow and Finch near the pavilion, and Chijioke sat on a stump not far from the kitchen door, a whittling project on his knee.

I rolled my translation into a scroll and tucked it under one arm, shuffling into the glow of sunset and standing beside Chijioke. Little wood shavings flew as he attacked the piece of wood furiously, all the while keeping his hazel eyes trained on Sparrow and Finch. Sparrow had changed into a more expected ensemble for lawn darts, a light, breezy dress of ivory that made her look appropriately angelic. It was clear she and her brother were winning, but judging from Amelia's giggling, the loss wasn't upsetting the guests. They only had eyes for each other anyway, Mason and Amelia giving no attention whatsoever to the twins or, apparently, their aim.

"Do you know where Mr. Morningside might be?" I asked, watching a stray wood shaving land on my boot.

"In his usual spot, I'd wager," Chijioke grumbled. I watched the knife drive in and out, an instant later a fin where once a shapeless nub had been. Gradually the lump was beginning to look like a fish.

"He isn't there, I looked," I replied. "How can you carve so quickly without looking?"

"Don't know, lass, just helps me relax." He flicked the knife twice more, adding delicate little scales to the fish. Finally, he glanced away from the lawn bowls, but not at his carving. Instead, he gazed up at me. I had been staring quite rudely at his handiwork. As soon as he looked at me he turned away again, and I heard him give a sigh. "It's for Mary. For when she returns. She said fish were lucky; she kept a charm of one in her pocket to rub for good fortune."

"It's very nice," I told him. "Were you two . . . I mean, was there some kind of understanding between you?"

It was the first time his knife slipped, and the edge missed his thumb by a hair.

"An understanding? No . . . Well, maybe. A word here or there, but never the right ones. That was my blunder." He cleared his throat. "That would have been nice to have. An understanding, that is."

Mary's absence made me miserable, but I had known her only a short while—Chijioke and the others must have been suffering terribly. Three-hundred-year contracts. How long had they been here? It was selfish of me not to think of it, and to lose myself in another obsession so quickly. Here he was, carving her a lovely token while I did nothing but plot revenge against a rich father I had never met.

"I don't blame you, you know," he said, carving and glaring at Finch and Sparrow again. "She made her choice, too. Someone was hurting and she wanted that fixed, and nothing anyone said would've changed her mind. That's just how she is. Was."

"Is." I tried to sound resolute. We were quiet for a moment, but I wasn't ready to leave in search of Mr. Morningside yet. This was important, too. Mary, Chijioke . . . They had become my friends, and I owed them more than passing consideration. I hoped to fix their general opinion of me very soon. "I did everything right to bring her back," I said, and my voice faltered, not because I doubted myself but because the failure stung. "I followed Mr. Morningside's instructions to the letter. It was the same spring, the same man giving the riddles, the same wish. . . . I don't know what went wrong, Chijioke, I'm sorry."

His shoulders bunched up and the carving stopped. Then I heard another sigh, this one more forlorn than the last. "I believe you, lass. Her kind are ancient and hard to really know. Someone might have needed her more than you this time. Who can say? Mary will return to us when she's good and ready, aye? All I can do is hope these Upworlder bastards will be long gone before then."

"Why do you hate them so much?" I asked, going to his other side and kneeling in the cool grass where it was not snowing wood chips. The sun flared as it lowered, and I shielded my eyes again, watching as Sparrow managed a perfect toss.

Chijioke muttered something dark and unintelligible and then spat in the pile of wood shavings to his right. He squinted at the Upworlders and returned to his blind carving. "Adjudicators are dangerous and odd-like, same as us, but they and their followers have got that self-righteous stink on them. We're the evil ones, aye? What rubbish. Justice is justice—whether they deliver it or we do. We take souls and so do they, our methods are just different."

I followed his steely gaze, and while the sight of the twins gave me that cold feeling inside, it was hard to imagine them being killers. That was unfair, of course; I had learned to stop judging on appearances alone. Sparrow stood just behind her brother, rolling her eyes as Amelia missed yet another easy shot.

"Do they have a house like Coldthistle?" I asked. "I thought angels and the like would be in Heaven or something."

He chuckled and tossed his head, giving me a sideways glance. "I forget that there's still so much you have to learn, lass."

"I'm trying," I said, admittedly exasperated. "It really doesn't help that I was raised on a Bible and stories that don't fit anything I've seen."

"Aye, you *are* at a disadvantage there," Chijioke replied. With the half-finished fish carving he pointed to Amelia—in red, of course—and her husband-to-be. "What do you see when you look at those two?"

"Must I look?"

He laughed again, or snorted, really, and nodded. "Indulge me, lass."

"Very well." I rolled my eyes at him and then studied Amelia and Mason for a moment. I noted that they were doing very badly at bowls, and that of the two Mason seemed to have more aptitude for it, but he frequently made a bad shot because Amelia insisted on draping herself across his arm. "I see two fools oblivious to the fact that they're being soundly beaten, and that if they wagered anything on the match then surely they will lose it."

Chijioke tapped his chin thoughtfully with the wooden fish and swayed his head side to side. "Granted. Granted. But I see two people who are so in love with each other they're not likely to care about losing at bowls or losing coin. I see true love."

"Goodness gracious." I glanced up at him, and the look he gave me in return was hooded. Unreadable. "Have you spent even a moment alone with Miss Amelia Canny?"

"I have not."

"Firstly, I cannot recommend it. Secondly, she has already confessed to me that she did something horrible to win that man's affections," I explained. "How can that be true love?"

His smile broadened and he gave me a wink, tapping me on the forehead with the fish. "There are the things that humans see and write down, and there are the things that really happen. Nobody ever said they have to be the same thing."

"Ah. I take your meaning," I said. Finch had noticed us watching, apparently, and disengaged from the match, walking toward us at a leisurely pace. I stood and felt Chijioke puff up like a nervous hound as the Upworlder approached. "So the Bible is, what? A misunderstanding? A clerical error?"

Chijioke sprang up next to me, his knife back to work on the fish for Mary. "It's the best a few could do to describe what the many couldn't or wouldn't see. We all make mistakes, Louisa, some are just bigger. A lot bigger."

"You're not going to stab him, are you?" I muttered.

That at least made him smirk, but only briefly, for soon he was glowering again. "Adjudicators come in threes, Louisa, so keep your wits about you."

"Threes?" I frowned and watched as Finch slowed his steps toward us. "Sparrow might think I'm hopelessly stupid, but I *can* count. Where is the third one?"

"I haven't the faintest clue," he said. "Which is why this makes me nervous."

"Does that mean you're going to stab him, then?"

"Stand behind me," Chijioke added, edging out in front of me. "If he tries anything, he'll get a walloping."

"He hardly looks like trouble. . . ."

He gave a slight shake of his head. "Oh aye, and that's because you have never witnessed a Judgment."

"A what?"

Chijioke didn't answer. Whatever Finch had seen on or near us had made him change his mind. He stopped abruptly, face falling, before he turned on his heel and returned to his lawn bowls. I felt his presence a moment later at my side and my unease appeared with him. Mr. Morningside had found us, and he loomed tall and narrow next to me.

He nodded politely to Chijioke and then gave us both a brilliant white smile. The sun was almost completely gone behind the horizon, and Amelia whined as they decided to end the game in time for a wash-up and supper. Dimly, I heard Mason

Breen congratulate Finch and Sparrow on their win, but I was deaf to whatever they said afterward.

"A game of bowls among friends," Mr. Morningside crowed, leaning back and adjusting his fine silk cravat. The diminishing light turned his black hair to glossy raven's wings as he took in a deep, loud breath through his nose. "A crisp evening. The splendor of nature. The fading luster of spring . . ." He extended his hand, sweeping it in front of him. "What a satisfactory sight."

But he was not looking at the horizon or the trees, or the game of bowls, or even my face. I swallowed, feeling cornered even in the open air. Mr. Morningside had seen the parchment rolled under my arm, and all of his appreciable attention was bent toward it.

Chapter Fourteen

he dining gallery glowed softly with candles, the twinkling melody of cutlery on plates and crystal glassware floating lightly beneath the conversation. It had been months since I had last served at a formal supper, and I struggled to maintain the proper attention to detail and regimen. Lee, Mrs. Haylam, and I stood to the side near the serving board, waiting for just the right moment to dash in with more wine or to retrieve a fallen handkerchief.

The pace of it made me itch. Lee did not seem any better off, fidgeting at my side. We watched Miss Canny, her betrothed, and his father and business associate dine on white soup and roast loin of pork studded with cloves, the smells so rich and tempting that my stomach growled in protest. Our meal, by contrast, had been a cup of stew made days ago, filling but not nearly as decadent as the spread being served now.

Amelia wore dazzling pins in her hair to match her scarlet gown. I couldn't help but stare at her and wonder what it was like to own so many frocks that a new one could be donned for each part of the day. Mason Breen and his side of the family dressed far more soberly, in simple grays and browns, though the cut of their suits and the quality of the fabric hinted at their wealth. Mason Breen's father, Mr. Barrow Breen, had the look of a sailor, with very tanned and weathered flesh, and gnarled knuckles. Such men were commonplace where I had grown up, which led me to believe he might be one of the newly rich, perhaps a man who had made his fortune in exports. The two men shared a strong familial resemblance, both with bright shocks of blond hair and pale gray eyes. Mason was quite handsome, angular and austere, and his father simply looked like an aged, tired version of his son.

Their business partner, Samuel Potts, had a swarthier appearance, also sun-dappled and leathery, with shaggy, thinning gray hair and a monstrous beard. His suit, while fine, fit on him strangely, as if he were a bear wrestled into a waistcoat.

"I do find that young Mr. Finch very agreeable," Amelia was saying. She had managed the bulk of the conversation at the table, which did not seem to upset any of the men. They listened dutifully and drank just as intently. A dark rosy stain was spreading across Mason's cheeks.

"His sister is far less . . . Well, she is rather opinionated, is she not?"

Samuel Potts grunted into his wine, ruffling his mustache.

"Where did they say they were from again?" Mason Breen asked, helping himself to more pork.

"London," Mrs. Haylam said suddenly, startling us all. The room fell silent at her single, barked word. She gave a mild, faked smile and added, "By way of Calcutta. Merely passing through, I'm afraid."

Amelia recovered from the shock of Mrs. Haylam's

interruption with a giggle. "Now that is a shame. It is excellent to make new friends, they could even attend the wedding—"

"Out of the question," Mr. Barrow Breen grumbled. "The very idea!"

"Oh, it was only a silly suggestion," Amelia replied, but she hid her face, concentrating on her dinner plate. "I cannot see the harm in—"

"Girl, I know what you see; you see whatever it is you want to waste my money on next," he thundered. The hall rang with the boom of his voice, and Lee and I both flinched, then shared a look. He raised both tawny eyebrows and then rolled his eyes slowly toward the table. I tried not to laugh.

"At least we won't have to put up with it for long," I whispered, and I saw him smile.

"I won't have you speaking to my betrothed that way!" Mason had finally spoken up, jumping to his feet and rattling the table. The wineglass perched on the edge near Samuel Potts upended, and he roared in surprise, shooting up out of his seat and grabbing for something to wipe at his soiled shirt.

"Quickly now," Mrs. Haylam directed, snapping into action. "Help Mr. Potts, Louisa."

I turned to the board behind us and took a clean napkin from the folded pile and dabbed it in a glass of water, rushing to the bushy man's side. He snatched the napkin out of my hand and shooed me away, rubbing furiously at his clothes.

"This wedding is enough of a farce without that brainless

ninny inviting strangers to gawk at our lives!" Barrow Breen shoved a finger in his son's face, which was immediately batted away.

Mason was as tall as his father and now puffed himself up to be even larger. "How . . . How dare you, sir? How dare you?" He whirled and motioned to a dumbfounded Amelia. "Come, Amelia, we do not have to endure this."

She gave a soft little pout and rounded the table on tippy-toes, taking Mason's elbow and following him out of the room.

In the aftermath there was only silence. Mr. Breen breathed so erratically I could see his shoulders jumping up and down as he struggled to contain himself. Samuel Potts continued to work fruitlessly at his shirt and then scoffed, throwing the napkin down on the table.

"Just a short dessert, then," Mrs. Haylam said brightly, as if nothing at all had happened.

Lee and I stared at her in disbelief, then scurried to change out the plates and remove the soup and pork from the table. There was trifle and pudding, but the men only picked at their portions in the ominous residuum of the argument. Tea was brought and ignored, and finally the men filed out, the atmosphere clearing as if a storm had passed.

"A delightful bunch," Lee muttered as we cleared the table and helped Mrs. Haylam return everything to the kitchens.

I had always liked the dining hall, as it felt cozier and more human than some of the other rooms in Coldthistle, but now it felt stained, as if the family had left behind an imprint of sorrow. Mrs. Haylam stayed behind in the kitchens on our last trip to direct Poppy on what could be saved and salvaged for the pantry. Lee and I remained in the dining room, washing and sweeping.

"I would not want to marry into that miserable family," I replied, peeling off the tablecloth. I sighed at the massive wine stain on one side, dreading the time it would take me to clean it. "I don't care how rich they are."

"Amelia obviously does," Lee said. He swept under the board and chairs, making a little pile of crumbs near the open door. The dining hall was at the back of the house, around behind the staircase and looking out onto the north end of the lawn and the spring. The house was mostly quiet, but above us I could hear pacing, and I wondered if Amelia was having trouble sleeping after the fight.

"She was poor once," I told him. "It makes you ruthless."

"Does it?" He said it softly, but I heard the implicit accusation.

"Yes," I replied, undaunted. "It can grind you into dust, having nothing, it isn't noble or romantic, and it's humiliating to know villains like *Mr.* Barrow Breen get to wallow in luxury and still turn out to be unbearable heels."

Lee swept silently for a moment, then paused and turned to look at me as I rolled up the tablecloth for the wash. "And if you came into money? Would you be different?"

"I don't know," I said. "I should probably learn to hate myself."

"You would do something good with it," he assured me, and swept the pile of crumbs out into the foyer. "I like to think you would do something good."

I'm trying, I thought, silently considering my bargain with the Devil. I will.

I was exhausted by the time Mrs. Haylam excused us. Lee disappeared at once, dodging out of the kitchens and into the darkness outside the house. He narrowly missed Poppy and Bartholomew, who slumped inside to rest while Mrs. Haylam did the final locking up.

With so much dessert left behind, she allowed us to each take a bit of trifle with us up to bed. It was the best thing I had eaten in a long time, but I could hardly taste it. While I battled the fatigue muddling my mind, I thought about what Lee had said. Would I really do something good with a fortune of my own? I didn't quite know. . . . Of course it was tempting to imagine oneself as a gracious benefactor, foregoing decadence and living modestly as a philanthropist, giving money to orphanages and turning patron to some needy ward. But I could not say if that was my secret truth. Perhaps my secret truth was that I wanted to finally have something of my own, to spend money however I saw fit, to own a great house and fill it with ridiculous gowns and trinkets.

I would not know until that secret truth could be my reality. Croydon Frost and the money he owed me was reality, one that crept ever closer as Mr. Morningside read over the first translation.

Lee was right, I told myself. I would take Frost's money and help my friends. If they did not want to live with me then I could buy them all houses of their own. How amazing it would be, I thought, to give them the gift of freedom.

In the morning I would bother him about bringing my father to the house, but in that moment I craved only sleep. I finished the trifle, spooning up the last of the cream and shuffling into my chambers. Closing the door, I rested against it gratefully for a moment. In the corridor I heard the familiar scraping gait of the Residents as they began their nightly patrols of the house. I crossed to the bed and left my little empty cup on the table, then changed into my bedclothes with leaden limbs. Crawling into bed, I shifted the curtain to my right aside and gazed up at the stars for a moment, letting the bright moonlight bathe my face.

I must have fallen asleep immediately, but woke soon after, roused by what sounded like crying. Sitting up in bed, I moved the curtain on my window aside again and peered out into the darkness. From there, I saw only the eastern side of the lawn, part of the barn, and the newly built pavilion. Nothing obvious stirred in the yard, and I waited for a moment, listening, thinking that the horses had been startled or a hawk had found a mouse in the fields. But the cry came again, this time clearer and certainly human.

Kneeling, I pressed my face to the cool glass and squinted. There was movement at the very edge of the strip of woods behind the pavilion. I swore it was so. I waited still longer, and this time it was a long, pained wail. A girl's voice. Had Poppy gotten out of the house and into some kind of trouble? It didn't sound like her, but I couldn't imagine who else would be out in the forest crying. Mrs. Haylam had warned us to be careful, to stay in the house, but I ignored her advice, putting bare feet to cold wooden slats and searching for a coat. I had been given an old, quilted housecoat that was tattered and worn, but as it was nearly summer, it would suffice.

I shrugged on the coat and padded to the door, then opened it slowly and checked for any wandering Residents. Down the hall, one drifted up the stairs, just the bedraggled tips of its feet hanging there before it glided up to the floor above. After a moment, I darted down toward where it had been and raced toward the foyer, hoping it would be too late in sensing me. Though I had not often navigated the house in the dark, I trusted that the kitchen door would be the most expedient route. It was also likely to be empty, since Mrs. Haylam and Poppy had their rooms elsewhere. Coldthistle remained silent, filled with the kind of uneasy tension that came in the dead of night.

The kitchens were empty but the door leading out had been locked. Of course. Mrs. Haylam was feeling particularly touchy about security with the Upworlders around. I fished the spoon necklace out from under my chemise and closed my eyes, steadying my breathing. I didn't think of my father but of the person in need outside. My thoughts raced. What if Poppy had been lured to the woods? Would the Upworlders really try to harm her? Or perhaps Amelia and Mason had sneaked off for some mischief in the spring and twisted an ankle. . . . Whoever or whatever it was, I knew I would never get back to sleep with them wailing outside my window.

The spoon grew hot in my hand and changed as I squeezed it, re-forming into a key. I unlocked the kitchen door and crept out into the moonlit yard. It was far brighter than normal, lending me plenty of light to see by as I tiptoed through the grass. No commotion came from the barn as I passed, but that high, scared cry came from the forest again. This time, I could make out words. . . .

Heeeelp me! Please, help!

The girl was crying. She sounded so pitiful, so lonely. . . . Tendrils of familiarity tugged at my heart. I knew the voice, I could *swear* I knew the voice. So I approached the forest edge, carefully, the pavilion to my right and back, Coldthistle looming over my left shoulder. There was no path into the woods here, for the only trail cut through farther to my left and led only to the natural spring. As I neared the forest I heard the spring bubbling distantly, and the chorus of frogs and crickets that took up near its moister grounds filled the air with their song. A twig cracked under my foot and I froze, clutching the spoon necklace with both hands. Without my meaning it to, the spoon that had become a key had now, in my fear, become a knife.

That was all right, I decided, swallowing back the little voice in my head that told me to turn back and go immediately to bed. Another voice joined that one, the same that had risen in me when I first met Finch and Sparrow.

The woods are no place for you tonight, child. Turn back.

I did not relish the thought of a woman's disembodied voice living inside me, and so far it had not protected me from anything at all. Sparrow and Finch had not harmed me, though admittedly this did seem like a far worse circumstance. I hesitated, clutching the knife, wondering if now was the time to listen to that voice before it was too late. A chill ran through my bones and I swiveled to look back at Coldthistle. Nobody had followed and I did not see any Residents watching me from the windows. The place looked dead, just a black and shadowed husk that seemed as unwelcoming as the forest. The frogs and insects chirped louder, screeching like a bow singing across a too-tight string. The hairs on the back of my neck stood up. Danger. I would go inside, I thought, I would heed that warning voice at last.

But then the cry came again and I gasped, spinning and plunging into the forest.

Mary.

Chapter
Fifteen

ranches sharp and stinging clawed at my face, but I knew my purpose now and nothing would stop me.

Mary was hurt. Mary was in danger. I would not let her slip through my grasp. Knife still in hand—for who could say what had given her cause to cry?—I followed the sound of her voice whenever it rose again. She had ceased calling for help and instead wept softly. My heart ached, and I panted, running, ignoring the burn in my chest and the cutting branches scraping at my cheeks.

The forest was deeper than it looked from a distance, but I soon reached a tiny clearing. Thank God for the moonlight, else I might have stumbled and broken my ankle as the ground dipped into a shallow divot. A few larger rocks were strewn around the clearing, and there was Mary, kneeling, clinging to one of those boulders. I ran toward her, elated and afraid, then dropped to her side. Her face lit up as she caught sight of me and she flung her arms around my neck, still crying.

"Louisa! You came!" She held me tightly and I held her back.

"Are you well? Did you fall?" I held her at arm's length, inspecting her from head to foot. She had her same wild brown hair and green eyes, and those freckles clustered thickly over her nose, the same gentle Irish lilt to her voice. Her garments were travel stained and her hem and boots were caked with mud, as if she had walked a long distance. A light lavender cloak was bunched around her neck and shoulders, and she used it to dab her wet face. Her cheeks were too hollow, as if she had gone hungry, and it made her eyes look only larger and more innocent.

"I tripped," she said, and gave a weak laugh. "So clumsy, can you believe it? This close to the house and I had to get tangled in my own feet."

"Is your leg badly hurt?" I asked. It didn't look twisted or swollen, but then her skirts hid most of her lower half. "Where did you come from? I went to the spring to summon you ages ago; did something go wrong?"

Mary gave a relieved laugh and wiped more at her face, then leaned against the rock and gazed into my eyes. She reached up and touched my hair, and I felt a surge of hope. I had not failed her completely. She was back, and now things might be the slightest bit more normal, if normal existed at Coldthistle House.

"You were perfect," Mary assured me, taking my hand and squeezing it. "I was stuck in the Dusk Lands, it was just dreadful, and then I heard you call me back, call me through. But . . . I wasn't ready to come back. I needed time. Time for myself."

I nodded and looked away, a little shy. "Of course. I'm . . . I'm terribly nosy, I'm sorry. After what happened with Lee . . . Well. Nobody could expect you to be jumping at the chance to return. I'm sure I'm the last person you wanted to come to your aid."

Mary seemed calmer and began to shimmy up the rock, putting careful pressure on her left foot. I jumped up and helped, letting her lean against my side as she stood. She winced, but otherwise looked ready to be upright.

"You came," she said softly. "That's what matters. Oh, I'm sure my leg is not as bad as I thought. I'm just so tired. . . . It was a long way. I thought the walk would help me, you know, help to put things right in my brain."

"You walked all the way from Waterford? That . . . How?"

She giggled and swatted my shoulder. "No, Louisa, not all the way. I wanted to walk the last bit to . . ." Mary chewed over her answer for a long moment and then shrugged. "I wanted to walk the fields, get a feel for my home again."

"In the dead of night?" I teased.

Mary's answer was cut short. Her eyes widened as we both heard a bloodcurdling call emanating from deep in the woods. We froze, looking at one another. I had never heard anything like it—a high, unearthly wail, almost the scream of a Resident but less hollow, filled with the raw throatiness of an animal. It was not a wolf, or if it was, it was an unnatural one.

"I have a knife," I whispered. "But let us hasten; you are in no fit state to fend off an animal. . . ."

"Hurry," Mary agreed with a little hiccuping cry, pulling on my shoulder.

The shrill animal scream came again, and closer, and my spine rippled, warning me, primal fear of *whatever the hell that was* taking over. Heavy footsteps shook the clearing and the trees behind us as I tried my best to carry her toward the house. The thing was running now and Mary forgot her injury, taking my hand and yanking me across the clearing.

"We must hurry," she shrieked, panting. "D-do something, Louisa, you must change, change into a bear, into anything—"

"Can you shield us?" I was panicking. A bear? How could I possibly do that? I could hardly change a spoon into a sad little knife! "Are you too exhausted?"

"I—I can't. I—"

The creature broke through the trees and into the clearing, crushing a sapling under its massive foot with ease. My instinct to run was overtaken by sheer terror as a beast, upright as a man but furred as a wolf, crashed into the open. I opened my mouth to scream, huddling against Mary as she, too, stared in open-mouthed horror at the creature. It was taller than a large man by at least a yard. Ripples of scarred muscle burst through its brown-black fur in places, and its face was pointed, almost fox-like. Narrow, glittering purple eyes found us at once, shining brighter as it chose its prey. I was trembling so fiercely I could hardly stand, but I did what I could, shoving Mary behind me, shielding her with my shaking body.

My eyes traveled slowly from its face to its hands, those, too, like a man's but longer, capped with razor-like claws. A black sash around its middle rippled as it went low and then pounced, leaping toward us with a snarl. We must have both screamed but I couldn't hear my own voice, not as its thick arm collided with my shoulder, knocking me to the ground.

There was a ringing in my ears as I tried to sit up, pain dulled by fear as I stumbled away from the tree I had hit and raised the knife. The creature had rounded on Mary, ignoring me completely, raising one of its clawed hands and preparing to strike.

I couldn't say when the knife had transformed into a pistol, but it had. My terror as I flew through the air must have forced the change. Whatever caused it, I did not care, raising the gun and firing, reeling back as the bullet grazed the side of the creature's face. It roared, that same horrible, animal scream filling the clearing. I clapped my hands over my ears, deafened, watching in mute horror as it swung toward me, purple eyes brighter even than the moon above.

Now I had drawn the creature's attention and I had no idea what to do—the pistol held only one shot and I scrambled to change the spoon yet again, this time into a knife, a spear, anything. . . . But I was too unfocused, too panicked, and the beast was upon me, its black nose tracing the shape of my head before it snorted and showed me its fangs.

And it *spoke.*

I closed my eyes, feeling death near, smelling the musky scent of its fur and the grass and brambles caught in its coat. One crunch of its teeth and my throat would be ripped to tatters. Blood dripped down its sharp cheek from where the bullet had torn open a wound.

"*Nebet, aw ibek,*" it growled, or something that sounded like those jumbled words.

How it spoke, I know not, but the voice was from the pits of Hell itself, full of malice and unnatural tremors. It turned away from me, but not before grabbing the pistol from my hand and crushing it in its great fist. I lunged, trying to reach for it, the one weapon I might have boasted against the beast, and then gasped, a flash of light blinding us all.

The creature snarled again, and when I could finally see through the haze of gold filling the clearing, I saw the thing go on all fours and sprint away into the forest. The ground shook at its going, trees creaking and groaning as it rent them in its retreat. I rubbed at my eyes, stumbling forward to try to find Mary, but she was not alone.

Finch stood over her, a pair of immense white wings flaring from his back before they folded behind his back and vanished. A glow remained around him, the obvious source of the flash that had startled the beast and made it flee. I touched my neck, feeling the raw spot where the beast had ripped at the chain on my necklace. It was gone—spoon, knife, gun, whatever it was, it was gone.

"What was that thing?" I murmured, hoarse.

Mary got slowly to her feet, helped by Finch. He was still dressed in his slim gray suit, but his hair looked rumpled from sleep.

Frowning, he turned and looked toward the path of destruction left by the creature as it escaped. "I only caught a glimpse of it," he said, guiding Mary to lean against his shoulder. "The sound it gave was enough. I thought it better to blind first and get a good look later."

"It . . . It was like a wolf or, or a fox, but so much bigger," I stammered. My back ached from colliding with the tree and my hands were still shaking from shock. "What if it comes back?"

"Then I will deal with it again," Finch said. He looked sure, but I detected a jumpiness in his gaze, his eyes shifting side to side as he held Mary. "We should get you both back to the house."

"Are you hurt, Mary?" I asked, watching as she stared around at the edges of the clearing, vigilant.

"I . . . I don't think so," she said. "But I fear my leg will not allow me to return on foot."

"That is no trouble," Finch replied, and motioned to his back. "Climb on my back. I'll have you both to safety in a moment's time."

"I am quite capable of walking," I said with a sigh. "And besides, you could not possibly carry us both."

"Don't be ridiculous." Mary had sidled to his back and hooked her arms gingerly about his neck. He reached for me as soon as she did, sweeping me up into his strong grasp and launching into the air. Neither of us had time to properly react, those same huge, white wings sprouting from his back as if they were weightless, as if they were made of pure light.

I let out a shriek of surprise, scrambling to hang on to his shoulders as we flew up and away from the forest, leaving the forest floor far behind. Cool night air rushed over us, and my heart raced with terror all over again. It was more than just surprise, it was also dread, and the chilliness his presence always gave me. Well, and I had never been whisked through the air by a being with *wings*.

We landed safely in the yard just outside the kitchens. The door was still open, but now Mrs. Haylam was on the other side. Her face, twisted in fury, soon fell as she saw that it was not just me and Finch, but also Mary. I tumbled out of Finch's grasp clumsily, wrapping my housecoat tightly around me as Mrs. Haylam rushed to Mary and herded her into an embrace.

"At last," Mrs. Haylam was saying over and over again. It was the closest I had seen her come to tears or even joy. "At last you have returned to us. But you must be so weary."

Mary wilted, boneless with exhaustion.

"I won't ask what this was all about until tomorrow," Mrs. Haylam said in a deadly whisper. Her one good eye locked on me and I pressed my lips together. "Mary is home; that earns you clemency for a few hours."

She gave Finch an equally sharp look and then guided Mary toward the kitchens. I saw Chijioke inside, his brows knitted with concern as he scooped Mary up and brought her away from the night's chill.

"A 'thank you' would suffice," Finch muttered, long after Mrs. Haylam had gone.

"How about a spot of tea and a 'thank you'?" I asked, trooping wearily into the kitchen.

"Are you sure that's wise? Your housekeeper seems cross."

"I'm already in trouble, what could it hurt?" I gestured him inside, then went to the range and checked to see that a low fire was still burning. With a wick, I went about the room, lighting a few stumpy candles and placing them on the table. There was pudding still in the pantry, and I retrieved it, laying out a bit of food while I fetched the kettle.

Frosty needles still prickled in my gut, but I ignored it, rationalizing that he had just saved my life and Mary's, and so I could put up with the discomfort for the length of a cup of tea.

"Thank you," I said, back to him as I fussed with the cups. "But how did you find us? No one else heard the commotion."

"We . . ." He trailed off, and when I glanced over my shoulder, I found he had seated himself at the table, but would not meet my eye. His dark mane of hair fell in front of his eyes and he traced a circle on the table with one finger. "Sparrow and I are watching the house. It's part of why we are here. We came to observe, and I know that sounds incredibly intrusive, but perhaps you can understand, given . . ."

"Given that a ruddy huge wolf just attacked me in the woods?" I finished. "Forgiven. And if it means anything, I don't mind you so much. The others . . ."

"It's a shame. A damn shame."

Scrutiny. Mr. Morningside had mentioned that he was not looking forward to their poking around. He would probably be furious if he knew they had been floating about the house at night.

I managed a tired smile and measured out the tea, listening to Chijioke and Mrs. Haylam fuss as they brought Mary up the stairs to her room. "Should you be cursing?"

"Oh, don't be fooled by the wings," he said with a wink. "We can be dangerous."

"That's what everyone promises me. What shall they say now that you saved my life?"

His mirth faded and he flinched, dropping his elbow onto the table and his chin into that palm. "We were close once, you know. You are a newcomer to our worlds, so all of this must be deeply confusing. There was more than just passing civility in the old days. We were allies, those of our world and of Henry's. We had to be. Now we just exist in a kind of . . . tense civility. I hope it can last but I fear it will not."

"It is hard to imagine you and someone like Chijioke getting along. He is not fond of your kind, not even a little." I filled the cups and let them steep, finding small comfort in the fragrant tea steam that drifted up from the darkening surface. "What caused the . . . How would you describe it? Rift?"

The promise of tea helped, even if my hands were still shaking. When I blinked, I saw the beast's purple eyes and maw.

That hellish voice would forever darken my dreams.

I joined Finch at the table, grateful for the rest the chair provided. It was only then that I noticed my hands were skinned and scratched, and drops of blood stained the housecoat's sleeve. The blood of the beast. I shivered.

"We can talk of cheerier things," Finch murmured, noticing.

"As if that were possible," I said. My hands smoothed around the teacup, absorbing its warmth. "I have seen all manner of horrors here, but never have I seen a wolf like that."

Finch took up his cup, too, holding it with both hands just under his chin. "There have been no wolves in England for hundreds of years. Maybe that hound I've seen skulking about the house has gone feral."

"Do not tell me what I saw," I told him sternly. "It was a wolf of a kind, taller than a man, with glowing eyes, and it could *speak*. Truly you did not see the thing properly if you could mistake it for Bartholomew. Besides, that dog is more interested in napping than hunting these days."

I heard Mrs. Haylam's pointed boots clicking on the floor outside the kitchen, and then she swept inside. She had come to retrieve a basin and some rags, which she did, but not before making her displeasure known. Standing in the door, she hitched the basin higher in her arms and nodded toward the kettle.

"Clean this up before morning," she said curtly, then left in a huff and a whirl of skirts.

"Do not trouble yourself with my well-being, Granny," I mumbled to where she had been. "Just a bump or two, nothing to fret about."

Finch sipped carefully at his hot tea and tilted his head to the side, watching me. "If I may be so bold, Louisa, you are not like the others here. I get the feeling that you would not just follow Mrs. Haylam or Henry blindly."

I shrugged off the praise. So far, I had done too much of what Mr. Morningside wanted. What would Finch think of me if he knew I had just that day signed a contract vowing to help him? Well, that was private. He did not need to know about my father, and I had promised to keep the journal and its contents a secret.

"How could I?" I looked into my teacup, hoping he could not sense the deception. "He was wrong about my friend Lee."

"Right. Exactly. That's good—I mean, not good that he was mistaken—but you should bring that up at the Court. It's important that we have the truth, and that you give honest testimony."

"Testimony?" I laughed. "Mr. Morningside is under the impression that this is some kind of party. . . ."

"He would be. I doubt he's taken anything seriously in his life, which is how we got into this mess in the first place. Just reap souls, send them on their way . . . how hard could that really be? Why does he have to make a mess of everything?"

Sighing, I stood and drained my teacup, then carried it to

the deep porcelain tub beside the range to wash up. I hadn't exactly seen Mr. Morningside sending souls anywhere but into birds, but perhaps that was what Finch meant after all. I said nothing to contradict him. Finch's chair scraped across the tiles as he stood and brought his cup to sit next to mine. The cold knot in my stomach only hurt worse the closer he came.

"Did I say something to offend you?" he asked softly.

"I'm . . . tired. Tired from the day's work, tired from that ordeal in the forest, and tired of all of you speaking in circles above my head." It came spilling out of me in a rush of words; whatever thread of patience I had left had finally snapped. I leaned hard against the washbasin and covered my face with both hands. It took just an instant before I could muster the will to take up a rag and rinse out the teacups. "I did not mean to lose my composure."

Finch returned to the table and brought me the rest of the porcelain we had used as well as the spoons. I stared for a long moment at the tea-stained curve of one of the spoons, feeling heartsick at the thought of that creature bounding off into the forest with the one Lee had given me. Another wave of hopeless exhaustion crashed down, and I wondered if the next time I closed my eyes I would simply drift off to sleep standing up.

"I would be more worried if you weren't overwhelmed," he said, and out of the corner of my eye I could see him give a polite bow before he moved toward the kitchen door. "Try to rest if you can. I wish I could say the days will get easier, but I would not want to give you false hope."

Nodding, I dried the teacups with a worn cloth and listened to his retreating steps.

"Aye, I will try to rest," I said. "Good night."

Good night. I had to grimace at the thought—it would be just as well if I stayed there at the basin until dawn came and I was needed in the kitchens again. How could I sleep soundly knowing that monster was out there? Could any of us stand against it? I shivered and tidied the kitchen, then pulled the door shut and stared across the room into the dark foyer. If that thing came back for Mary, mere doors would not stop it. I had to console myself with the idea that Finch and his sister would continue watching the house, and perhaps if the beast returned they would see it before it could strike.

It was cold comfort, and when I returned to my chambers and slid into bed, it was a long, lonely time before restless sleep allowed me to escape and dream.

Chapter
Sixteen

Year One

𓉘𓏏𓏜 𓈖𓏲𓏤𓈖𓏤 𓂋𓏤 𓀀𓏥

Journal of Bennu, Who Runs

*I followed the river north and composed in my head messages
to my family.* Do not worry, *they began,* I will return soon.
*These would be lies, but they would not be the first I told. My
mother and sisters already disliked my fervent devotion to gods
they did not recognize or respect. They worshipped as everyone
else did, and thought me foolish for bowing low to the river, to*

the bee, to the very palms that sheltered our house.

If they knew that no more than a shared vision of Meryt and Chryseis's had sent me on this task, they would lock me up and lose the key.

Still. Composing the messages made me feel better, because if I was allowed to write such things or even see my family again, then it meant I had survived. How far would I have to go? How would I know when I arrived? The book and satchel grew heavier as I stumbled along the banks of the river. The ground sloped up and down, sometimes cluttered with reeds and shifting stones, sometimes open to the sun, and occasionally cooled by the shade of date palms. Would the guide I had been promised meet me at the next village, or the next? My belly demanded food and my thirst had become such that I tasted blood on the cracked edges of my lips.

As night fell on that first long day, I stopped in a small gathering of homes near a flooded bend. It was a farming community, and with the day's work over, the villagers had returned to their homes to relax and drink honeyed beer.

I swatted at the mosquitoes swarming my arms and prowled the homes quietly, hopeful for a sign. The land grew hillier as I traveled away from the water. A woman sang to her child, the haunting melody drifting out through an open window. My feet felt raw, my body on the verge of collapse. And then, cause to hope! I noted the red-and-white paint flecking off the bottom of a brick house. It was just a modest place, not much more than a squat hut, but a snake had been painted to the left of the door, and though it was old and faded with age, I knew what it meant.

Sanctuary.

"Hello?" I called, and tapped lightly on the wooden door. "A friend is at the door. I kneel in the river to pray. I wash the feet of jackals. I do not go to the temple, I do not speak the names."

It was dark inside, and I wondered if nobody waited within. Then a light and a single eye appeared at the crack in the door. A gruff male voice said: "Are you lost, child?"

Smiling, I hitched the pack higher on my shoulder and replied, "My feet are on the path."

The door opened, as I'd hoped it would, and I slumped gratefully inside. The man who greeted me was old and hunch-backed, and he leaned heavily on a cane that was little more than a branch. A few leaves still clung to the top. He limped across the straw floor to a table surrounded by three stools. He had farmer's hands, strong and scarred, and though his furnishings were meager, the smell emanating from his small brick oven was excellent. Of course a man who worshipped all of nature's beauty, as we did, would have a special touch when it came to farming the land. I had no doubt his crops grew better and hardier than all the rest.

"Thank you for your hospitality," I said, setting down the satchel with a sigh.

"Don't thank me yet, boy," he replied. "Meti is my name, but my daughter will soon be back. She will not want you here."

I hesitated near the door, my stomach giving a loud rumble as I did so.

"Ha. We can fix that," the man, Meti, said. Then he waved his hand toward the oven. "Take a bowl. Help yourself. We have more than enough to eat."

"Mother and Father always provide," I murmured, rushing to the oven. It was rude to look so desperate, but I had no shame in my weariness.

"They do. Lean times come for others," Meti said. "Not for us."

I filled my bowl and began to eat the fish stew. It was redolent with onion and garlic, and I washed it all down with gulps of thick, sweet beer. It was not food fit for the pharaoh, but it was more than enough for a tired traveler.

As I finished my second bite, the door banged open and a homely young woman walked in. She had Meti's same narrow eyes and skinny frame. Her black hair was braided tightly back from her forehead, and she frowned at me and then at my satchel.

"No, Father!" she said at once, dropping the basket of onions she had been carrying. "No more of this! These visitors only bring trouble."

"I told you so." Meti cackled from the table. "Bring me a cup of beer; I am thirsty, too."

The daughter stomped up to me and poked a finger in my face. "Finish that food and drink that cup, then you must go."

"Hush, Niyek, hush. Let him stay the night."

"No!" She whirled on her father, bringing him a cup of beer and slamming it on the table. "You are too old for these ridiculous people and . . . and their make-believe!"

He pointed to the overflowing basket of onions, each bigger and more well-formed than the last. "Is that make-believe, child? When the drought did not touch our crops, was that ridiculous, too?"

Niyek scoffed and threw her hands into the air. "That is because I prayed and made offerings day and night to Tefnut, not because of your cult."

The old man did not raise his voice; he simply sipped his beer and shrugged knobbly shoulders. "The other villagers prayed to her. What good did it bring them?"

There was shouting outside. Doors opened and shut, and I could hear growing confusion as villagers emerged from their houses. Niyek ran to the small window at the door and peered out, her hand held out behind her as if to keep us silent.

"More strangers," she said with a grunt. "More trouble."

The beer in my stomach soured and I dropped the bowl and cup on the table near Meti and then joined the girl at the window. She shoved me aside angrily and pointed at the satchel.

"Take your things and go before you bring more problems to this house," she hissed.

The old man stood unsteadily with his cane and hobbled over to us. There were screams then, and a sound like the shaking of leaves after a sudden wind. It was the whip and whoosh before a storm. Someone outside was in anguish, wailing as if in mourning.

"Out the back, then," the man told me, taking me by the arm and guiding me toward a curtain near the brick oven. "There have been raiders lately; they know our granary is full."

"Maybe I was followed," I whispered.

"Why would you be followed?" Niyek scrambled away from the window, chasing after us. "Do you see, Father? Now you have brought a criminal into this house!"

"Be quiet, girl."

Meti ripped the curtain aside and pushed me out into the cooling night. I smelled smoke and heard the distant crackle of flames. The village was burning.

"Get out of here," he said, silhouetted against the light in the house. "Put your feet on the path. Mother and Father will guide you."

Then he was gone, muttering to his daughter as they debated what to do. I crouched down behind the house, moving the curtain aside just as their door exploded in a blinding flash. Two hulking figures entered. They had the shape of men but were unnaturally tall and emanated such a bright light it was difficult even to glance at them, men with yellow hair and bodies that glowed like embers. Great white wings spread behind them as they wrestled Niyek and her father to the ground.

"Where is the writer?" Their voices were so loud, so piercing, *they made my own head throb.*

The writer? Great Snake, did they know about the book? Did they mean me? To think that I had brought this evil down on innocents. . . . They wanted me. I huddled behind the curtain and prayed, wondering if I had the strength to run after a long day of travel and only a bit of food. My feet were covered in new blisters and my shoulder ached from the burden of the book. Niyek shrieked, and when I looked again, one of the glowing creatures was kissing her. . . . No, not kissing her . . . Some kind of light stretched between his open mouth and hers, stealing the sound from her screams.

"She is not confessing. They do not know anything," the other creature said. He looked disgusted.

"They must!" The man holding Niyek gave her a shake and the light poured from his mouth to hers brighter, brighter. . . . Meti cried for mercy for her, for them both, and then wept as Niyek went limp. The skin around her lips bubbled and burst, and the flesh on her face grew shiny before it melted like wax.

A third figure burst through the door then, alight with that same unnatural brilliance.

I clutched my stomach and let go of the curtain, lurching toward the spiky bushes behind the house. Niyek's exposed skull lingered in my mind, a curse now, a curse I had brought down on myself for seeking their help.

"Did you hear that?"

The men inside must have noticed my rustling in the bushes. I

*shouldered the pack and dragged bleeding feet across the ground,
running as fast as I could. They would find me. They would
find the book, and I, too, would be nothing but a puddle of
melted flesh, a fate I dreaded but perhaps deserved.*

———— ❦ ————

My punishment the next morning was to spend hours mucking
out the horse stalls. Mrs. Haylam sent me out to the barn first
thing in the morning without a crust of bread or a sip of tea.
She must have known it would take longer to clean up after the
horses if I was weak with hunger.

It was a mild sentence, due in no small part, I was sure, to
Mary. Leave it to her to beg for understanding on my behalf.
I had not argued when Mrs. Haylam handed down the verdict
in the kitchen, since even I had no idea if I deserved to be punished for the previous night's terror. There had been warnings
about leaving the house at night, and though I had found Mary,
I had also immediately failed to protect her. I couldn't help but
wonder if part of my current misery had come about because of
Finch's heroism.

My day was to get no better, and in fact, mucking the stables might be considered the high point. After I finished, I was
expected to wait on Amelia Canny while she chose trimmings
and bunting for the wedding, a task I would not wish on my

cruelest enemy. I had no interest in her or her betrothed—each hour I spent away from the cellar was another hour wasted. While I dealt with horse dung, the clock ran down on my time to translate the journal.

Two hours after I had begun, the task was finished, and I wiped off my soiled boots and let my rucked-up skirts down. I needed a bath, badly, and something to eat. Cleaner now, the stables smelled strongly of horse and hay, with the sweeter note of grass and clover. The day was a gloomy one, the late-spring sun retreating behind a heavy swell of clouds. Still, that did not make it much cooler, and I felt damp all over with sweat.

At the very least I could justify a bath before meeting with Amelia—she would only complain about her serving girl reeking of horse.

I heard a soft tread on the boards above me, as if someone had just climbed into the hayloft. That had been my haunt for most of the autumn as I adjusted to my job at Coldthistle House, but I had no idea that others were also using it as a hideaway. Quietly, I circled around the horse stalls to the hay-strewn floor of the barn, finding the ladder to the loft was lowered. Someone was indeed above, and it sounded like he was crying.

There was no voice of warning this time, at least, but still, I had learned my lesson about bolting after the sound of sobs. It was broad daylight, however, and Bartholomew dozed outside. I could hear his grumbly snores, and satisfied myself by swearing he would wake and alert if any massive wolf creatures came dashing into the yard.

I put one foot on the hayloft ladder and waited. "Hello up there? Are you well?"

"It's only me."

Chijioke called back, a note of pain in his voice. I climbed up slowly, giving him the chance to shoo me off. But I reached the top and hoisted myself into the loft without him saying another word, and I found him pacing the low-ceilinged attic, a sheen of tears still sparkling on his cheeks.

"I could use the company," he said with a sigh. He stopped near one of the low triangular windows and leaned against the beams. "I've no idea what I did wrong, Louisa. Or if . . . Sod it, why must this all be so confoundedly complicated?"

"What is?" I asked gently.

He touched his forehead to the broad beam above the window and his shoulders heaved, but he did not cry. "Mary . . . I know not what I did to vex her."

"I only saw her last night in the woods," I said. "What happened? God, I can understand if she's cross with me after all I did, but you had nothing to do with it!"

Chijioke shook his head and ran a hand over his black hair, resting his knuckles against his nape. "This morning after breakfast I went to see her. I gave her the fish carving, aye? And she . . . Oh, Louisa, she said she didn't want it, and that she was too tired to see me just then."

Now he sounded on the verge of more tears, and I rushed

over to him, putting just my fingertips on his arm. He leaned ever forward, as if curling up into a ball, wiping at his face as silent tears coursed down his cheeks.

"I had no idea you two were so close," I said. "I suppose I don't know a lot of things. But perhaps you should simply believe her, mm? If she is too tired, then . . . Well, she *died*. One can hardly blame her for wanting a rest. I'm sure she will come around when more time has passed."

He shook his head fervently, pushing away from the window and turning to face me. His brows furrowed and he stared at the space over my left shoulder, as if too shy to meet my eyes. "No. . . . No. I looked in her eyes as she said it, as she gave me back the gift. There was nothing there. Nothing. Like . . . like she couldn't even see me."

"I'm terribly sorry," I said, feeling pressure build in my chest. This was my fault. They had been finding some kind of joy in each other, and then I had come along and selfishly stolen it away by agreeing to a bargain I did not fully understand. Now she was back, but quite obviously changed. "Do you want me to speak with her? Let me help, please; if there is anything I can do, I'll do it."

Chijioke took in a great, spluttering breath and then let it out, at last nodding his head and looking away toward the window. "If you *did* speak to her, don't tell her I asked you to. It would help to know . . . If it's all past hope, then I'd like to know."

"I'm certain it isn't," I told him, and he walked with me back toward the ladder. His tears had slowed. "You did not see the beast that attacked us, Chijioke, I'm hardly in my right mind after it, and it was intent on hurting Mary. She must be in shock."

"Aye," he said, helping me down the ladder. "I had thought to comfort her."

"We all face fear so differently, she may be trying to spare you. You lost her once, and almost lost her again last night."

"Indeed, lass, I heard you fired a gun at the mad creature that came after ye. Very brave."

"Hardly brave, just desperate," I replied with a shrug. "It was Finch who frightened the fell thing away."

Chijioke gave a snort of derision at that and followed me nimbly down the ladder. Together we walked toward the open barn doors, where the cloud-dampened sunlight poured in. Poppy's hound was waiting for us, snuffling in the hay curiously with his big brown ears flopped over his eyes. He looked up at us and sat, giving a quiet *boof*.

"Mrs. Haylam must be looking for us," I sighed. "I'm to meet with Amelia, but not before a bath."

"I wasn't going to say anything," he teased. "If you wait a moment, I can distract Haylam so you can slip by. I'll make up some— What the devil?"

Chijioke trailed off, taking one step out of the barn and into the yard. I had heard the footsteps and panting, too—little

Poppy ran across the yard toward us, braids bouncing, hands still dusted with flour from the kitchens. She nearly collided with the dog as she skidded to a stop, looking between us with huge eyes.

"Slow down there," Chijioke said, patting her back. "What's all this haste about?"

"You both must . . . You both must come now." She gulped for air, then flung her hand back toward the house. "Amelia is dead," she whispered. "Dead."

"An accident?" Chijioke asked. "How?"

"No accident; it must be murder." Poppy shook her head. "You must both come inside and quick."

Chapter Seventeen

t was more than grim to find that Poppy had not exaggerated. Miss Amelia Canny was in fact dead, lying on her back in her bed, hands curled up on her chest as if she were an insect, her skin an oddish gray color. I had never seen anything quite like it. It was as if every drop of moisture had been squeezed from her body, or sucked out through her mouth somehow. That same mouth was open permanently in terror and her eyes were shut, though thick liquid oozed out of the creases.

As I looked at her, my guts twisted sharply, that ghostly woman's voice filling my head again, emerging as if it were my own thoughts and not that of an unseen, unwanted interloper.

This will be you, it said. *Run.*

"Her eyeballs *exploded*," Poppy whispered. I couldn't tell if she was horrified or impressed. "I don't think we've cleaned up something like this before."

We certainly hadn't. I felt more and more sure that I needed to find a way to protect Poppy, Chijioke, Mary, and Lee, especially if there was some kind of murderer on the loose. Just because they were touched by magic, it did not mean my friends were invulnerable. I closed my eyes, trying not to imagine myself dead and desiccated in my own bed. We stood in a semicircle around the bed with Chijioke in the middle. He groaned and pinched the bridge of his nose.

"Och, this was not supposed to happen," he muttered. "They were to marry first."

"Why?" I asked. "Why does it matter? She was going to die here eventually, yes?"

Poppy leaned around Chijioke and stuck out her lip at me. "Did you do it?"

"Me!?" I laughed with exasperation. "Of course not, I was in the barn mucking out the stalls and then with Chijioke. I couldn't have done it."

"It wasn't any of us," he cut in flatly. "Unless you have some secrets I don't know about, Poppy. This doesn't exactly look like your work."

She tiptoed closer and leaned over the body. I shuddered, my stomach growing weak at the sight of Amelia. I had not liked her, certainly, but the look of a dead body was still nausea inducing. That, and it was hard to believe that a girl so young could deserve this end. She looked like a husk of a body, shriveled and frail.

Gradually, it dawned on me that this meant we were all in danger. If nobody on the staff had done this to Amelia, then who had? What would stop them from coming for us?

"We should tell Mrs. Haylam and search the house," I said, turning away from the gruesome sight. "There must be an intruder or—"

"Or it's one of those bloody Adjudicators," Chijioke bit out.

"Odds are this is their idea of a joke."

"Come now," I scolded, pointing to the bed. "You really think Finch could do something like this? He risked his life to help Mary and me last night. I know you don't like him, but—"

"Sparrow is very mean," Poppy said. "She could do it."

"Exactly." Chijioke began to pace, then went to Amelia's writing desk and began rummaging through it. We had closed and locked the door behind us on the way in. "You don't know them, Louisa. You don't know what they're capable of."

"Ha. Fine. If you know them so well, could they do that?" I asked, still pointing at Amelia. "Are they known to fly about sucking the life out of people?"

Chijioke paused with one of Amelia's letters in his hand. He tilted his head to the side, eyeing me over his shoulder. "I . . . Maybe. I don't know."

"Perfect!" I threw up my hands and stormed past him. It was time to alert the rest of the house.

"I've never seen a Judgment, but they can and do kill, Louisa, that much I know." He slapped down the letter and followed. "Poppy? Stay here. Don't let anyone through."

"All right," she said lightly, sitting down next to Amelia's corpse and swinging her legs.

We locked the door behind us and left. Fortunately, the corridor outside her chambers was empty. The men had gone down to the spring for a soak, allowing us a narrow window to decide on a plan. Two Residents drifted down the stairs toward us, then turned and hovered outside Amelia's door as if on guard.

"I need to ask you a question and I don't want you to judge me for it," I said softly, giving the Residents a wary glance. "Is it . . . possible that Lee could have done this?"

I felt guilty even considering it, and while I still worried about Lee, part of that worry extended to what this house and its dark secrets had done to him. What the book had made him become. Maybe finding a way to release him from the book's power was as much about protecting all of us as it was about protecting Lee from himself.

Chijioke chewed the inside of his cheek and went swiftly down the stairs with me. I was at least happy to find that he wasn't offended by my suggestion. Before Lee's death and resurrection, he had been a gentle young man, but it was clear that coming back had changed him. I didn't relish the idea that he was randomly killing guests, of course, but it seemed foolish not to at least entertain the idea.

"That's a question for Mrs. Haylam," he replied as we reached the foyer. "You best prepare yourself for her fury. This will not be a pleasant afternoon."

"It's just so strange," I said with a sigh. "Finch and Sparrow were told to keep out of our business. Would they really do something so . . . so inciting?"

"I'd ask Mrs. Haylam that, too, lass."

We did not find the housekeeper in the kitchens, but as we left and turned toward the dining room we heard her come in behind us. She must have read the urgency on our faces, for at once she stopped wiping her hands on her apron and squinted, then marched right up to us.

"Something strange has happened."

"Amelia is dead."

Chijioke and I blurted it out simultaneously, then both fell immediately silent. I had no idea what to expect from the old woman, but for an eternal moment she glared hard at Chijioke. She inhaled deeply through her nose and then pressed her hands together.

"Where is she?" Mrs. Haylam finally asked. I was not foolish enough to mistake her calm tone of voice for anything but the deepest disappointment. Her entire body was rigid, like a hound that's scented a rabbit.

"In her chambers," Chijioke said. I let him explain the rest, too. "Poppy found her, but it's none of us that did it. I don't know *what* could have done it. She's all dried up and wrinkly, and her eyeballs, well, they popped."

Her good eye glittered at that.

"And the men?"

"Still taking the waters," he said.

She nodded for what felt like an entire minute, and then she took Chijioke by the forearm, pulling him closer. "You will go to town and raise Giles St. Giles. Louisa, you will help me forge a letter. Miss Amelia has cold feet and fled the house, we do not know where she has gone. That will keep the men busy looking while we clean up this mess."

"But why? You're going to kill them anyway." I couldn't help myself, and the words just came tumbling out stupidly. Mrs. Haylam reeled back as if I had slapped her. "Why not just have done now and get it over with?"

"That is not how we do things in this house," she hissed, baring her teeth. "Now do as I say, you idiot girl."

Chijioke shot me a warning look and then hurried away. I decided it would be best to heed that warning, and followed Mrs. Haylam as she swept through the foyer and up the stairs. The front door closed in our wake, and Chijioke was gone, off to rig up the cart and ride to Derridon. While we climbed the stairs, I fretted with my apron, feeling naked without the spoon around my neck.

"It pains me to ask this," I said carefully. "But does Lee have powers now? Powers we haven't seen him use before?"

Mrs. Haylam did not wave me off or chide me; she weighed the question, head swaying back and forth as we reached the first-level landing. "The gift of shadow can be unexpected," she told me. "Unnaturally long life is assured; greater strength is a common boon, too. I have never heard of one imbued with shadow turning healthy beings to husks."

"But it's not impossible," I pressed.

"He will be questioned, girl," Mrs. Haylam said irritably. We climbed another staircase and another, then found ourselves outside Amelia's locked door. The housekeeper fished her huge key ring out and found the proper one. "And I will be having a long talk with our Upworlder *guests*, too."

The Residents hovering outside the door came closer as if drawn by her mere presence.

"Go," she told them calmly. "Alert me when the men are returned."

The shadow creatures billowed away, off to find windows and vantages. They paid me no attention as they went, but the hall felt warmer in their absence. I watched her fit the key in and give a shove with her shoulder. At once, the smell of death wafted out to meet us and I winced.

"Chijioke said it could be something called a Judgment," I said, hesitating to go in and be met with more and worse odors.

It did not seem to bother Mrs. Haylam, who locked us in and marched right up to the bed.

"Long has it been since I beheld a Judged body," she said, leaning over Amelia. She inspected her so closely that it made me feel ill. I couldn't imagine putting my face that close to a corpse willingly. "The Adjudicator seeks a confession and the soul will give it no matter what. All guilt is revealed. I do not know if death arises from the extraction or from the Adjudicator's will to annihilate."

"That sounds awful," I whispered. Again, I could not imagine Finch doing such a thing. Chijioke could warn me a hundred more times about him, and still I would only be able to judge Finch on his actions toward me. By those standards, he had been nothing but kind.

"Do not be fooled by pretty words and shiny halos," Mrs. Haylam murmured, peeling one of Amelia's eyes open. I turned away. "They are the shepherd's violent hand of justice, seekers and executors of truth. Amelia Canny's crimes would more than justify her doom in their estimation."

"Her crimes . . ." I shook my head, going to Amelia's desk and looking at the scattered letters and books there.

"Killed her rival," Mrs. Haylam said coldly. "Her servant saw it happen, and confessed her suspicions to a priest. She was not believed, of course. What does a silly serving girl know, mm?"

"Lottie." Amelia's diary sat at an angle on the desk, but I had no urge to look inside. I did not want to know what lurked in the mind of a girl twisted enough to kill for marriage and money. "Amelia was awful to her; I would have a vendetta, too."

"Poppy, go and tell Mr. Morningside what has happened. Please assure him that it is all under our control now, and that he will need to provide a bird to Giles St. Giles and Chijioke." Mrs. Haylam stood up from her inspection and crossed to the desk, rifling through the letters for a clean piece of parchment and a quill.

"Did Chijioke go to Derridon?" Poppy asked, hopping down off the bed and skipping toward the door.

"He did; now be quick, child."

When we were alone, Mrs. Haylam reached for Amelia's diary, opening to a random page and setting it before me.

"You have steadier and younger hands," she said, shoving quill and parchment at me. I was beginning to resent being forced to write for the owners of the house. "Do your best. Not too much or they may notice the penmanship is wrong."

I sat down and puzzled over the note, listening to Mrs. Haylam wrap Amelia in a bedsheet. What would I say if I were her and I had doubts about the marriage? But Amelia didn't have doubts, did she? She had wanted Mason and his fortune so badly that she had killed for it. Then I remembered the fight at dinner we had witnessed, and I bent over the parchment, dashing off an apology.

My dearest love— Your father's rudeness has given me pause. Why does he hate me so? If I am to be a part of your family, then I demand respect. I must think, Mason, my love. I must be certain that this is what I want.

"That will do just fine."

I jumped, startled by the old woman appearing at my shoulder. She found a vial of Amelia's perfume and dabbed it on the letter, then returned to the bed. The dead girl had been covered, wrapped up, and rolled into her bedsheet and two blankets.

Mrs. Haylam waved me over, taking up the body by the shoulders while I hesitated near the foot of the bed.

"Help me carry this to the kitchens, Louisa, then be off and have a bath. You stink of manure."

Chapter
Eighteen

Year One

𓊪𓏭𓏛 𓈖𓄿𓏛𓈖 𓅓𓏥 𓂋𓏤

Journal of Bennu, Who Runs

I began traveling by night to escape the scorch of the sun. Perhaps it was only my imagination, but the book felt easier to carry in the darkness. The strange men who had attacked Meti and Niyek did not find me that night as I hid in the bushes, and I did not see them again when I continued my journey north.

For five days my passage was slow but smooth. I avoided

villages until I became desperate for food and drink, then stole what I needed come nightfall and skulked back into the wilds, sleeping under any rocky outcroppings I could find, sheltered by palm and samwa, huddled under a filched blanket. It was not comfortable or easy, but I was safe. I was safe until I made a terrible mistake.

I had wrongly assumed I had more time to reach the coast before the rainy season began. It was not so. A sudden downpour caught me unawares just as I reached the split in the Nile. Soaked and cold, I changed course away from the river and toward the nearest town. Giza would surely have safe houses with shelter and food; there I'd wait out the storm and dry off before pressing on to the sea. It had been five days since the glowing men came looking for the "writer"—by now they must have given up the search.

To assume such was foolish, but I was hungry and wet and tired, every bone and sinew aching from the weight of the book. And so I risked the streets of Giza, head down against the rain, just one of many men hurrying to get out of the damp. I found a safe house on the edge of town, not far from the abandoned stalls of a market. A few onions had been left behind on the ground, and I scooped them up for later out of habit.

The shelter, marked with the red-and-white-striped serpent near the door, was open to all. It was quiet inside, seemingly abandoned, but a few braziers burned low, the scent of incense floating thick on the air. It was a simple brick building in the *style of a temple, an empty altar the feature of the main room, with a gathering place and a basket heaped high with offerings. In a shallow room beyond I found a kitchen, the remnants of an evening meal left uneaten but warm on the hearth. I should have considered that conundrum more carefully; I should not have been the fly so eager to tangle itself in the spider's web. But hunger and cold make mincemeat of sense, and I dropped the satchel in the doorway, rushing forward to gobble up the bread and soup left there for seemingly no one at all.*

I should have felt the twinge on the air. I should have sensed the imprint of death, the cool whispers of souls recently parted from their bodies. But I knew only the relief of a full belly and the promise of a warm bed away from the rain.

"Good work." I heard the words emerge like a scrape on stone from the shadows behind me, and I froze, mouth still stuffed with food. The words were not for me. Whoever had made the abandoned feast was there now, watching, three young women in simple linen dresses all hugging each other, eyes wet with tears as they shivered and cowered.

I looked at the girls for only a moment, for a huge, hunchbacked figure lurked just outside the kitchen. I wondered where this thing could have been hiding, big as it was, its bulk wide enough to obscure the girls huddling in the temple. It was shaped vaguely like a woman, but cruder, as if hastily slapped together out of clay. Shreds of blue-and-white fabric clung to its shoulders, its skin the color of sun-bleached bones.

The satchel with the book lay between us, but I could not move. I had looked into the creature's face, and the moment I saw what was there, my entire body became paralyzed not with fear but with evil magic. The cup of beer in my hand dropped to the floor, splattering us both. The creature lunged toward me, showing more of its terrible visage as it dipped into the light. It had but a small slot for a mouth, the entirety of its long face glittering with eyes. No, not eyes, I saw as it lumbered closer: wasps.

Mother protect me, I pleaded, staring down now what I knew was the bringer of my death. The wasp wings fluttered like eyelashes, all of them in unison, dozens of insects, striped and somehow allowing this thing to see. It stopped when it reached the satchel, hands opening and closing as if in childlike delight. Bending its massive frame, lank silver hair slipping over its forehead, the creature gave a gurgling laugh and put its hand on the satchel, then turned its face up toward me. My body went even more rigid as the wings of its eyes ceased fluttering, all of its attention on me.

"A hundred servants on a hundred hunts, and at last the writer is revealed."

"Writer?" I whispered, mouth dry. "I am no writer. . . ."

"Silence."

The girls behind the creature gasped and cried harder, but I could not make another sound. The beast's command had stolen my voice away, my throat closing as if filling with sand. If only I could claw at my lips or scream for help or do anything but watch in mute terror as the beast neared, taking up the satchel and reaching its other hand toward me, slowly, slowly, wrapping its hot fingers around my neck. My eyes bulged, lungs desperate and empty, the crushing force of the beast and its fingers making sparks of light dance in front of my eyes.

Those horrible wasp eyes were nearer now, and I could hear a faint, droning hum . . . a hum from a bottomless pit. A deathly hum, a terrible hum . . .

"A new sun rises," it hissed, drawing out the word, tongue flicking out to lick at a lipless mouth. "See darkness now as your sun sets."

There was a crash and the girls screamed. Everything became dim and distant as I choked and lost the will to fight. Suddenly I was free, released from the creature's merciless hold, and sliding to the floor. I felt the satchel underneath me as I fell, and covered it with my body as if I could somehow protect it that way.

I heard a trill like a pack of jackals laughing in my ear; there was hot, wet warmth on my face and then nothing, just the black embrace as I tumbled into oblivion.

When I opened my eyes again, the dark brick ceiling was above, a stuffed mattress below me. Each part of me protested as I sat up to find that I had been placed in a corner to rest, dawn breaking as the altar glowed softly with candles, ribbons of gray incense smoke rising in slow streams. The three girls in their simple dresses were cleaning the floor and walls with rags stained red through.

Pools of blood dotted with gore stretched across the floor toward me. In the middle of the room lay the body of the many-eyed creature, the wasps unmoving, for it was dead. Something or someone had torn its jaw completely open, and it hung down unnaturally, yellow teeth broken, the monster now giving an eternal scream.

I was too exhausted even to recoil, leaning back against the wall and breathing a sigh of relief when I noticed the satchel and my burden had been placed next to me on the mattress. My clothes, too, were covered in blood, an awful odor rising from the stains.

"You're awake, that's good." A young man, naked from the waist up, emerged from the kitchen doorway. He was tall and well-formed, torso crisscrossed with old scars that cut lines through the fur on his chest. Stepping smoothly over the creature's carcass, he came toward me, using his teeth to pull a bandage taut as he wrapped a gash on his right arm. "How is your throat, friend?"

"Are you lost, child?" I touched my neck, feeling the rawness in my voice.

The man paused, letting the bandage tail drop out of his mouth. He leaned back and laughed. The light from the altar made his dark brown skin look gold. I noticed then a pattern of tattoos on his arms and shoulders, rows and rows of formal hieroglyphs inked into his skin expertly as if by a scribe. "My feet are on the path. Do not worry, Bennu, I am here to look after you and take you the rest of the way."

I sighed and said a silent prayer of thanks. He left and returned with a small cup in his hand; it was perfumed like flowers and goat's milk, and hot as he handed it to me. Kneeling at my side, he waited until I had a steady grip on the cup.

"Drink that, it will ease the pain."

He had a northerly accent, a proper one, as if he had been raised and educated in one of the noble houses of the upper kingdom. "Did Meryt and Chryseis send you?" I asked him.

"In a way. Drink." His eyes were odd, not brown as I expected but a very deep purple. "You're a hard boy to find, Bennu, and that is good. They're looking everywhere; always now they are seeking, seeking. Our temples and safe houses from Buhen to Maydum have been raided. It was with the Mother's luck that I found you when I did."

"Raided?" At once, the tea, or whatever it was, calmed my burning throat. The pain in my back and feet eased, too, and I drank more, chasing the comfort. "Have the priests of the old gods sent their numbers against us?"

"No, this is something new," he told me. "Something worse. These are creatures the likes of which we have never seen. They bow to someone called Roeh, who takes the guise of a farmer, though he is no simple peasant. More and more they appear from the east, these Nephilim and Adjudicators of Roeh."

"And you?" I asked. "What do I call the man who slays beasts with wasps for eyes?"

He smirked and smoothed scarred hands back over his fore-head and hair, which was black and had been braided neatly, close to the scalp. "Khent," he said, bowing his head gracefully. His sharp chin and nose reminded me of statuary. "There will be time for introductions later, Bennu. For now, you must rest and regain your strength. We leave in three hours, for the task is urgent and we have very far to go."

As I toiled away at my translations in the cellar, the house exploded into commotion above.

The men had returned from their time at the spring, Amelia's note was discovered, and every room in Coldthistle House seemed to be filled with Mason Breen's demented wailing and his father's thundering shouts. Even through layers of wood and brick and carpet I could tell two camps were emerging—Mason was beside himself with anguish and organizing a search. Mr. Breen, on the other hand, was lobbying to forget the whole business and press on to London.

Nobody would leave, I knew that much, but I hoped they would soon scatter to the woods to look for Amelia and leave us in peace. With any luck, the odious Mr. Breen and the wolf creature with the purple eyes would meet and solve one problem handily.

On second thought, I did not hope for the monster's return. No, I prayed that it was far, far away, so frightened by Finch's blinding light that it decided to leave us alone forever. Though it was musty and a bit dark, I welcomed the solitude of the underground library. There had been more than enough excitement for one morning, and I was beginning to worry that one week would not be nearly enough time to finish the translation for Mr. Morningside.

"At least," I muttered to myself, dashing off the period on a finished entry, "the material is never dull."

I found myself being absorbed into this boy Bennu's adventures. Mr. Morningside's interest in the journal was also becoming clearer the more I read—there were mentions here and there of Adjudicators, and I could only assume that Bennu had been party to some ancient and apparently still standing grudge. Finch had mentioned war and struggle, and I had to wonder if this journal contained secrets about Mr. Morningside's enemies that he would find valuable. I still had no earthly idea how it all related to his trial, or how he had known the journal was important in the first place, but the only way forward was through.

My eyes had begun to tire from working steadily away with nothing but a few blue-flamed candles to keep me company. Hours had passed, and the house above had become quieter as the men scattered to search for Amelia. She was probably already on her way to Derridon in a cart, off to have a visit with

Chijioke and Giles St. Giles, presently to find her soul residing in an enchanted pigeon.

"I hope they choose a vulture," I said, pushing back from the desk and standing. A bit of exercise would put me to rights, so I made rounds of the room, shaking out my cramped fingers as I perused the odd bits and bobs hidden away here by Mr. Morningside.

I could have spent entire weeks poking my nose into every corner of that place. There were books in languages I had never seen before, and jars filled with a liquid that shied away and sloshed to the far end of the container when I neared. He had seen fit to save an entire massive tome filled with nothing but pressed thistles. I wandered past the fireplace and approached the corner of the library not far from the door. Again, I saw the painting of four figures leaning against the shelves, and I approached, gingerly, as if by some magic the people painted there could see me on the other side of the canvas.

Leaning down, I found the picture had been partially covered by a dust cloth, an old white brocade thing that hung down in a dramatic swoop. I pinched the edge of the fabric and lifted it up, studying the painting and its strange subjects. There were three men and one woman. The woman was dressed in what looked like the drapey garments seen on Roman statues. She was exquisitely beautiful, garbed all in bright magenta; there was even a slight pink tinge to her skin. The man beside her was standing rather close, as if they were familiar, perhaps husband

and wife or brother and sister. He wore a big black cape that covered most of his body, and he also wore a mask made of wood, covered in twisting vines that described the eyes and mouth.

The other two men were apart, one standing and the other seated on a low ivory sofa. I could not make out much of the standing man, for though his face had been painted, it lacked any kind of features. It was just a blank swath of flesh, with no eyes or mouth or nose. Horrible to behold, I thought, cringing. A man should have a face, and a painted man with no face should not be able to fill a girl with such pointed unease. Seated near the faceless person was an elderly person, of jolly complexion and plump. He quite distinctly resembled the shepherd that had taken me in when I tried to run from Coldthistle House. And while he had treated me with kindness then, looking at this re-creation of him made the flesh creep across my skin. It was not a benign smile he showed, but a hungry one, the glint in his eyes tipped ever so slightly with madness.

"Ghastly, isn't it? Not the sort of thing you want hanging in the front hall."

I leapt back, frightened, hands flailing out in front of me instinctually. Mr. Morningside had entered on silent feet, watching me from the door with his arms crossed over his dark, striped coat.

"Hard at work, are we?" he added with a laugh.

"My hand needed a rest," I replied with a weak shrug. "But I completed more entries for you."

"Ah! Good news at last!" He strode merrily to the desk, leaning over it to inspect my work. He paged through the translations, humming with appreciation. "Fine job, Louisa, a very fine job. I almost feel rotten for teasing you."

"Indeed," I said, sarcastic. "How did Amelia's betrothed take the news?"

Mr. Morningside puffed out his lips like a horse neighing and shook his head, still reading over my work. "Not well, as one might expect, but no punches were thrown, thank goodness. It's a nasty business, what we do, but we can and should keep it civil if at all possible."

I said nothing, knowing I'd only come out with more cheek.

"Don't feel bad for Mason, Louisa. He isn't here because of his charitable works."

"I know that," I said testily. "I don't think anything about him at all."

"Good. What do you think of it?"

"Sorry?" His head was still low over the pages, eyes scanning quickly.

With a grin, Mr. Morningside flicked his head to the left and back, and I realized with some trepidation that he meant the painting. "The art. You seemed quite taken with it a moment ago."

I blushed, hating that he had caught me snooping. "Who are they? I recognize the shepherd, but who are the others?"

"Relics, all of them," he said flatly. "Remnants of a bygone era."

For a moment I stared at him, trying to pierce through that breezy smile to the man behind it. "The faceless one is you, isn't it?"

At last he looked up from the pages, and I almost wished he had not. I recognized it for what it was—a predator reassessing its prey, as if the doe had fought back and charged the hunter.

"What an interesting opinion," he purred.

"It isn't an opinion. The portraits outside your office . . . those are all you, aren't they? You appear differently to everyone. You're an old man to Poppy and something else to Mrs. Haylam, though I don't know what," I replied, sticking out my chin. I turned and pointed at the painting. "That's you and that's the shepherd. Who are the other two?"

Mr. Morningside appraised me closely for another moment and then shuffled the papers in his hands, putting them in a neat stack on the desk. With the air of a teacher bored to death of his student, he crossed to the painting and lifted the dust cover off it.

"They were mentors, of a sort," he explained. He, too, seemed drawn to the painting, staring at it as I had earlier. "I never knew them well, not like the shepherd knew them. Back then I was very young, hardly more than an idea made manifest." He put back the cover rather roughly and strode toward me, taking up the translations and glaring at me down the length of his nose. "It doesn't matter, Louisa; they're gone."

"Gone? Do you mean they're dead?"

He chuckled and shook his head. "You cannot kill a god, girl, only convince it that continuing to exist is folly."

I wanted to know more, so much more, and I tried to choose my next question thoughtfully, for I knew he would do everything he could to dance around a direct answer. Before I could say another word, Mr. Morningside winced, gathering up the papers and holding them close to his chest as if he were suffering a sudden pang. His face became tinged with green, like a man on the verge of sickness.

"Blast it all, he's here," he muttered, drawing in a deep breath through his teeth.

"Who?" I asked, following him to the door.

"Shepherd," Mr. Morningside growled. He looked at me with pity then, or perhaps sorrow. With his eyes softened that way, he almost appeared sympathetic. It was hard to imagine anything ruffling the Devil, but clearly—clearly—I saw fear in his gaze. "I suppose we must hurry, Louisa; my trial is about to begin."

Chapter Nineteen

s soon as we reached the landing, Chijioke burst in through the front door of the house. The chaos left behind by Amelia's disappearance lingered, though now there was even greater cause for action. In the kitchen, I heard Mrs. Haylam shouting orders to Poppy, and Bartholomew barked out his frustrations with the noise. Chijioke had lost his coat somewhere, charging toward us in his shirtsleeves, sweat glistening on his forehead. Through the open doors outside, I spied the cart and horses still waiting in the drive.

"Sir," he said, breathless. "They're here, the—"

"Yes, Chijioke, I am aware." Mr. Morningside gave him a mild smile and a pat on the shoulder, then gave each of us a look in turn. "Now, both of you, please let Mrs. Haylam know that I will be along shortly. We must all remain calm, as this is little more than a formality, thanks to Louisa."

Chijioke turned toward me, giving a soft "huh."

Was it really that surprising that I could make myself useful?

"I don't expect it will take long. Chijioke, if you would be so kind, please encourage Miss Canny's acquaintances to take the carriage to Derridon. There have been sightings of her there and of course they will want to investigate those claims."

Nodding, Chijioke bounded up the stairs. Above us, I could hear the men arguing, and judging from the proximity, they were doing so in Amelia's rooms.

"What if they don't come back?" I asked.

Mr. Morningside laughed and laughed, then shook his head at me as if I were a child speaking out of turn. "They always come back." Then he swatted me lightly on the nose with the papers in his hand, sweeping back toward the green door that led to his office. "I will need to look over these translations and change into something more suitable. Tell Mrs. Haylam to prepare light refreshment on the lawn for the shepherd and his retinue. I will do my best not to keep them waiting."

I gave a quick curtsy out of habit and rushed toward the kitchens, nearly colliding with Poppy as she bounced back and forth between the range and the large table in the center of the room. My message seemed awfully redundant, considering that same table was already heaped high with a dazzling array of tea cakes, tiny sandwiches, and bowls of fruit. There was even a luxurious pineapple there, decorated to look like a peacock, with cloves for eyes and fresh flowers for the feathery tail.

"Don't just stand there gawking, girl, help! Mary is still recovering, so we will be short a pair of useful hands." Mrs. Haylam, surprisingly, looked flustered, perhaps for the first time in her life. She bustled as nervously as Poppy, loading up trays with mincemeat pies and sparkling teacups.

"Mr. Morningside said to provide light refreshment in the yard," I said, not knowing where to put myself in the midst of so much chaos.

"Well, what does it look like we're doing?" Mrs. Haylam snapped, pinching my earlobe as she whooshed by. "Help Poppy with the tea, please, and fetch some brandy, too. Slice some lemons very finely, child, as that is all the shepherd will take with his tea."

I found Poppy struggling under the weight of an overladen silver tea service and took it up for her, laying it out neatly on the table. Several lemons were produced from the pantry, and I took pains to cut them into minuscule wedges, fanning them out prettily on a plate with the sugar and cream.

A mess of heavy footsteps pounded on the staircase out in the foyer. I peeped out while Mrs. Haylam was busy washing a stain from her apron, and saw Mason, his father, and Samuel Potts trooping across the worn rugs to the front doors. I had barely glimpsed Mason since Amelia's disappearance, and I was shocked to find him strolling along as if nothing had happened. In fact, he was distracted by a necklace in his hands, a locket that he had opened and run a thumb over fondly. It was fruitless to guess at what was inside, but perhaps it was a cameo of Amelia and he was simply using it as a remembrance. He noticed me staring, his blond head coming up sharply as he fumbled, blushed, and shoved the locket into his waistcoat pocket.

I curtsied to cover my rudeness and said gently, "She's certain to turn up soon."

"Yes, of course. Thank you," he said, but there was no hope or kindness in it.

That was just as well. I felt cruel lying to him, providing hope that did not truly exist. The men disappeared and Chijioke with them. Faintly, as the doors closed, I heard him explaining the way to Derridon and giving suggestions on where to look for Amelia.

Soon after, the "light" spread we had prepared was ready to be presented. My stomach was in tight, gurgling knots as we began ferrying the food from the kitchens to the lawn. When we stepped out into the hazy sunshine, Chijioke had just finished putting out a series of wicker chairs and three low, outdoor wicker tables. I paused with a tray of cakes and clotted cream, taking stock of those who had come for the Court.

They did not look particularly intimidating, but Mr. Morningside had made sure to pound into my head that appearances were nearly always deceiving. Indeed, the tableau before me might have been a merry Sunday gathering of friends—the shepherd had changed out of his woodsy flannels and into a more formal suit, but it was still a far cry from Mr. Morningside's indisputable taste. Indeed, he had even brought along his tattered cap, a rustic counterpoint to his brown summer coat. His daughter, Joanna, was also dressed more formally, wearing a pretty pale blue muslin dress tied under the bust with a pink satin bow. Her buttercup-yellow hair was pinned up and braided under a sweet straw bonnet.

Joanna helped the shepherd into his chair, then stood next to him, squinting around at the house curiously. Their patchy-furred herding dog, Big Earl, had come, too, taking a day away from the sheep to stand guard at his master's side. Big Earl had eyes only for Bartholomew, who paced and snuffled in the shade of the barn.

Finch and Sparrow were there of course, too, dressed in matching summer tweeds of gray and light green, Sparrow again wearing trousers, her long dark hair coiled up and pinned, the braids intertwined with ribbons the color of spring grass.

My first thought, as I approached, was that they all, with the exception of Sparrow, looked delighted to see me. It was growing hot as the day wore on, and I must have looked tired and sweaty as I set down the first tray, for Finch sprang forward to help me.

"That's not necessary," I told him softly. "You're our guests."

"Louisa . . ." The shepherd leaned forward in his chair, round cheeks ruddy from the heat. He smiled at me, but it did not touch his eyes. "I am not surprised to find you are still employed here. Still, it is reassuring to see you in good health. Hmm, now this one I do not recognize. . . ."

I glanced over my shoulder, watching as Lee emerged from the kitchens with the tea. He glowered up at the sun, hair overgrown and mussed, clothes rumpled. I tried to give him an encouraging smile while Finch described to the old man who exactly Lee was and the strange circumstances that had led to him being a permanent fixture at Coldthistle.

The shepherd harrumphed, hurrying to make his point

before Lee arrived. "Things are changing rapidly, I see. Henry has much to explain."

That cold ache in my bones returned, and the knots in my stomach tightened painfully. I dreaded the thought of testifying against Mr. Morningside, particularly where Lee was concerned. No, Lee had not belonged at Coldthistle House—that *was* a mistake—but it was my own actions that had led to his demise and return. I knew speaking it all aloud would fill me with shame and regret, but maybe I deserved to feel those things again and again.

Beyond that, it seemed ludicrous to take a side against Mr. Morningside when I had accepted his help, making a deal to provide those translations that he thought would prove his innocence. I had not meant to play both sides, but unwittingly, I had.

"Are you well, Louisa?" Finch asked, coming to me and placing a hand on my elbow. I flinched away. "You look terribly pale."

"Just too warm," I mumbled, tearing away to help Lee unload the tea. He had seen Finch's familiar touch on my arm, and his frown had turned into a sneer. "Ignore him," I whispered to Lee, snatching up the emptied tray and fleeing toward the house. He followed.

Lord, but this was a mess. I wanted to disappear. Maybe nobody would notice if I ran straight through the kitchens, up the stairs, and into Mary's room. I could hide there with her, and while the day away talking, talking about her and where she had gone, talking about anything but this confounded trial.

When we reached the kitchens, Mrs. Haylam was just leaving. She had managed to get the spot out of her apron and collected herself, no longer so harried but regal, head held high as she strode out into the yard, hands empty, leaving Poppy to scurry behind her with a platter of buns.

"This is ridiculous," I said, ducking into the cool shade of the kitchen. There was still much to bring out for the guests, but I leaned against the table, tarrying. Lee went to the basin and washed already clean hands, then used the water on his hands to smooth out his wild hair.

"I wish they would go," he replied, keeping his back to me. "Just being near them makes me feel ill."

"Mr. Morningside swears they will be gone soon, but that only seems like wishful thinking. Who knows how long this so-called trial will last or what the outcome will be. Mr. Morningside seems preoccupied with it all, as if it might go badly."

Lee let out a vicious laugh at that and twisted around to look at me. It was odd to see him so angry, as if the sweetness of his face protested this new, meaner temperament. His lips had always been formed as if to smile permanently, this scowling and snarling unnatural.

"Good. I hope he suffers." He stalked to the table and took up a tray of sandwiches.

I sighed and reached out, placing my fingertips on his forearm.

"No, Lee, you don't want that," I told him. "Not because he doesn't deserve it—because he does—but because of what it will mean for us. He says they're here to scrutinize us, and Finch himself said they have to do some kind of observation. They won't leave. Finch or Sparrow or both will stay behind to watch him. And it won't just be him; if they're in the house, then our every move will be observed. That's how Finch found Mary and me the other night—they're patrolling Coldthistle at all hours."

That gave him pause, and he put the tray back down for a moment. He stared at the place where my hand touched him, and his scowl fell for just a moment. I knew our faces were the same—helpless. Sad.

His curly head lowered, and when he looked up at me again his lips were straightened in a determined line. "I don't want those things around here, Louisa. My guts are always drawn up like I'm going to vomit. It's . . . hard to sleep now, but even harder with them here."

"I'm sorry," I told him.

"Don't be sorry," he said hotly. "Just help me find a way to make them leave."

I nodded and took my hand away, helping him lift the tray of sandwiches and then finding something of my own to carry. I did not tell him that instead, I was trying to find a way for all of *us* to go. "Mr. Morningside wants me to testify on his behalf, and Finch wants me to speak against him. I . . . could lie, but I'm not certain that's such a good idea."

"Why not?" he pressed, walking slowly to the door with me. For the first time since he had returned, he looked hopeful. Excited. "What does it matter if it will get them to go?"

I hesitated in the doorway. A bank of low clouds had moved in, settling across the sky like a heavy gray curtain. Finch spotted us lurking and gave a little wave to me as he stood next to his sister. "Because I'm not certain lying is an option, Lee. I don't think they will let me make up stories, and if I do, I'm afraid it may get me killed."

Chapter
Twenty

r. Morningside did not appear at all during the "light refreshment" on the lawn, and it was growing dark by the time Mrs. Haylam urged the visitors to move into the pavilion. She had timed it all perfectly—the shepherd and his friends disappeared into the big white tent just as Mason Breen, his father, and Samuel Potts returned from Derridon.

I was dispatched to serve them supper in the dining room while Chijioke and Lee tidied up the mess in the yard and put away the wicker furniture. It was all accomplished like the smoothest sleight of hand—one group disappearing before the other could notice them, everything still running more or less smoothly while we accommodated two separate parties.

As I brought cold ham and an array of salads to the dining room, I couldn't help but wonder what was taking Mr. Morningside so long. Hadn't he only gone to change his clothes? Was this some calculated trick to make the shepherd wait and establish his dominance? Whatever it was, it only made me hopeful that it would grow too late for the trial to begin that night. I had already worked a full day, and I wasn't sure I had the presence of mind to outwit an Adjudicator when I longed so for bed.

The elder Breen and Samuel Potts stayed just for a moment, long enough to snatch up a few cuts of meat and wine before retiring, grumpy and mud-spattered, to their rooms. Out in the foyer, I heard Poppy hurrying to find wash clothes and a basin for them while I continued serving Mason Breen. He was quiet for a spell, chewing slowly, drinking his wine lazily and with aching, exhausted movements. It was like he was moving through sludge.

"I suppose we must go to Malton tomorrow," he finally said, sighing into his ham. His sleek blond head was low over the plate as he poked at his food. "After everything we . . . After so much turmoil. I cannot believe Amelia would humiliate me this way. I always stood up for her. I *always* stood up for her."

Please go to bed, please go to bed, please go to bed . . .

"Sir, if I may—"

"Of course," he said with a snort. "Does it look like I have anyone else to talk to?"

I bustled over from the serving board and poured him a bit more wine. If he kept drinking that claret steadily enough, then it would get him upstairs and asleep all the faster. He grunted in thanks as I refilled his glass, and then immediately began sipping.

"I did not know Miss Canny well," I began, taking a step back and cradling the decanter with my palm. "Not at all well— in fact we only spoke at any length once—but she struck me as a strong-willed young lady. We grew up not far from each other, and as she revealed to me, in poverty."

Mason moved with more urgency at that, his head turning

swiftly toward me. There was a small red wine stain on his lip. "Did you indeed?"

"Aye, sir, my accent is not what it was, but Dungarven and Waterford are not far apart," I said. "Having all that new wealth, joining a great family like yours . . . I can only imagine it was—is—intimidating for her. I know for my part it would be hard to change so much; it would feel like maybe I was betraying my old family. My old friends. It's like becoming a new person."

Gradually, Mason smiled, a dimple creasing his cheek as he gazed a little drunkenly at me. "I hadn't thought of it like that. My only fixation has been her hatred of my father, and one can hardly blame her. . . . He is an acquired taste. He only wants what is best for me, but he cannot see that Amelia wants me for *me*, not for my money. Or at least I think she does. Damn it all, why did she have to run like that?"

He swore under his breath and pushed the claret away, then reached into his waistcoat pocket and pulled out the locket I had seen him fussing with earlier. Snapping open the hinge, he sighed and cooed over the little piece of jewelry. At that distance I could see the thing better and noted that one side contained a tiny painting of Mason, and on the other side was a young woman. A young redheaded woman who did not in any way resemble Amelia.

Amelia's rival, the one she had murdered to get to Mason.

"Who is she?" I asked lightly. When he glanced at me, I gave him the most dim-witted, vacant smile I could muster. "She is quite lovely."

"Enid," he breathed. The claret had put him on the verge of tears. "I adored her. *Father* adored her. She fell down the stairs and broke her neck at our country home. I found her when we came in from a hunt. It was the worst day of my life."

I said nothing, watching as he downed his cup and then closed his fist around the locket. Darting forward, I poured a bit more claret for him, which he also guzzled.

"But then Amelia was there," he slurred. Now he had two dimples as he gazed dreamily over at me. Poor sod. He was gone. "She was so constant, so understanding. I grieved Enid for months and months, but Amelia never wavered. Even after that ugly business in New South Wales, she stood by me. I liked that. She was never as pretty or accomplished as Enid, but she loved me with a kind of desperation that made me feel safe. Have you ever had that? Has anyone ever loved you that way?"

"No," I said flatly. Did I want that? It sounded exhausting. "You are very fortunate to have found two such women."

"By God, you're right." Mason tucked the necklace away and stood, unsteadily, grabbing the table for balance before stumbling a few steps toward the door. "I *am* lucky. Amelia will come back. That's who she is—devoted. Utterly devoted. Thank you, this . . . I needed this. Is it a great bother if I take the rest of that claret up with me?"

I smiled and handed him the decanter. "Just be careful going up the stairs, sir, they are rather steep."

"And I'm slaughtered, I know, you don't have to tell me," Mason said, hiccuping. He turned and fumbled his way toward the foyer, all of his limited concentration bent on keeping the wine upright. That he would make it back to his chambers completely upright was looking less and less likely.

It was a relief to be alone, and I took my time tidying the mess the men had left. The longer I took, the later it became, the greater the chance I could escape up to bed without being asked to do more chores. But I was not to be that lucky. As I extinguished the last of the candles and wiped away the wax, a shadow darkened the room. Mr. Morningside. He waited in the archway leading to the foyer, his tall, slim silhouette unmistakable.

"Louisa," he said sharply. "Finish in here and then go to the pavilion. Do not go inside, do you understand me? Wait until you are summoned."

My eyes were drooping with fatigue as I shuffled toward him, arms laden with dirty napkins and the tablecloth. "How long must I wait?"

"As long as it takes," Mr. Morningside snapped. He vanished before I could reach him, though I had clearly seen him carrying my stack of translated papers. I spied nothing but the tail end of his coat as I made my way slowly from the dining room to the kitchens. Nobody but Bartholomew was there, the hound dozing on his back, all four paws curled in the air.

I gave him a scratch on the chin as I passed, dropping off the washing in the pantry and taking a fresh apron. It was an empty gesture, but just putting on something clean made me feel better and more awake. I ate one of the untouched meat pies on my way to the pavilion. Two blazing torches burned outside the tent, not bright enough to illuminate the entire yard, but enough to give me a clear destination. I welcomed the cooler air, the scent of fresh grass and pine bandied about by the light wind. Even without rain or frost, Coldthistle became something more sinister at dusk. Its slim parapets and slivers of windows became darker even than the night itself. The house was not its true self in the daylight and seemed almost to grow larger at night, as if it could drink the shadows to become strong.

I did not look back at the windows as I approached the tent, but I did hope that Mary was not alone in there. It concerned me that we did not yet know the identity of Amelia's killer, and Mary, still recovering, would not be able to fend off an attacker. Poppy had gone to fetch bathwater for the men, and surely Mrs. Haylam would be smart enough to set the Residents to watch. Everything seemed piled on top of everything else—the Court, the guests, Mary's return, the creatures in the woods, Amelia's death, my deal with Mr. Morningside and the revenge that might come of it. No wonder I felt fit to fall over and collapse of exhaustion at any moment—it was enough to make anyone dizzy with distraction.

But my purpose in that moment was clear, or at least, it

ought to be. I pictured Lee's hopeful face as I mentioned a way to rid ourselves of the Adjudicators. He was already living— "living"—with so many changes, the least I could do was set him free of the pain their presence caused. And yet that would require lying, lying to Finch, who had already heard me say that Mr. Morningside had been wrong about Lee. There were rules here I still did not understand—was he supposed to be infallible? Of course that would be so. Chijioke and Poppy had such pure faith in his decisions. . . . Did they waver in their dedication now that they knew he had been mistaken once?

As I reached the pavilion, I shuddered, thinking of what I had read in Bennu's journal. No doubt what he had witnessed were creatures like Finch and Sparrow using their powers to pass judgment. There were always three, Chijioke had said, and three were mentioned in Bennu's account. If I lied, would one of them pull the truth out of me and my very life with it?

I hovered near one of the torches and waited, hands clutching one another nervously. There was nothing for it—I would have to lie, I owed that much to Lee, but I reserved the right to anticipate that moment with anxiety. Fidgeting. Pacing. I heard low voices in the pavilion and grew more and more curious about what they might be saying inside. At the same time, I grew aware of the darkness around me. The small island of light around the torch felt safe, but as the sun vanished on the horizon, I couldn't bear to stray too far, watching for any signs of movement along the edge of the woods and the pasture to the east.

A strong wind came up from the west, rattling the leaves in the forest and making them shimmer louder and louder, the scent of distant wood smoke overwhelming my senses with childhood nostalgia. It smelled of home. *Home.* Or whatever occasional comforts I had experienced there, mostly alone or with my imaginary friend. I closed my eyes against the feeling. When I opened them again, the torch beside me roared, fighting the wind. Another sound, like the gale in the leaves but softer, whispered along the fringe of the forest. The nearness of the torch made it difficult to make out anything far away, and I moved out of the light for a moment, waiting for my sight to clear and then watching as the bushes and saplings deformed, shaking, moved by something traveling along the trees.

My skin prickled, whatever it was moving quickly, concealed by the darkness and the density of the brush but visibly coming closer. Nobody else was outside but me, and I huddled closer to the torch again. What if it was that wolf creature? I was vulnerable out in the open like that, and totally defenseless. I tiptoed toward the pavilion's opening, preparing to dash inside the moment the monster showed itself.

The moon glowed softly, a sliver missing, the dense cloud coverage in front of it diminishing its light. No, I would have only the torch to protect me. I took the far torch out of its holder, brandishing it in front of me as I peered into the shadows, then began to advance. Whatever moved among the trees came closer, and closer still, the shivering of the leaves so loud now that I felt it echoing at the base of my spine, a trill of fear and danger rippling up toward my neck. The torch blazed but my skin was cold with fright. No squirrel could make trees bend that way. A shape no bigger than a man materialized out of the woods, running at speed toward me.

I panicked, gasping, retreating to the safety of the pavilion and holding the torch at the ready. Whoever it was ran with incredible ease and swiftness, with not the grace of a man but of a deer or fox. I knew the moment the figure saw me that they had the advantage, for I was almost blind with the torchlight so near to my face. They had seen me watching them and stopped, stooping as if to pounce, then turned and fled back to the safety of the forest.

I heard something soft thud in the grass. They had *thrown* something at me.

Perhaps foolishly, I hazarded a few steps out into danger. The voices in the tent grew softer as I padded along the grass, sweeping the torch this way and that, looking for whatever object might be hiding in the weeds. The leaves at the edge of the woods rattled again and I glanced up, freezing in place, but it was only the person plunging back into the bushes.

"Hello?" I called. "I see you! I see you hiding out there! Who are you? What do you want?"

Nothing. Just the crackling of the torch in my hand and the hoot of an owl.

"Announce yourself!" I cried again.

I stumbled forward, watching for movement in the forest. All was quiet, but I advanced anyway. I felt bolder now that I had chased them off. The toe of my boot collided with something in the grass and I knelt, running my palm over the ground until I felt a bump and my fingernails scraped over a huge, curled leaf.

The leaf had been bundled around something and knotted with a piece of long, dry grass. Standing, I held the strange parcel up to the torchlight, pulling away the tie and unwrapping the leaf. I almost dropped the thing in surprise.

A spoon. *My* spoon. It was mangled and bent at odd angles, as if a giant had tried using it. Obviously someone had tried to work out the kinks, but to no avail. The necklace chain dangled from the loop at the end of the spoon, broken. I pocketed the spoon, mystified, and turned back toward the pavilion, nearly missing the design in mud on the leaf.

I unrolled the leaf, pressing it to my thigh to keep it from snapping shut again. Whoever had found and returned the spoon had tried to write a message on the veined, rough surface of the leaf. It was done in shaky, childlike smears of mud and read:

SO RY.

Sorry. I gazed up from the leaf to the woods, dumbfounded.

"Hello?" I called once more, wondering if just one more try might get me a response.

"Louisa! There you are!"

I shoved the leaf message in the pocket with the spoon and

whirled, trotting toward Mr. Morningside as he took loping strides toward me. He had come from the pavilion, and he looked to be in good spirits. He squinted and inspected the forest behind me, then laughed.

"What are you doing out here? Mrs. Haylam doesn't want you wondering around after that shock you had in the woods, and neither do I. It isn't safe here right now, you know that." He took me by the shoulder and guided me back toward the pavilion. "Don't tell me you were thinking of running away."

"No . . . No, I just thought I saw something," I mumbled.

"Were you startled? Shall I give you a moment before we go in?"

"I should be all right. But what am I expected to do?" I asked. We had returned to the opening of the pavilion. The pennants above us snapped in the wind while I put the torch back in its place.

Now in the light, I saw that Mr. Morningside had dressed exquisitely for the occasion, his suit pinstriped with iridescent silver and red, his ebony silk cravat studded with a ruby-encrusted broach in the shape of a bird's skull. I felt woefully drab by contrast, my fresh apron now stained with soot and grease from the torch. He walked me to the flap in the pavilion and held me at arm's length, seemingly unaware of how underdressed I felt.

"It shan't go on much longer this evening, Louisa. I know you're tired." He ducked inside first, then waited for me to join.

"You only need answer a few short questions, mostly about the nature of the translations you've been doing for me. If you get nervous or afraid, just say you need more time to think."

"Wait," I whispered, and he hesitated with the canvas in his hand, his head lowered to clear the short door. "Should I tell the truth? What if I say the wrong thing?"

Mr. Morningside gave me one of his big white smiles and shook his head. "You just say whatever you think is . . . Well, *your* version of the truth. One man's truth is another man's lie, what you see is not necessarily what I see, and what I believe is not what you believe. Does that make things more clear?"

"No," I said with a sigh. "Not at all."

His chuckle vanished into the pavilion with him, and I took a deep breath, stepping forward. That single step into the tent felt like walking off a cliff, and that was apt, because what I found inside would leave me stunned and reeling.

Chapter
Twenty-One

had not expected an ordinary tent, but this was altogether astonishing. It felt as if I had stepped into a fairy glade, dark and cool, tiny twinkling lights of every color dancing on the air above us. They were connected to nothing, freely lending their blue or rose or yellow glow before skipping off to light another corner of the pavilion. Even the boundaries of the place were hard to describe, as there seemed to be no walls or ceiling, just a shroud of black mist encasing us in air that smelled as sweet and honeyed as an apiary.

When I had rebounded from the shock, I gazed around in wonder at the volume of attendees. Where had they all come from? The pavilion was bustling with activity, men and women, young and old, some in long black cloaks and others in shimmering gowns of ivory. To my left was a long wooden table with plenty of goblets and decanters, though food looked scarce. A banner hung over that table with a large embroidered version of the pin I wore for safe passage. But the banner did not have the I AM WRATH script across it, just the serpents. Those who hovered around that table wore the black cloaks; those in white clung to a table at the far end of the tent, near a raised dais. That table had a banner on it with a simple coat of arms, four quadrants, two with wings and two with sheep. To my right stood a third table, but it was completely empty. Nobody lingered near it. A banner hung above that table, but it was simply black and tattered, as if long forgotten.

Our entrance did not put an end to the din of conversation, and I glanced around sheepishly for any familiar faces. At last I spied Chijioke in a sea of black cloaks. His garb was far more brilliant—a scarlet coat, wide in the shoulders, with billowing sleeves and a diamond pattern down the front. He wore a small round hat, too, and his eyes glowed like red coals, as brightly as they had when I watched him doing his ferrying ceremony in Derridon.

I hurried over to him, amazed at his appearance. When he caught sight of me, he looked equally stunned.

"Ah, lass, I was curious indeed to see what the Court would make of you," he said with an inscrutable smile.

"Make of me?" I asked.

"You cannot hide what you are in here," he said, gesturing to the room. "No magic, no incantation, no spell would be strong enough to mask your nature. That is why I appear as I do, and why you appear as *you* do."

I felt a fool as I looked down at my own frock, gasping when I found my dowdy servant's clothes and apron were gone, replaced by an evening gown of green silk with a pattern of tiny vines. A light-as-gauze fichu was tucked around the neck, replacing the plain, sturdy one that had been there before. Chijioke had a good laugh over my surprise.

"What? You've done this before?" I reached for one of

the goblets behind him on the table, trying to find my own reflection.

"No, but your reaction is the best I've so far seen. Here," he said, taking the goblet and holding it so I could get a look at myself.

My hair had changed, too, swept up and braided into twisty ropes that secured a tall headdress of leaves and antlers. And my eyes . . . they were completely black, vast and startling, and I turned away from my own reflection in revulsion. There were plenty of other things and people to gape at. Chijioke stayed by my side, then handed me another cup, this one filled with what tasted like ice-cold honey wine.

"Where did they all come from?" I asked. "I saw no one enter the grounds. . . ."

"That surprised me, too," Chijioke replied. "But there is a door in the back, by the judge's seat. It leads to . . . well, lass, all kinds of places. I think the shepherd wanted a whole mess of witnesses just in case Mr. Morningside tried to wiggle out of the trial."

I had almost forgotten that I was there to testify. Through the milling crowd I spotted Mr. Morningside and watched him proceed through the pavilion toward the dais at the other end of the tent. His magnificent suit did not transform, but *he* did, his image flickering as if one were rapidly turning the pages of a book and catching glimpses of illustrations here and there. One instant he was an elderly man with a curlicue beard, the next he was as I knew him, then the next he was childlike and rosy-cheeked. Before my very eyes, the Devil was showing his hundreds of faces.

"Can I hide here with you?" I murmured. "I do not want to be questioned."

"I don't envy you, Louisa," he said, finding his own cup. "But my time will come soon, too."

"And will you tell them the truth?" I pressed. "About what happened with Lee and his uncle? About Mr. Morningside's mistake?"

Chijioke's easy smile died and he looked to his feet, red eyes suddenly dimmer. "I . . . hadn't thought about it. The truth seems wisest."

"It seems wisest until it doesn't," I said with a sigh. "What if they leave the Adjudicators to spy on us because Mr. Morningside isn't doing his job properly? Don't you think whatever the punishment is, it will be for us, too?"

He nodded, slowly, raising the cup to his lips and leaving it there as if the liquid inside could give him the answers he needed. "I'll chew it over, that's for certain. Don't look now, but I think you're being summoned."

The chatter in the tent had died down. In that silence, I turned and found a path had been cleared toward me. A tall, liquid gold figure stood in front of us. It was sexless and ageless, just the shape of a man or woman with skin like burning aurous fire.

"Louisa."

It was Finch, recognizable only because of his voice. When I looked past him, I saw two other figures like him, featureless but gold, waiting at the raised platform. Seated there above them in an ornate wooden throne was the shepherd. He hadn't changed a jot.

"Yes, all right," I muttered, putting the cup back on the table and turning quickly to Chijioke. "Wish me luck?"

"You won't need it," he said with a chuckle. "You have your wits."

I wasn't so sure about that. I felt completely disoriented, assaulted from every direction with strange images. It was like stumbling onto a foreign shore and being expected to know the language and customs within minutes. Could I not stand a moment and just breathe it all in? Get my bearings? No, I was being marched through the tent, all eyes trained directly on me.

There were no words of encouragement from Finch; he simply walked ahead of me and then motioned to the empty spot next to Mr. Morningside. Gradually the conversations behind us started up again, but now I knew they were all about me.

"Well, well, well." I glanced up at Mr. Morningside, whose ever-changing eyes swept from the antlers on my head to the hem of my green silk gown. "Are you ready?" he asked. Even his voice was strange, reflecting the different faces that pulsed in and out, each word pronounced by a man younger or older.

"Do I have a choice?"

"Not really." He winked—or one of his faces did—and then cleared his throat, tucking his hands behind his back and beaming up at the shepherd. Three golden figures joined him by the throne, flanking him like a small army.

"Is that the third Adjudicator?" I whispered.

"Hm? Oh, no, that's the dog," Mr. Morningside said, rolling his eyes. He was not whispering back but bellowing all of this loudly enough for the room to hear. "Always found it ironic, making the voice of God masquerade as a mutt. Bark, bark, heed my word! Bark, bark, fire and brimstone!"

Could that thing really be Big Earl? The shimmering tall man to the shepherd's right squared his shoulders. "Dogs are the noblest creatures in the kingdom. It is my privilege to take their form."

"A privilege to piss on fence posts and sniff your own arse? Noted."

"That's *enough*." The shepherd put his hand up, and both of them were silent. The only difference I could divine, looking up at the bearded old man, was that his voice sounded richer and louder, like the thunder of horses charging.

He drew in a long breath and gave his speech not with force but with a kind of disappointed melancholy. "We are here to ascertain whether Henry Ingram Morningside is guilty of dereliction of his duties. Long ago, in an effort to create peace between our two sides, it was agreed that he would ferry on the souls of the wicked and damned, that doing so would suit his dark nature and prevent crueler urges from being indulged. For our part, we agreed to look to the souls of the good, and to intervene with the wicked only in extreme cases. These are simple terms and simple duties, but they carry unsimple weight. This balance we have achieved can be broken, Henry, and the consequences of such imbalance hurt us all."

He turned his pale eyes on me from where he sat in his throne, his legs too short even to reach the floor. "Are you here willingly, my dear?"

Oh. It was my turn to speak. I felt small and frail under the pressure of so many expectant eyes, but I lifted my chin and tried to reply as loudly as I could. "I am, yes."

"Finch tells me you have quite the story to tell," the shepherd said. He smiled, smug. "Do you agree to tell your truth here, when instructed, and to speak with honesty and integrity? You may refuse, Louisa, if that is your preference."

"N-no," I said, cursing the stammer. "I agree."

The shepherd leaned toward me, and at once that nasty, icy feeling in my bones returned, so acute and intense that I went rigid, then felt my knees threaten to fail. I struggled to keep my eyes open as he told me in clear, short bursts, "If we suspect you of lying, you will be submitted to Judgment to discern the truth. Is that clear? We will enforce our ancient agreements by any means necessary."

"I . . . I . . ." The cold was so terrible I was half convinced I would see my breath puff out in white clouds as I hesitated.

Judgment. I knew what that meant. I knew what a lie could do, the pain and death it could bring.

"That won't be required." Mr. Morningside spoke up. He held up the papers I had translated, flashing them high for everyone to see. "I am submitting my own evidence. Thanks to Louisa's marvelous skills of translation, I will soon have the location of the long-lost third book."

He handed the stack of parchment to the shepherd, who leaned back in the throne, shying away as if the papers might pinch. "That's impossible."

"This is ridiculous!" Sparrow exploded. She rushed forward to intercept the papers, but Mr. Morningside flicked them away. "Theatrics, pure theatrics! This is nothing more than a vulgar distraction!"

"On the contrary," Mr. Morningside said smoothly. "It's entirely relevant to the proceedings. We're here to determine my fitness, yes? My competence? The missing book and the Lost Order are linked, and I will prove it to you." He pivoted and addressed the shepherd directly. "You cannot call into question the competency of a man who has done what you have tried and failed to do for centuries!"

The shepherd stood up and the excited noise of the onlookers died at once. He leaned far out of his throne, and as he glared at Mr. Morningside, I saw not an old man but a warrior, aged, perhaps, weathered, but glowing with as much white-hot fury as the blazing figures around him. I shrank back, afraid, regretting that I had chosen this side, and that I had ever been asked to choose one at all.

Silence. Then the shepherd broke it like a clap of lightning and something in the room snapped. "Give those to me."

The tension evaporated. Mr. Morningside handed over my work and then said nothing, offering no more insults or mockery.

"If what you say is true—" the shepherd began.

"No!" Sparrow was quick to interrupt. "You cannot possibly—"

"*If* what you say is true and these findings are authentic," he continued, dismissing her with a look, "it will indeed alter the nature of this Court. I will study what you have here, Henry, and determine the best course of action. That is all."

The Court erupted in outrage and excitement. The reactions were quite obviously split between two halves of the room, the loudest protests coming from Sparrow, who stormed back and forth across the dais, haranguing her brother for not warning her that this was coming. I couldn't help but feel sorry for Finch, who had no way of knowing what Mr. Morningside was up to. Perhaps she had expected him to pump me for information, but I had only offered him the mistake with Lee, a dry crumb compared to the far tastier morsel I had concealed.

"Off we go," Mr. Morningside said cheerily, taking me by the elbow and dragging me through the near riotous crowd.

"Don't need anyone trying to take your head off before you can finish that journal."

"Should I be worried about that?" I asked, dodging the curious, penetrating looks of strangers, all of them swarming close to us as we tried to leave the pavilion. I flinched away from them, wishing I could disappear quietly, not on the arm of the person who had just caused such a flurry of anger and wonder.

"About Sparrow? No. Maybe. She's always been an embarrassing lunatic, ever the loose cannon, but it's only gotten worse with Spicer gone," he told me. We at last reached the exit and he half tossed me outside and into the darkness. He followed, and instantly his appearance subsided into the familiar one with wild black hair and golden eyes. "Which reminds me, I should find out what that imbecile is up to."

"Is he the third one?" I asked. "Spicer? I know that name somehow. . . ."

"Yes, he's *the third one*," Mr. Morningside said impatiently. He took off toward the house and I tried to keep up, worried that if I were left alone Sparrow might come looking. "His absence is conspicuous and I don't like not knowing what it means. They probably sent him to dig up dirt on me somewhere, or maybe he's gone in search of the Lost Order. Whatever it is, it's suspicious."

I was too tired to make sense of what he was saying. Once inside the kitchens, we startled Bartholomew awake. He had been sleeping by the range for warmth. I stopped at the sight of him and knelt down, rubbing his ears until he stuck his nose in the air and touched it to my chin. *The noblest creatures in the kingdom.*

"What are you doing? Did I dismiss you?" Mr. Morningside whirled around, looming over us with his hands on his hips.

"I want him to sleep in my room tonight, or at least outside my door," I said sternly. "There's a monster in the woods, someone killed Amelia, and those insane golden people want to suck out my soul if I lie! Forgive me if the thought of sleeping alone is impossible."

His eyes softened and he glanced away, nodding as he turned toward the foyer. "Peace. Peace, Louisa. Of course. Take the dog. I suppose I have been . . . a touch neglectful of the house. Mrs. Haylam is looking into it, but I'll do my part, too, Louisa. Take Bartholomew; I shall walk the grounds. If there is a wolf and a murderer in our midst, then they will be found."

Chapter
Twenty-Two

t was late when I opened my eyes and found the door to my room ajar. Bartholomew must have left, and I was all alone. I shivered in the darkness. One of the candles I had left burning was still clinging to life, just a smear of wax with a dying flame flickering out beside the bed. I still felt so tired, though I must have slept, and distant from myself, as if my thoughts were an arm's length away at all times.

Laughter. Distant laughter. It was too late for anyone to be up at this hour. . . . I longed to go back to bed but felt drawn to the sounds of celebrating. Clinking glassware. Amiable conversation. Had the guests in the pavilion stayed and moved their merrymaking into the house? I doubted Mrs. Haylam would allow such a thing. Taking up the little candle stub in its holder and pulling on a shawl, I tiptoed out of bed and down the hall.

The black ragged tails of Residents disappeared just ahead of me. There were three of them, all heading down the stairs toward the foyer. I passed the bird paintings cluttering up the wall, though the images seemed hazy, my eyes bleary with exhaustion. A dread cold hung over the house, as if the warmer months were long gone, the depths of winter returned. I saw my breath on the air and felt my skin prickle as it did in the moments before the sky broke and snow fell.

I followed the Residents, always just a step behind, watching them float ahead of me and toward the kitchens. Perhaps they, too, sensed something was amiss. The laughter was far off again, too far off, moving whenever I drew near. With chilly bare feet I crossed the foyer and peered into the kitchens, seeing the ghostly fringe of a Resident drift out the door and onto the lawn. Where the devil were they going? I had never seen any of them leave for the grounds except Lee. Faster I chased after them, faster, shielding the candle flame with one hand as it threatened to die.

The air outside stung, but the laughter was getting clearer. Oh, but it sounded like a jolly gathering indeed. The Residents sped across the grass, swift, black shapes that went with no hesitation to the pavilion and then forced their way inside. My heart ached. It felt like a joke I was not privy to, like a conversation whispered in the next room, a conversation you know is pure gossip and all about you. I ignored the candle flame, running hard, slipping across the lawn before better judgment could intervene and send me back to bed.

When I plunged into the tent it was brightly lit, though dyed silvery blue. All the wonder and beauty of it was gone, replaced by a deadness on the air and a horrible smell that made me gag and press my wrist over my mouth. The trestle tables had been removed. The pavilion seemed to go on forever, a long, horrible gauntlet of enduring that stench. It was worse than the docks at low tide. Worse than the stables on a hot day. It was old, bad flesh, a butcher's cart in high summer. It hung around me thick as a fog, but at last I had found the source of the laughter.

There, at the far, far end of the tent was the gathering. I recognized everyone from behind—Mr. Morningside, of course, and Chijioke, Mrs. Haylam, and Poppy, but also Finch, Sparrow, the shepherd, and his dog. What could possibly make them all so happy? And why would they go there to have a revelry in the middle of the night?

It was all wrong. It was a dream, a nightmare, and I knew it then but to my horror found that I could not wake myself. I was locked into this endless walk and would not break out of the dream until I saw it through.

And so I ran on and on, feeling breathless and hopeless, convinced that I would never reach my destination. They were laughing harder now, uproariously, and the smell was so aggressive I could only breathe through the fabric of my shawl, and even then tendrils of the stench clawed at the back of my throat. At last it was over and time slowed, and it was like watching them underwater, their voices distorted and low, the laughter insane, forced, only for my benefit.

I stopped dead. It was a joke I wish I had never been in on. Their faces were messy with gore; they had been eating sloppily. My body was on the table in front of them, all of it torn open, unrecognizable but for the face. And there my eyes were missing. I saw then that Poppy was holding my eyes in her palm;

she squealed with too much delight and popped them into her mouth.

"Her eyeballs exploded!" she giggled, gray juice running down her chin.

There was almost nothing of me left, just the head with its empty sockets, Big Earl rooting around in the viscera left on the table, his jowls slick with blood. Even the shepherd had feasted, his lips limned in red, eyes wild and ecstatic as he chewed and chewed.

I tried to back away, feeling my stomach give out and my limbs go soft, but Mr. Morningside took me by the shoulder and pulled me in. I could smell the reek on him, see stains all down his once immaculate suit.

His brow knitted with concern as bloodied fingers tilted my chin up and he studied me intently. Mr. Morningside pouted and let his head fall to the side. "Are you lost, child? *Are you lost?*"

"Are you awake, Louisa? Louisa! Wake up!"

I was. I was? Strangely, my eyes were already open, but only then did normal sight return. And I was still choking, gagging. I coughed, hard, nearly crashing my head into two pairs of concerned eyes. Poppy and Bartholomew both sat on the bed, leaning in close enough for me to feel their breath on my face. My chin felt wet. I couldn't stop coughing. What was the matter with me? Could a dream really be so powerful? I wiped at my chin, expecting to find an embarrassing amount of drool from the night; instead the back of my hand came away stained with pink foam.

Shit.

"Why are you spitting up pink stuff?" Poppy asked, poking at my hand. "That is very unusual, Louisa. Are you ill? Shall I call for Mrs. Haylam? She will know what to do!"

"No!" I said too loud. Too panicked. I grabbed the shawl draped on my bedside table and wiped furiously at my mouth. God, there was a lot of it. "It's . . . a Changeling thing."

Poppy's brows shot up. Bartholomew did not look convinced. "Is it? That must be very inconvenient."

"Oh . . . it is," I said, forcing a smile. "It, um, happens sometimes when we have a bad dream. I have been meaning to ask Mr. Morningside about it; he does know a lot about Unworlder things."

"That is a grand idea," Poppy replied with a laugh. She bounced her way across the bed and the dog followed, though much more slowly. My lap was blazingly hot from where Bartholomew had spent the night guarding me. I looked to the door, shuddering, convinced I could still smell that awful stench, as if it lingered from the dream at the back of my mouth.

"Oh!" Poppy twirled at the door, leaning on the frame and sticking a knuckle between her teeth. Her eyes darted nervously about the room. "About why I came to wake you. Yes, well, you should really hurry and clean up your face. You have a visitor, Louisa."

"A visitor?" I pulled the blanket up, hiding the soiled shawl underneath. "Who would come to see me?"

"Your father, silly. He's waiting downstairs!"

I had asked for this, and yet it was the last thing I needed.

Pink foam. Foam. Just like in the journal, the two girls . . . Oh God, and now my father, my real *father. My real father who abandoned my mother and left us to suffer poverty and degradation, who left me for a drunken half-wit to berate and abuse. Oh God. Oh* God.

It took longer than usual to get dressed, as I not only wanted to buy myself time but also make certain I looked presentable. There was little I could do to gussy up a servant's simple bodice, skirts, and tucker, but at least I could make sure my apron was straight and my hair nicely plaited. While my nerves gathered like a storm at the edge of the horizon, I tried to take a modicum of satisfaction in making him wait. Croydon Frost. What did I expect? What did *he* expect?

Not a long-faced, lank-haired plain girl with black eyes, I wagered. Most fathers must imagine their daughters to be great beauties. Lord, did he have a surprise in store.

I walked calmly down the hall when I was ready, or ready enough, reminding myself not to seem too eager. I confess, there was a part of me consumed with a giddy curiosity. Even if he was a vile, abandoning cur, I couldn't help but feel a tad excited. It was a solved mystery, a gift opened at last on Christmas morning, or maybe not; maybe it would be the shock of a snake waiting in the grass to bite.

Mary's door was shut as I passed by, and I paused outside, then tapped on the door. I heard nothing inside, but tapped again and said softly, "I promise to visit later. There's so much I need to tell you. Rest well, Mary."

I was stalling and I knew it. But I also had an advantage while I lingered upstairs. The first floor looked out onto the foyer; they shared the same vaulted walls and ceiling, the same horrendous bird art. So I moved back a few steps and then slowly toward the banister, peering ever so gradually over the edge, trying to spot the man before he spotted me. I felt owed a look at him, a long look, one that lasted for whatever duration felt necessary. Maybe it would dispel the fear. Maybe it would give me courage.

And there he was. My first impression was that he was extraordinarily tall. He had removed a glossy top hat, revealing black curly hair speckled with silver. A long dark coat embroidered with green trim with an attached cape hung from his lean frame. Three modestly sized fabric bags were lined up beside him, and he had a small birdcage tucked under one arm, though I could see no bird in it. His face was . . . Well, not like mine exactly, but I could certainly note the resemblance. His eyes were also dark, even blacker than mine, and he, too, had a narrow face. It was dominated by a hawkish nose, too big, some would say, but it balanced a square, cleft chin. All in all he was not necessarily handsome, but striking, and stood with a casually authoritative tilt to his hips, as if, after mere moments, he belonged in this place.

He shifted the birdcage to his other arm and let his eyes roam around the room, and that was when he saw me.

It was time to go downstairs and come out of hiding. I pretended like I had not been spying on him, but of course my pale cheeks flamed with embarrassment. That would not do. I pulled my shoulders back and marched down the stairs like a queen about to address her subjects. He had sent a letter groveling for my acceptance, after all, and that meant I had the upper hand. I had begun to wonder if he was suffering from some terrible illness and wanted to make amends before he passed. Men always became frightfully concerned about their reputations when death hovered near.

"There you are," he said as I reached the bottom step. The severity of his face changed, and he gave a full-bodied sigh, brows tenting with relief.

"Does Mrs. Haylam know you're here?" I asked, keeping a safe distance. I crossed my wrists primly in front of my waist. There would be no leaping into arms or embracing today.

"She does," he replied. He put down the birdcage carefully on the floor and took a few steps toward me, gesturing with his top hat. "I . . . told her to wait on accommodations. It is your decision whether I stay or go."

I had expected him to have an accent like mine, but travel

or time had worn it down, altered it, until it was not Irish or anything else, but uniquely his own.

"Then Mr. Morningside extended an invitation," I said. "I had no idea it would reach you so soon; this is all very . . . hasty."

"Oh! Oh." He bit down hard on his lower lip and worried the edge of his hat with both hands. "There was no invitation, Louisa. I came on my own." He must have seen the rising fury in my face because he held up a hand as if to keep me from lunging. "Please don't be angry. Please. I just needed to see you with my own eyes. If you want me to depart at once then I will."

I closed my eyes, feeling my hands turn into fists, the nails biting hard into my palms. The nerve of this man. The enduring nerve. I took in a deep breath, promising myself it was not worth throttling him then and there. Still. I was hurt, beyond hurt, aching in a place in my heart I didn't know existed. Breathe. *Breathe.* "How did you even find me?"

"I hired a few men," he said with a shrug. "They started in Waterford, spiraled out from there. They found your old school, but the headmistress had not seen you in months. There were only so many towns near enough to walk to, so they started again there."

"You hunted me down like a thief," I murmured, icy. "How flattering."

"How this would all look when I found you was not my most pressing priority," he said, gaining a little sternness of his own. But he backed it down, hanging his head, playing the beleaguered father. "I suppose I should have given that more thought. I'll go."

"No!" I hated myself for how fast it came out, how little control I had over the word. "No . . . Not yet. There are things I want to know, things I want to hear from you, and then you can be on your way."

"I had hoped to leave with you," he admitted. "Foolish, I know, but one does dream. What father does not want to spoil a child who deserved spoiling all along?"

"You don't know me," I shot back. "You don't know what I deserve."

"Well then, I should like to change that." My father, for he was that—the resemblance could not be denied, especially now that I saw him more closely—came toward me. He stopped a polite span away and bowed at the waist. "Croydon Frost; our meeting and these introductions are long overdue. Longer than you can possibly imagine."

"I can imagine. I was alive for all of it." But I gave a short curtsy and sighed, sweeping by him and inspecting his luggage. The scent of pine perfume drifted from his possessions. "Don't expect me to, I don't know, love you or something. Or act like your daughter."

"Very well."

From the kitchens, I saw both Poppy and Mrs. Haylam spying on us intently. They did not even attempt to hide their interest. "And when I ask you to leave for good you had better do it."

"I understand," he said, but I heard the sadness in his voice.

"I have work to do here, so I can't spend all my time with you. I'm quite busy, you know, so don't expect courtesy." He said nothing, but there was agreement in the silence. I picked up one of his bags and gestured to Poppy. "Mrs. Haylam can decide where to put you. Welcome to Coldthistle House."

Chapter
Twenty-Three

"an you believe it? It's . . . I don't know if there's a word for it, Mary; it's outrageous!" I was storming back and forth across poor Mary's room, complaining her ear off about the sudden appearance of Mr. Croydon Frost. "To come here without my consent! To send that ridiculous letter asking for my permission and then to totally ignore it! And to think, I was going to invite him, only to rob him of course, but still! I hate him, Mary, I hate him already!"

The tirade ended with me flopping next to her on the bed, where she was bundled up, back to the wall next to her window, a book opened on her lap. She looked much better, her cheeks fuller and red with health. It was such a good turn for her that I almost forgot the fury in my heart.

"Calm yourself," she said, taking my hand and squeezing it. I could tell she was eating up all this gossip, however, green eyes sparkling with interest. "You have known the man five whole minutes; perhaps it is too soon to judge what might come of this."

The only good thing that might come of it was a fortune to spend getting all of us away from the ugly perils of Cold-thistle House. It would be a lonely life to fleece my father only to spend it in solitude with no friends to share in the wealth. I grinned at her and shook my head. "You're too kind, Mary, nobody deserves you. Except perhaps Chijioke." That glow in her cheeks redoubled and her face fell. "No, forget I said that! I'm sorry, truly, it isn't my place to pry. . . ."

"He told you about the carving," she said, looking away toward the window. "I wish he hadn't."

"I have no idea what was going on between you two and it isn't my business. The only thing I *will* say is that he's been a wonderful friend to me these past months. Lee has decided he despises me, which is his right, and I would have been terribly alone without Chijioke to keep me company," I said. "Just . . . Well, here you are telling me to give things time, and now I will say the same to you."

Mary nodded and patted my hand. "Then I will take my own wise advice."

I left the bed and went to the window, pulling the half-drawn curtain aside. Mason and his father were in the yard having a talk, not a friendly one judging by the boy's fevered gesturing. The casement had been left open, and there was a woodsy scent on the air.

"It seems no one here has good luck when it comes to family," I said softly. "I should tell him to go. Hating him is exhausting."

"You could try forgiveness," Mary suggested.

"No," I sighed. "That sounds exhausting, too. Besides, I don't believe in forgiveness. A thing either bothers you or it doesn't; forgiveness is for the other person, to make them feel better about being cruel or selfish."

"And yet I'm sure you would like Lee to forgive you."

I flinched. She was right. "That won't happen, and it shouldn't."

Mary closed up her book and folded her hands over it. I could feel her staring at me, but I wouldn't take my eyes away from Mason and his father. "Why are you so determined to suffer?"

"I don't know," I whispered. "I wish I knew."

Thunk.

"Hey!" I jumped back from the window. Someone had thrown a rock, narrowly missing the glass.

"What was that?" Mary asked, leaning out of bed.

I pulled the curtain completely aside and opened the window wider, letting in a gush of humid air and the sulfurous tinge from the nearby spring.

"Did you need something, sir?" I called down. The two Breens were the only people I could see on the lawn, and one of them must have thrown the rock.

Mason searched the windows for the source of the voice, then spotted me and shielded his eyes, frowning. "Hello up there. What did you say?"

"Did you need assistance, sir? I heard the rock you tossed this way. . . ."

"Rock?" He shook his head and glanced at his father, who looked equally confused. "You must be mistaken! Perhaps it was the house shifting or a bit of grit on the wind?"

House shifting indeed.

"My apologies for bothering you, sir," I called back, leaning against the sill to watch them closely. If they tried to trick me again I would catch it.

"How odd," Mary said, gazing over at me. "Do you think he's fibbing?"

"Obviously," I muttered. "There are two more men I wouldn't mind asking to pack and go."

Through the closed door to Mary's room I heard Mrs. Haylam's voice. She was calling, or rather shouting, my name. I slammed my head back against the wall, frustrated. Could I not have one moment of peace alone with Mary? Was that so much to ask?

"Duty calls," she said sadly, reading my thoughts.

"As ever. Will you be terribly cross if I go? I promise to come to you again soon, friend. I've missed you so much, it lifts my spirits to see you getting better."

Mary reached out her hand and I crossed to her, squeezing her warm little fingers and smiling. "I will only be cross if you stay away too long."

"You're an angel," I said, turning to go. "Or . . . well, whatever the equivalent would be, you know, for us."

Her amused laughter followed me out the door, and I tried to hold on to it, tried to wrap it around me like a shield. At least she was on the mend; everything else may have been odd and confusing, but her steadfastness gave me a drop of hope.

I took the steps quickly, aware of a strange emptiness in the house. Other than in my horrid dream, I had not seen a single Resident all day. They had been swarming Mary's door previously, most likely to protect her from whomever killed Amelia, but now they were gone. Then I remembered my conversation with Mr. Morningside, and wondered if they had been sent to scour the grounds for the wolf monster. That made sense, considering they could cover far more ground than any of us on foot and blend inconspicuously into the shadows of the trees.

Mrs. Haylam waited, foot tapping, in the foyer. She looked haggard, tired, with noticeable smudges of purple under her eyes, her bun drawn up more tightly than usual. All bad signs.

"Have you seen to Mr. Breen's room?" she asked without a word of greeting.

"Yes, ma'am," I replied obediently. I was in no mood for a fight, and neither, clearly, was she.

"And the washing from yesterday, you hung it up?"

"Yes, and the pantry is swept." Half-heartedly, I added in my head.

Mrs. Haylam's good eye swept over me as if it could detect deception. She nodded then and pointed to the green door behind me. "Mr. Morningside wants you back to work. You can socialize later."

I gave her a polite curtsy and turned toward the door, then stopped and told her as she returned to the kitchens, "Thank you for giving my . . . For giving Croydon Frost a room."

"Don't thank me, girl. If it were up to me, he'd be sleeping in the barn."

"No arguments there," I said, and I heard her cackle before I opened the green door and let it swallow me up.

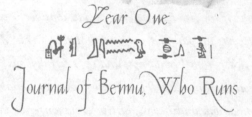

Year One

𓀀𓏏𓈖𓏤 𓈖𓅓𓈖𓄿 𓎼𓃀 𓇋𓆑

Journal of Bennu, Who Runs

We made land briefly at Knossos before gaining passage to Pylos aboard an Athenian merchant ship. I had never been at sea, and at first the constant rolling and rocking made me ill for hours on end. By the time we reached Pylos, I felt like an accomplished sailor, accustomed to the sway of the deck and growing fond of the fresh salt tang on the air.

Nothing could prepare me for the beauty of Pylos, with its crystalline waters and the crisp white houses piled on the coast, explosively green fir and cypress trees hugging the towns like a thick emerald shawl. Arriving at dusk, we watched as the city above began to glow faintly with lanterns, then guard fires lit along the walled walkways as we began our climb buffeted at our backs by the cooling sea wind.

"It will be good to sleep on firm ground again," I said to my companion. We both wore voluminous ivory hoods that draped around our necks. They served to hide his unusual markings and my heavy satchel.

Khent peered at me from under his deep hood, smirking. "And it will be good to eat mutton again. I tire of all this fish."

I had noticed his peculiar eating habits in Knossos. He ate almost no onions or barley with his meals, and he took his meat and fish off the fire long before I would consider it edible. But then he was an odd sort in general, I found. He often heard things clearly that I could not, and slept fitfully, waking at the tiniest disturbance. But he was otherwise an amiable traveling companion, and I was grateful to no longer be facing these dangers alone.

We took our time entering the city proper, for our legs had become accustomed to the sea, and it felt good to walk and stretch, and to look about and see more than just turquoise in every direction. I was winded and ready for rest when we passed under the gates. It was a time of peace, and we were not questioned, for we blended in well with the busy ebb and flow from the docks.

"It will be more difficult to find shelter here," Khent warned me. "Mother and Father are worshipped everywhere, but here temples to the old gods are more vigilant. We may be better off at an inn."

"Our safe houses are being watched," I agreed. "They are not safe anymore."

Khent nodded, and together we pushed through the crowds lining the streets. The market had begun to close, and merchants and buyers alike were beginning to close up and head home. "I do not know how far Roeh's influence has spread, but the Dark One has servants everywhere. Necromancers and poison-fingered demons, beautiful women that lure you away and rip out your heart in the night . . . We will be hunted from every direction, my friend. The sea was a reprieve, but that refuge is no more."

"The Dark One," I murmured. I could see Khent searching for shelter, eyes canted up as he checked each passing door for signs of an inn. It seemed, too, as if he were inhaling more, sniffing, as if his nose could lead him to a safe destination. "Meryt and Chryseis spoke of him once, but only in whispers. I don't know how anyone could worship an evil thing."

"We are not so different," Khent replied. As we left the market square, flanked on all sides by tall, shining white buildings, the crowd thinned but the smell of cooking food intensified. My stomach roared, soured from too much dried fish and hard bread on the boat. "Mother and Father command trees and creatures, wondrous beings who spring from water and air. But they command the boar, too, which sometimes kills the hunter, and the oleander that poisons the hound. It is said the Dark One's servants only come for the most nefarious among us, but his servants are new to this world, and I do not trust it will remain so forever."

"Evil hunting evil," I murmured, thoughtful. "That is not so bad."

Khent laughed. He had an infectious laugh, a giddy sound that was completely unique to him. It sometimes reminded me of hyenas giggling to one another on the plains. "Are we not performing evil in their eyes right now? We are servants to other masters, more powerful masters, and if Roeh and the Dark One want to see them destroyed, then I would hesitate to call either of them 'friend.' Ah! Here."

He stopped us outside a small inn. The sign had been defaced, but I did not read enough of the language to know what it said. It was loud inside, filled with early drunks, the perfect place for two quiet young travelers to disappear. Nobody would hear us above the din of the men, mostly sailors, who boasted and played dice and exchanged insults, keen for a brawl.

We found the innkeep slumbering in the corner while his wife and daughter hurried to refill cups and deliver steaming bowls of fish stew, olives, and bread to the sailors.

Khent half shouted, banging his fist in front of the innkeep's face, and I assumed he had asked for a room. The man jumped awake, sallow-faced and saggy, with thin black hair and a patchy beard.

They haggled briefly, the innkeep glancing between us suspiciously, then he handed over a key and snatched the coin out of Khent's fingers before we could change our minds.

"Charming fellow," Khent sneered, dragging me away from the back of the inn and toward a table at the hearth. "Keep your voice down; we don't know what prejudices lurk among these people."

"I am too weary to speak much anyway," I said, joining him at the small table and falling onto the bench like a sack of bricks. The strap of the satchel had carved a deep runnel in my shoulder, a purple-and-black bruise that only grew worse with each passing day. Sometimes Khent offered to carry the bag, but I had been tasked with delivering the book, and so I never allowed him to keep it for long.

"No, I suppose you will just take out that little journal of yours and scribble away," he teased. He signaled to the innkeep's daughter, who blew a strand of sweaty hair out of her face and wandered over. Khent spoke to her gently, politely, and at once I saw the change in her—she was obviously grateful to have two quieter, calmer customers. He gave her a coin at the outset, and that pleased her, too.

"Why do you write in that thing so much? One book not enough for you to carry?"

"I don't know," I said, gazing into the fire. "I just want to remember that I did any of this, that I . . . that I mattered. At first it was just a daily log of what had transpired, but now it feels like more than that. I don't want this story, my story—our story—to just disappear. We have seen terrible and wonderful things, and those sights should be recorded."

Khent nodded, grinning at the girl as she returned with two foaming cups of beer. She blushed under his attentions, and it was not difficult to understand why.

"Well, your penmanship is a disaster," he said when she was gone. "What sort of scribe taught you? A blind one?"

"It isn't a disaster," I shot back, defensive. "Nobody can read it. It's a language of my own. Shorthand. All of these curiosities and secrets should be kept, but they are not for all eyes."

His eyebrows rose at that, and his dark purple eyes glimmered over the cup of his beer. "Not bad, Bennu. You're full of surprises."

"As are you, my friend." The beer was not cold but it did taste wonderful, enough to wash out the salty residue in my mouth leftover from the sea. "What are those marks on your arms? Where did you come from? You have the look of a nobleman's son and you do not sound like anyone I know in my village. You speak perfect Greek. What sort of scribe taught you?"

He gave that strange wild laugh again and sipped his beer. "I like you, Bennu the Runner, I like you very much. And to your question—it was a royal scribe who taught me, and that is all you must know for now."

We remained at the inn for two nights, two blissfully

uneventful, restful nights. Khent still slept fitfully, but that did not bother me. In fact, I was glad to have someone so watchful at my side. The book I carried attracted bad luck like honey attracted flies, and his vigilance afforded me better sleep. We hard hardly left the inn at all, which let me carry the bag less, and my shoulder began to heal. But we could not stay forever, which became obvious on the third morning, when I woke from night terrors, pink spittle rushing from my lips.

Khent saw it, for he always woke well before me, and at once he donned his traveling cloak. "It is time we moved on," he said solemnly.

"What does it mean?" I asked, climbing regretfully out of the blankets and cleaning my chin on a basin rag. "I have seen it before. The girls who sent me on this journey, they were praying by the book and had visions. . . ."

"It's Mother speaking to you," he said, and handed me my cloak. "It means we need to leave."

And leave we did, by the north gate, hitching a ride with a wealthy goatherd who allowed us to ride on his cart for the hillier, more treacherous stretches leading from the city. My feet were glad for the goatherd, but he could only take us into the countryside, a place greener than I had ever seen before, with rocky hills dotted with fluffy sheep and grazing goats. We sheltered that night in an abandoned herder's shack shaded by tall pines. It was strange to be so far from home, to look out onto grassy hills and not the familiar serpentine rushing of the Nile.

Khent retrieved bundles of grass from the shallow woods behind us and helped me pile them into bundles for sleeping. Then he made a small fire outside the shack, and we sat and watched the stars emerge, each of us munching on goat cheese given to us by the helpful herder. A shape appeared in the sky as we ate, a winding thing that slithered its way in front of the stars, higher than a bird might fly but not by much. It was massive, black, with faint stripes of yellow and red. I gasped and pointed, mouth full, watching it glide effortlessly.

"A Sky Snake," Khent said, grinning. "A good omen; my heart is glad to see it. We will follow it, and soon; we should leave while we still have the cover of dark."

I huddled under my cloak and tried to sleep, but the hillside soon grew cold, too cold for our meager fire to banish, and I felt vulnerable, the rickety old shack offering a clear view of us curled up inside. I do not think I slept until I heard the song.

It was quiet at first, haunting, a mother's lullaby turning sour at the edges. Sad. The woman who sang it sounded like she was in mourning. But it was beautiful, and for a while I rested as if inside it, comforted by its soft, winding verses. Then listening to it in dreams was not enough, and I woke up, refreshed. I could not say how much time had passed, but the moon was out and full again, almost garish as it hung shining in the sky.

The Sky Snake was gone, but the song had come, and so I climbed out from under my cloak and stood. It seemed wrong to leave the satchel, for it was mine to protect, so I hoisted it onto my shoulder and winced from the pain, then shook off the discomfort and went in search of the song. I felt compelled to find it, called to it like a gull called to the sea. It drifted out from the shallow forest, and in I went, feeling the pine boughs brush against my cheeks as I blindly searched, using my ears and not my eyes to go by.

The song grew louder. It had words yet it did not, or I did not understand the words; they folded in on themselves. And then the woman would sing a note, a high note, one that plucked at my heart, stirring a longing there that almost brought me to tears. Why was she so sad? I had to find her.

A tiny brook wound its way through the trees, and my feet splashed in it, the water leading me to a large, rounded rock, and there she sat. I had never seen a woman so beautiful in all my life. She was dark-skinned and plump, with wide, catlike eyes, and she wore nothing but black hair that fell like a shroud and pooled around her feet. Her knees were drawn up to her chest as she combed her fingers through that hair and sang, her lips shining as if painted with gold.

"Are you lost?" I asked.

"No." She broke off the song with a giggle, those dark, pretty eyes fixed on me. "Are you?"

She beckoned me closer and I went, certainly in love. I had never wanted to hold a person so much, to feel their body pressed close, to know their touch, their scent. . . . Her eyes had sunk hooks into mine and I easily scaled the boulder she sat on, feeling a strange, silky tendril snaking along my legs. I dropped the satchel. What did the book matter when this being existed?

"What is your name?" I asked, desperate. "I must know it."

With one finger under my chin she smiled, showing me three sets of pointed teeth. That was beautiful, too, and just the brush of her fingertip felt as if it could cure me of all ills. "Talai," she cooed, "but you will only live to say it once."

Her long black hair had wrapped around my ankles. I could feel it tightening there, holding me, and then more of it slithered across my arms and up to my shoulders, trapping me like a silken black web.

"Talai," I repeated, but her spell was beginning to break. The too-tight hold of her hair around my legs and arms shocked me back to myself and I struggled, yanking my limbs this way and that. She only smiled wider in the face of my panic and tears, moonlight sparkling on her many, many teeth.

She began to pull me closer, closer, and nothing I did ended her steely grip. Out of the corner of my eye I saw another snaking tendril of hair wrap around my satchel and pick it up. It was out of my reach, and I screamed, hoping that Khent in his vigilance would wake and bring help. I had failed us both with my foolishness, and now this creature had the book. . . .

Her breath, foul and sharp, washed over me. I gagged and closed my eyes, unwilling to watch the horror of her face coming near. That huge, devouring mouth was on me, sealing to my face like a leech, unbearably sharp teeth tearing into my skin. She was silencing me, silencing me forever, though still I screamed and screamed into her throat.

The forest floor shook under us, and for a moment I felt reprieve. The creature froze, the lightest, stinging kiss of its teeth prickling against my flesh. I could not breathe the hot sour air in its mouth, but at least it had been distracted by the noise. Then the clamor came again, and again, trees around us swaying as if knocked about by a giant. From behind came an ear-rending scream, a canine shriek as if a hundred jackals howled in unison.

Thrum. Thrum. Thrum.

Footsteps. What greater terror had come to finish me and this monster off together? I went limp in the creature's grasp, crying harder as the boulder under us trembled, threatening to dislodge and send us tumbling to the ground. But I did not tumble—in fact, I was lifted, not by the unnatural hairs of the singing creature but by hands, massive ones, strong and almost human.

Then I was tossed aside, ripped out of one creature's grasp and thrown by another's. I rolled onto the springy grass of the forest and panted, flipping onto my back and scuttling into the cover of the trees. The thing that had saved me was taller than the tallest man, covered in mottled gray-and-black fur with a stripe down its back and large, pointed ears. Blessed earth, it was impossible to believe my eyes, but I had seen such a thing before, hundreds, thousands of times—it was Anubis himself, not stone but flesh. Stranger still, its shoulders and arms, muscled like a man's, had faint markings beneath the fur. Khent's markings.

Talai shrieked at it, hissing, standing on top of the boulder fearlessly and flinging herself at it teeth-first. The jackal creature—Khent, or so I hoped, for I did not want to be its next target—caught Talai easily by her throat and squeezed, wringing a wet, gagging cry from her. He slammed her into the boulder, and though she was stunned, she quickly gained her feet and backed away, toward the trees, hissing and spitting, her neck already blackened with bruising.

Anubis reborn gave chase, following after the woman as she dashed into the darkness. I heard a terrible roar and another scream, and then the sounds of their battling grew fainter and fainter, until at last I was alone with the quiet bubbling of the brook. Bleeding, terrified, I climbed to my feet and scrambled after the satchel, lifting it with both hands and limping back toward the herder's shack.

I found it in splinters, nothing but our cloaks left among the shards.

Chapter Twenty-Four

"I need you to skip to the end."

Mr. Morningside paged through my latest translation, a piece of iced lemon cake in front of him, which he diligently ate in between appraisals of my work.

"This is all fine, excellent, really, but I must know where it ends," he said, slapping the packet of papers down onto the desk in front of me. My eyes hurt from squinting in the candlelight for so long, and my fingertips were stained with ink. I sat back and stared numbly at the journal, my head swirling with questions. "Where do they go?" Mr. Morningside added. "Where do they stop? Find that and translate it. The rest," he said, flicking his brows and stabbing his dessert, "is just icing on the cake, my dear."

I glared up at him, annoyed by his cheery demeanor.

"My father is here, did you know that?" I asked, crossing my arms over my middle. "You never wrote to him. . . ."

"I was planning on it."

"You never wrote to him." I scoffed and looked away from him, choosing to stare instead into the blue flames in the library's fireplace. "I can't believe this."

"Which part?" he asked, finishing the cake and licking the crumbs from his fingers.

"*All of it.*" I gave up, piling my forearms on the desk and resting my forehead on them.

Mr. Morningside gave me a patronizing pat on the shoulder and stood from where he had been perched on the desk. "You wanted him here and now he's here, Louisa. I really don't see the problem. Do you want me to try talking to him?"

"No," I mumbled. "You will only make it worse."

"That's harsh." He paced in front of the desk; I could hear his riding boots pitter-pattering across the rug. "Is this going to be too much of a distraction for you? It does not matter how persuasive the shepherd finds those journal entries—at some point you will be asked to speak and I need you at your best."

I dragged my head up off the table and gave him my most hollow-eyed stare. "Do I look like I am at my best?"

No longer pacing, Mr. Morningside tucked his knuckles under his chin and said, "Very well. I see now that I have been pushing you too hard. The Court cannot long be detained, but what would you need?"

"A day," I replied after a moment's consideration. "Just . . . one day to sort things out with my father and finish this work for you. A day without tasks from Mrs. Haylam or having to attend your bizarre trial. A day like that and I may feel . . ." Better? Human? Normal? What would I feel? "Ready."

He nodded and danced quickly toward the desk, smacking it with his palm. "A day I can grant you. Tomorrow is yours, Louisa; do with it what you will." This bargain seemed to please him, or at least satisfy him, and Mr. Morningside brushed by me with a whistle, walking briskly toward the door that led out to the endless corridor and his office. "Oh! And you have one less thing to worry about," he said as he opened the door.

"What do you mean?" I twisted in my chair to face him.

"I know who killed Amelia."

That made me sit up straighter. "Was it Finch? Sparrow?"

"Sparrow? Ha! No, dear girl, it was Mary. Ah well, Amelia was going to depart us anyway; now we must just decide what to do with the rest of them. . . ."

He made to close the door on that but I shot out of the chair, racing across the room toward him. "Mary?" I blurted. "But how is that possible?"

Mr. Morningside grinned and peered out from the crack in the door, just one bright yellow eye visible as he purred, "I don't pretend to truly know even my oldest friends, Louisa, and neither should you."

I was no longer certain of many things, but one thing I knew in my heart was that Mary could not be a killer. Nothing about her gentle aspect and goodness told me she was capable of turning Amelia Canny into a dried-up husk with liquefied eyeballs. Rather than freeing me of one concern, Mr. Morningside had simply added another to the growing pile.

Mary, a killer. Those three words rolled around in my skull all through that day, rattling 'round and 'round while I served Mason, his father, and Samuel Potts their luncheon, and while

I helped Chijioke gather kindling from the edge of the woods, and while I sat, silent and stumped, all through our dinner. Mary did not join us; she now only had a little bit of broth in the morning and before bed, but otherwise kept to her room and rested. I did not see my father, either, though Poppy announced to us at supper that he knew marvelous much about flowers and had given her a thrilling lecture on dandelions and all their medicinal properties.

"How nice for you," I had told her, dazed.

Mrs. Haylam shushed her, perhaps thinking I did not want to be bothered with stories of my father, which was true, but my real distraction centered around Mary. It didn't make any sense. Why lash out at Amelia? They had probably not even met, and nothing I had ever learned about Mary or her abilities led me to believe she could murder someone in that horrible manner. *I don't pretend to truly know even my oldest friends.* Was there wisdom in that? My eyes roamed the table, falling on first Mrs. Haylam, then Poppy, and finally Chijioke. I did not claim to know any of them intimately, but did I really know so little about the people in this place?

Whether I liked it or not, I had grown to trust Poppy and Chijioke, Chijioke in particular, and maybe that was a mistake. If Mary could suck the life out of a young woman and not say a word about it, then perhaps everyone else was just as changeable and unpredictable, too.

I retired to bed that night with my head stuffed full of

uncomfortable questions. Now I dreaded the nighttime, convinced that each time I slept, some new, vivid nightmare awaited. But that night passed relatively peacefully, with only vague dreams of a woman's voice in the distance; she sounded scared and sad, but I never quite knew what she was trying to tell me. It was bliss to wake after a full night's rest, and it cajoled me into believing the remainder of the day would unfold just as nicely. I dressed hurriedly and ran downstairs for a quick breakfast. There was still no sign of the Residents as I went.

Mrs. Haylam presented me a plate of back bacon and buttered bread with no commentary.

I sat at the table by myself, listening to Chijioke sing to himself a little tune as he shooed the horses in the barn, his distant song wending its way across the grass and into the kitchens through the open door. It was fixing to be a hot, hazy day, the house already resonant with sticky warmth.

"Is Chijioke going to town today?" I asked idly.

Mrs. Haylam scrubbed an old vase at the basin, her slim back to me. "The Breens are intent on going to Malton. They believe the sightings of Amelia there are promising."

"Ah. And the Residents? Where are they? I've seen not a wisp of them lately."

"I have dispatched them to the forest and surrounding pastures," Mrs. Haylam explained, a little tartly. "They are ranging as far as my magicks allow, searching for your mysterious man wolf."

I stopped midchew, remembering clearly the journal entry I had just finished for Mr. Morningside. Bennu's description in his writings matched what I had seen almost exactly, and I was beginning to think we had encountered the same creature. My silence must have perturbed Mrs. Haylam, for she slowly turned at the waist, her good eye skewering me like a well-aimed arrow.

"Any more questions?" she murmured.

"It's just odd," I said, picking at my bacon and spinning my teacup while I gathered my thoughts. I was not supposed to discuss the work I was doing for Mr. Morningside, but obviously she knew I was up to something with him. Perhaps a vague gesture at the truth might suffice. "I've been doing a good deal of reading, you know, to try to learn more about this new world I live in. . . . Mr. Morningside's books are rather instructive."

"They are."

"Do you think it's possible that monster that attacked us is, I don't know, one of us?" I thought of the mangled spoon in my pocket, of the sad little note reading "SO RY" in a messy, wibbly script. Something didn't fit. "Could it be reasoned with?"

"Reasoned with?" She rounded on me, losing her temper. Her nostrils flared, one tendon working furiously on the side of her face as she pointed the damp vase at me. "That thing tried to kill Mary. If you hadn't gained your senses for half an instant and shot at it, who knows what would have happened?"

"Well, it was Finch who actually—"

"*I don't care who did what, I only care that you two fools sur-vived.*" It was the closest thing to concern she had shown for me in a long time. Perhaps ever. Her furor ebbed, and she turned back to the basin, calmly washing the vase once more. "I know you don't appreciate that there is, or was, an order to things around here, but some of us are doing our best to maintain it. That order does not have room for a mangy, flea-bitten . . ."

I couldn't make heads or tails of the rest of her sentence, but it damn well sounded like she knew what that monster was. Even its proper name. I pushed my half-eaten plate away and stood, sliding smoothly out the door toward the foyer. If Mrs. Haylam knew what that thing was, then so did Mr. Morning-side, and if she wouldn't tell me then perhaps he would. I had leverage now, in fact: his precious translations.

"I should start my day," I said as I left, feeling petty and tri-umphant that I had left behind a small mess to clean up.

"I dare say," she drawled, her shoulders bunched up in irrita-tion. "Enjoy it while it lasts, girl."

Enjoy was a strong word, but I did intend to make the most of my short freedom. I had so far avoided my father, but the con-frontation could no longer be avoided.

I planted myself in the west salon next to the foyer. It was commonly used for reading or taking tea in the afternoons, and it was only a matter of time before Croydon Frost found me there. Poppy mentioned over supper that he had spent most of the day there writing letters and perusing a book of poetry. While I waited near the windows, I watched the clouds pass low over the forest. The little path leading to the spring was always dark, like the crack in a cliff wall only into deep shadow. I usually avoided the spring, as guests liked to congregate there, and now I felt even less inclined to visit. The Residents were indeed flitting among the trees, and I watched them weave silently on their patrols, hunting for the creature prowling unseen.

There was a hot, building pressure in my forehead, and I recognized it for what it was—the strain of too many questions and an aching dread. Sailors often complained of pains before a storm, and this was no different—something horrible waited on the horizon, I could feel it, but I was powerless against our inexorable slide toward calamity. I did not believe Mr. Morningside's trial would go as flawlessly as he anticipated, and I did not believe Mary had killed Amelia. A storm was gathering above us, and nobody but me seemed to notice the building, angry clouds.

"It's an extremely finicky process, enfleurage. . . ."

I pulled away from the window, turning to find Croydon Frost picking his way across the carpets toward me. He was dressed as exquisitely as Mr. Morningside, making no attempt to hide his wealth, with a well-cut deep emerald suit in velvet, and glossy riding boots. His puffy silk cravat was patterned with moss-green roses.

"You are attempting to preserve delicate things, re-create

something ephemeral and vanishing. The tallow must be imbued with a flower's life over and over again, the fat hungry for the fragrance, not sated until it has devoured dozens, sometimes hundreds of blossoms." He paused halfway across the room from me and pulled a small glass vial from his pocket. Holding it up, the crystalline bottle shimmered in the sunlight. Something moved along his shoulders, bright and strange, but I could not tell what it was until he shifted closer.

"And then, when the fat has had its fill, we come to this." He opened the cork on the vial and approached, handing the tiny bottle of perfume to me. Even before it reached my hand I could smell the indelible, light beauty of lilacs. It was almost otherworldly, how perfectly he had captured the essence of the flower. My eyes fluttered shut, and I held the bottle just under my nose, breathing in pure summer.

"A gift," he said softly. "A woman is not fully dressed until she has her *parfum*."

I opened my eyes and stared down at the bottle. No wonder this had made him rich. I wondered how much this little vial would fetch, and slipped it into my apron pocket next to the bent spoon.

"Thank you," I said. "It was very— Oh *God*, what is that?"

The thing on his shoulder skittered around from behind his neck to the arm nearest me. It was a spider, a huge, hairy spider the size of a bird, brilliant purple and pink, as if dyed to match some garish ball gown, and a small chain like a leash was secured around its middle. It was, quite frankly, the creepiest personal effect I could imagine. Carrying a bloody great spider on a chain everywhere? Was I really related to this person?

I recoiled, backing into the window and holding the curtain in front of me.

"Oh, this?" Croydon Frost laughed, urging the creature down his forearm to his palm, where it seemed to regard me with its many eyes, one fragile furry leg in the air swaying. "She's quite harmless, I promise, just a stunning creature I found on my travels."

"It doesn't look harmless," I murmured, cowering.

"Do you think I would let her crawl all over me if she were prone to biting?" He grinned and held her out closer to me. "Go on, it's not like the fur of a cat. It's completely unique."

I had no desire to touch it, but seeing it in greater detail was morbidly fascinating—it had a spiral pattern on its back and I could not believe how bright and pretty its pink and purple stripes looked in the sunlight. Carefully, I reached a finger out and stroked one of its furry legs.

"Ouch!" I snatched my hand back in horror. "It bit me!"

"My apologies." He stumbled away, shielding me from the spider with his other hand. "She's never . . . That's not like her."

It felt like a bee's sting, and my finger immediately became red and swollen where the creature lashed out.

"Is it poisonous? Oh Lord, am I going to die?" I felt immediately sweaty, cradling my hand defensively to my chest. How perfect. Closing my eyes against the pain, I went rigid, listening as the woman's voice I had been hearing drifted toward me again, soft, like music from a neighboring room.

Run, child. Run, the slumber is ended.

"No, no, be calm, they're not poisonous, you should be just fine once the swelling goes down," Croydon explained. I almost didn't hear him, focusing completely on the voice that came not from without but from within. Who was she? Why did I keep hearing her words of warning? She had been right last time, and I took a small step back from Croydon.

He sighed and shooed the spider back up his arm, where it seemed to watch me, peering around his neck, little black eyes glittering with interest. Or hunger. Maybe I had proved a tasty bite.

"And here I had hoped to win you over." He strode to the windows to my right, placing his hands on his hips and surveying the lawn.

"Resist the urge to bring a spider next time," I muttered.

"At least we know I'm a spectacular failure in all things," Croydon joked, but he sounded genuinely miserable. "Consistency is important."

"Don't expect me to feel sorry for you. Nobody made you fail me and Mum, you did that all on your own." I glared down at my wound, wondering if it would scar as badly as the marks left behind by the book. He said nothing, but I felt him gazing at me with desperate eyes. Forgiveness. That's what he wanted, what everyone wanted, but I had no intention of giving it to him. "Seventeen years of neglect is not rectified with a perfume bottle." I marched over to him, fishing the vial out of my apron pocket and thrusting it forward. "You can have this back. I don't want to be bribed, I just want you to answer my questions."

"And money, I expect you want my money, too." He sounded colder now, angry. His black eyes narrowed as he looked down his beak of a nose at me. "That's nothing to be ashamed of. You're my daughter—you have my eyes, you have my curse, you will also have my vices."

It was so strange to see him, really see him, and know that we shared a kinship, for I felt nothing at all for him, no daughterly warmth, no familial connection.

"Why did you leave us?" I demanded, searching his face. If he lied, I would push him through that bloody window, spider and all.

"I didn't know what you would become, if you would be odd like me," Croydon replied flatly. "Without me . . . Without me you had a better chance of living a normal life."

"A poor life! A miserable life with a drunk of a father!" I prodded him in the chest and he touched the spot as if burned. "So you *are* a Changeling?"

Croydon Frost considered the question for a long moment, and his eyes went hollow, almost dead, as if he had momentarily slipped into a trance. Then swiftly, before I could react, his hand flashed out, capturing mine and lifting it. He studied the bite on my finger, shiny and red, and then let go.

"I want to give you an inheritance," he whispered. There was life again behind his black eyes, swirling, burning life.

"That doesn't answer my—"

"But you will have to choose, Louisa," Croydon interrupted sharply. "You can have wealth or knowledge, and one is infinitely more valuable than the other. That is a promise you can depend upon."

I shook my head, hoping he saw that same, determined fire behind my eyes now. "No," I said resolutely. "I want both."

"Both," he repeated in a growling whisper. What I saw then in his gaze frightened me. He was not disgusted by my greed or intimidated by my stand; he instead reveled in it, a kind of mad intent simmering in his eyes, like a thrumming kettle about to scream. "Then you will have both, daughter, but not here. Not now. You will meet me in the pavilion tonight, midnight, you will come alone, and you will have all your questions answered, and more. Some answers, I suspect, you will wish to forget."

Chapter
Twenty-Five

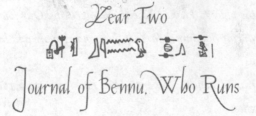

Year Two

𓂀𓏏𓈖 𓏛𓏏𓂝𓏏 𓊖𓂝𓏏 𓏏

Journal of Bennu, Who Runs

I could track the months of our journey on my face, in the fading of the circular scar around my mouth and in the dark beard that had begun to cover it and darken my entire jaw. When I saw my reflection in puddles now, I saw not a naive young boy but a man, seasoned and changed by a year of endless peril.

Khent, too, had grown a beard, though due to his strange

nature, it grew far thicker and wilder than mine, mottled as if to match his beastly counterpart's pelt. He weathered the winter with greater ease, seemingly hardened against the ice and wind that drove at us constantly as we crossed a narrow channel by boat and continued north along the coast of this strange island. Its people were hardy, friendly, though coarsely dressed by our standards. They had strange blue markings in paint and ink on their bodies, and buried their dead in fields of raised furrows. When trade became necessary, we communicated with them only through hand gestures. We ranged over these areas quickly, keeping to ourselves as much as possible, mindful not to step on the sacred barrows of the locals, following the Sky Snake when it appeared, resting in crude shelters of branch and stone when it eluded us.

"Do you think we are the first of our kingdom to the south to find this place?" I asked Khent one morning. Our journey's end felt near, for how much farther, how many more odd lands could we cross?

It rained steadily. Khent's hood had long ago become soaked and useless.

"I think it will not matter, because we will never see home again to tell the tale."

Months ago that statement would have wounded me, but I saw the wisdom in such skepticism. We had barely survived to this point; a return trip might kill us both, if only from exhaustion.

"A long rest," I said softly. "That is what we both need."

"I could sleep forever," Khent replied with a snort. "Mother's mercy, I have forgotten what comfort feels like."

"And I have forgotten what it feels like to be dry. We will be among friends soon," I told him. "And then we can sleep to our hearts' content."

I had never seen such wet days. Even during the rainiest seasons of home, the storms came in short bursts, never these days upon days of dreary damp. It kept the pastures lush, and we hopped many low stone enclosures where huge brown sheep grazed and watched us go by. The villages were few and sparse, though some had larger rings of low stone houses and even markets, markets that endured through the persistent fog and rain.

The morning wore on, the terrain stagnating, rolling field after rolling field, and in the distance what looked like a fortress from afar. As we neared it, I saw that it was merely a collection of pillars artistically arranged, some balancing straight up and down, others placed on top, almost like roofing slats.

"A sacred place," Khent whispered. We had both stopped to marvel at the circle of stones. "It looks like a bunch of, I don't know, doors. Gates."

"Maybe we should go another way," I suggested. "If it's sacred we could be trespassing."

But he ignored me, hefting his pack and pointing above us. "There. You see? She wants us to go this way."

"The Sky Snake is a girl now," I teased, following with a

sigh. I had grown stronger over the months, but the pack still weighed heavily on my shoulder, and the bruises and scars there from the burden would never fade.

"She was sent by Mother to guide us, mm? It just seems right."

The stones loomed larger, gray and dappled, gates for giants. I had stood in wonder at our own great sphinxes and pyramids, but this, too, was a marvel, simple, stoic, but awe-inspiring to behold. Khent pushed on, running his hand along one of the massive stones and ducking underneath into one of the gates.

"We could shelter here," he said, gazing up at the gray sky.

"I don't like it," I replied, glancing in every direction. "It's out in the open. And if it's sacred . . ."

"All right, Bennu, you win. We will find somewhere else," he grumbled. "If only this accursed rain would end."

We passed under one stone gate and into the circle where it was clearer. Those who had built the sacred circle had left markings in the grass and bits of stone, swirls and circles, intricate and precise. I wondered if we should be walking across them at all, but Khent did not hesitate, casting his head back and watching the giant snake above us, angling his path toward its tail.

"See how she flies more quickly?" Khent called to me through the rain, pointing. "We must be close. She's eager to take us there."

"Eager? Ha. If she wants to get there faster, she could allow us to ride."

"That's the spirit," he joked. "You are Bennu the Runner, yes? Not Bennu the Flier."

"You *gave me that name! I see no reason to abide by it.*"

We both laughed, and my heart gladdened from the sound and from the sudden change of fortune in our favor—the rain lessened to a far more tolerable drizzle. When we were again in silence I heard the distant humming of bees, and cast about for hives. There had been few insects at all with the steady rain, but now I heard what sounded like a massive swarm.

Khent put out a hand, my chest bumping into it as he tilted his head to the side. He had heard it, too. We had not yet crossed the clearing in the stone circle. Had we angered the locals and invoked some kind of curse?

"A swarm?" I whispered, clutching the satchel with trembling fingers. "From where?"

"There, to the south; do you see those shapes that move across the clouds like cranes?"

"Bigger than cranes," I murmured. "Swifter, too."

They were indeed creatures of the air, though as large as men and hurtling toward us at great speed. Before I could see them clearly or speak another word, Khent grabbed me by the shawl and pulled, urging me into a run.

"Look above you, friend. Do you see the moon? We are in no position to make a stand, not in daylight," he huffed. He was faster than I was, and I struggled to keep up. Reaching over, he pulled the satchel from my shoulder, and I was grateful to be relieved of it as we fled.

"We cannot outrun them," I panted, glancing over my

shoulder and feeling my heart stutter, not just from the chase but from the sight of three winged monsters diving toward us. I shrieked and ducked my head as one swooped low, a hard talon scraping across the top of my hood.

We dove toward one of the stone gates, finding meager cover from our pursuers.

Khent dropped the satchel between us, backing up against one of the pillars and grabbing me close to his side.

"That sound," he whispered, staring up with wide, frightened eyes as the winged things hovered and circled, the hum of bees loud enough now to drown out all other sounds in the valley. "Wasps. Wings. Servants of Roeh, no doubt, but none like I have ever faced."

"They're chanting," I replied, cowering at his shoulder. "What are they saying?"

"I don't know." Khent ducked down and peeled off his own pack, rummaging inside and coming up with a crude bronze knife he had bartered for days ago. "And I don't care. Chanting will do nothing to stop the bleeding."

I did not share his confidence, staring up in mute terror. There were three of them, each with six massive white wings. The feathers looked more like knives than tufts of soft white. One pair of wings stretched around from the shoulders, covering their faces; another pair of lower wings wrapped around to hide their feet, almost demurely, their torsos draped in white shrouds threaded with gold.

And they had not come unprepared. Each of them wielded a sword, a long, honed blade of pure silver.

Sanctus, sanctus, sanctus . . .

The chanting was like a drone, a drone intertwining with the rising hum of the bees. That sound emanated from within them, as if they were being held aloft by the power of hundreds of buzzing little creatures. Khent brandished the knife, daring one to come forward.

"Watch our backs," he hissed. "We mustn't let them flank us."

"Khent, we are outnumbered. Look at those swords."

"I have noted the swords, Bennu; watch our backs!"

"Sanctus!" One of the creatures, face still hidden, screamed its chant louder, a piercing call that preceded its charge. I felt the wind on my face as its massive wings beat the air, diving down and forward, sword raised. As it neared, the wings obscuring its face parted, and I fell back in fear against the stone pillar. It was a man's face, or would have been, but for its maw, larger and hungrier than any normal man's mouth. There were no eyes, no eyes at all, just a crown of jagged shards protruding from its skull, bleeding gold.

"Back!" Khent lunged with the knife, and the winged horror parried.

They traded blows until Khent earned a lucky slash, catching the thing's sword arm, forcing it back to scream and chant and hold its gushing wound. It was only a temporary victory, as the other two came to retaliate, screaming their chant at us in a rising chorus, slashing blindly with the swords.

"Agh!" Khent staggered into me, cut. "The book. Protect the book . . ."

"I won't let you die," I shouted, taking the knife and propping him up.

But they were too strong. The creature Khent had wounded dove again, this time revealing its clawed, hideous talons. It risked flying low enough to duck beneath the stone gate, and crashed into us with so much force my lungs felt as if they would explode. We were being crushed into the stone, Khent scratching and punching at the thing's back. Then it scrabbled in the dirt at our feet until its talons found the satchel. It released us, mud splashing as it kicked up, satchel clutched in its feet, and climbed high into the air.

"No!" I lurched after it, running, arms flailing as I cried and cried. "No!"

We had come so far! How could we come so far only to lose the book now? A year. A year of evading death and starvation, nations and tribes found and crossed, seas braved, only to stumble and fall with victory in sight. My knees gave out and I fell, defeated, not caring now if those things slashed me to pieces.

Behind me, Khent roared in agony. They were going to kill him.

I stood and decided to face them, for I should rather die defending my friend and on my feet. The creatures had descended, dancing in and out of range of the knife, taking easy, cruel slashes where they could. Khent leaned against the pillar, bleeding badly, and I could see his strength fading as he weakly jabbed with his weapon.

"Leave him alone!" I shouted, throwing myself in front of Khent.

Their huge mouths grinned as they readied their swords, preparing to give the death blow. We all four of us paused, for the sound of humming bees had dimmed with the departure of the monster who had stolen the book. That sound returned, and fast, too fast. I turned just in time to see a ball of white slam into the earth beside us, cratering, a shower of white feathers filling the air.

The book tumbled out of its grasp, abandoned and intact in the mud.

But how? I would not release Khent but ducked us both down as a shadow draped itself over the stone circle. The cry it gave deafened me as it descended, like a hawk the size of a mountain screaming to its hatchlings. Through half-lidded eyes I saw the colossal red-and-black tail flecked with yellow. I saw its clawed hands, its wings the size of clouds, its pointed face, beaked like Horus, a decoration of feathers and scales cresting over its forehead.

Steam rose in sinuous gray ribbons from its nostrils.

The Sky Snake. It stamped the ground, shaking the pillars. Khent's eyes rolled skyward, and he nudged me, weak but alive.

"The book," he whispered. "We run. Now."

I pitched forward, scooping up the book into my arms and putting every last ounce of strength into my legs as we pelted away from the stones and into the wide field beyond. There was no solid earth to run on with the Sky Snake pounding out its anger. I heard the screaming chants and glanced behind, watching as the monsters were flung through the air. The Sky Snake was toying with them now, and snatched up one with its beak, tossing it up before snapping it clean in half, a rain of liquid gold pouring to the sacred stones below.

"I cannot . . . I cannot go any farther," Khent wheezed, tumbling to the wet grass and rolling onto his back. The cuts were everywhere. I shrugged off my shawl and began tearing strips off it, binding his wounds as best I could, listening to the stones creak as the Sky Snake slammed one of the monsters into a pillar. It was right of us to run—for the very gate we had been sheltering under collapsed, the cross stone sliding faster and faster until it smashed into the ground, pulverizing the winged thing beneath it.

"I will not leave without you," I said. "We will find a village and rest until you are healed."

"Don't be stupid, that will take too long. You must go on, Bennu, you must take the book north."

"No!"

That same massive shadow drifted over us again, and I watched through the drizzling rain as the Sky Snake launched into the air again and then coasted across the field toward us, landing lightly, though even that shook the ground like a clap of thunder. It lowered its head, watching us with its intelligent bird eyes, a high chittering chirp vibrating out of its throat.

"Thank you," I said to the creature. It had come close enough to touch, and carefully, with nervous and shaky fingers, I put my palm on its feathers just above the black beak.

The Sky Snake shook off my hand and craned its long neck, touching the tip of its beak to Khent's head. It bumped him as gently as it could, then flung its nose backward, gesturing from where we lay to its back.

"I . . . think it wants us to go with it," I murmured. "Can you stand?"

Khent groaned and coughed as I got to my feet and urged him up, up, balancing the book satchel under one arm and him with the other. My clothes were stained heavily with his blood, and his eyes drooped as I helped him limp toward the Sky Snake. He put one hand on its scaled and feathered belly, giving a wan, exhausted smile as he patted it in thanks.

"Well, friend, it appears you will be Bennu the Flier after all," he growled, and climbed onto the great beast's back. He grew still there, his breath just a weak flutter. Blood soaked into the Sky Snake's back as Khent stared up at the rainy heavens, dying.

Chapter
Twenty-Six

he Residents returned to the house. I heard them scratching and scraping outside my door, moving up and down the corridors, back to their usual evening prowls. I picked anxiously at the bandage on my finger. The spider had drawn no more than a drop of blood. The stinging had stopped, but the damn bite itched like mad. It was time to keep my appointment with Croydon Frost, and I could only hope he would leave his nasty little pet somewhere else.

"Go," I breathed, pressed to the crack in my door, waiting for the Resident outside to grow bored and float away. "Just please, go."

I hadn't left myself much time to get down to the pavilion. The Court had been postponed for that evening, giving the shepherd time to look over the translations Mr. Morningside provided. From everything I had heard of courts back home, this one seemed to function much the same—slowly and inefficiently, with constant stops and starts. That suited me just fine. I dreaded the moment I would be called upon to lie or tell the truth.

At last, the Resident moved back down the corridor, stopping briefly outside Mary's room before continuing on to the landing, where it turned right and traveled up the stairs and out of view. I gently opened the door and slipped out, tiptoeing as quickly as I dared. It was hard to escape the sensation of being watched in Coldthistle House, but that feeling had only felt more drastic lately. The Residents were particularly watchful now that Mrs. Haylam had tasked them with finding the monster in the woods. I, too, paused outside Mary's room, pressing my ear to the door frame but hearing nothing, not even a snore. Ah well, hopefully that meant she was sleeping deeply.

I rounded the landing and hurried down toward the foyer, taking pains to be as silent as possible as I passed in front of the green door. Clouds had rolled in at dusk, threatening rain, and without the moonlight I could see almost nothing as I made my way carefully through the mansion. A whispered conversation seeped out from under the kitchen door. I had almost chosen to go that way, as it was the easiest route to the barn and pavilion, but stopped short when I noticed the voices. How the devil was I supposed to get out now? The front doors were agonizingly loud to open, creaky and huge.

So I waited once more, shimmying up close to the kitchen door and listening, recognizing Mrs. Haylam's and Mr. Morningside's voices at once. I had caught them mid-argument, and Mr. Morningside did not sound at all pleased.

". . . for you to question me on this is really amazing, Ilusha. I saw what I saw, and I know what it means for us. What it means for her."

Ilusha? Was that Mrs. Haylam's true name? It seemed so . . . so *beautiful* for her, but then, everyone was young once. She paused before answering, and her voice came out in such a fierce whisper that I almost could not make it out.

"This has the marks of your mischief all over it, *maskim xul*, and I do not like to be left in the dark where your schemes are concerned. What would you have me do? Spirit her away? We are far beyond such contingencies."

Mr. Morningside scoffed, and I heard him begin to pace. I pressed closer to the door, wishing I could see inside and read their body language. Instead, I could rely only on my ears. Time was passing. I needed to get out of the house and to the pavilion, but my instincts told me to listen longer and be patient. There would be no leaving until I found out who this "her" was, though the sinking feeling in my gut told me that I already knew her identity.

"Did she find something in that journal? She has been asking unexpected questions."

Mr. Morningside responded with a laugh. "The *Abediew*. She knows of it. The Runner encountered one and described it."

"*Henry.*"

"I know! I *know*." He was half shouting now. "And I still have no idea how it got here. They were extinct well before the Schism."

"I told you I had my suspicions about her, but you refused to listen. I'm beginning to think maybe this Court is necessary after all. This is growing beyond your control, and I will not endanger this house and all those we chose to look after just so you can assuage a guilty conscience and entertain a fancy!" I had heard Mrs. Haylam cross many, many times, but this was something else. She sounded almost desperate. Afraid. "If she is what you say she is," Mrs. Haylam went on. "*If.* Then what do we do?"

"Then we take the necessary precautions. *Tabalu mudutu.* We can't risk it," he said.

Oh God, he was leaving, and he was heading my way. I flattened myself against the wall next to the door, hoping against hope that when it opened I would be concealed.

"I *will* protect this house," Mrs. Haylam was saying as Mr. Morningside approached the door. "We have survived this way for a long time. Why endanger that now?"

There was movement on the staircase across the foyer. Lee. He had appeared, wraithlike and silent, on the bottom step, nothing but the wet glitter of his eyes visible in the darkness. I saw him open his mouth to say something and quickly I hushed him with a finger to my lips. A shake of the head. *No. No, don't give me away!*

My heart had almost stopped. The hinge creaked as the door swung open, smashing hard into my foot. I caught the knob before it could bounce back and hit Mr. Morningside, alerting him to my position. Still, he seemed puzzled by the door and turned to inspect it. . . .

"Sir!" It was Lee. Bless him. His shoes rushed across the carpets, and when next he spoke it was just beside the door. "I, um, I had a question for you, sir, about the Residents."

"This should really be directed to Mrs. Haylam," Mr. Morningside muttered. He sounded exhausted. "What is it?"

"Mr. Brimble? What's going on out here at this hour?"

They were all three in the foyer now, and Lee cleared his throat, stumbling his way through an explanation. "Well, it's only that . . . It's that I saw something on the third floor, I thought you might want to see it."

"Now?" Mrs. Haylam demanded after a delay.

"Yes. Yes, now, obviously. It's . . . urgent and all that."

Had I become the actual wall? I had stopped moving, stopped breathing. Lee's performance wasn't exactly worthy of a standing ovation, but Mrs. Haylam sighed and told him to get on with it. Their voices grew softer as he led her away toward the stairs, and a moment later I heard the green door shut. Alone.

Thank you, Lee.

I dodged around the door and dashed through the kitchens, hoping I wouldn't trip over Bartholomew and send him yelping. Mrs. Haylam had not yet locked up the house, thankfully, and I was spared the time it would take to turn my mangled spoon into a key. Moving with both speed and grace proved challenging, as I was sure it was well beyond midnight now. But I wanted to make good use of Lee's diversion, and I managed to squeak out the back door without anyone being alerted. The grass was cool and wet as I skulked across the lawn, keeping a sharp eye out for any Residents sent to wander the grounds.

The pavilion was visible only because of its bright white exterior. Without a shred of moonlight, it was impossible to tease apart house from ground from woods. A single light remained on in Coldthistle House—it was on the third floor, perhaps the result of Lee's haphazard lie. I owed him—more than one—and I bit down hard on my lip as I flitted across the lawn toward the tent; I knew now, and knew it for certain, that if it came time to lie and save Mr. Morningside's reputation, if only to send the Adjudicators packing, then I would. I had no idea if Lee and I remained friends, but he deserved some kind of repayment for his help. Help I almost certainly did not deserve.

It wasn't until I was a few paces from the tent that I noticed the soft, whispering sounds rising from the ground. I slowed my steps, picking up my skirts and squinting down at the grass. Oh *God*. I slapped both hands over my mouth, preventing the scream that welled up from deep inside. Snakes. Garden snakes. Hundreds of garden snakes had emerged from their hiding places, slithering quietly across the wet grass, all of them streaming toward the pavilion. I took one more step, trying to avoid the snakes, and flinched. My boot had crunched something. Several somethings. Slowly, slowly, terrified of what I would find, I knelt, looking more closely at the ground and what had snapped under my shoe.

They were worse than the snakes. Spiders. My stomach flipped over.

Run, child. Be gone from this place.

Oh, but how I longed to listen to the whispery woman's voice in my bones. How I craved the warm cocoon of bed. Lord, I would even trade one of those too-real dreams for this black morass of snakes and spiders that gathered before the tent as if called by some unheard song. And I had seen—or rather read of—this before. Had Bennu not seen something similar?

Of course the journal was not a coincidence, I had decided that long ago, but to see first that wolf creature, then the pink foam out of my own mouth, and finally this . . . I hugged myself, hesitating at the opening to the tent, skin crawling as I stood among the eight-legged and the scaled. It was as if I were taking Bennu's journey in some part, reliving steps of his odyssey toward . . . Toward what? I had so little left to translate. Now I wished I had stayed longer in the cellar and finished it after all.

Toward my father.

There were warnings everywhere. I checked my apron pocket, making sure the spoon was still inside. Its weight was a small comfort, for it had saved me in the past. I had been living in darkness for too long, I thought, reaching for the opening of the tent. Whether it killed me or enlightened me, I needed to know how this—Mr. Morningside, the journal, the Court—all fit together. His whispered conversation with Mrs. Haylam only made me that much more determined. They were talking about me. I had heard the fright in her voice. *She* was scared of *me*.

I took one giant step across the writhing carpet under my

feet and crossed into the pavilion. It was as I remembered it, and that was a relief, though it was completely empty but for one figure. The trestle tables remained, each with its pennant, and the raised platform was there with two thrones, the space on the right side conspicuously vacant. I heard a low thrum, too, that I had not noticed before. It emanated from a curtain behind the platform, and reminded me of the purr of a cat.

Croydon Frost stood down at the opposite end of the tent, staring up at the dais and the empty space there on the stage.

I walked toward him slowly, the fairy lights dancing above me making my hands speckled with color. My clothes, transformed into the long green ball gown, shushed softly across the thick carpets laid down. The tables set for banqueting struck me as haunted now, sad and forlorn without their revelers. And the pennants that hung down, too, struck me as melancholy, particularly the one all in black. It looked more like a funerary setting than a celebratory decoration.

The path leading to my father felt like an eternity. Without the guests, the pavilion felt bloated in size, cavernous. Bleak. I glanced behind me, but none of the snakes or spiders had followed me inside.

As I neared, I remembered that he, too, would appear different, for the Court revealed all creatures, and forced them to be their true selves. I assumed he would look much like me, being a Changeling, and indeed, I noticed an adornment on his head much like mine, antlers and vines reaching high above his hair.

His was a far greater crown, big enough to befit even the largest stag. He wore a long, ragged black cloak, pricked here and there with leaves, and I felt a twinge of relief when I saw that his spider was not there crawling back and forth across his shoulders.

"No spider? That's considerate," I said as I came closer. "I thought you brought her everywhere."

"She doesn't belong in this place." Even his voice had changed; it was darker, more resonant, not loud but oddly powerful enough to send a tremor through the earth. I stopped short, suddenly afraid. He turned, deliberately, allowing me to take his full measure. There was a green mask of vines on his face, one I had seen before in a painting. He pulled it off with a harsh tug, revealing skin of smoke and ash. His eyes were large and black, with tiny red cores that found me at once. The crown of antlers was not a crown at all, but part of his head, and the hands that held the mask were long, extended by claws fit for a lion.

"She does not belong in this place," my father repeated, handing me the mask. "And neither, my child, do you."

Chapter
Twenty-Seven

What are you?"

It was all I could think to say. His presence, his voice, made me tremulous and short of breath. This was not the person I had seen in the house. It did not seem possible that we two could be related, that we two could be the same thing.

"There are many answers to that question," he began, dragging his cloak of shreds and leaves toward the dais. Croydon Frost placed one clawed hand on the wood, scratching deep welts into it as he gazed up with his black eyes into the vacant space above. "One answer will make you weep. One answer will make you laugh. And one answer will fire your blood for battle. I will give you all of those answers and more, but first you must do something for me."

"I don't owe you anything," I said, trying to remember who he had been in my mind before. *Neglectful father. Deserter. Coward.* "I . . . don't even have to stay here and listen to your silly babbling."

He chuckled at that, and outside, out on the grass, I heard a wretched echo, the spiders and snakes shivering back and forth, making their own horrible laughter.

I was so distracted by the commotion outside that I almost didn't hear his softly spoken question.

"Are you lost, child?"

Stunned, I stared at the back of his crown, my mouth opening and closing on a gasp. "My feet are on the path."

I said it as a habit, having read the call and response over and over again in the journal. In the journal. But how could he possibly know what was in there?

"I don't understand," I murmured, backing away. "H-how do you know about that?"

"There should be a third throne here," Croydon Frost said coldly, ignoring me. "Here. In that empty place. That is where my throne should be, where it would be, if they had not taken my kingdom away from me."

I took another small step backward. "I do so hate all this cryptic nonsense. You and Mr. Morningside are a real pair when it comes to that."

His shoulders bunched at the name, and he gave what sounded like a feral growl. "Do not compare me to that *usurper*."

"Fine, I won't compare you, but you told me I would get answers tonight and so far you've only offered more questions. Who are you? And I mean really—who are you? You're not some wandering perfume maker, that's obvious. I'm beginning to doubt Croydon Frost is your name, or that you're my father. You're not here for me at all."

More laughter, more whispers amid the grass outside. I shivered, ending my retreat, when he turned and glared at me, those small red hearts in his eyes glowing like candle flames. His face looked gaunter and stranger, as if it were stretched thin around a deer's skull.

"On the contrary, I came here for you first, Roeh second, and He-Who-Lies-In-Wait third."

Him. Roeh, the shepherd. The lier-in-wait could only be Mr. Morningside. I looked down at the green mask in his hand and swallowed hard, aware then that I needed to choose my words carefully. God, I had wanted this man here to shame and rob him, and now I was the one in trouble.

"Where is the woman?" I asked, innocent. "There were four of you in the painting I saw. Where is the fourth?"

The scarlet beams in his eyes flared.

"Gone," he said simply, the smoke billowing around his hollow cheeks dying down momentarily. "She was pure and selfless, and this world of darkening deeds swallowed her whole. There will never be another like her, nor can there be. There are no souls left pure enough to deserve her."

Lies, lies, little child, all lies . . .

The voice echoed in my bones, and I tried hard to conceal its effect on me. Nobody, least of all this dangerous stranger, needed to know I was hearing whispers of warning.

"So what do I call you?" I murmured. "I'm not stupid enough to think the Devil's name is *Henry*, or that you, whatever you are, that you are called Croydon Frost."

"He does exist, or he did. I took a page from your employer's book and . . . *commandeered* the life of Croydon Frost, wealthy merchant. He is a useful disguise. You may call me Father," he replied with a slight bow of his head. "All Father of the Trees, if you prefer the formality, but 'Father' will suffice."

This was who Bennu and his cult had worshipped. Mother and Father, only now "Mother" was somehow gone, according to him.

"Does that make you a god?" I asked.

He smiled, but it was a horrible thing to witness. "There are no gods left anymore, my child, only monsters too stubborn to die."

"So a god can be killed?"

"Killed? No, but weakened? Made to surrender? Oh yes." His hands curled into fists at that, and he seemed to grow larger, as if the anger buried in that remembrance fed him. Then he breathed out and diminished, though he was still an intimidating size. He roamed to the trestle table with the black pennant hanging above it. Reaching up, he pulled on the fabric, a black sleeve coming loose, revealing a more colorful flag underneath. It was a stag's skull with many purple eyes, rose- and green-colored vines twisting around its antlers.

Placing one hand on the table, he leaned heavily against it, as if he were losing strength and growing tired.

"Ask your questions now, child. I am weak from many long years of slumber."

I fidgeted with the little vines on my skirts, my mind working out two problems simultaneously. There were plenty of questions to ask, but the rules had changed, and quickly, and now I had to adjust and find a way to survive this. His arrival at this place signaled something terrible, that storm I sensed on the horizon, screaming in fast. Even if he was weakened, he was dangerous, dangerous and terrifying. It was upon us, I realized, the thunder and lightning and crashing winds beginning any moment. I did not know if I could control this man, this god who had diminished into a monster, but I had to at least manage him.

There were innocents at Coldthistle, Mary and Poppy, Chijioke and Lee, and I had no intention of letting them get hurt when the storm reached its peak.

"Am I the only one?" I asked. "Your only child?"

"No," he said matter-of-factly. "But you are the only one who matters, the only one who developed the gift."

"So you abandoned many of your children," I muttered.

He twisted, one black-and-red eye staring at me over his shoulder. "Your human lives and concerns struck me as unbearably petty. And fleeting. Is that offensive? Human lives pass in the blink of an eye. I had been sleeping for centuries; I was far too restless to care for one or two or three humans."

"I see. I'm useful to you now because I inherited some of your powers," I said. It almost felt good to realize this man, or *thing*, was as vile as I'd expected. It made it easier to dislike him, and inside that hatred was protection. He did not quibble with my observation, so I went on. "How do you do that? Change into other people, I mean. I can do small things, change my spoon into a key or a knife, sometimes a gun if I really need to, and I can translate things. But could I really become someone else?"

At that, he turned around to face me completely. He looked caught off guard, and if I squinted, sad.

"He taught you nothing. Of course. He must be terrified of you, of what you could become." Grinning, he spread his clawed hands wide. "You are my one true child, and it would be an insult to my blood if you could not do all that I can. Let me see, there was a rhyme the druids once sang. *A drop of blood, a lock of hair, lands you in the Changeling's snare.*"

"I need someone's blood and hair to mimic them?" I pressed.

"Spill the blood of another or have them spill yours, and that is power enough to create their image," he said. "But you will not *be* them, only appear and sound like them. It's a mirage, child, nothing more."

I would store that away for later, a useful trick if I could manage it.

"And what about pink foam? I . . . had a dream, and the next morning I had spit up something dark pink. What does that mean?" I asked.

"That can happen when our kind experience a particularly potent vision," he said. "Whatever you dreamt that night could be prophecy."

I shuddered. Prophecy? My friends and employers eating me alive was *prophecy*?

He approached me, the black mist rising from his face and robes contorting as he walked. Soft echoes surrounded him, as if he wore a cloak of ancient whispers. He reached out toward me and I froze, paralyzed by the strangeness of his eyes and the undeniable power that rolled off him in terrible tendrils. His talons traced the edge of my jaw and I inhaled quickly, trying not to tremble, trying not to show him my fear.

"There is a war coming, Louisa. The usurpers thought they could keep me safely sleeping for eternity, but their magic is weak now and it is time to reclaim what we lost. I wish you could have seen our world before they annihilated it. Druids, fae, creatures of mist and water and vine, a vast palace of root and stone, protected by the Sky Snake and the Tocahuatl . . ."

I nodded, feeling as if he had put me under a spell. It sounded like fantasy, like impossibility, but I had seen enough these past months to question everything I had learned as a child. "I . . . I read about some of it. In Bennu's journal."

He laughed, sending another ripple of excitement through the snakes and spiders outside the tent. "That was just a piece, just the tip of the spear. Imagine a kingdom encased in branch and leaf, all of its people asleep, doomed to wander in an eternal nightmare. Then imagine that one day the oldest of those people wakes up. There's a crack in the branches, a bit of moonlight seeps through the leaves, and the people inside the nightmare slowly wake up."

I said, "They put you to sleep because they could not kill you?"

He let go of my chin, and it seemed then that he frowned, overcome with grief.

"Do not be fooled by anything He-Who-Lies-In-Wait tells you. You are not his friend, Louisa, and you are not his employee. You are but a pretty curiosity to study, a rare butterfly pinned under glass." He sighed and folded his clawed hands in front of his waist. "But I will take you away from this place. You will be made safe before my great war begins."

I shook my head, holding out my hand to him. The marks left behind by the book were not erased by the magic of the pavilion. "I can't leave. The only thing allowing me to come and go is this pin Mr. Morningside gave me. I'm bound to the book."

His melancholy lifted, his eyes glittering then with interest. "So you have seen it. Touched it. Remarkable. And he gave you this pin? Then he knows you can handle the book without perishing." He paced furiously, sharp brows drawn down in concentration. "We have even less time than I thought." Then he stopped and spun to face me, eyes glowing brighter and brighter still. "You must bring me the book, Louisa. I will release you from its dark power, but first you must bring it to me and bring it in secret."

Chapter
Twenty-Eight

The spiders and snakes outside the tent grew suddenly restless, and this time it had nothing to do with laughter.

"Someone is coming," Father whispered.

He took me by the wrist, yanking me to the front of the pavilion. I ran alongside him but felt dazed, as if the new history of this man and his kingdom weighted me like a physical burden. Could it all be true? Could he really be the victim of some plot between the shepherd and Mr. Morningside? It seemed insane, but I could not deny that Bennu's journal confirmed the story. He and that boy Khent had been ruthlessly pursued, all because they carried something valuable to the Mother and Father.

We burst out of the tent, insects and snakes scattering like they had been fired out of a rifle. At first I did not see them, but then, I followed the origin of the fleeing creatures to where Sparrow and Finch descended from the sky. Their wings were but a flash as they landed, and instinctively I placed my hand over the spoon hidden in my apron. They had not harmed me yet, so why did I distrust them so?

"These pitiful fools," Father hissed. "They are as blind and meddling as their leader, but perhaps more easily dispatched."

"Wait," I murmured. "Dispatched? They come in threes; did you kill the third one?"

"Quiet now," he said, but he was smiling. "I am still vulner-able here. They mustn't know."

Sparrow came out of her descent at a sprint, then marched right up to us. We had reverted to our far less glamorous appearances, and "Father" was once again Croydon Frost. He gave her an amiable, almost goofy smile and a bow from the waist. My bones ached with cold, the urge to shiver uncontrollably growing stronger as they came so near.

"Awfully late for a stroll," she said between gritted teeth. "What are you two up to? I thought the housekeeper imposed a curfew on all her maids."

"There's no need to be so hostile," Finch murmured, taking his sister by the arm and pulling her back. She would not budge. I glanced up at my father, noticing the tight tendon in his temple, fearing that if challenged he would do something regrettable. Now that I knew the truth, that he was capable of "dispatching" one of the Adjudicators, I had no idea what the parameters of his temper might be.

"Stop giving this creepy little chit so much leeway, brother; she's one of them, and we're here to investigate them, not invite them over for tea cakes and ices." She said it all without ever taking her eyes off me. I almost wanted to laugh, for she was so convinced that I was the troublemaker, when in truth she stood before a cloaked god, one clearly obsessed with revenge upon her kind.

"You're right," I said plainly. "We are not friends, and I am breaking curfew. Shall I fetch a rod so you can administer a beating?"

"That would be a good place to start," she growled, leaning over me.

"I haven't done anything to you," I replied. "Why do you hate me so much?"

"Hate you?" She laughed and tossed back her thick yellow hair over her shoulders. "I was created for this purpose, to find truth and dispose with lies. There is mischief afoot in this house, and I know you are part of it, girl. What were you two doing out here?"

"Sparrow, please, calm down—" Finch reached for her shoulder but she shrugged him off again.

"He's my father, all right?" I sighed. Just saying that much seemed like it was giving "Father" a victory. At my side, he smiled benignly, an impressive mask. "I never met him when I was a child. He came here to meet me, to find the daughter he never knew. I'm sure it gives you no small pleasure, finding out I'm not only a lowly Unworlder but an illegitimate one at that."

Sparrow's sapphire eyes narrowed dangerously, and in that moment she did not look angelic at all. Before I could react or speak, her hand darted out, closing like a vise around my neck. I gasped and flailed, but she was far stronger. Her thumb pressed hard on my neck as she dragged me close. "That is only half the truth, you little liar, there is no deceiving me. I invoke the right of Judgment—"

I did not hear the rest of what was said. Sparrow opened her mouth wide and a beam of searing gold light blasted out of it. Vaguely, I sensed that both Finch and my father were shouting, but I was not there. There was only blinding, brilliant white light and then a moment of nothingness as I floated. When my eyes adjusted to the blast, I was in a cold white room, with nothing in it but a table, and I was on that table. The surface of it felt like hot needles against my skin, and whenever I chanced to move, the scraping and stinging were unbearable.

I cried out, but there was nothing I could do—secured to the T-shaped table like Jesus to the cross, iron manacles over my ankles and wrists. Sparrow was there, I could feel her, all around me like a vapor. This was not a place of brick or stone, but a prison inside my own mind.

"What were you doing in that tent?"

Her voice emerged from the walls of the mind prison, from the very air. I struggled for breath, lost in a panic. Did the rules of the world apply here? Was there a way out? I squeezed my eyes shut, fighting a sharp urge to blurt out the truth. When I tried to speak I choked on it. Lying. Lying wouldn't work here. . . . I thought of the girl in Bennu's story, of her face melting off like hot, bubbling wax. . . .

"Meeting my father!" I screamed it. My voice was raw and crazed.

"What did you discuss?"

It was like I could taste her voice, as if I were breathing her in, letting her see into the darkest, most secret corners of my soul and mind. I had to get out. I would not let her win. I tossed and flailed, hurting myself as I banged against the stabs of the table. My head turned back and forth as I tried to fight her off, but it was no use. I stopped, panting, squirming with the notion that she would at any moment have the whole truth from me. My eyes traveled down my shoulder and arm to my hand, where the two scars on my fingertips lingered and where there was also a bandage. A bandage from a spider bite.

This time I had no trouble conjuring the terror and desperation to transform. Father said it was possible. What was the rhyme again? *A drop of blood, a lock of hair, lands you in the Changeling's snare. . . .*

Please work, please work!

It was agony, becoming someone else. *Something* else. It was like the pains of growing into an adolescent body but more intense, and in reverse, my flesh and bones too big for what my powers forced me to become. I was shrinking, skin on fire, bones snapping in my ears. But then it was over, and while I still ached everywhere, I was not myself. I was small and so, so fast, and I popped up off the table. I could jump! Lord, but could I jump.

I heard Sparrow screaming in outrage, and the light blasted through me again, and then, miraculously, I was free.

Incredibly free. Freer than I had ever been. The table and room vanished, and I dropped into the grass with a soft thump.

New legs. Six new legs! The grass felt like velvet as I sped away into the night, listening with a hammering little heart to Sparrow's tantrum. I had outwitted her, and while Finch tried to quell her and my father burst into laughter, I also heard her launch into the air. She was coming to search for me.

I did not go to the forest, but straight back to the house. There were poorly fitted doors and windows aplenty, and I would find a crack big enough for my spider body somewhere in the shadows. It was a marvelous, exhilarating trick, this transformation, but I could already feel myself growing tired. Magic came at a price, and exhaustion would soon claim me. I hurried along the edge of the house until I reached the kitchens. The yard seemed like a vast, terrible forest, everything expanded into a size I found hard to fathom. At last I crawled to the kitchen door, squeezing through the crack between it and the stone tiles. It was a tight fit, but I managed it, somersaulting out of the spider's body and into my own, crashing into the table and rolling to my side.

Naked. Stark naked.

Of course. A spider would not need clothing or boots; it all must have dropped into the grass the second I evaded Sparrow's Judgment. I held my banged head gingerly and stood up, grabbing the table for balance, looking over the edge of it and directly into Lee's face.

"Oh, hello," he breathed. He had been eating a jelly pastry and slowly lowered it from his mouth, wiping a few crumbs from his chin.

My pulse had not stopped racing since landing in that horrible white room, and now I wondered if my heart would simply implode from the strain. I carefully placed one arm over relevant areas and cleared my throat, attempting to stand nonchalantly in the shadow behind the door.

"Awfully late for tea," I murmured, blushing so hard it hurt.

Lee put down his pastry and remembered himself, covering his eyes with one hand. "I told you, I can't sleep with those Upworlders around."

"Right," I whispered. "I think I'd like to be rid of them, too."

"Would they by any chance have something to do with, um, all this?" he asked, and I could hear the poorly restrained giggle.

"Good guess." I sighed and sidestepped my way around the room to the door. Sparrow might be angry enough to risk Mrs. Haylam's ire and search the house, and I was eager to put as many doors, bricks, and large dogs between her and me as I could. "And if you happen to see her or Finch in the near future, you did not see me. In fact, if anyone asks, I was not here, and I was certainly not naked."

Lee nodded, still covering his eyes, but I could see a smile peek out from under his hand. "Shall I also forget the part where you exploded out of a spider's body?"

I opened the door and slid around it into the foyer. "Yes," I said with a wince, using the door as a shield. "Yes, I think that would be best."

Chapter
Twenty-Nine

ike Lee, I did not sleep a wink that night. Each time I closed my eyes I imagined myself back in Sparrow's white room of pain, her voice everywhere around me, outside of me, within me. What would have happened if I'd stayed to be tortured? Lying had felt like an impossibility, and only my powers had saved me from revealing the truth to her. Now I knew why Chijioke had warned me so thoroughly; they were dangerous, very dangerous, and not to be trusted.

But then, who *was* to be trusted?

The book. He wanted the book. In Mr. Morningside's journals I had learned it was called the Black Elbion, but in my mind I only ever thought of the word *BOOK* in huge, ominous letters. I reluctantly called the man I'd known as Croydon Frost Father in my head as I considered his motivations and his ultimate desire. He had come here in disguise, and he had already lied to me repeatedly about who and what he was. And he had murdered or at least incapacitated Sparrow and Finch's third companion. Mr. Morningside had told me quite clearly that endangering the book meant endangering his existence, and that without him the world would fall into chaos. Had that been a lie, too?

I felt so, so tired, pulled in every direction. Everyone wanted something. The problem now became: Who would get what they wanted, and who would become my enemy? If I helped Mr. Morningside find the location of this book he wanted so badly, then I was striking a blow against my father, and perhaps even against the world I belonged to. If Father was to be believed, then there was a kingdom of Dark Fae and all sorts out there waiting to be found, cursed to sleep forever by Mr. Morningside and the shepherd. Would that place be destroyed altogether if they found the book that sustained it?

After Sparrow's attack upon me, I certainly felt no allegiance to the shepherd. But nor did I feel any kinship toward my father. Perhaps others would want to find that their estranged family member was actually a god, but it only filled me with dread. He was embroiled in a centuries-long dispute, which meant I, by extension, was caught up in it, too. He spoke of war, and I did not belong in a war. Now I would be required to choose a side, and the most obvious side was the Devil's. After all, we had signed a contract, one that might just see me out of Coldthistle for good. But then, my plan had to shift now, for there was no telling if I could still get so much as a penny from Father.

The safest way out, I decided, was *out*. Not just for me, but for all of us. But did I really trust Mr. Morningside to honor our agreement? He had admitted that releasing all of his employees would be a major inconvenience. Perhaps he had no intention of seeing our bargain through.

There came to be only one truth I could depend upon entirely: I needed to extricate myself from this tangled web of grudges, deceit, and magic. That extrication, however, would require just a little more deceit. I would strike a deal, a new one, and not with the Devil but with my father: the Black Elbion for my freedom, and enough coin to get me comfortably to London, and from there? Comfortably normal.

It would be risky handing over the black book to my father, but then, how far would he really get with it on the grounds of Coldthistle? He was surrounded by enemies, and even if he wore his disguise while he tried to waltz out the door with the book, Mrs. Haylam would surely notice someone toying with her magicks.

I came to my decision when it was not yet dawn. A smidgen of night yet remained, perhaps enough to find my way to the upper floors, to the great, empty ballroom there only to house the book. Getting there without being seen was a cumbersome task, of course, but now I had the means to do it. Or at least, I had the means to get to the book, but perhaps not the way to leave.

Searching the room, I ran my hands along the sills and under the bed, hunting and hunting until I found what I was looking for—a fly.

It gave a half-hearted attempt at escape, but I quickly scooped it off the windowsill and into my hands, apologizing softly before smashing it to bits. I wiped off the black stain on the carpet and went to the door, opening it just a crack. The corridor was empty, but I knew that any moment a Resident might float by on its rounds. Taking a deep breath, I braced for the pain to come, pouring all of my thoughts into the fly, into its shape and size.

Somehow it was less uncomfortable this time, or I was prepared, and with a soft pop my skin and bones contorted, reshaped, shrank and shrank until I was just a tiny buzzing thing tripping through the air. More than the pain, the sensation of bobbing along with wings was disorienting, walls, floor, and ceiling all magnified and yet hazy, the slightest puff of wind blowing me completely off course. As I bumbled my way down the hallway, weaving clumsily, I nearly flew headlong into a Resident. It had emerged from the staircase above, silently turning the corner and drifting toward my room.

I narrowly avoided its blurred edge, the barely there gust of wind it created sending me spiraling toward the wall. It stopped, cold, black presence spinning slowly until its little shadow eyes found me. Nearer and nearer it came, until its face was level with me, following my path, floating next to me as I pumped my small wings desperately, heading for the staircase.

For a moment it followed, then lost interest and floated away, taking with it the chilly air of unease and dread. The effort of flying and of keeping this form was beginning to tax me greatly. I fought the exhaustion, buzzing my way up the stairs, and up again, and seeing in almost all directions I spied another Resident, though this one did not come to investigate. Still, even with that boon I was running out of time—any moment my strength would fail and my true shape be revealed.

My sight was nearly gone, blackened with weariness, when I reached the long, vaulted ballroom at the top of the house.

I flew as far as I could, invigorated by the emptiness of the room. There were no Residents guarding the book! They were practically making this too simple. On and on I coasted, until I reached the place where I had last beheld the book. And I stopped, and I fell, and I tumbled into my own human body as I landed in the dust.

There it was—not the book, but the shape of it stamped into the grime. They had moved it. I stood, naked and furious with myself. Of course they would move it. Had I not heard Mrs. Haylam and Mr. Morningside's whispered conversation? They were nervous, and the book was too important to leave out in the open with so many suspicions lingering in the air.

I wrapped my arms around myself and shivered, miserable. This had all been for nothing, and now I had to find a way back to my chambers without a stitch of clothing. After two transformations in one evening I was beyond tired, my reserves of vigor more than tapped. I turned and tiptoed out of the ball-room, cursing my stupidity but also floundering in my mind, casting about for some new plan.

Peering out into the upper halls, I waited for a Resident to come swooping down and find me. Looking around the corner, I saw one waiting at the end of the corridor, its ugly, big-mouthed face turned away from me. I took the opportunity and dashed to the stairs, running and running, not caring or slowing down until I reached my floor. God, I was lucky, for there were none that I could see, and I rushed down toward my door, then froze—ah, of course, nobody could be that fortunate. A Resident hovered just outside my door, waiting, though it, too, was focused on the room itself, as if it sensed that I was not where I should be.

The door just to my left opened, a bed-frazzled Mary squinting out from behind a candleholder.

"What are you doing up?" She gasped at my state and pulled off her own dressing gown, tossing it around my shoulders and herding me inside. "Why . . . Why on earth are you wandering the halls at night like that?"

I let her pull me away from the door as she shut it, and I tried not to sound too catatonic with relief as I shuffled with her toward the bed. "Thank you, Mary, I'm sorry, I don't know what got into me. I . . ." *I have no good reason to give you.* "I must have been sleepwalking."

"Sleepwalking!" Mary laughed, carrying the candle to the bedside table and sitting, leaving plenty of room for me to take the other half of the bed. "Louisa, if you are prone to such things, you must really learn to dress properly before bed."

"Go ahead, laugh," I said, sighing. I snuggled down into the warm housecoat and tried to relax. It didn't work. My body was almost agonizingly spent, but my brain would not stop turning over and over the uncertainties hanging over me. "Mary,

I know this probably isn't the time to ask, but I need to know something. . . ."

"Amelia," she said sadly. Mary's green eyes grew dim, and she looked toward the window and the moonless night. "I'm well again, Louisa, and I should be back to work, but Mrs. Haylam does not trust me anymore. She thinks I stepped out of line, you know, that I killed Amelia. But I didn't! I swear to you, I had nothing to do with it."

I reached for her hand, squeezing it hard. "I knew it! I didn't believe for a second that you would do such a thing. And anyway, are you even capable of that? I only ever saw you shield people with your powers. Shield me."

Mary smiled shyly, tucking her knees up to her chest. The candle made her skin glow softly, and it was a relief to see her so rested and well, it lifted my heart just a little, and that did a world of good. "I think they just need to blame someone, and if they don't point a finger at the shepherd's people, then it will keep the peace. They don't want to start a war, and I suppose that means I must be punished."

"But that's awful!" I blurted. "I think it was Sparrow. She's horrid. Just tonight she tried to Judge me or whatever it is, and if I hadn't found a way to escape I think she might have, I don't know, taken it all the way."

"Oh, Louisa, you mustn't trust them. I know it sounds cold, but there's a reason our kind never get along with them. We're not the same, and we must stick together." She gave me a gentle pat on the hand. Her eyes brightened, and she looked filled with sudden excitement. "I mean we must stick together, Louisa. You and I."

"What do you mean?" I asked. "You're my friend, Mary, even though I am often a very bad friend."

"You mustn't say that." Mary sighed and put down the candle, now clasping my hand with both of hers. "Listen to me, we're different, you and I. Chijioke and Poppy, they are nice, of course, but they are Unworlders."

My brow furrowed as I searched her freckled face. "And so are we."

"No, Louisa; they take us in, even protect us, but I'm born of a fairy's spring, and you're from Dark Fae blood as old as memory itself. This"—she gestured to the room, the house— "this is theirs. We're visitors as surely as the shepherd and his flock."

She wasn't having me on, her frown never subsiding into a teasing laugh. "Why have you never told me this before?"

"Because . . ." She shrugged, letting go of my hand. "Because I was safe before and they trusted me. Now I don't know what to do or where to go. Why would I want to stay here with people who think I'm capable of murdering for fun? And anyway, does it matter? I've told you now and that's what counts, right?"

"Amelia was going to die anyway," I said. "That's why she was here."

"Not like that. Mrs. Haylam says there is an order to things, and now she thinks I violated that order. They won't kick me out, of course they won't, but she will never look at me the same way again." Mary sighed and jutted out her lip. "I hate that."

After a moment, I stood, the full brunt of my exhaustion hitting me hard. I needed to at least lie down, though sleep would do me wonders. I hesitated next to the bed, lost, feeling sorry for her but also afraid. Every moment that passed I knew even less about myself, and about where I stood in the world.

"If I can find a way to leave and take you with me, would you go?" I asked.

Mary's green eyes widened, lashes fluttering. "Oh yes. Please, Louisa, could we go? But where would we go?"

"I . . . don't know that yet. I believe I've found a way to come into some money soon; perhaps I could use it to take us far away. To London. Or farther. I know it sounds far-fetched but I really am trying, and I think my plans just might work."

She hopped out of the bed and flung herself at me, hugging me hard. I walked with her to the door, and she embraced me again as I turned the knob and peered out into the hall, checking for Residents. There was nobody there, though I could feel that dawn was close, and I would get very little rest.

"Nobody," I told her. "Here," I added, shrugging out of her housecoat and handing it back. "Almost ran off in that, wouldn't want to accidentally steal your good-luck charm."

Mary had begun to turn away, then laughed. "My what?"

"Your lucky charm," I said. "Chijioke said you always have it on you. To rub for good fortune."

"Oh." Her brows knitted again and then she smiled, a strange, hot glow on her cheeks. I had forgotten my nakedness, aware then that she was fidgeting nervously. "Right. The, the . . ."

She was acting very strangely. *I wonder . . .*

"The coin," I supplied, giving a falsely teasing wink. "How could you forget, *Mary*?"

"Yes! Of course. Brain must still be asleep, ha! My lucky coin, aye, don't you run off with it!" She shook the housecoat at me playfully and I blinked, hard, feeling my heart plummet to my toes. I stared at the back of her head as she turned toward the bed, and a cold, merciless rage flooded through me, suppressed only by the lump in my throat.

A fish. Her good-luck charm was a fish.

I left, striding quickly toward my room. Behind me, I heard her sweetly calling, "Good night!"

"Good night," I choked out, flinging open the door to my room. I sank down at once, curling up on the cold, hard floor. The tears were immediate and sobering.

A drop of blood, a lock of hair, lands you in the Changeling's snare.

"Which did you take, Father? Blood or hair?" I whispered into my hands. Mary. God. Where was the real Mary? What did he do to her? How long had he been masquerading in her image?

I stood and wiped blindly at the tears on my cheeks. The bed felt nearly as cold as the floor, for there was no comfort to be found that night. I pulled the blankets up to my chin and bared my teeth to the darkness. "It had better be the lock of hair, Father. For your sake."

Chapter Thirty

acing "Croydon Frost" early the next morning was unbearable. I served him tea as he read in the west salon, that horrid pink spider straining its chain as it watched me from his shoulder. It looked eager to hop on my face and take another bite.

Perhaps I had a future on the stage, I thought, putting on a kindly smile as I waited for him to choose a pastry from the tiered plates. His suit that morning was black, simple, with a celadon-green cravat, a tiny leaf holding the silk ruffle in place. The smell of pine drifted from his clothing. He sat with one leg resting on the other, stirring a cup of tea, long chin jutted out thoughtfully as he perused the selection.

"I wanted to propose something," I said quietly, making a big show of glancing around the room to reaffirm that we were alone.

He grinned up at me, at last taking a scone from the tray. Now when I looked at his narrow, handsome face I could see nothing but the stag skull beneath it, as if the flesh he wore were only a thin and fading covering that would slip any second, revealing the true monster. It took every fiber of restraint I had to keep from smashing him over the head with his own teacup.

Where is Mary? What did you do with her?

I was bargaining from a position of weakness, for as soon as he discovered I knew the truth about Mary he would have dangerous leverage. He had seen firsthand how dearly I admired her, and the knowledge of her true location was invaluable. If I did not play this game carefully, I would lose before it even really began.

"I am listening," he said, inhaling deeply.

He did not eat his scone but rather abandoned it on his saucer. I took a step closer, loathing every minute I spent in his presence. My plan had altered in the night, but my original goal remained. I had to leave Coldthistle House for good, and avoid the mess he was determined to make.

"The book," I whispered, giving another conspiratorial look about. "I'll find a way to get it for you, but I want something, and I want it up front."

"Money?" Of course he knew, the clever bastard, having heard it from my own lips last night. He smiled like the cat that got the cream, making death by teacup that much more tempting.

"Not just money," I replied hastily. "A fortune. Enough to start over, enough for me to take Mary and my friends far away from here and begin a new life."

"Intriguing," he purred. "Go on."

"It won't matter if you give me the money first, since I want this bond to the book severed for good. I won't leave until you help me with that, and that requires the book." I sighed and put on my best fearful little girl face. "It will be very dangerous for me, do you understand? I'm risking everything to get you that book, so no tricks. Once I have my coin and you have what you want, then I'm finished. I don't want any part in . . . in what you have planned."

There were low voices in the foyer, the sound of men chatting to one another. I turned away and busied myself with the teapot on the table near the windows, waiting until the Breens and Samuel Potts left through the front doors. When I spun back around to face my father, he was staring blankly into the distance, still stirring his tea, as if he were a man lost in thought and I was not there at all.

"I wish I could change your mind. When these pretenders have been overthrown and the kingdom restored, we could look after it together. You could go home, to your real home, and be among beautiful creatures just like yourself." He sounded wistful, but I did not trust it for an instant.

"You said yourself there's a war coming, and I am not a soldier. No, a quiet life will suit me better. Perhaps I shall marry, or get a dog. May I ask why you can't take the book for yourself?" I asked. "You must be far more powerful than me; surely you could survive its touch."

"I'm weak, not nearly at my full strength," he said calmly. "If you slept for over a thousand years you may find yourself waking with a slight crick in the neck and a stiff walk, too."

He was lying. If he was strong enough to masquerade as Mary for hours on end, then he could damn well walk up the stairs and pick up the book. I had been tidying up the spilled sugar on the table when it occurred to me: he *could* take the book. In fact, he had probably tried already. But they had moved it, and now he was relying on me to discern its location.

"There is one complication," I said slowly, sweeping up the sugar with my palm.

"And that is?"

"The book . . . Mrs. Haylam moved it somewhere. I think they know something strange is going on, and I don't know how to find it without drawing attention." I dusted off my hands over the tray with the teapot and fetched the tiered biscuit plate.

The chair creaked as he leaned forward, uncrossing his legs. I could feel him searching the back of my head, trying silently to persuade me to turn around. I ignored him, worried that the slightest twitch, the wrong blush, would give me away.

"You must be smart now, daughter. If this is a true proposal, and we are to strike a true deal, then I must receive something in return for the money," he said. "They trust you here; turn that to your advantage."

You're using me, just like you used Mary.

"You're not drinking your tea," I pointed out lightly. "Is there something wrong with it?"

"Not at all. But I do not want tea, my dear daughter, I want revenge."

"Indeed," I said, brightening up and plastering on a fake smile for him. When I turned he had not moved and had not touched his tea. The pink-and-purple spider on his shoulder continued to stare at me, and I couldn't help but think it was strange. I had never seen a spider behave so placidly. "And I'm sure you will have it. I fear I must be going now, if you don't need anything else. Mr. Morningside is becoming anxious about his translations."

"I'm sure he is," my father replied with a deep chuckle. He sat back in his chair and sighed, relaxing, finally taking a single slow drink from his cup. "I wouldn't keep him waiting. I overheard the housekeeper fretting about the trial tonight. He does so deserve to know the ending before his world comes crashing down around his ears."

"I've just had the most incredible story from that ridiculous little kiss-up Finch."

Of course the moment I sat down to work Mr. Morningside appeared, swaggering into the library with his usual grace. This time, however, he looked as if he had not been sleeping. I relished that a touch, since I knew now that he had kept back crucial information from me. As much as I disliked Father—and I disliked him intensely—I couldn't shake the sense that he was right on a few things, one of those being Mr. Morningside's affinity for keeping pets. Was that all I was to him? A charming novelty? One of the last Changelings and therefore valuable only because of the rarity? And if so, did that not mean he would be loath to let me go? There were stories warning against deals with the Devil for a reason. I was increasingly worried that he would break our contract, or find some loophole within it to keep me from what I wanted.

He strolled to the desk, sitting on it, as he usually did, and grinned down at me. My eyes rolled up to meet his and I sighed. I knew precisely where this was headed.

"It wouldn't have anything to do with spiders, would it?"

"How did you guess?" Mr. Morningside had a good laugh over that, gasping for breath when he was finished. "Honestly, I wish I could have seen the looks on their faces!"

"So do I," I muttered. "Tragically, I was busy escaping Sparrow's overzealous accusations."

He sniffed and drew out his handkerchief, embroidered with his initials of course, and dabbed gently at his forehead. Apparently he had laughed himself into perspiring.

"She's a brute. Always has been. If Spicer were here, he would keep her in line, but Finch never says a thing, too much the devoted brother. Still, it invites the question, why were you out so late last night with your father?"

I glanced away, fumbling for a plausible lie. During my time at Pitney School, I had learned that the most believable lies not only held a grain of truth but also contained a shred of incriminating information. A sparkling-clean story never fooled anyone.

"We were taking a walk around the grounds," I said. "He wanted to talk to me away from everyone else and tell me about my mother . . . about their courtship. I thought meeting him would make me hate him, but there is something there that I find intriguing. He is my father, after all; it would be a shame not to at least hear his side of the story. It will not hurt my chances of inheritance, either."

"There is no need to hide such things or go skulking about in the night; I will not tease you for finding common ground with your own flesh and blood," he said with a chuckle. "But I do apologize for Sparrow's behavior. I wish I could say I'm shocked, but this is utterly believable. Spicer would wring her neck; I'll make certain he hears about all of this."

I flinched, wondering if he had any idea that this Spicer person was more than likely dead. Was it worth taunting him with it? While I weighed my options, Mr. Morningside made the decision for me. He straightened his lovely maroon jacket and leaned one hand on the table, letting out a plaintive breath.

"They don't make them like that anymore," he murmured. I had never seen him like this, boyish, almost *dreamy*. "Spicer was one of the shepherd's first servants. We were close. He never developed that wretched moralizing streak the others have. He never judged me simply because we were on opposite sides of things. Ha, he only judged me for my very bad decisions. Of which there were, and continue to be, many."

I nodded along, growing more and more ill at the lie sticking behind my tongue. "His name sounds familiar. I think I read about it in your book."

"Yes." Mr. Morningside snorted, tucking his handkerchief away. "That was his copy, from better days when he actually visited. The shepherd has apparently had him chasing this book of Bennu's all over creation. Old boy will be furious when he realizes it was all a wild-goose chase."

We both fell silent, sitting amid the crackling of the hearth flames and the distant voices above us that echoed through the house. I enjoyed it, in fact, simply sitting there being, as I had come to like that hidden library, and it was a rare moment that he treated me like a friend and not a fool to be manipulated. It was hard to imagine him being friends with one of the Adjudicators, but then I had learned far stranger things in recent hours.

"This book," I said, tapping the cover of Bennu's journal, "why does it matter so much? I'm not just blindly translating this for you; I *have* been paying attention. You and the shepherd, the Dark One and Roeh, you were rivals, but you were also fighting this Mother and Father, weren't you?"

He gave me a gentle but snobbish smile, one that clearly communicated how little he thought of my investigative skills. *Oh, I know so much more, sir, just you wait.*

"That's why there's an empty table at the Court. If the table is vacant and the flag is black that means they must be gone or dead. You have a book, the shepherd has one, and now you want theirs. Why?"

That drew his eyebrows up in surprise and his smug smile

faded away. He was looking at me differently now, as if he was only really seeing me for the first time. "It's the principle of the thing," he said flatly.

"No, it isn't," I scoffed. "When have you ever been principled?"

"Ha! Very droll. All right, but the answer might surprise you," he said, wagging his finger at me.

"Try me."

"I don't like what we did," Mr. Morningside told me, a haunted shadow darkening his normally vibrant yellow eyes. "It was a bloody business, brutal, and I listened to the shepherd when I shouldn't have. They were first, you know, the Mother and Father, they were old, old beings by the time he and I appeared. They had many names, many incarnations, but their true followers just called them Mother and Father. At first I thought we might all get along. I didn't need their worshippers and they didn't need mine."

"So what changed?" I asked, leaning onto the desk.

"What changed? Everything. The shepherd wanted more, more followers, more praise, more power. That was when our rivalry began, when it all became Satan or God, Hell or Heaven. We were both collecting worshippers so quickly, and we stopped caring about what they called us or what they did in our names. It . . . made something snap in the Father, I think. He was a god of tricks and trouble, the embodiment of nature's chaos. And while we bickered and settled our differences he grew and spread, unchecked. Something had to be done. There were disagreements, of course; I thought it was cruel to unite against him, but what could be done?"

I swiveled in the chair and nodded toward the painting. "But there are four of you. What happened to the Mother?"

Mr. Morningside drew himself up and shrugged, shaking his head quickly and running his hand over his face. "I wish I knew. She was the only sensible one among us, I think. One day she just . . . vanished. Bennu must have taken her from Egypt to wherever he wound up, but there was no trace of her after that. Things with the Father only got worse. He went mad. So the shepherd and I made an alliance of convenience." His voice lowered to nothing but a choked whisper, his eyes wide and staring as if a flood of awful memories had taken hold. "It was a bloodbath. We gave him no choice but to surrender."

He glanced up at me then, and it was the most honest, the most vulnerable I had ever seen him. His hand shook a little as he passed it over his face again. "That's why there are so few of you left, and why I've tried so hard to chronicle the Dark Fae and, well, take in any that I find."

"Guilty conscience," I murmured, using Mrs. Haylam's phrase.

"Guilt is not a strong enough word for what I feel, Louisa." Mr. Morningside stood and jerked on the bottom of his coat, sucking in his cheeks as he watched me. "Does that answer your question?"

He did not rush me as I came to my own conclusion, one that startled me even as I said it. "You don't want to destroy the book. You want to protect it from the shepherd."

A slow, wan smile spread across his face, chasing away the haunted shadow in his eyes. "It gladdens me to know you at least think that much of me."

"But then, why this?" I asked, running my palm over the journal. "You're handing him the key to destroying my people forever."

The Devil's smile deepened and he leaned toward me, eyes dodging toward the journal under my hand. "Clever, Louisa. Always too clever. That's why I came to see you. I know you're about to finish the translation, and I need you to make a few small . . . *adjustments*."

Chapter
Thirty-One

Year Two

𓇯𓏏 𓈖𓈖𓈖𓈖 𓆓𓂝 𓏲𓏏

Journal of Bennu, Who Runs

We arrived at the fortress at dawn, descending through a skylight
surrounded on all sides by twining, reaching branches. It looked
as if we were landing in a great wicker basket with the bottom
cut out, but as we neared the ground I saw that the fortress went
deep underground, too, a wide, stone spiraling staircase disap-
pearing into the earth. Outside the walls stood a forest so dense

and green that it looked like a single, unbroken sea of emerald.

I rolled from the back of the Sky Snake drenched from the rain, but that did not matter. At once, I tended to Khent, pulling him down, helping him limp, bloodied and sagging, toward . . . Well, I did not know where we were expected to go or whether we were expected at all. The Sky Snake departed before I could give it so much as a single pat of thanks, and soon its long black tail was again whipping along among the clouds.

The courtyard seemed deserted, silent but for an incredible racket of frogs. There must have been a swamp or river nearby, for it sounded as if we stood in the chorus of a million singing creatures. I had not noticed that a heavy bronze gate guarded the descent into the earth, and with a noisy clanging it began to move, receding into the wall and opening the way.

"Can you walk?" I asked Khent, but he had long since lost the ability to speak and simply moaned and rolled his head against my shoulder.

I had dragged him but a pace or two when two figures appeared, climbing up out of the depths of the inner fortress. Too tired to temper my response, I stood in openmouthed surprise at the sight of them, for they, like so many things I had seen on my journey, were utterly new to my eyes. They were human from the waist up, young women, each armored in what looked like smoothed wood chased with leaves, the straps of which were secured around their necks and arms with thick white webbing. Their skin was pale pink, and though they had big, pretty eyes as any maiden might, each had six more than they should, four smaller purple eyes curving up toward their white hair. Long plumes in every color were tucked into their braids and they had pieces of bone lodged in their ears and noses. That was all strange, but stranger still were their lower halves, not human-like but jutting out far behind them to accommodate eight legs. Eight massive, furred legs striped in pink and purple bands.

It was as if some twisted alchemist had taken the top of a woman and mingled it precisely with the body of a tarantula, and where woman met spider hung a long woven cloth painted with an elaborate deer skull with eight eyes. The strange design reminded me of the very book I had carried so far.

Both armored creatures carried wooden spears, and the one on the left, whose hair was longer and braided in twisting ropes over one shoulder, pointed the tip of that spear at me.

"Who is this that rides a Sky Snake into our midst and brings a bloodied companion? Speak, strangers, or be food for the forest." She did not need to shout, for the threat was more than enough. Her voice was husky, and her lip curled in anger.

"My name is Bennu," I said, trembling. I carefully pulled the book from its satchel and heard both women gasp. "Mother sent me. I followed the signs over a great, great distance. Please, we have come from half a world away, do not forsake us now."

"No! No . . . you are welcome here," the same creature said, giving an impressively elegant bow despite her strange configuration. She nodded to her companion, who skittered back down

into the earth. She emerged a moment later with a trio of help-
ers, who looked much like me but for their entirely black eyes.
"We will tend to your friend, and you will give us this precious
gift—"

The three assistants took hold of Khent and carried him away
before I could say anything. He gave me one last look, fevered
and afraid, and I worried then that our tribulations were not
yet at an end. As he was led away a commotion erupted below
us, and soon a whole group of black-robed men and women
arrived in the courtyard from below. Their faces were painted
with elaborate designs and tattooed with green spirals. One
stepped forward, an elderly man, and elbowed the spiderlike girl
out of the way.

He smelled strongly of the woods, of pine and nettles, and
when he smiled his teeth were dyed a hideous green. "It will be
taken to Father at once. You will join us."

"What is this? Get back to your swamp, Green Healer; the
Mother's very essence is in that thing and it will go to her priest-
esses first."

She leveled the spear at him but he hacked up a laugh and
pushed it away. "You have precious little power while she
remains on papyrus," he hissed. He spat when he talked, and his
right eye twitched constantly, his round shape and pointed face
reminding me of a tick. "Father will know what to do. He is,
after all, eager to be reunited with his bride."

I felt numb all over. Of course I knew the book was

irreplaceable, but to think it carried Mother herself? My relief
at having safely brought her so far was swiftly extinguished.
The Green Healer yanked the book out of my arms and stumbled
back, not anticipating its weight. The other robed figures closed
around him, and they all oozed as one back down into the for-
tress.

"This is an outrage," the other spider guardian muttered. "We
cannot allow it, Coszca! Mother will not be herself. She will not
have her full strength until she is released."

"I know, Cuica, I know. You." The one who had pointed her
spear at me, Coszca, pointed her weapon at me again and nod-
ded toward the stairs. "Follow us. I do not trust those druids;
their love is for Father and, I fear, for Father only."

We rushed down the stone stairs, and I was relieved to find
the passage lit all the way down with gouts of flame shooting up
from gaps in the walls. The entirety of the fortress was painted
with murals, most of them forest scenes, but some showed the
Sky Snake and the half women, half spiders as they triumphed
in battles. I gave the pictures little more than a glance, for the
women were much faster than I, and used the walls as naturally
as the stairs to travel down. A wider landing came into view,
and off that a door that led into a shadowy place I could not yet
see.

The women tore ahead, breaking through that archway. I
heard them scream an instant later as I stumbled through the
opening. The druids had been waiting there. They tossed massive

nets over them and pelted them with stones. The women fought, trilling loud, beautiful cries as they thrust their spears again and again. More druids smothered me with their cloaks, picking me up and hoisting me away.

I did not see what became of the warrior women and could only hope they would be shown mercy for doing nothing but demonstrating loyalty to their Mother.

I, too, fought as the robed men and women forced me along an unseen path. The ground changed from stones to mud, and my feet sank deep, sucked down by the wet earth, the mud covering me up to my knees. I smelled the primeval oldness of the forest, the perfume of dense trees and rotting leaves, and then, finally, they released me and pulled their cloaks from my face.

Before me stood a tree. I could not describe it even if threatened with death, for it was both dead and living, black and yet unburned, flourishing with leaves except those leaves were like daggers dripping poison. The druids shoved the book I had carried for so long back into my arms, and I cradled it like a beloved child. Then the robed figures vanished, leaving me to tremble in that place alone.

And then they came.

They emerged from the tree like worms from the earth. More shadow than mass, they slithered out from between the groaning cracks in the trunk before making their way to the clearing. The roots of the tree were as thick around as horses, broad and gnarled, never touched by man and rarely even glimpsed by him.

The creatures came out of those roots gradually at first, but as twilight dipped into evening, they arrived at a steadier pace, a slow drip that became a constant stream. . . .

Father was real. Mother was real. It was all real. I reminded myself that I had no allegiance, that Mr. Morningside had been kind but that he had also lied, that the shepherd had been kind but he had also sent his cruel Adjudicators, and that Father had been generous with truth but equally generous with lies.

I had no allegiance, so why was it so difficult to choose the side that counted most: my side.

I needed more. More proof, more assurance that I was doing the right thing. It took no more than passing a note to Lee during lunch to set my plan in motion. He was not necessarily part of it, but I needed one last thing from him, a favor for me that I hoped would wind up being a favor for many. By then, it had gotten around that I had thwarted Sparrow, and that she had not shown her face since the humiliation of a spider popping out of my clothes and evading Judgment.

"Lass, that was pure art." Chijioke had retold the story at least three different times over the meal. I laughed along, but only half-heartedly, knowing full well that this meal might be the last I shared with them. My heart ached to tell him the truth about Mary, to relieve his worries that she had passed him over. He had been wooing my master deceiver of a father, not the shy, kind young woman we both liked so much. There would be time for that truth later. I did not plan to leave Cold-thistle House alone. If Mr. Morningside actually kept his side of the bargain . . .

The thought of reuniting Chijioke and Mary was almost too pure, too good to entertain. And it was a vanishing possibility that still lay at the end of a long, long tunnel filled with spikes and traps and twists and angry gods.

"Just: wham! And a ruddy great spider flies out of your apron! Legendary." Chijioke doubled over with laughter. Poppy could hardly breathe she found it all so funny. Even Bartholomew, awake for once, snuffled against the girl's leg.

"Serves her right," Mrs. Haylam said from the range. She was toasting a last bit of bread for herself, and then turned to the stew pot to fix herself a bowl. "Your powers of transforma-tion have certainly grown leaps and bounds since your father's arrival. It sounds like he's taught you much."

I could not read her tone, so I simply nodded and minded my food. "His presence has been most instructive."

She glanced over her shoulder at me, staring for a long, long time. "The Court should finish its business this evening. I look forward to a bit more peace and quiet around here once they all pack up and go."

"What about Mason and his father?" I asked. "Are they

staying with us much longer?"

"No, Mrs. Haylam says I should take care of them just as soon as Mary's well," Poppy said brightly. "That mean old Samuel Potts did bad, bad things to folks down in Few South Ales and it's time he paid for it. Right, Mrs. Haylam?"

"New South Wales, Poppy. And yes. I will need to have a discussion or two with Mary, and then she will return to work as usual."

I nearly choked on my mouthful of stew. Chijioke patted my back, trying to help me overcome the sudden coughing fit.

"Some water will set you to rights," he said, hopping up and hurrying to the spigot out in the yard.

I took the opportunity to pass a note to Lee under the table, tapping his leg with it until his eyes opened wide and his hand closed over mine. Our gazes met, and I held his for a moment. He frowned, looking worn, frayed around the edges, his eyes no longer so brightly blue, his hair dull and greasy. It was not that he was no longer handsome, but that the strangeness of the new life I had thrust upon him did not suit him at all. What I was about to do was as much for him as it was for me. Or so I told myself.

Lee took the note and smoothly transferred it to his inner coat pocket. When Chijioke returned, I faked a few more coughs and accepted the water from him, drinking deep.

"Thank you," I said, putting up my plate and cup before giving Mrs. Haylam a quick curtsy. "May I go? The library needs dusting, and Mr. Breen left a mess of books in there yesterday."

"See to it, then," she sighed. "But be washed up and ready for the trial. It will commence at sundown."

Sundown. Right. That was more than enough time. I glanced back once more at Lee and smiled before I left and crossed the foyer, going swiftly up the stairs and up again to the library, which was actually not as dusty as it could have been and tidied nicely. It didn't matter; I just needed somewhere private to speak to Lee. I might have asked Chijioke or Poppy to help, but Lee was the least attached to the house and to Mr. Morningside, at least in an emotional sense. He was tied to the book forever, yes, but I hoped to change that, and anyway, he did not seem to have any love for Coldthistle.

What I had to say would make Chijioke panic, and Poppy was too much of a loudmouth.

I waited for only a moment or two, pacing nervously in front of the windows. The sun had come out and harshly, leaching all color from the lawn, which needed rain and had begun turning brown in places. Lee entered the library and gave a soft tap on the wall to let me know he had arrived.

"There you are," I whispered. "Shut the door!"

"What's going on, Louisa?" he asked, doing as I said but only after hesitating, squinting suspiciously.

"Listen, there are a hundred things I wish I could tell you right now, but there isn't time to explain it all." I rushed to him and took him by his cold hands, leading him through the stacks of books to the back of the library, where once we had spoken of our families, of dashed hopes and sins long past. It had been a lifetime and a half since then, or so it seemed, for he did not look at me with hope or joy any longer, only skepticism. "This is going to sound mad, but you must trust me. My father is not who he says he is; he's an old god, a terrible one, and he's very, very dangerous. He didn't come here for me or for reconciliation; he came to start a war. The shepherd and Mr. Morningside defeated him long ago, and now he wants revenge."

"An . . . old god? Is it possible?" Lee raked his eyes over me as if in disbelief that I could be the daughter of such a thing. I couldn't blame him. "How do you know all of this?"

"The pavilion; it reveals your true self, and I saw what he was when I met him inside," I explained, tumbling over my words in my haste. "Everything he told me is confirmed by a journal Mr. Morningside has had me translate. He came here to start trouble, and I'm terrified that all of you will get caught up in it and hurt. Which is why I need you to make sure that you, Poppy, and Chijioke do not go to the Court tonight."

Lee pulled back, still studying me closely. His brow furrowed and he tilted his head to the side as he said, "Why? What do you think will happen?"

"Something bad," I replied hotly. "Something bad will happen because I am going to *make* it happen. I'm not smart or strong enough to get rid of my father, but Mr. Morningside and the shepherd will know what to do."

"You're going to stab your own father in the back?" Lee cried. "Isn't that awfully cruel?"

"You don't know him," I said, closing my eyes tightly. "You don't know him, Lee; he's not anyone to pity or admire. I don't care if he's a god or a ditch digger, he cannot be trusted. He's been impersonating Mary."

His eyes blew wide and he shook his head. "No. . . . No!"

"He has. Why is she locked in her room all day? Have you ever seen them in the same place? She spurned Chijioke and forgot her own good-luck charm. These are not accidents, Lee, *think*."

"Mary is your closest friend here," he whispered. "You must have told him all kinds of things. . . ."

"Precisely. But I discovered the deception, and as far as I know, he has no idea that I'm wise to it," I told him quickly. "He wants the book, the Black Elbion, and in exchange I'm to receive a fortune and freedom from the book's grip."

His head sank low and he gave almost a yelp of helplessness. I took his hand, squeezing.

"Don't do that," I said, desperate. "I won't give it to him, Lee. I wouldn't risk it. But I must know what he intended to do, and I must know that betraying him this way is the best path forward. He is downstairs right now, in the west salon, reading. Can you keep him there?"

"What do you intend to do, Louisa?" he asked, pulling his hand away. "You won't find the book—they moved it. . . ."

"I know that, Lee. I don't want it. I need to get in his rooms and have a look around, that's all."

"The last time you did something like this you nearly died, and I *did* die. Why on earth would I let you try that again?"

I threw my head back in exasperation, spinning and pacing from the window and back to him, chewing my knuckle. "Fine. Don't distract him; I'll do it on my own. Just please, promise me that you will keep everyone safe in the house tonight. Promise me, Lee—it's important. Whatever happens, I want to make sure you're all protected."

He rolled his eyes and grabbed me, pulling me in for a tight embrace. I made a soft *oof* sound of surprise, then returned the gesture.

"I won't let you do this alone. God help me, I believe you. You never lied to me before. I know you tried to save me from Mr. Morningside, even if it . . . didn't go as planned." He leaned back, holding me at arm's length. "Are you sure this is the right thing to do? I'll be very cross if you go and get yourself killed, too."

I managed a small smile, and swallowed the urge to cry. "I'm only trying to stop a war and outwit an ancient god of the forest. How hard could it be?"

Chapter
Thirty-Two

ather's chambers were the very definition of neatness. His bags were arranged in an orderly row under the window, his suits packed in the wardrobe, a leather case with rows and rows of little glass vials sitting on the desk. Most of the rooms in Coldthistle were arranged similarly, with a wardrobe to the left upon entering, a small bathing area connected to a sitting area on the right, and a writing desk beyond, the bed across from the desk and a window center to it all.

The air was thick with his now familiar woodsy cologne, though other whiffs of perfume danced across my nose. My heart raced as I tiptoed to the desk, inspecting the dark leather case. There were three rows of ten little bottles, each fixed with a handwritten label describing the scent within. This was the life's work of Croydon Frost, a man who was probably rotting in a ditch somewhere, his face and fortune stolen by a mad god.

I peered into his bags but there was nothing of interest there, just jars of insects for his spider and a few changes of undergarments. Nothing. For a "man" of wealth and taste, his traveling style was practically ascetic. But I had seen him handling correspondence, so he must be storing his post somewhere. I returned to the desk, poking lamely at the black case. The bottom of it did seem rather thick, but no tray of bottles sprang out of it no matter what I did. Was it a false bottom?

Running my fingers over the entire thing produced no result. Out of desperation I began picking up each of the vials and checking underneath. And there it was—on the second row of bottles, third from the left, a round depression that looked out of place. I pushed down on the circle and heard the false bottom unlatch, a tray springing out from under the vials.

Stacks and stacks of letters were revealed, and I began paging through them at random. Most were leftover correspondence of Croydon Frost the actual man, for the penmanship did not at all resemble the letter I had received from Father. Underneath those notes was an expense ledger and under that a series of folded papers. I spread them flat on the desk, glancing at the door, reminding myself that I did not have all afternoon to spy through his things.

At first the pages just looked like nonsense, lists of names with lines drawn haphazardly between columns. Then I looked closer, realizing that they were not random at all but organized in chunks. Family trees. At the very top he had listed his own name and then jotted down women he had taken as lovers over the years. And, although the records went back only twenty years or so, there were many name. Dozens. I flipped the page. Hundreds. My stomach tightened, a sick feeling spreading through my body as I read the names over, searching for my mother. Most of the names were crossed off, which I could only assume meant they were dead.

The troubling part was just how many names were struck

through, and the sheer number of his own children who had mysteriously died young.

My God, in the twenty years since he awoke, he has been breeding offspring and then eliminating them.

I searched desperately for my mother's name, and in doing so came across a family tree that looked painfully familiar.

1793: Deirdre Donovan _____ Brandon Canny

Daughter: ~~Amelia Jane Canny~~

Mary *had* killed Amelia. Mrs. Haylam had been right, only not in the way she thought she was. Was it sheer coincidence that Amelia had been here, too? That she was, *God*, my half sister? That was his latest kill; other girls remained between Amelia and me, and there were others after, but no other child on the list had their name *circled*. Just me.

He hadn't been lying about that; he really was here for me. I had no idea if I would ever find this list again, and did my best to memorize what names I could that had not yet gotten the strike-through. *Auraline Waters, Justine Black, Emma Robinson . . .* I could never have imagined in my wildest dreams that I had this many half sisters. The busy, miserable cheat.

Perhaps I could warn them if my scheme tonight did not go as planned. But then, if that happened, I would not live to write those letters. I thought of all those crossed-off names and wondered if he would kill me, too, after getting what he wanted. He needed the book, and maybe he really was too weak to handle its burning touch, but once he had it I would no longer be necessary.

I left before I could be discovered, a renewed sense of purpose putting wings on my feet. It was late afternoon. Not much time now. I rushed down the stairs, breezing by one of the Residents, who didn't seem puzzled by my emerging from Father's room. After all, it was my job to change over the bed linens and empty the chamber pot upon request. My timing was perfect, for I met Lee just as he came scurrying out of the west salon.

"Oh thank God," he panted. "I couldn't keep him there much longer, Louisa. Mrs. Haylam needs me—apparently the Breens are getting squirrelly. They checked Malton and Derridon and found nothing, of course. They're becoming convinced we know something about Amelia. She wants them *taken care of* soon."

"No!" I pulled him toward the wall, lowering my voice to a whisper. "If Poppy tries to do anything, we all die, do you understand? Mary isn't here to shield anyone."

Lee swore under his breath, nodding and leaving me as he trotted off toward the kitchens. "I'll see what I can do. Did your, um, chore go smoothly?"

"I found what I was looking for," I told him resolutely. I very nearly said *My feet are on the path.* What had come over me? "Remember—tonight, nobody goes to the trial."

"Right. You can count on me, Louisa. We can keep them safe."

Then he was gone, pushing through the door and into the kitchens. I went on my way, too, rounding the corner and finding Father still tucked up in his chair, reading, his faithful spider companion wandering back and forth across his shoulders.

"I have good news," I said with top brightness. Of course, as he turned and looked at me I made a big show of checking the room for any listeners. It was stupid, but I needed him to think I was pulling off a grand scheme for him, not *on* him.

His smile was wolfish as I approached, thin face dominated by that satisfied grin.

"How did you do it?" he asked, giddily interested.

I leaned over his chair, keeping a wary eye on his spider friend. "I nicked Mrs. Haylam with a knife while we prepared lunch. It was easy enough to get what I needed from Mr. Morningside after that."

Then I winked and he practically collapsed with laughter. I shivered, remembering the ugly echo of the spiders and snakes that seemed to laugh with him outside the pavilion last night. His eyes twinkled, and I could almost see the red pinpricks there, concealed by his guise.

"I've hidden it in a safe location, and as soon as it leaves the house the Residents will realize it, so we must be careful. I will bring it with me to the Court and leave it under the table. *Our* table," I said, making things up as I went. It was a plausible story and apparently one he believed. "Tonight, after the trial, I will bring it to you. I suggest you attend. What I have in store for Mr. Morningside will please you greatly. It will be a night to remember."

Another wink.

"You are the sort of daughter every father hopes for and rarely gets," he said fondly, chuckling again. With his spindly fingers he reached into his coat pocket, withdrawing a long, wide slip of paper. A banknote. "There will be more," he said, handing me the money. It was for a bank in London, and the sum was more than I could digest. Ten thousand pounds. A girl could live off that for the rest of her life.

"Enjoy it," Father said.

While you can, I added silently. I saw the coolness in his eyes as he handed over the note. He knew it would not be mine for long, that as soon as he had the book I would be useless and therefore a burden. I tucked the banknote away in my apron pocket, folding it and sliding it against the spoon.

"I will wait outside the tent or risk being revealed," he murmured. "I wouldn't want them to know of my return too soon."

"Oh, trust me," I said with a beaming smile. "Nobody will be looking at you, not when I make utter fools of our enemies. But it would be wise for you to conceal yourself. Listen nearby and you will hear me give the signal."

Father sighed and reached up for my face, touching his thumb to my chin. I went rigid to avoid recoiling and giving myself away.

"My beautiful daughter, what did I do to deserve you?"

Nothing, I thought, my smile cracking. And everything.

If this was what a bride felt like on her wedding day, then I never wanted to be faced with marriage. But this was that permanent, that unavoidable—I had come to it, and my nerves were on fire.

"Are you afraid, my dear? You're trembling."

Mr. Morningside stood beside me, flickering in and out of his many faces, every color of skin, every possible combination of features. I tried to look at him, but I was racked with uncertainty, finding that courage was fleeting now that we were in the pavilion and the Court had reconvened. Instead, I looked straight ahead at the dais, at the empty spot where a third throne should be.

Had I become a radical? A rogue element? I didn't belong at the center of so much turmoil.

"Yes," I told him truthfully. "I'm terrified. Do you think anyone will believe us?"

One of his faces smiled, and it bled onto all those that came into view next. "Take heart, Louisa, I will be the one Judged this night. We have done all that we can. Nobody will know where the third book has gone. You burned the journal, did you not?"

"I did." And I had. After our last meeting in the cellar library I had done as Mr. Morningside asked and tossed Bennu's work into the fireplace. For a long time I watched it burn, feeling as if I had deeply hurt a friend I had never even met.

"Good." He stared placidly out over the milling crowd. "Then only you have the secret. I wouldn't want it any other way."

I flinched. This was not only the night I betrayed my father, but the night I perhaps lost Mr. Morningside's regard. Forever.

"Just don't forget our deal," I said. "I did as you asked."

One of his less regal faces lifted a brow at me. "Getting nervous I'm going to slip your net, Louisa? We put it in writing."

"And you've never used a loophole to your advantage?" I asked with a snort. "You'll really let them go?"

One eye on a new face—a sly, handsome one—winked. "You will just have to trust me, won't you?" He paused, and I thought perhaps the conversation was over, but then he said softly, "You didn't *actually* hold up your end, you know."

I spun on him quickly. *"What?"*

"The journal," he drawled. "You skipped some entries."

"Because you told me to!" I cried.

"Don't panic, Louisa," Mr. Morningside said with a chuckle. "I'm just pointing it out."

The shepherd sat low in his throne, his gold, liquid angels surrounding him, all of them in the midst of a heated discussion. The translated pages that Mr. Morningside had given him days ago were piled on the shepherd's lap, his fist tucked up under his chin as he took counsel. I could hardly see any of it. My mind was spinning. According to Mr. Morningside, I had broken the contract, which meant he might not let us go at all.

Suddenly, my pledge to help him against the shepherd felt far less important.

Mr. Morningside said nothing about the bag hanging from my shoulder. He either didn't notice it or didn't care to comment. This was not a carpet in front of me but a precipice, I thought, wishing I could roll back time and do everything differently. I should have shut the door in my father's face the moment he appeared. I should have trusted myself, and trusted that a man who'd run out on his infant daughter was not to be heard or seen or respected. I might have told Mr. Morningside Father's secret, but selfishly I had assumed I could handle this all myself. Whether that was true or not was about to become painfully apparent.

The tent was as dazzling as ever, the fairy lights bouncing and shining, everyone glittering in their dark, beautiful robes or their ivory gowns. Even the angels burning on the stage were lovely, suffusing the back half of the pavilion with their light. The crowd of onlookers drank and laughed, though they stayed largely relegated to their own kind; no brave mingling would happen on that night.

"Let us begin."

The shepherd's voice boomed out over the crowd and everyone fell silent. I took the moment of distraction to break away from Mr. Morningside. He had already begun to walk toward the dais anyway. Dodging toward the long, empty trestle table with the black pennant, I stuffed the book in the flour sack under the table and then just as swiftly fell into step behind Mr. Morningside. We reached the empty space before the stage and I heard the tent flaps rustle. I glanced over my shoulder and gasped.

It was not Father, as I'd expected, but Chijioke. He ducked into the pavilion and searched the crowd with his glowing red eyes. I tried to turn away, but he had spotted me and began weaving his way toward us, pushing people out of the way when they did not move fast enough for his taste.

"What are you doing here?" I whispered, slapping his arm lightly. "Get out of here. Now."

"Ha. Lass, the moment Lee told me we were to stay shut up in the house I knew you were going to do something stupid. The only thing I want to know is, just how stupid are we talking here?"

I shook my head subtly, for the shepherd was talking directly about the translations and eyes were beginning to seek me out in the crowd.

"Leave, Chijioke, I'm begging you. Nothing good will come of this trial. I'm trying to protect you."

"Are you in some kind of trouble?" he whispered.

"I am in every kind of trouble." I took him hard by the shoulder and inched away from Mr. Morningside. "They're calling me forward. Look at me. No! Look at me. Chijioke, when the commotion starts you need to get out of here."

"Louisa Ditton, come forward."

The shepherd's dog had summoned me, and I gave Chijioke's shoulder one last squeeze before ripping myself away. He tried to grab my hand but I was gone, pushing through the thin barrier of people between me and the empty floor, going and taking my place, for good or bad, next to Mr. Morningside.

I felt a chill ripple across the air and knew without looking that Father had come. His eyes were on me. I clasped my hands together to keep them from visibly shaking.

"I have reviewed these journals," the shepherd began. He looked as weary as I did, but his eyes were alert, bouncing back and forth between me and Mr. Morningside. "They are most interesting. They are also incomplete."

"Where is the book, you snake?" It was Sparrow, obvious from the venom in her voice. She prowled to the edge of the stage, pointing at us. "Your precious Changeling pet weaseled her way out of telling me the truth of it, but that will not happen again."

"Save your accusations for me, Sparrow; this girl has done nothing but comply with my requests—requests that serve us all," Mr. Morningside said calmly, almost cheerfully, in fact. He plucked another sheaf of papers from inside his coat and strode to the dais, handing them up to Sparrow. She snatched them out of his hand with a grunt, taking a glance before passing them to the shepherd.

"That's the good bit," he said with a chuckle, rocking back

onto his heels. The crowd murmured with interest, and I could feel them surging closer to our backs. "We now have the location of the third book, and once it is recovered, another Court can be convened to decide what must be done with it."

"A pyre is its rightful fate," Sparrow muttered. There were sounds of both agreement and dissent in the crowd. "Perhaps the Black Elbion should go on it, too, Beast."

That drew cries of agitation from the audience. The shepherd was reading the documents and quickly, flipping through page after page after page, his eyes jumping up and down. His expression grew gradually more somber, until he reached the end, and melancholy turned to anger.

"What is this?" He drew his eyes up slowly from the page, settling them not on Mr. Morningside but on me. "Girl, you swear that this is what you read in the journals? Do not lie to me."

I swallowed hard and drew back my shoulders, staring directly into the face of a god and lying. I had gotten good at it, apparently, after all that practice with Father. It didn't feel good to lie, not when I was growing more and more worried that Mr. Morningside would break our bargain. "I swear it's the truth."

"It is," Mr. Morningside said at once.

The shepherd gradually shifted his unseeing gaze to Mr. Morningside, squinting. "The resting place of the third book, the secret location we have agonized over for centuries, is Stoke-on-Trent? Is that really true?"

"Absurd!" Sparrow shouted. The flames of her body leapt, erupting higher as she stalked over to the throne, trying to read over the shepherd's shoulder. "This is a diversion! A trick! Morningside knows the real location but wants it only for himself." She dropped down to her knees suddenly and clasped her hands around the shepherd's knee. "Let me invoke the Right of Judgment. Please, let me do it. You know it is right."

He drew in a long, slow breath. Beside me, Mr. Morningside fidgeted, but I suspected it was just a show. Still, when I happened to look at him, I did notice a sheen of perspiration on his many changing faces. Was he truly nervous? Did he doubt that our plan would work?

While the shepherd deliberated and the crowd grew more and more agitated, I risked a glance over my shoulder. Father was outside waiting somewhere. Just knowing he was close made me tingle with fear.

"Very well." The shepherd stood, and as he spoke, I could see tears of regret sparkling at the corners of his eyes. "Step forward, sir; the Right of Judgment has been invoked. You will give us the truth, and no lie will go unpunished."

Chapter
Thirty-Three

saw his knees tremble as he took his position, kneeling in front of the stage with Sparrow's shining golden form poised above him.

There was no way of knowing what was under the shifting glitter of her face, but I knew in my heart that she was smiling. For my part, I could do nothing but squeeze the life out of my hands as I waited for it all to be over. The pavilion had become deathly silent, with only the faint pulsing of the portal behind the stage providing any sound at all. Even the crickets and frogs outside had gone quiet, as if the whole world sensed the grave significance of this moment.

Mr. Morningside chuckled as Sparrow, with great dignity and solemnity, took him by the chin, tilting his head upward.

"Give us a kiss, darling," he purred.

"You're disgusting," she muttered. "I'm going to enjoy watching you squirm."

"As if there was any doubt of that at all," Mr. Morningside laughed. "Do pardon the brandy on my breath; it was a tense night, you see."

Sparrow ignored him, but she was rattled, a slight jitter in the hand that held his chin. Then she leaned down and brought her mouth close over his, and as I saw his eyes roll back and his body go slack, I felt a pang of empathy, remembering how terribly her Judgment had hurt. Was that what I looked like when she did the same thing to me? It was awful. If I did not comprehend the circumstances, I would have believed him dead. Occasionally his body jerked this way or that, the whites of his eyes flickering, the crowd reacting to each tiny twitch.

I turned and found Chijioke in the sea of faces, pressing my lips together tightly as if I could silently apologize for what he had to witness. If he only knew what I'd done, that Mr. Morningside had every possibility of passing this test. That we had rigged the game. That I was now as complicit in his devilish schemes as the Devil himself.

The silence was the hardest to bear. Sparrow's voice must have been screaming through his head, but we heard none of it. The shepherd watched intently from his throne, leaning forward, elbows on his knees as he, too, reacted to every spasm of Mr. Morningside's body.

The tension grew, a thick white beam of light stretching from Sparrow's open golden mouth to his; a high, whining sound, like a bird holding a shrill note, emanated from the light. It became so loud, so piercing, that most of us held our hands over our ears. I thought my head might explode as the beam of light intensified, too bright to look at, and the sound ripped through my brain like a razor.

"Ah!" The spell was broken at last, and Mr. Morningside's eyes rolled back into place. He gulped for air, falling to the ground and panting.

"No!" Sparrow shouted, stomping out a tight circle. "He . . . He must be lying! He must be! Can't you see this is some trickery? How did you do it?" she bellowed. "HOW DID YOU DO IT?"

"Enough, Sparrow, leave him be. You have had the truth from him," the shepherd thundered, slicing his hand through the air. He no longer looked like a dowdy old farmer, but a wise and commanding elder. "We must accept Mr. Morningside's answer, unlikely as it may be."

I breathed a sigh of relief and watched Henry climb to his feet. He fixed his coat and cravat, giving Sparrow a shaky but cocky bow.

"A real treat, my dear. Let's do it again sometime."

"Then we will depart at once for Stoke." Finch spoke up, going to his sister and leading her back up onto the dais. "This is a great gift of knowledge. We cannot punish him for sharing it with us. He has accomplished what none of us could, and surely that establishes his competency. He did not have to share this at all but he did. That, more than anything, proves his allegiance to our ancient agreement."

The crowd seemed largely to share Finch's sentiments. Mr. Morningside began to swagger back toward me and I took him by the wrist, squeezing hard.

"Honor our agreement," I whispered. "Do it now. Tell me the contracts are dissolved."

"Not right now," he replied with a shrug. "We should be celebrating. . . ."

"I need to know that you're going to keep your promise."

But Mr. Morningside laughed me off. Perhaps he did not see how serious I had become, or maybe he did not care. "It's in writing, Louisa, what more can I say to you?"

"You can say you won't back out through a loophole," I shot back.

"Clearly you do not know me as well as you think you do, to even imagine I would promise such a thing." He was laughing again and it made my blood boil. I was lying and scheming *for* him and this was how he treated me? "A bargain was struck, Louisa. I will say no more on it."

"No," I said. I dropped Mr. Morningside's wrist and turned. It lacked the conviction I wanted, and nobody noticed me moving toward the stage. "No!" I shouted it this time and the clamor died down. Mr. Morningside's smile abruptly faded and he sneered at me.

"What are you doing, Louisa?" he whispered.

"He told you the truth," I pushed on. My hands were sweating profusely. The earth felt like it was moving underneath me, like I might be sick at any moment. My throat was closing in panic, but I went on, determined now to see my plan, not Henry's, through. "He told you the truth, sir, but I did not."

"I *knew* it." Sparrow was elated, springing toward me with a throaty laugh.

"Shut up," I spat, glaring at her. "The truth is that Mr. Morningside does not know the location of the book, but I do."

Henry's eyes found mine and he shook his head urgently, mouthing things at me that I could not and would not obey.

"I lied to him," I said, and that was a lie, too. He had told me to conceal the location, to keep it to myself until he asked for it. This, at least, would somewhat exonerate him. "That's how he passed your Judgment, Sparrow. He honestly knows no other location."

"Why would you do this?" the shepherd murmured. He didn't sound angry, exactly, just sad.

"Because the book is gone," I called back. The pavilion became one massive gasp. "It's gone, forever. Only one person has its knowledge because he devoured it. It's in him, in his mind, in his blood, and I have delivered him to you. Tonight."

It was no longer gasps I heard but outraged shouts. *Liar!* was the most popular response to shout at me. I stood still, absorbing it all, letting them curse at me and fling insults. For once, Sparrow was reduced to stunned silence.

"There," I said, turning and pointing. I had half expected Father to flee altogether once he divined my intentions. But no, he had arrived, moving to the center back of the pavilion. All eyes raced to find him, and a ripple of fear and excitement followed his discovery. He stood looming over the others, taller and larger than them all, the ashy mist rolling off his face darker and more sinister than I remembered it. The fairy lights seemed to dim around him, as if shying away.

"Blood and thunder," Mr. Morningside swore, diving toward me and taking my arm. *"What are you trying to do, Louisa?"*

"Unhand my daughter," Father said, so softly and surely that I almost could not hear him. But all had gone quiet, for everyone wanted to hear what he would say. Under that curiosity I sensed a rising fear, and I noticed more than one person in the crowd begin to edge toward us, preparing to run for the portal.

"You were defeated." The shepherd's voice shook with emotion, his angels gathering around him. "Your kingdom sleeps eternal."

"Does it?" Father laughed, taking the flour sack and the book within it and hoisting it over his head. "Night fades, slumber breaks, and now those you betrayed are waking up. My daughter is one such child, one of mine, the first and last children, and she has brought me a magnificent gift." His gaze fell on Mr. Morningside, who had not taken his hand from my elbow and was, in fact, squeezing it hard enough to bruise. "I smell your fear, Lier-In-Wait; remove yourself from my daughter or I will tear this book in half before your very eyes."

Mr. Morningside released my arm, taking one giant step away. I heard his noisy swallow of fear and looked to him, lip quivering with shame.

"That's not possible!" Chijioke rushed forward from the

crowd. His face was pained, his red eyes filling with moisture. "Louisa!"

"Do it, you old bastard," Mr. Morningside jeered. "You lack the courage."

Now the crowd broke in earnest, screams rending the air as I was pushed this way and that, the onlookers running for the way out. An empty no-man's-land appeared before Father, a swath of carpet that no one dared to tread.

"Defend us, defend us all!" the shepherd shouted, and his Adjudicators sprang to life, each of them gliding above us on massive white wings, their golden bodies almost blinding as they charged.

"How could you do this to us?" Chijioke begged, snatching up my hand and shaking me. "How?"

"Peace, good man." Mr. Morningside had waded back toward us through the sea of bodies streaming toward the portal. He slapped Chijioke on the shoulder and gave me a wink. "You underestimate our dear Louisa."

"*She betrayed us,*" Chijioke thundered, and it tore at my heart.

"Did she?" Mr. Morningside, holding his shoulder, turned him back toward Father and the melee ensuing.

The angels descended on him, golden arms rippling, reshaping into scythes and shields. They amassed before him, preparing to dive, shining weapons held high. Father seemed to grow larger, bolder, the swirling dark mist around him gathering like smoky armor. Sparrow gave a mighty cry and swooped down toward him, scythe slashing. He smashed his arm through her golden shield, shards of bright metal showering the last of the crowd to flee. They screamed as she did, though her cries were loudest, Father's talons ripping across her throat as he grabbed her by the neck, then tossed her across the pavilion. She slammed into the pole nearest us, shaking the ground and the tent, her limp body sliding to the ground in a heap.

"No!" The shepherd vaulted off the stage and ran to her. He lifted her head and she moaned.

Finch was the next to give his shout of battle and charge Father, and I stumbled toward them, not wishing harm upon someone who had been so kind to me. But he was joined at once by Big Earl, whose hand had become a lance. He landed a glancing blow before Father knocked them both across the pavilion and over our heads.

Chijioke made as if to run in and fight with them, and I grabbed the back of his red coat, yanking him away. "Don't, it isn't worth it!"

"The book!" he cried. "We must get it back!"

"You dare send your fledglings after me," Father shouted, taking up the bag again and brandishing it like a dagger. "You will pay, you will pay what you owe, the blood of those you love, the blood of your people, the very foundations of your kingdoms will shiver before they fall!"

Chijioke ducked as if to shield himself as Father gave an ugly laugh, pulling the flour sack away and tossing it over his shoulder. He held up the book, black, slimy, decorated with the crossed eye, and those left dazed and watching and recovering in the tent gasped. Even Mr. Morningside went rigid at my side, but then the charm faded. My Changeling powers could not withstand the potency of the pavilion, which revealed all things in their true form.

"Ooh." Mr. Morningside stood up, nodding approvingly. Father's face fell; he must have felt the weight of the book shift and its size adjust, for it was not the black book, it was nothing of consequence at all. "*English Bards and Scotch Reviewers*," the Devil teased. "Is that from my library? Good choice."

The book was hurled into the air, aimed directly at me. I had no time to dodge, and it hit me squarely in the gut. I doubled over with a grunt, Chijioke wrapping his arm around me in support.

"I thought you were a real shit for a moment there," he said with a relieved laugh. "Another work of art, that."

"Don't gloat just yet," I wheezed. "I had half a mind to turn on Henry, and Father is still an ancient god. . . ."

Yes, he was, and we soon learned the consequences of it. Roots exploded through the bottom of the tent, wrapping around our calves and ankles, bolting us to the ground. Father was coming toward us, stalking across the pavilion with his claws flashing and at the ready.

"You ungrateful, faithless deceiver!" he bellowed. His voice filled the entire tent, shaking it, his wrath terrible as the roots began to pull, taking us slowly into the churned earth. He would suffocate us, I thought, but my fate would surely be worse. I had believed him when he told me he was weak, and now I would pay the price for my trust. Chijioke struggled against the roots beside me. I reached into my apron, pulling out the spoon and bending it to my will. If only I could turn it into a knife for just a second, just long enough to cut free of these roots . . . But it was no use. The pavilion was fighting me, keeping me from even the most basic transformation.

Even Mr. Morningside was powerless against the pull of the earth. I could see him trying to blink forward, but when he managed it, another root lashed out, taking hold.

Father was upon us, his cloak of mist and leaves billowing out around him. His black-and-red eyes were only for me, the ugly skull face twisting into a hideous smile.

"You were going to kill me all along!" I screamed, defiant. "Now's your big chance!"

"Yes, foolish child, and I will relish it. . . ."

The mist reached me, cold and paralyzing, wrapping around me as if to choke me while the roots took me into their annihilating embrace. Chijioke clawed at the ground, wheezing, finding no purchase and no strength against the fury of nature. Distantly I smelled smoke, and heard a soft, almost dance-like crackling. Father reared up, claws sparkling; they flashed red and purple and yellow in the fairy lights before they came for my face.

He managed only one swipe, a single talon grazing my cheek, hot blood pouring down my face. But then there came a crack, clear as lightning, and Father froze above us, then collapsed to the side in a heap.

A bronzed young man stood over the fallen body, chest heaving. He was dressed only in rags, heavily scarred, with strange tattoos covering his arms and shoulders. Was I going mad? It wasn't possible. . . .

There was no time to wonder or speak as a gout of red flower bloomed to our left. Then came the smoke. Then the fire.

The pavilion was going up in a blaze.

Chapter
Thirty-Four

moke carpeted the pavilion as the lower edges of the canvas burned away, the flames leaping higher and higher, spreading to the ceiling. The roots went suddenly slack, and I glanced toward Father—he was still out cold. I climbed to my feet, helped up by the mysterious young man who had interceded on our behalf.

The shepherd limped toward us, holding up Sparrow. Finch and the shepherd's dog were well enough to walk, and followed, then aided us in gaining our feet. Cursing, Mr. Morningside ran first toward the front of the pavilion and then changed his mind, joining us again in the middle.

"It's . . . it's too hot. We cannot go that way!"

"Out the back!" Chijioke yelled, gesturing for us to follow. "And if that fails, we take the portal."

"Where does it lead?" I asked as we moved as one slow group past the tables, the stage, and around toward the very end of the pavilion.

"Leeds Castle," Mr. Morningside shouted over the crackle of flames. "Which is only slightly better than burning to death."

The tattooed man at my side grabbed my hand, pulling hard. He was shaking his head, trying to speak to us, but I did not understand the language. It was like nothing I had ever heard before, and I looked to Mr. Morningside helplessly.

"Can you understand him?" I cried.

We had reached the portal, which was little more than a curtained doorway. I heard its pulsing magic behind the fabric, and wondered what lay beyond. But the back of the tent had suffered fewer of the flames, and Finch sprang forward, using his weapon-like arm to slice through the fabric and give us a way out. The smoke was rising, choking us, my eyes and mouth burning from it, heat licking at us from every direction as the fire swept toward this last safe bastion.

"Something, something, something surrounded, I don't know. My Egyptian is not what it used to be," Mr. Morningside muttered, shoving us toward the cut in the tent. "Yes, my friend, the flames *are* surrounding us, good of you to notice. Come on, whatever it is can wait!"

But the stranger was intent on making us listen, drowned out by the fire and Mr. Morningside's calls for us to leave while we still could. We stumbled out into the night, scattering, all of us gasping for clean air as we put distance between us and the blaze. Then I stopped, panicking, whirling back toward the tent.

"No!" I cried. "We have to get Father out!"

Chijioke grabbed me and held me fast as I attempted to rush past and into the fire. "It's going to collapse, it's madness to go back in there."

"He has the book," I said, extricating myself from his grasp. "And he knows where Mary is, he must! He used her hair or her blood to impersonate her. That's how it works. We can't let him burn!"

Perhaps that was what the stranger had been trying to communicate all along, for he took one long look at me and bit his lip before turning and charging back into the pavilion.

"Wait!" I screamed, trying to follow. Chijioke pulled me back again. "He helped us." It was too smoky, too hot, but I knew we could not let Father perish. I had no idea what it would mean for all the creatures of his world, of his kingdom, and I so badly wanted to see Mary again.

"I'm only doing this to get Mary back, the bastard," Chijioke muttered. He pushed me away roughly and was gone, joining the boy in the tent, disappearing into the swallowing flames.

"I won't let them go alone; this matters to us, too," Finch offered, sweeping past us. His body was human for only one more instant before he, too, pushed through the opening in the tent, a flash of gold blinding me before the smoke overcame him.

"Ah. So that's what he meant by surrounded."

Coughing, smoke still eating at my throat, I saw what Mr. Morningside had, that three men had emerged from the darkness, each of them holding a bayoneted rifle. Lee was right; they were more than squirrelly; they were avenging Amelia's honor. I stared into their eyes one by one, and saw only the intent to kill. They were drawn to Coldthistle House, after all. I doubted we were the first to see the ends of those rifles.

"Gentlemen," Mr. Morningside said, spreading his hands wide. Somehow he still looked dapper and self-possessed, even while covered in soot, his hair wild and uncombed. "To what do we owe this pleasure?"

"Where's Amelia?" Mason took a few tiny steps forward, brandishing his weapon.

Behind us, I heard the men calling to one another in the tent. There was a terrible, heart-stopping *crack* as one of the interior beams gave, snapping in half. The moon shone brightly above us, not full but impressively mirrorlike, its light gleaming off the metal barrels of the guns and knives.

"Can you not read, Mr. Breen? She left this place. You may search my pockets; I assure you she is not hiding in there," Mr. Morningside chuckled. "But in all seriousness, this can be resolved without the use of arson or murder."

"Them girls in the house didn't say much neither." It was Samuel Potts, spitting, hammering back his rifle and lifting it to his shoulder. "You're a creepy bunch, eh? Who's to say you didn't bring harm to that girl? We've searched this whole forest, the whole bloody county, she's not 'ere. What'd you lot do with her?"

A shower of fiery canvas and wood exploded into the sky, falling down on us like scarlet rain. They were running out of time in the tent and we were running out of time out here. The shepherd huddled over Sparrow, the dog curled up between them, showings its teeth and growling at the men. That seemed to make the elder Breen nervous, and he kept his gun trained on the dog, waiting for it to lunge.

I was tired and aching, my cheek bloodied, my ankles skinned and raw. My patience felt paper thin, and then it tore, a strangled cry breaking from my throat as Mason took another daring step and poked his bayonet toward me. It nearly stabbed my hand. And I stared down the gun, knowing what came next, remembering the shot as it ripped through Lee, remembering it as if I were living it again. His terrible cry. The sound of his body hitting the floor. The press of his uncle's body against mine as he tried and tried to snuff out my life.

It would be different this time, I told myself, closing my eyes. It had to be.

"Louisa . . ." Mr. Morningside had tried to nudge me but I did not move. I was concentrating, dipping deep into what little vigor remained in my body, finding a last reserve of strength and a welcome burst of inspiration.

To become smaller was pain, most certainly; to become bigger was agony. My skin erupted, bones lengthening, flesh sprouting fur as I became not woman but beast, massive and terrifying to behold, wielding hands with claws and a snout with fangs, and purple eyes that could pierce the night. I had drawn his blood, after all, a lucky shot, a graze of the cheek.

My scream startled the men as much as the transformation, and they fumbled backward, clumsily bumping into one another as the whites of their eyes flashed. I could smell *everything*. Fear, the ash, the smoke, the musk of perspiration and the pine tang of the trees, the sweet grass and the blood welling from Sparrow's wounds. The blood ignited something in this thing I had become, and I gave another jackal's cry, lumbering toward the men, claws ripping at air and then, I hoped, at flesh.

The moonlight felt like silk on my furred body as I sprang into violence. It was exhilarating even as it was exhausting. They lost their footing as I charged, and I tore into Samuel Potts first, clawing a gash in his chest that exposed bone to starlight. More blood, and more. This form could not get enough of the rich, coppery smell. Pain seared across my left side, and I yelped, spinning, batting Mason back as his bayonet sank into my hide. There was another stab and I flailed blindly, catching the elder Breen on the chin. He flew backward, but not before discharging his weapon. The bullet was fire in my chest, the blood that poured out of the hole hotter still.

My strength was failing, my grasp on the transformation slipping. Another stab. Another. I heard Mr. Morningside bellowing at my back and I saw him, briefly, charging at the men when all their bullets had been discharged. My vision blurred, trees becoming sky becoming moon. It was so itchy all over, so warm, but then, horribly, very cold.

I reeled, stumbling, falling from hind legs to fore, and then slowly I felt small again and the pain was worse, much worse, not endured by the body of a massive beast but that of a young and frail girl.

There were voices all around me, a man's cry of pain, and then another. I rolled onto my back and stared up longingly at the sky. The moon was so, so bright and beautiful. I tried to reach up and touch it, but there was no way to move my arm.

Mr. Morningside was suddenly at my side, trying to herd me into his lap. He shook me once, hand on my cheek.

"Stay with me, Louisa. Stay here."

No, I thought, closing my eyes into restless bliss. It's time.

Chapter
Thirty-Five

"Are you lost, child?"

I had read about jungles but quite obviously had never seen one with my eyes. The humidity came first, like a damp caress, and then the sound of water playing over stones. Fronds arced above my head, explosively bright flowers lining the ground in such abundance I could never have counted them all.

The voice. I knew that voice. I turned toward it, away from the glory of the jungle's palms and blossoms, and found the source of the voice and the water. There was a waterfall, an entire wall of waterfalls, and a woman walking toward me. She was the most beautiful person I had ever seen, tall and strong, with well-muscled arms and thick legs. Her skin was dark purple, so dark it was almost black. Her hair, pink and long, was coiled and pinned into a heart shape on her head, the plaits dotted with jewels. Most incredible of all were her eyes, the predominant pair wide and pink, though she had eight eyes in total, with smaller ones curving up along her cheekbones.

"Are you lost?" she asked me again. Her voice was like music, melodic and soft, a voice I had heard before when it came from my bones.

I moved toward her as if reeled in on a line. I wanted to be near her. *Be* her.

"My feet are on the path," I told her. "At least . . . I thought so. Where is this?"

"You will only be staying for a little while," she said with a warm smile. She towered over me as she approached, dressed in a simple pale dress, the color of summer peaches. "But do not worry, dear one, you will see me again."

"I don't want to go," I said. Vaguely, I knew that wherever I was supposed to be was not a happy place. Was this the Dusk Lands? If so, it did not seem so bad after all. Staying there, in that paradise, sounded much, much better. "Can I not stay here with you?"

She laughed, scrunching up her many eyes playfully. "Oh, no, for this is nowhere, an in-between place, and no home for a young girl such as you." Her ears perked up and she tilted her head to the side, sighing. "Ah. Well. It is almost time for you to go, but you must remember one thing when you awake. . . ."

"The other place is ugly. I don't want to go."

Again she giggled at me and shook her head. "You will make it more beautiful; that is your path. And remember this, dear one: do not forget me. See this," and here she pressed one finger to the swollen bite on my hand. "See this and remember."

"I . . . will try," I said. "How do you know it is time for me to go?"

Her image began to waver as if it were only a mirage. I took in one last smile from her as she looked sadly toward the water-fall. "Because I sense his power again, and if they have done what I think they have, that means you have gained a gift and a burden. Remember, dear one, remember . . ."

"By God, it worked! You absolute genius, it worked!"

Breath flooded into me hard enough to make me choke. I sat up, coughing uncontrollably, spitting up so much pink foam that the men around me recoiled in unison. I was alive—had I died? Where had I gone? I looked around, realizing whatever I had just seen was already fading from memory. No matter how much I tried, I could not think of even a single detail.

I was lying in the grass still, gazing up at a dozen faces lit by the moon. Mr. Morningside was there to my left, hugging Chijioke with bruising enthusiasm. All of the familiar faces were there: Mrs. Haylam, Poppy, Lee, Finch, and the dark-skinned stranger. Only the shepherd and Sparrow were missing. And Father. Where was Father?

Putting a hand to my chest, I coughed one last time and studied my fingers. They came away from my apron stained with blood and pink froth. Someone had draped a jacket over me for modesty.

"I was dead," I said weakly. "How . . ."

My eyes drifted to Mrs. Haylam, but she simply shook her head.

"Chijioke ferried your soul back into your body before it could escape," Mr. Morningside told me with a gentle smile. His hair was even wilder now, and flecked with blood. "Although it took, well . . . How do you feel?"

"Strange," I murmured. Very strange. I was me, certainly, but I felt different, stronger, as if just flexing my hand or moving my head was an invigorating exercise. The urge to transform everything in the near vicinity was there, too, and a sense that I was seeing more clearly, with new precision. And there was a pit in my stomach, one made of anger and regret, and deep, dark memories. The grass seemed to bend toward me, as if responding to my hovered palm.

Before I could say another word, Finch sprang to his feet. He stumbled away from us, his mouth covered with one hand as he pointed an accusing finger first at Chijioke and then at Mr. Morningside. "What have you been doing, Henry? This boy . . . he can ferry souls to other bodies? This is not your power to command! Those souls are meant to move on, to embrace death. . . ."

Mr. Morningside and Chijioke shared a look, one I could not fully read but one that did not seem optimistic, and then in a blink both men rose and gave chase. But Finch was gone, fleeing, lifting into the air and out of their reach before they could get to him.

They returned slowly, Chijioke eyeing Mr. Morningside with his lip between his teeth. "We should not let him escape with that knowledge. . . ."

"It is what it is," Mr. Morningside said grimly. "The truth was bound to out eventually."

I hardly knew what they meant, and could not muster the energy to untangle the knot.

"Where is Father?" I asked softly, casting around for where he might be. "Did you save him in time?"

"That's . . . the tricky bit," Chijioke said. He was having trouble meeting my eye. "It was the only way to bring you back, Louisa."

Mr. Morningside took my hand before the panic really gripped me. My eyes flew to his and my mouth dropped open. No. *No.* They couldn't have done it. How could they have done it?

"Where is Mary?" he asked gently.

And I knew. At once I knew. "Oh God," I whispered, closing my eyes tightly. "She's in the fortress. In the First City. He imprisoned her there after she returned from the Dusk Lands. It's like I can feel parts of him in me . . . his thoughts, or memories, bits and pieces of it." Tears bubbled up, spilling in hot torrents down my face. I squeezed his hand, willing it not to be true, willing my father's blighted soul out of my body. "I need . . . I need to think. I must be alone."

"That's not a good idea right now," Chijioke said, intervening when I tried to stand. My balance almost gave out, but then I found my feet. "You shouldn't be alone until the shock wears off."

"And who is responsible for that shock?" I shot back, furious. Softly, Lee cleared his throat and I half sobbed, half sighed. "Of course. Of course you would let him make the decision."

"Louisa, it only seemed fair," Mr. Morningside told me, placing a careful hand on my back. I shrugged away. "You must not be cross with him. This is a good thing, yes? The book is preserved, Mary is found, and the soul of your people has a new start. A second chance."

I nodded, knowing all of that was true and right, knowing also that Lee deserved to decide my fate as I had decided his. And yet . . . And yet . . . It hurt. Maybe it would hurt less upon reflection, but I doubted it.

"I'm sorry."

The stranger had spoken, his voice rough but not unfriendly. I turned gradually to face him, taking in his huge purple eyes and markings. More than that, I saw the still healing wound on his cheek, a slim red line, a line that might be left by a bullet grazing a cheek. But I understood him—how? Of course. I sighed. With my father's soul had come his knowledge and his power.

The language sprang to my lips as easily as English. "I know you," I said wearily. "You were Bennu the Runner's companion; you guarded him from Egypt to the First City. You're an Abediew, a moon jackal called Khent. But how did you survive this long?"

"I slept when the kingdom slept, when Father slept," he said, scratching at the back of his neck sheepishly. "I woke not long ago to find the fortress frozen in time, everything as it was, and yet Father was gone. Tracking him took many months, many, many months, and when I at last found him it was too late. I was . . . too late to warn you."

"That's why you only attacked Mary in the woods," I murmured. "Because it was him." My hand slid into my apron pocket, closing over the bent spoon. "And you tried to return my spoon. With . . . an apology. Of a kind."

He ducked his head, eyes as furtive and gentle as a chided dog's. "I do not yet speak your language well, but I will learn."

"You should rest, lass; your body and soul need to mend," Chijioke said. There was a bird cradled in his hand, not dead but weakened. Was that where my soul had been while they found a way to entwine it with Father's? I felt ill, and yes, as he said, exhausted. I longed for bed but dreaded utterly what my dreams had in store.

Chapter Thirty-Six

"Drawing up more contracts?"

For once in a long while, I found Mr. Morningside's office door wide open. I waited just outside, watching him bending over his desk while he wrote languidly across a fresh parchment. He smiled but did not look up from his work.

"Not this time, dear Louisa. This is a bit of important correspondence, a letter I was hoping you might deliver to an acquaintance in London."

We had not spoken outright about my leaving, but the knowledge of it was in the air. Everybody seemed to know I would go even before I said a word about it. Perhaps Poppy had glimpsed me packing my meager belongings and sorting through Father's possessions, and that was indication enough that the rumors should start. I didn't mind.

"Here." Mr. Morningside finished the letter swiftly. It was not very long, and he closed it with one of his flourishing signatures, then dashed it with drying powder and folded it. "I would say this isn't urgent, but please give it your full attention when you get to the city. Something has not sat right with me for quite some time."

The folded note was still warm from his hand when I took it and tucked it into the folds of my skirts. "Who is it for?"

Mr. Morningside leaned casually against the edge of his desk and coaxed one of his birds onto his hand. It was a dainty finch, and it climbed onto his fingers with a soft cheep. I don't know if it was nostalgia or anxiety, but I felt suddenly sad and a little afraid. Was this the last time I would stand in this strange office and smell the scent of his books, tea, and the dusty pleasant perfume of so many fluttering wings?

"I'd like for you to visit the shop where I purchased Bennu's journal. I want more information about who brought it in initially."

Nodding, I felt another wave of fear. Leaving had felt like a way to extricate myself from all the confusing mysteries of the house, but it seemed the mysteries would never end. This would be one last favor, I told myself, and then I would be done. "I thought about that, too. How did the journal leave the First City? Someone must have taken it, perhaps a thief or . . ."

"Yes." Mr. Morningside looked distracted, his eyes fixed over my shoulder. "Let us hope it was a thief. My alternate theories are far less harmless."

I turned to find that Chijioke and Poppy had been summoned. The little girl with the marked face had her hands deep in her pockets and swung side to side, grinning up at me. Chijioke, by contrast, could not even for an instant meet my eye.

"Well. The time has come, Louisa, to discuss the dissolution of their work contracts," Mr. Morningside said, striding briskly into the foyer and standing between us.

At once, Poppy's face fell and she hid her eyes behind spread fingers. "You're . . . You're going to make us leave? But why?"

"Did we do something wrong?" Chijioke quickly added.

"Wrong? No, not at all. You have both been exemplary employees," he said.

"Then why must we go?" Poppy whined, but she sounded on the verge of tears. "Who else would take me in?"

I cleared my throat with some difficulty and knelt, but she did not come nearer. "Why, I would take you in. I have some money available to me now, Poppy, and I wanted all of you to come with me. You don't have to stay in this wretched place anymore; you don't have to kill people or do Mrs. Haylam's bidding. And you, Chijioke, would you not like a house of your own?"

He chuckled and crossed his thick arms across his chest. "Wait, lass, is this your idea of a gift?"

"It isn't wretched here!" Poppy scampered back and flung her arms around Chijioke's leg, hugging it. "This is my home. It's where I belong!"

"That's not true," I said, but I could already tell this was a battle I was going to lose. "Just because it's the only thing you know doesn't mean it's the best place in the whole world for you."

"We *like* it here, Louisa. I like it here." Chijioke shook his head, giving me a pitying smile. He put his hand reassuringly on Poppy's little shoulder. "I've no desire to live in a city. I wouldn't be able to breathe there."

I stood and went quiet, saying nothing until Mr. Morningside ushered Poppy toward the steps leading up and out of the cellar. "There is no need to fuss, Poppy. I am not sending you away, only allowing Louisa here to collect on her end of our bargain."

Chijioke took the girl's hand and pulled her toward the stairs, giving me a glance over his shoulder. "I'm sorry, lass. No offense, but you might've asked. I would have gladly told you I've no desire to leave."

And then they were gone. I had the letter in my hand still but it felt like nothing, like I held nothing at all, and that that emptiness was my reward in all of this.

"Lee?" I heard myself say softly.

"Mrs. Haylam knows of no way to untether him from the Black Elbion. Leaving its circle of power would kill him, Louisa." Mr. Morningside took a few strides toward the stairs, and waited to speak again until the door up above us latched. He looked at me sidelong and sighed. "You know, I almost wish they had agreed to leave with you. I do so fear what the shepherd might do next."

Fighting the numb feeling in my body, I squinted and watched him pace. "What do you mean?"

"Finch . . . What he saw . . . They were never to know that Chijioke has the ability to transfer souls from vessel to vessel. I'm meant to be banishing the souls here to death permanently.

Instead, I may have . . . tweaked the rules. Slightly." He ruffled his dark hair and puffed out his lips. "I would be more nervous, but for having you on my side."

"Your *side*?" I laughed, mirthless. "I will deliver this letter for you, but then I want nothing to do with you."

His face went still and unreadable, like one of his flickering masks from the pavilion. "You might now have the luxury of money, Louisa, but you do not have the luxury of anonymity. The shepherd will hear the story from Finch. He will know just as I do that you have Father's soul inside you. Pretend you can run all you like, girl, but ancient wheels have a way of turning, and old, ugly wounds have a way of opening up again."

I shook my head. No, no . . . he was wrong. I could go to London and live a normal life. I could free Mary and then find a way to be myself again.

"I suppose time will tell which of us is right," I told him softly.

He walked by me and took hold of his door, closing it after him as he began to leave me standing alone in the foyer. "Time will tell indeed, Louisa, but I do not think we will have all that long to wait."

At least in one respect he was correct; time really did move swiftly as my departure from Coldthistle approached. As ready as I was to leave, I felt ambushed by it. This time, there was none of the hope that I would be leaving with my odd friends in tow, which made the leaving all the more difficult. On that fateful day, a carriage waited outside for me, and with it, the promise of a new life. I had more possessions now than I had when I arrived, inheriting Father's bags and leather case, and the cage with his pink-and-purple spider.

Poppy had wanted me to leave it behind, eager for another pet. Bartholomew panted at my side, leaning against my legs as I waited for Mr. Morningside to emerge from his green door. My heart felt heavy, the urge to cry pressing constantly at the back of my eyes and throat. Why did it feel so hard to leave? I alternately hated and tolerated this place, but now . . . now . . .

"You will take care of that spider, won't you, Louisa? It looks very rare," Poppy said, crouching down to look into the cage. The spider lifted one leg as if in greeting.

Whenever I looked at the thing or someone mentioned it, my head hurt, as if there was some memory trapped in there, punching its way out. I would remember eventually, I thought, for Father's influence came and went. It would take time, I decided, to sort through his knowledge and memories, to find a balance between the anger that had defined him and the struggles that had defined me.

"You must give her a name!" Poppy said excitedly, jumping up.

"Hm," I replied, tapping my lower lip. "How about Mab?"

"Like the queen," she breathed. "I like it!"

Then she was flinging herself at me, hugging me hard around

the waist until I returned it. And I did in earnest, finding I would miss her bouncing around on my bed, waking me from ugly dreams. I scruffed Bartholomew's ears and he whined, as if offended I was trading in one guardian hound for another.

"This won't be the last time we meet," I told the dog, patting his head. "Something makes me sure of that."

"Well, I will guarantee it." Mr. Morningside had arrived, sparkling as always in a pristine ice-gray suit and silver cravat. He sidled up to me and bowed, which was his habit now, and extremely irritating. He must have noticed the sour expression on my face. "You're more than a maid now, Louisa; you're a young woman with a fortune in her pocket and the soul of an ancient god. You will soon have a great house in London. You will experience the Season. This time next year you'll have marriage proposals coming out of your ears. So please, for the love of all that is dark and disastrous, learn to enjoy a man bowing to you."

I couldn't help but smile, and even allowed him to take my hand and kiss it. He then straightened and carefully reached for the pin on my frock, the one that had given me freedom. With a sigh, he undid the clasp and pulled it free, showing it to me in his manicured palm.

"You know I have to take this. You never did finish all the journal translations. A deal is a deal, Louisa."

"Because you told me to get to the end," I said, rolling my eyes.

"Yes, I did," Henry murmured, a bit sadly. He avoided looking at me, pouring his focus into the pin. "Yes, I did. And now I think again we have come to the end." Brightening, he closed his fingers around the pin and tucked it into his pocket. "Until we meet again, that is. Chijioke will drive you as far as Malton. I trust you won't get in any trouble there?"

I gave a thin laugh and nodded toward the staircase behind him. "I will not be alone."

They had dressed Khent in one of Mr. Morningside's old suits, and he looked exceedingly uncomfortable in it. To the rest of us, however, he looked quite dashing, groomed, wounds seen to, his beard shaved off to accommodate more modern English tastes. He had a pack over his shoulder, one of my bags, and a sturdy shawled coat under one arm in the event of rain.

"Do look out for fleas," Mr. Morningside said with a wink, strolling toward the kitchen door, where Mrs. Haylam had appeared. I had no idea how long she had been watching us, but her one good eye was distant, hooded. She had been largely silent during my recuperation, only drawing breath to complain that she was shorthanded again and to bitterly admit that because I had died, the book no longer held sway over me.

The marks on my fingers had faded away.

Khent joined me in the foyer, picking up another bag and looking as if with his size and bulk he could carry all of them without strain. He took up a polite but vigilant stance behind me and to the left. I picked up the spider cage and one bag, hesitating. Lee had never appeared, but then, I would never dream of asking him to.

"Well," I said, drawing in a deep breath. "Thank you for . . . for everything you've done. I don't think this is good-bye, and truly, in my heart of hearts, I hope it isn't. When we retrieve Mary, I will give her your wishes. You may all be seeing her shortly if she decides to return."

"Oh, I hope she does!" Poppy squeezed her hands together as if in prayer. "And if not, you had better let us come see you, Louisa. I want to go to London! To the First City! All of it!"

Mrs. Haylam grunted. I could tell she was eager for me to go. After all, I had upset the balance. There was an order to things at Coldthistle House, an order I never seemed to understand. Mr. Morningside had been bending the rules he and the shepherd had set down, and I couldn't help but wonder if the trial was only the beginning of his problems. That it might put my friends in danger, and that they had refused to join me in leaving, was the hardest jab to bear.

"Of course you can visit," I chuckled. "Anyone is welcome, only, I have no idea where I will go. I must see to Mary, but then . . ." I shrugged. Anything was possible, wasn't it? "I will write."

"Yes, you will." Mr. Morningside winked at me from the kitchen door. "Now, be off, or Chijioke will be a bearded old man by the time he returns."

Now that it came to it, I did not want to go. But I picked up the last of my things and turned, following Khent out the door. It felt odd to be leaving with someone I hardly knew, but having read what he had done for Bennu and knowing that he had tried to warn me against Father, endeared me to him for now. It was a relief, at least, to have company, to forge ahead with this new life and this new soul aided by someone who knew the ins and outs of our curious world.

"Good-bye!" Poppy called after us. She and Bartholomew chased me to the door, waving like mad. The dog bayed, throwing his nose into the air as he wailed. "Write soon! Very soon! In fact, write when you get to Malton, and then every town after that. . . ."

"She's saying good-bye," I told Khent in his language. "She's, um, very precocious."

He grinned and gave me a sidelong look. "That was obvious in any language."

Chijioke met us at the carriage, pulling me into a bone-crushing embrace before hauling my bags onto the driver's seat. When he was done, he took a small wooden fish out of his pocket and gave it to me while Khent secured our bags for the trip.

"For Mary," he said, blushingly. "The real one."

"She'll love it," I replied, tucking the fish away. "You will know the moment we find her."

Nodding, Chijioke gave me a quick kiss on the cheek, then leapt up into the driver's box. "We can say good-bye at Malton, then I can do my weepies on the way back without you there to tease me."

I was about to take the fish and the spider cage with me into the carriage, but I heard a soft scuffle on the stones behind me. Like a shadow, Lee had come, emerging from the foyer headfirst, as if peering out to see if I had already gone. I lifted my things up for Khent to take, my hand on the door, my body twisted around to face Coldthistle.

Lee walked over to me slowly, eyes darting. Foolishly, I had thought that we were even, that now that he had decided my fate we would share some kind of intense and unique bond. But it was not so. And it was unfair to expect parity, especially when his resurrection had come with a price and so much pain, and mine had resulted only in greater power and understanding. It simply wasn't fair, and my heart ached for the things that could have been between us were life kinder.

On a whim, I reached out my hand toward him and he took it, his fingers cold, his posture careful. I had no idea what to say, the immensity of feeling swelling in my heart almost too much to bear, choking me. There is what the heart wants and what reality demands, and they are often as incompatible as snow and fire.

I took the spoon out from the chain around my neck. It had been repaired by Chijioke only recently, but I pulled the necklace off and placed it in his palm, closing his fingers around it.

"This has brought me such exceedingly bad luck," I told

him in a whisper, tears making my voice ragged. "Please chuck it off the roof or bury it in a deep, dark hole. For both our sakes."

Lee gifted me a small smile and nodded. "I thought I was so gallant, stealing that thing for you. My first act of larceny. No wonder it's cursed."

"Take care of yourself, Lee, please. I'm sorry."

He shoved the spoon into his pocket and pulled his shoulders back. "Don't be, Louisa. I'm not sorry we met, but I am sorry to see you go."

Then he hugged me, as suddenly as he had in the library, and I sank into that feeling for as long as propriety allowed. When it was over, he left in a hurry, disappearing into the house with a shadow's lively, cunning step.

It was time to go.

Khent helped me up into the carriage, holding out his huge hand for me to take and then following me inside. It was humid and quiet inside, Mab the spider sitting between us in her cage. Chijioke cracked the whip. I sighed and sat back in my seat, and watched Poppy chase us down the drive as we at last left Coldthistle House behind. I closed my eyes, listening to the gravel crunch under the wheels, feeling as if the mansion was watching me go, feeling as if it was giving a silent scream of frustration that I had managed to escape.

I did not know if I was free of the place, but I was on a path, and that was something. The sprawling parapets and long black windows of the house grew more distant as we made our way along the lawn.

The farther we went, the better I felt, as if a fog were lifting from all around me. I leaned against the window, memorizing the last of it, wondering if the melancholy weight in my heart would ever lift.

My eye caught on something as we passed from field to forest and turned toward the main dirt road. They had burned Father's body, a tiny black sapling already sprouting where the ashes lay. A black mist hung around it, and as I looked, the clouds brought on the wind opened up and a hard rain began to fall, a rolling roar of thunder threatening from a distance.

Epilogue

The driving wind and rain whipped hard at our faces. Even without Bennu's journals, my feet would have carried me to this place, a path I knew in my bones now that Father's soul was entwined with mine. To other eyes, human eyes, the road would not reveal itself, hidden as it was by tangle upon tangle of thick trees and shrubs, the path rising from the forest floor up to a long rock causeway carpeted with water. That water became falls, the rushing sound at our feet as noisy as the storm above.

"Watch your step!" Khent called over the commotion. The stones were slippery, treacherous, but I navigated deftly, as if I had walked the way a hundred times or more.

Through the wall of the downpour I saw a shape emerge, taller and grander than the trees to our right. To our left, the falls plunged toward a roaring froth of foam and sharp boulders.

The shape rising above us looked like a giant wicker basket, just like the one described by Bennu in his journals. Khent had not arrived at the city through this route, but he had taken a similar path when he fled, and his bare feet hopped across the wet stones with more grace than mine. He took my hand as the path ahead widened and became steep. If I squinted past my scarf and the rain, I could just see the outline of a pair of huge silvery doors.

"Do you think more people inside will have woken up?" I asked him. We spoke in his native language, but his English was improving by the day.

Khent shook his head, his face obscured by a sturdy hood and cowl. "I have no idea. Who can tell what Father's death and resurrection will have done?"

That felt like the repeated refrain of these recent days. Chaos. Uncertainty. Outside the walls of Coldthistle I felt almost naked, as if some vital part of me had been stripped away. I wondered if my confidence would ever really come. Whatever the case, I pushed on toward the doors, helped by Khent's steadying grip.

We reached the entrance to the city, the silver doors choked with vines and moss, the intricate carvings almost completely obliterated. I put my hand on the doors, expecting nothing, only to feel at once the old mechanisms engage, a loud, long creak rattling through my body. My instinct was to duck, but I held fast, breathing hard, pushing just a little and finding that the door gave inward. We dodged inside, and the moment we did, the storm abruptly ended.

Within, the air was warm and moist and fragrant, stifling but beautiful. Birdsong echoed off the round walls, the open courtyard similar to the shape and size of a coliseum. I gazed about, awestruck, feeling at once terrified and at home. *Home.* I did not intend to stay, and I did not know if I belonged there or if Father's soul was simply reacting to the familiar grounds, but for a moment, I relished that warm and welcoming sensation.

"Louisa?"

I turned at the sound of her voice. It was a little thing, but so, so comforting. Mary called my name again, stronger this time, and I ran toward her across the green stones. Archways splintered off in every direction, leading to what I could not see, and in the middle of the courtyard were the stairs leading downward that Bennu had described. The city felt utterly empty, as if only we three existed inside of it. Mary stood from where she had been sitting, her skirts dirtied and torn. When we met and embraced, my face was wet now from tears and not the rain.

"You came! You're here! How could you be here?" she cried, squeezing me hard.

I pulled back and sighed, noticing the obvious chunk of hair missing from the right side of her brown locks. "There is so much to explain. . . . So much . . ." I was breathless, elated.

"Oh, but you're soaked!" Mary said, clucking her tongue. "You must be near freezing!"

"Hush and stop worrying about me," I laughed, and waved her off. It was so good to see her face again, her shining eyes and freckles, and know that it was truly her. "You're the one I'm concerned about. . . . How did you stand to be here all this time?"

"I tried to leave, I truly did." With a frown, she gestured to the doors behind us. They had closed again. "Louisa, there is no way out! The walls are too high, and there are things that stir below, things I can only hear but do not wish to meet."

"I scaled the walls but only as a beast, else I would not have had the agility for it." Khent stepped forward at that, grimacing, and touched my shoulder gently before heading resolutely toward the staircase. "More folk must be waking," he said, and I watched Mary stare at him, dumbfounded. "Stay here until I can make certain they are . . . amenable."

"You'll be careful." I did not mean for it to sound like an order, but it was.

Khent grinned and tossed his head. "They will give me no trouble."

For a moment Mary was quiet, watching him go, her brow furrowed. "How did you get here, Louisa? There was an awful man who took me from Waterford before I could think a single thought. He took my hair and locked me up in here and would not tell me anything! And who is that person? What language are you speaking?"

I put my arm through hers and shrugged. Where to begin? "As I told you, there is so much to explain, but we should not do it here. I think it's a story for later, when we are all safe and dry and warm. It would be best told far, far away from here."

"Oh, please," she cried. "Please. It has been so boring waiting here. . . . It felt like an eternity. There are only so many times you can recite poems and ditties to yourself before it all becomes a sad jumble."

"Well, what I have to tell you is certainly not boring," I

laughed. Then, remembering what I had carried so far and through so much wind and rain, I dug into my pocket and came up with a little carved wooden fish. "Here," I said. "Chijioke made this for you."

"For me?" Her cheeks blossomed with color. She took the fish and closed her fingers around it, blinking hard. "And . . . does his little gift come up in this wild story of yours?"

From below, I heard a disarmingly hearty laugh. Perhaps Khent had not encountered trouble after all. I steered Mary slowly toward the stairs and waited, looking down into the darkness and wondering where exactly we would all go, where exactly I would find a home.

"It does," I told her. "I only wonder if you will believe it all."

Acknowledgments

This was not by any means an easy book to write, and there are many people who need thanking. Firstly, Andrew and the team at HarperCollins, who demonstrated saintly patience while I finished and finished and finished. Olivia Russo organized such wonderful travel opportunities to promote the series, and did so like a total rock star. I also want to acknowledge the design team, who put so much time and energy into making *House of Furies* look and feel beautiful. Daniel Danger and Iris Compiet did amazingly, of course, and I'm grateful to them for their creativity and passion. A huge thanks to my agent, Kate McKean, who continues to be the rock of my professional life. Matt Grigsby and Oliver Ash Northern, thank you for helping me make some wickedly cool promotional materials for the series.

To my family—you all know how much you mean to me, and the love and compassion you showed me while I raced to write and rewrite this book is nothing short of amazing. Next time let's not have a family emergency while I'm in deadline hell, okay?

Brent Roberts was instrumental in helping with aspects of Christian lore, and Amanda Raths provided major help with the Egyptian translations; thank you both for your generous assistance.

Image Credits

Victorian border on pages ii, iii, vi, vii, 1, 8, 18, 25, 31, 40, 50, 57, 69, 80, 91, 102, 109, 119, 128, 139, 154, 169, 179, 194, 205, 218, 230, 242, 262, 276, 288, 298, 308, 316, 328, 340, 355, 369, 381, 389, 397, 411, Teaser pages 1 and 5 © 2018 by iStock / Getty Images.

Wall texture on pages ii, iii, vi, vii, 1, 8, 18, 25, 31, 40, 50, 57, 69, 80, 91, 102, 109, 119, 128, 139, 154, 169, 179, 194, 205, 218, 230, 242, 262, 276, 288, 298, 308, 316, 328, 340, 355, 369, 381, 389, 397, 411, Teaser page 4 © 2018 by iStock / Getty Images.

Rusty wall on pages 7, 30, 68, 108, 168, 204, 261, 307, 354, Teaser page 4 © 2018 by iStock / Getty Images.

Photographs on pages 7, 30, 68, 108, 168, 204, 261, 307, 354, Teaser page 4 © 2018 by Shutterstock.

Illustrations on pages 2, 113, 155, 180, 249, 277, 341 by Iris Compiet.

Turn the page for a sneak peek at the final hair-raising novel

in the **HOUSE OF FURIES** series . . .

The war of the ancients is nigh—
and Louisa must decide whose side she's on.

Prologue

t was becoming less and less obvious where I stopped and he began. My father's dreams had become my own, and like his dark heart, they were ever terrible and troubling. I dreaded sleep yet fell into it with ease, a deep and dreamy slumber consuming me the moment my head touched the pillow. At times, in these dreams, I wandered the past—my past and his—watching as an observer, as an outsider judging my own choices and his.

But on that night, I explored a seemingly endless hall, high and arched as a cathedral, the walls and floor made of a black, twinkling glass. And while there was no explanation for it, I knew this place, and my presence in it, to be real. Though I slid through it in my dream, it felt as solid and true as the bones in my body and the blood in my veins. A real, true place, hidden somewhere, a church of starlight and mystery, with a tremendous secret churning like the determined and bloody chambers of a heart.

When I walked in that hall, I walked with my father's footsteps, his soul's presence in my body, his voice never far from my thoughts, as if he were there beside me, smirking, a question on his lips.

Are you lost, child?

I did not feel lost in that dream—in that strange, endless corridor. There was something at the end of the hall waiting for me, an answer, or perhaps an ending. I moved toward it with purpose and a trembling in my hands, for no ending came easily and no answer was ever given without a price.

Chapter One

was not strictly to blame for what happened at the Thrampton ball, though all those who witnessed the aftermath might claim otherwise. It would be hard to argue with their logic, considering I emerged from the house covered head to foot in blood, a small, dull knife still clutched in one hand. For a moment, it had been a sword, at times a shield; it became whatever tool of defense I needed it to be, shifting from honed to blunt at my will, bent by my Changeling powers—now more potent than ever.

For I harbored a god spirit in my body. It had been the thing used to resurrect me, and that was how all this trouble began in the first place. That was how a perfectly charming ballroom became an abattoir, a scene of horror and gore, guts in the punch bowl, screams of anguish splattered across the fine cucumber sandwiches.

I had not attended the Thrampton ball expecting to be ambushed, though there had been signs that something in London was terribly amiss.

The evening of the ball, I looked down at the stoop, littered with dozens of dead spiders, and instinctively reached behind me for the door. There was no mistaking what this meant—somebody with ill intent was watching the house, observing it—and us—closely, and now they were leaving a calling card. Not the polite, sensible sort of card like the one I had left with my long-lost half sister a few weeks prior. No, this was not a kind overture, but a warning. I wondered if it had to do with Mary. When we first arrived in London, she had been using her Dark Fae powers to shield our presence and the house. It was a precaution born of my anxious sense that we would never make a clean getaway from Coldthistle House. Too many dark events had transpired there, and she helpfully agreed to use the lightest shielding she could manage, a sort of mirage that would make us bleed into the neighborhood like a couple of boring, native residents.

But after weeks of all quiet, I had told her the protection was no longer necessary. How wrong I had been.

Toeing aside a few of the dead spiders, I flicked my eyes up to the gated perimeter of the lawn, seeking anything ominous that did not belong. But the fog was thick, and all those who were out late on the town were concealed by heavy black coats or gliding along in carriages, the mist making those carriages look as if they were pulled by nothing at all. By ghosts. I went back inside with heavy steps.

London was not at all what I'd expected.

For all its terror and strangeness, there had been a kind of peace at Coldthistle House. I would wake to near silence or the soft bustle of the staff and guests rousing, and I would sleep to the rumbling snores of Bartholomew the dog, or Poppy's voice as she sang herself odd lullabies, coaxing us both into dreams.

There was never peace in London, a fact I did not mind, as the traffic of the horses, cries of stray cats, and merry singing of the drunks wandering home at night made for distracting company. The noise kept me from delving too deeply into my thoughts and fears. It kept me from pursuing the growing number of voices in my head, those that had come almost the moment after my friend and former colleague Chijioke diverted my father's godlike spirit into my body, saving me from death.

Aye, the differences, the changes, did not bother me until the dead things began arriving on my doorstep.

The first had come the week before, a small and dusty bird wrapped in a handkerchief. Mary had been the one to discover it, shrieking as she opened the door to retrieve our wood and fuel delivery. The package had come, but the bird was on top of it, its coal-black legs curled up, its toes splayed horribly, part of the beak missing as if snapped away, a silver spoon impaled through its breast.

The second unwelcome surprise had come only two days later, while we entertained our neighbors, Mr. Kinton and his daughters. We had been enjoying a spirited round of whist, and then there was a knock at the door, and Khent excused himself to help our servant, Agnes, answer. They were gone for too long, prompting me also to take my leave from the game and join them in the front hall. Another strange thing had turned up—this time it was a child's toy in the shape of a shaggy black dog, its head torn off and left with the body. Khent and I had shared a glance that Agnes couldn't possibly understand.

I had a feeling we would share it again tonight when I retreated back into the house. But inside I found neither Khent nor Agnes, but Mary, her curling, reddish-brown hair braided neatly up, away from her ears and in a crown over her head. She wore a fine white gown and a green shawl draped over her shoulders. She rushed toward me, reading at once the pale fury on my face—I had only gone out to get a breath of air, nervous to attend my first social dance in the Ton.

"It's happened again, hasn't it?" she asked, her pallor matching mine.

Khent emerged from the shadows near the staircase, dressed for the dance in a becoming black suit and cloaked coat that hid his many tattoos and scars.

"What was it this time?" His low voice trembled with disgust.

"Spiders." My eyes slid between the two of them, and I walked to the staircase, leaning on the banister. I suddenly felt faint, and the whispering voices in my head rose like a restless tide. "A bird with the spoon, a dead dog, spiders . . . These aren't random warnings, they're messages from someone who knows our business here."

"I shouldn't have stopped shielding us, it must have been doing some good after all. Perhaps we shouldn't attend the ball," Mary said, biting her lip. "We could be in danger."

"Then we would be safer away from this house," I suggested. The hall glowed pleasantly with the sconces lit for the evening, a lingering scent of roast and baked bread remaining from our supper. Agnes and our housekeeper, Silvia, chatted in the kitchen, their work done for the day.

"I will fetch a broom," I added. "The spiders will frighten them."

"They have a right to know something is amiss," Mary replied, following me as I went to a small cupboard in the hall pantry. "Someone is trying to frighten you. Us."

"I know that, and I *will* tell them, Mary, just . . . in a manner that doesn't involve them stepping all over a pile of dead spiders."

I had snapped at her. She recoiled and slipped back toward the foyer, hugging herself tightly with the shawl. It had been happening more lately, my temper fraying, the endless battle to quiet the voices in my head turning me into an exhausted meanie.

"That was unfair, Mary, I apologize. I'm simply upset." And exhausted. And overwhelmed. I found the broom, carrying it quickly to the door and outside, glancing around again for signs of life on our property as I brushed the tiny black bodies into the hedges.

"As you should be," Khent grunted. His English had improved so much over our travels and subsequent move to London that he had only a trace of an accent. His penmanship still needed considerable attention, but that was far less of a priority. "From now on I will sleep outside. They will not feel so bold and clever when I catch them red-handed."

"That's absurd," I said, closing the door again and hiding away from the chilly fog. "We can take turns, can we not? Keeping some kind of watch."

"It almost makes me miss the Residents," Mary whispered, referring to the shadowy monster creatures that roamed our old home. They had kept a constant vigil, though I had from time to time managed to evade them. "I'm sure Mrs. Haylam would know some magicks to keep us safer —wards or something."

"We don't need wards," Khent replied, taking the broom from me and returning it to the cupboard. "We have . . ." He cleared his throat, checking over his shoulder to make certain Agnes and Silvia were not near enough to overhear. "Me. We have my nose. You've been kind enough to let me stay in this house, shelter me. Let me do something in return. Besides, you are . . ."

He was staring at me so intently, it almost made my skin itch. His unusual eyes pulsed with purple light, a side effect of his condition, the ability to shift into a jackal-like giant with razor claws and fangs. Then it dawned on me what he meant— me. My voices. My problem.

"Finish your thought, if you please."

"You should not take offense, *eyachou*. You have the voice of a mad god in you; that would test even the strongest Fae."

Mary took a step back from our bickering, still hugging herself.

"You know I hate it when you call me that." My temper was causing more of this, too, more fights, more disagreements. It burned to know that both Mary and Khent could see me struggling. I was supposed to be the head of the house, the one who had inherited the fortune that paid for our newer, shinier lives in London, a caretaker and someone to be depended upon. But it was becoming clear that my hidden fight was no longer so hidden.

I pinched the bridge of my nose and took a deep breath, shoving the voices away, trying to bundle them and lock them up tight. But it was like trying to pick up water, and one or two sly whispers always slithered free.

They question you. They dare question you?

The voices, quite obviously, were rarely friendly.

If I wanted my companions to consider me capable, then it was time to act like a leader. I pulled back my shoulders and calmly looked at them each in turn, folding my hands in front of my waist.

"We will attend the ball this evening, so as not to alarm Agnes and Silvia. Tonight, Khent will take the watch on the property, but tomorrow we will discuss a more permanent solution. In the morning, I will let our staff know that something is amiss and question them to see if perhaps they've noticed anything strange lately. Mary, maybe you would be so good as to write Chijioke? I'm sure he could either make suggestions of his own or talk to Mrs. Haylam."

Mary's eyes lit up at that. I had been surprised when she agreed to stay with me in London and not return to Coldthistle House. She had obviously made the decision with some regret, having discovered a kindling feeling for the groundskeeper of the boarding house. Their frequent correspondence since then had not slipped my notice.

"Diversion then," Khent said, giving me a toothy smile. "And libations!"

"One or two," I warned the Egyptian gently. "I shall remind you that this is not one of Seti's feasts." Khent had told me all manner of incredible stories about kings and queens whose names were as beautiful as they were unusual. I wondered if even half the tales were true, but he recalled them with such conviction and detail that I decided to believe. And anyway, it felt like a secret between us, these stories of ancient grandeur that he had witnessed firsthand. I was the only person lucky enough to hear these tales, their truth lost to time and, according to Khent, the persistent sandy winds of the desert. I attempted to read Terrasson's *The Life of Sethos* with him, but he insisted the inaccuracies were too much to bear.

He snorted and winked, and then held out his arm for me

to take. "His parties were tame compared to those of Ramesses. Have I ever told you about the time I ate two scorpions on a dare from His Radiance?"

Taking the proffered arm, I stepped with him out into the misty chill. "I do not think there will be scorpions to swallow at Lady Thrampton's ball."

"Vipers?"

"Nary a one," I said with a laugh. A few spider corpses remained on the stoop, but I tried not to look at them. A cold shiver slid down my spine.

Khent made a face, helping me down the short stairs in my dark crimson silk gown. Mary had been wise to bring a shawl, and now I was wishing for one of my own.

"Are we going to a celebration or a funeral?" Khent groused. "Damned English."

He would hear no rebuttals from two Irish lasses. We reached the gate at the edge of the lawn, and I grinned up at Khent, who seemed distracted by thoughts of grander, wilder fetes. With his rapidly expanding English vocabulary and friendly demeanor, I sometimes forgot that he had lived a lifetime ago and spent hundreds of years in frozen isolation, imprisoned by my father—by the cruel god now taking up residence in my head.

Turning down the lane toward our destination, he noticed my staring. Mary giggled softly behind us, but I ignored it. There was that shoulder-pinching sensation of being watched as we went, but I ignored that, too, chalking it up to the strangeness of living once more in the city and not in the secluded country fashion.

"What is it?" he asked, smirking. "That look makes me nervous, *huatyeh*."

Shrugging, I finally peeled my eyes away. "I'm simply glad you're free. And here. That we're all here."

The thick fog seemed to muffle and swallow our words. That feeling of being watched never left me, and as it persisted, a heavy dread settled over me. I had come so far, all the way to London, and made a new life for myself, one I had perhaps always wanted and dreamed of, but even now I was not safe. Even now, far, far away from Coldthistle House and its dark mysteries, I was hunted.

A group of women in white dresses so bright they cut through the fog huddled on the church steps across the road from us. I had noticed these women before on walks through Mayfair. Recently their numbers had grown, more clusters of white-garbed chanters appearing on street corners, shivering together like sheep on the moors as they braved rain and cold to sing or shout at passersby.

I couldn't help watching them now as we passed. Perhaps it was the fashionable thing to take a phaeton to the ball, but I preferred to walk and so did my compatriots. Khent craved the darkness and the fresh air on his face. Mary had been confined for a long time, too, and she enjoyed the exercise. Neither of them seemed to pay any mind to the chanters, but I did, squinting into the mist, listening to their shrill voices rise above the steady *clip-clop* of traffic.

"The shepherd guides you in love! Join the fold, join our flock—the shepherd, you are lost without him! You are lost!" Then they began to sing in unison, a childlike song about the safe embrace of the shepherd.

His arms keep out the wind; he forgives all who sinned . . .

That steel-edged shiver returned and so, too, did one of the voices in my head. I caught eyes with one of the chanters as she raised her voice to boom at us from across the road.

Are you lost, child?

The sound of evening hymns ought to bring comfort, but my stomach squirmed as if filled with snakes. Something was wrong, and either my own instincts or those of the soul in my head felt the danger keenly. I began to walk faster, as if I could outrun the man in my head and the strange women all in white, who watched, vigilant, as we disappeared into the dusk.

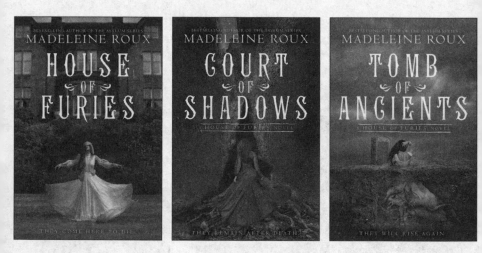